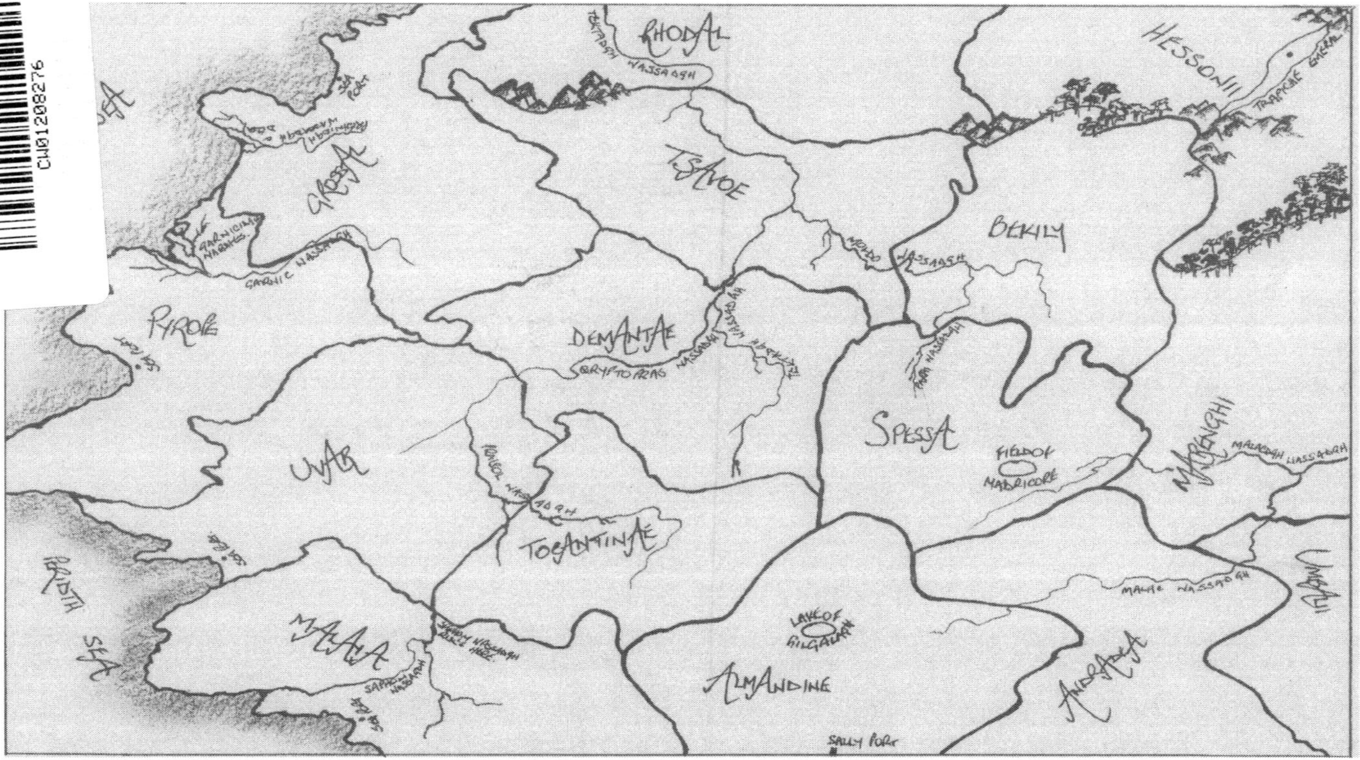
RHODAL
TSAVOE
BEKILY
HESSONII
PYROE
DEMANTAE
SPESSA
TOGANTINAE
ALMANDINE
MARENGHI
SALLY PORT

Copyright © 2010 C. McDonald
First published by Flying Pig Publications

Revised edition 2013
Copyright © 2013 C. McDonald
Published 2014 by Flying Pig Publications

The right of C. McDonald to be identified as the Author of the Work has been asserted by her in accordance with the Copyright, Designs and Patent Act 1988.

All rights reserved. No part of this publication may be reproduced, stored in a retrieval system, or transmitted, in any form or by any means without the prior written permission of the author, nor be otherwise circulated in any form of binding or cover other than that in which it is published and without a similar condition being imposed on the subsequent purchaser.

ISBN -13: 978-1494970161

ISBN: -10: 149-4970163

Book cover: Designed and Painted by
C. McDonald

For my children

Camille, Abigail and Joshua

Acknowledgments:

My grateful thanks for all of their help and encouragement to:

Max China – The Sister

Angelika Rust – Ratpaths

Atrament Speaks

The first book of the Noor trilogy

C. McDonald

Notes

Atrament Speaks.

Chapter 1.

Noor – the third trichotomy of the sparn.

Vivid colour stings the eye. Silvered whites, barley twisted greens, corals dappled with russet, garnish each root, trunk, branch, and twig. Fluttering in dance on every tree and bush, foliage of red, purple, blue and gold.
 Stretching far into the distance, bleached grass sways. The pale-blue stalks laden with heavy pink and lavender seed-heads tossed in the rising breeze. In the middle of the undulating landscape a small hill, ringed by a knotted mass of turquoise shrubbery, and always, and everywhere, a cacophony of whispering voices.
Coming out of the woodland onto the plain, the murmuring swelled. Ebbing and flowing with the fluidity of tidal water, the thousands faded in the long ago and final battle, but still bound to the land, spoke in rustling undertones. Hate. Regret. Loss. Longing. Love. All emotion, ravelled together in an unseen skein that never could, never would, be untangled, the quiet voices drowning in the air, carried away by a frisky wind, forever remaining.
Clara pulled the gostles up hard.
"See?" she pointed.
"I see it." Persimmony Clump, shifting uneasily in his saddle, let the reins slide through stiffened fingers in response to the haran stretching out its neck to graze. "Do not mean much though, do it? Do not mean he be not faded just because a hillock be where it should."
"We will find out," Clara urged the gostles forward.
Beckoning to the selected band standing discreetly some way off, Clump followed.

* * *

He had monitored the passage of his message bubble. Noted with satisfaction its rude delivery, and the Clara Maddingley person's shocked reaction to it. For a time, he was not certain she would obey. When hasty preparations for a journey began, he was confident she would come, and disinterested in mundane tasks of such beginnings, left off careful watch.

At intervals, he checked the steady progress of the troop through the defiant blaze of the final part of the year, coming in answer to his summons.

* * *

The unmistakable sound of rock, scraping against rock, signalled they had begun to clear the entrance. A bass tone rumbling, the words indistinct, filtered through the crack they had made, and floated, light as a dust mote, down to where he waited. Soaring without effort another voice, both soft and hard, full of authority and determination, cut it short.

It would take time to clear the way, time for the woman to negotiate the winding stair. Are not all things a matter of time, he reasoned, knowing the exquisite cruelty with which the weight of days crushed him with ever heavier force, grinding his being to fraying threads that must hold a while yet.

A sudden, niggling dread, soured the thrum of exultation experienced for some days. To speak face to face with another, even one from Lessadgh, after so long was daunting. Was there time enough? Time to imbibe, in one single draught, the infusion he had distilled to boost failing talent, and would its effect coincide exactly with her arrival? Would she accept the gifts he would tell her of, and one, he would not? Would she carry them out into the perfect light of Noor, where they belonged? She must, if they were to do their work.

Hesitant footfall on the stairs. No time left to ponder. With one great swallow, he took the potion, and withdrawing from the space he had prepared, went into the antechamber.

* * *

The entrance gaped open. Thick layers of draped cobwebs torn away, revealed rough-hewn steps going down into dark upon dark.

"We have spoken of this. You know, I must go alone, Clump. Be sure, I will call if help is needed," she said, in answer to the anxious look he wore.

He nodded reluctance, and sparking a fire crystal to brilliance, handed it to her. Taking hold of it, she thrust the flame before her and stepped inside. The smell of icy cold, and musty damp, rushed to meet her, and she could hear the rhythmic slap of moisture dripping somewhere. The stairs, uneven and treacherous, were carpeted with the muck of ages, and mossy growths had won the battle with fire crystals set into the walls. Glowing with frail dimness, they licked greedily at the light her torch gave out, all but dowsing it with hungry need.

Barely able to see, Clara made her way slowly, feeling for each tread with the tip of her toe. Making sure there was solid ground to put her foot on, before committing to the next step. Down, down, winding down. Any fears she had of this meeting and its outcome now forgotten, she focused solely on the challenge to reach the bottom safely.

Down, down, winding ever downward, noticing the air becoming a little warmer, and drier, though no lighter, until her toe could find no more steps. Balancing on one leg, stretching the other to its fullest extent, she arched her foot, and again, with her toes, felt to see what lay ahead.

"Nodgh credgh sloo memem. Nodgh pheludgh fam oblisudgh."

Thrusting the guttering brand to arms length, she swept it round trying to see who had spoken.

"Speak slow," she cried. "I am not well versed in the old language."

"Then I speak in the new. No chasm awaits, Lady. No trick for your destruction. You did well to answer my summons."

"I received no summons, nor do you have right to summon. An invitation was delivered to me. Had I wished, I could have declined."

"Couch it in whatever terms please you, Lady. Summons, invitation, neither would you have refused. Curiosity would have drawn you. Curiosity has ever been a trait of your human-kind, and will likely be its end."

"This place smells of stale blood, and broken bones!"

"You seek to quarrel with me? Or is it, perhaps, knowing something of my reputation, Lady, you fear for your safety? If so, do not fear. What good would your tired life force do me, when it surges sluggish? And your flesh, by the same token of great age, as Lessadgh reckons time, too tough for my taste."

"I am not reassured."

"You are wise. My given name is Amthyst. Many names, have I borne throughout the ages, though in these most recent times I am known by the name of Atrament."

"For now, you are merely a voice issuing from the dark."

"You believe me faded?"

"I am not fool enough to think a faded one could send a message bubble. There are options. If you are Atrament newly faded, it is not beyond the realm of possibility, you could have persuaded another to send it on your behalf. Or, this is perhaps, a joke in worst taste, contrived by some witless prankster? Or do you linger still? If final proof be offered, show yourself."

Light exploded, the white brilliancy of it intense and painful. In quick response, Clara dropped the fire crystal, screwed her eyes shut, and covered them with her hands.

"No need is there to shield your eyes, Lady. Never has this blaze burnt, or blinded. Look upon what you wished to see."

She slowly opened her eyes, and peeping through cracked fingers, waited for them to adjust before removing her hands completely. She appeared to be in a geode of massive proportions. Myriad amethyst crystals, growing close-packed together, studded outwardly curving walls and the domed roof soaring high above. Placed on various ledges, around and about, were skulls, so many skulls, with amethysts set into the empty eye sockets. In the middle of the vast and empty floor space, smoothed and polished by untold years of use, he stood.

Taller than any Faienya she had ever seen, and naked, but for a cloth draped casually beneath his stomach and over slim hips. Remaining quite still, he was movement. Unseen energy passing through hair, bluer than richest lapis lazuli, ruffled the fleecy halo standing about his head. Set above cheekbones, flat and broad, unblinking eyes flashed neon green with no white showing in them. Lean and lightly muscled, his body was completely patterned by glowing talent marks. Travelling one after another, so swiftly through his life force, they appeared to have no beginning or end, and burnished his coppered skin to bright rose-gold.

"You see me well enough, Lady?"

"I see you. From descriptions made in former times, you are not much changed. State your business with me."

"To the point. Very well, it is my wish to gift you."

"Gift me? With what?"

"Knowledge. The greatest gift any could bestow upon another. It is knowledge I would give into the palms of your hands."

"What can you know that is of importance to me?"

"Lady, to say I know all things would be a lie. To say, I know almost everything, is not far from truth. To say knowledge complete is mine concerning the Insane Child? Lady, that is fact."

"You lie," she cried, "You can know nothing of my boy."

"Can I not? I know you faded him." His words knocked the breath from her. Turned her bones to aspic, and heartsick in an instant. Folding in upon herself, Clara silently sank to the floor. "Is that not truth?"

"You gift me with torture," she managed to say.

"No torture of my doing. Guilt shakes you. Grief rends you. I see it is so. Easement for anguish suffered, is the gift I offer. The cause of the child's insanity, and better yet, who provoked it, is truly known to me. The knowledge I spoke of is here, concise, complete in a speak-cube. Answers to questions unanswered and, mayhap, to some un-thought of as yet."

"I must believe you, because?" she answered at last.

"Because, more comprehensive than any found in the archives of both worlds, I offer the history of Noor and Lessadgh. Because of the Insane Child, whom you loved to destruction, and his voice never to run through corridors of the Helm again, runs constant in the byways of your mind. What does he say in your waking? Your sleeping? Does he whisper? Does he whimper his pain? Or does he shout and scream it aloud?"

"Do not..."

"Lady, I must. And my gift you must accept, for one reason only. For you, there is nothing else. To carry assuagement hence, two further things you must take. The beginning of terror, I gift freely, together with a thing of beauty and obsession. How say you? Come, Lady, time runs short. I would have your answer. Say you yea, or nay?"

* * *

She clutched the casket tight. The coldness of the thing numbed the hand holding it, and spiked her breast through cloak and clothing. She hardly felt it. Stumbling, half crawling, Clara struggled to climb the darkened stairway, until Persimmony Clump, seeing white hair shimmering in the gloom below, ran down to help her.

"He be not faded as supposed, is he?" His encircling arm lifted her to her feet.

She shook her head.

"He offered no harm?' he asked, hauling her out into the day.

"No harm," though fractures in her heart gaped wide once more, and her mind felt splintered. "A little water, Clump, my throat rasps."

She drank greedily, aware his eyes travelled from her face to the bone white casket.

"You saw him?" he said, when she handed the flask back.

"Atrament as he was, not as he is."

"How so?"

"He had both arms," tiredness curdled her voice. "Most likely, talent needed to portray himself in his prime will be the fading of him."

"You spoke with him?" Clara nodded. "Then, for all eternity, let no other hear his voice," Clump said, quiet.

He took her arm, bellowing to the resting troop, "Seal the entrance firm shut. We must be long gone from this place before the darkling falls," and half dragged, half carried her to the cart.

* * *

Worn almost to transparency, Atrament crept out of the anteroom. In the middle of the now darkened floor-space where the simulacrum, so painstakingly created had stood, he lay down to wait for the process begun long ago to reach its conclusion. Soon electrons rotating around the nucleus of protons and neutrons, the axis of matter particles forming the insubstantial fabric of his being would falter, lose their orbit and collapse. Just the tiniest speck, indiscernible to the eye, would be all that remained, together with his voice, reduced to a rustling whisper, that would go running through the geode, and the underground canyons leading from it. And those who had kept company with him from his youth, perched on their ledges, would keep watch with the amethyst eyes he had given them.

"My enemies enemy," he whispered repeatedly.

Content the woman from Lessadgh was equipped to accomplish what he wished performed, the last true child of the Disobedient Ones waited.

Chapter 2.

The Way of Atrament? In error, others gave my name to it, not I. Know this, long established was the Way before ever I came into existence. How else could the Disobedient Ones have grown curious about carnal passion, and the burning nature of it? How else could a longing have developed to taste its unknown pleasures? And, in fulfilment of that desire, what other road could they have travelled to take on human form, and finally lie with the women of Lessadgh? I tell you, none.

Clump nodded to the casket she still held tight, "Best that thing be thrown back to whence it came, before the last boulder be set."

"No," Clara said, clutching it tighter. "It is a gift, given for a reason."

"A gift? What kind?" She shook her head. "For what reason?" She shrugged her shoulders. "Why would he gift you, a woman of Lessadgh, a place he loathed and despised? Think. What gift of his giving would not sow discord? The archives tell us that was ever his pleasure."

"Nevertheless, I will not discard it. Not yet."

"We shall speak of this later," he promised.

"Doubtless."

Clump snorted, and walked away, shouting. "Wedge the last rock well in place. Drag the brushwood removed back over it," and swinging into the saddle, glared at the casket for a long moment before kicking a command for the haran to get to its feet. Wrenching the beast's head round so hard, the quills along its proudly arched neck rattled, he goaded it forward, and took the lead.

Clara placed the box on the seat beside her, and picking up the reins, lightly flicked her whip over the backs of the well-rested gostles waiting in the shafts of her cart. In answer, antlered heads tossed, haunches tightened, and with a sudden lurch, they were away. The troop, their work finished, rushed to their mounts, and as always, came on behind.

* * *

Bone white, the casket gifted to her by Atrament. Bone white, and very smooth. Bone white, banded and studded with a dark, rough-textured material that had no like. Bone white. White as the skulls she had seen adorning ledges in the geode, but from this bone whiteness no amethyst eyes stared blank and unseeing. Her eye was constantly drawn to it. If the cart jostled over rough ground, her hand steadied it. Going over well-packed tracks, or even roads, her hand unconsciously sought it out.

On the rare occasions Clump spoke to her, distracted by thoughts of what lay inside it, dreading and yet eager to know, Clara answered automatically. Seeing her hand always rest upon it, he directed his speech to the troop, and then only to issue instructions. Fluttering between them, tension already spun fine, became lightly layered.

During the next days, ignorant of the purpose of the journey and its outcome, the troop felt that tension swell. Felt the oppressive atmosphere reach out to encompass them. As one, they drew rein, hoping distance would smudge its edges to nothing, but the unseen pressure becoming taut, became profound.

Darkness had stopped its tentative crawl, and begun to tumble down in earnest to smother the brightness of day, when through recalcitrant twilight, the pale green towers of the Helm could be seen. They were a welcome sight. Each one had reason to hurry inside its sheltering walls.

* * *

Clump jumped from his haran. Striding over the cobbled courtyard, lit by flaming fire crystals, Smu Hundghs with hides the swirling colours of smoke in night air, rushed to greet him, yapping soundless excitement. He shouldered them out of the way until he came to the cart, and waited for Clara to climb down, before grasping her arm.

"You lied," he accused, "you know what that casket contains."

"Yes," she admitted, shaking him off.

"And did not tell me?"

"A gift made to me, need not concern you, Clump. If it pleases you, I will tell you now. Three things there are, separate, but somehow bound. One of them to do with my boy, my William."

"Your boy?"

"He said, he knew the cause of his madness, and of the one who provoked it."

"Of course he would say such a thing," he railed. "Who does not know an open wound be the best place to slide a blade? Have you forgot; he is Atrament Emim? In the old language: dark terror. Those names were hard earned, Clara. Well you know it, and that his ambition knew no bounds. How he faded many, for no other reason than to steal away their talent, enabling him to seize power. Total domination was his aim, and it be my belief that monster would have eaten this world, and that of Lessadgh had he not been stopped. His name, and the Way he trod, is Anathema to us, yet you take heed when he says he knows something of your long gone child? Yes, your boy went away. William be absent these many years, but his leaving be no fault of yours."

Clara winced. "You know nothing, Clump."

"I know this. You must let the past remain the past. How else will you ever know peace? Mayhap, when your boy has completed what he went to do, he will return. Think on that."

"He told me, I could discover answers to many questions."

"He told you? If he told you, it must be so, be that your reasoning? Do not let emotion cloud judgment. Think again. Think with clarity. What truth could ever come from that quarter?"

"My mind is clear."

"I see it already made up. You be reckless, Clara." Leaning close to her, Clump spoke more quietly, "Always you have been so. The boy filled a childless void within you, yet it was reckless to take him down from where he was left. Reckless, to take the boy into your home, so much more to keep him in your heart once I had told you of the risk, of the dangers that would surely follow. Willingly, you made a fight yours, without knowing the cause or cost. Be that not reckless? But let us pass over many other reckless things you have done, and concentrate on the current. Reckless, and foolish, to go into the company of the dark one, it was. Had I known, he be not faded, I would have done more to prevent you going."

"You go beyond your station," she snapped. "It is not within your remit to prevent me anything."

"Very well, then I tell you what you already know. At times you are both foolish and reckless. Do not add further to the list already made by opening the casket. Let it lie in some secure place uncared for, un-thought of. Better yet, forgotten entirely."

"You forget to whom you speak, Clump."

"For that I beg pardon, Lady. I thought I spoke to my friend, Clara Maddingley, not the High Lord of the Helm."

"Am I not both?"

"Lady, you give me good reason to believe not."

Turning on his heel, Clump marched away. She watched him go, his cloak flying out behind him. Watched him go into the stables. Heard him cuss, and swear, at the boys to un-harness the gostles, and rub the harans down. Bellow at the troop to get to their quarters, and bother him no more that night, and she was, for a second, tempted to go after him, to try to heal the rift made in their long friendship. Icily cold, white-fired heat needled her numbed hand, bringing her attention back to the casket.

"Tomorrow," she muttered. "I will heal the breach with Clump tomorrow."

* * *

Stark, in contrast to opulent colours decorating her bedchamber, the bone white casket. Bone white, and lying on the table in front of her, untouched since she had placed it there. Clump's words had bitten deep.

You are reckless Clara. Always have been.

"Am I reckless?" she wondered out loud, as her fingers automatically found the emerald ring she always wore. She twisted it round, and round, the smooth warmth of the gold, the coldness of the faceted stone, strangely comforting. Round and round. Twisted once, twisted twice, and the table of the gem stroked, a sign of contemplation, or anxiety, to anyone who knew her well. "Or...do I dare what others will not?"

What risk is there in opening the casket? What risk, if Atrament told true? What risk, if he lied? She did not know. So much she did not know. The beginning of terror, what did that mean? What could it mean? Had the beginning of terror met its end, or could it be possible to unleash a tethered menace?

A thing of beauty, and obsession? Beauty no longer moved her in ways it once had. How, then, could such a thing touch her? Obsession, she admitted, held her fast, but only in relation to William, the child she had loved, and lost, and silently grieved for. The child killed by her own hands, a long kept secret thought to be known by her only, until now.

The speak-cube was the only item in the box that interested her. *Answers to questions unanswered, and mayhap, some to those yet un-thought of.* To know, at last, the cause of William's madness, and who had provoked it, for those answers what would she give? Everything. Everything. She would cause havoc in the world of Noor, and that of Lessadgh, to know those answers

"I am become a little mad to even think of such destruction," she whispered, wiping her face with her hands. "I am tired. Best make no decision until the brightling. Yet..."

Bone white, the casket. Tempting to look inside, to take the speak-cube, and denying them the light of day, leave the other things inside forever.

If I open it, will there be a cost? Who can say? To be wise after the event is not wisdom, it is experience. If there is a cost, I will pay it, and pray no other has to.

Bone white, the casket, cold-laced...and open!

Chapter 3.

Very tall in stature, well formed, and of strange intense beauty, such was the human shape assumed by the Disobedient Ones. The people of Lessadgh, believing the gods had come to dwell among them, willingly gave daughters to them to do with as they wished, considering it great honour to invest in godhead. Unions that never should have been, bore fruit. The women of Lessadgh died in birthing. From the beginning we, the progeny, were called Anwim. Devastators. Nevertheless, knowing what fate awaited them, daughters were still given.

Black. Red. Blue. Three little boxes, side by side, in bone whiteness. Each, rectangular in shape, no one larger than another, crystalline yet opaque, and giving no hint of what might lie inside.

Clara grimaced, recognizing Atrament had outmanoeuvred her.

"He foresaw what I would do," she fumed. "He forces me to the same choice as before. Take one, take all, to have what I most desire. Open one, perhaps, open all, to find it."

Back and forth, back and forth, her hand trailed slowly over the surfaces as if by touch alone, she could find the speak-cube. Tiredness gritted her eyes. Tiredness, clotting in her stomach, sent little spirals of nausea up into her throat. Her bones ached. The night was all but wasted, nascent the dawning day.

Will I while away segments with further indecision? I think not.

Choosing the blue box, she lifted it up. Held it on her out-stretched palm, turning it this way, and that, to see where the catch was located. A slight click. The lid flew up. The sides collapsed outward, and hung over her hand like a neatly dismembered package. Surprised by the sudden action of hidden hinges, she nearly dropped it. It took her a moment, or two, to see what had been hidden inside. On a bed of moss-blue velvet, moulded to keep the object in place, two long diamonds. Two long diamonds, shaped like fangs, secured to one another by a bridge of precious urilatum, the points wickedly sharp glittering in the half-light.

The beginning of terror? There is no sense to this thing. Some function it has, but what? Unless, unless it is a perverted weapon of some kind? Why, then, gift me with this vile object?

Placing it onto the table, she pushed it to one side to make the next choice. Lifting the red box next, she held it as before, understanding her body heat had somehow triggered the unexpected action of the last one. A slight click. The lid flew up, and the sides of the box collapsed. Immediately, she saw what lay within, and recognized it. With a little cry, she threw it onto the table with such force the object jumped out of its container, and went skittering across the polished surface to careen into its blue neighbour.

A thing of beauty, and obsession, fabulous, and infamously fatal, the ancient quiver. Miniature in size, its body woven from coppery-silver urilatum to resemble a basket, the top and bottom edges roped with rare green gold. Within, nestling upright in their stays, the darts. Elegant shafts of green gold, delicately engraved, and studded with fine gems, and fletches made from fine strands of drawn urilatum, each strand thinner than a hairsbreadth. This thing, this once coveted emblem of status, and wealth, this relic from the past, Clara knew.

Seen only a few times, many years ago, suspended from the girdle of Apatia, the vacuous, malicious child of faded Lingaradgh.

Heart-shaken, breathing heavily through flared nostrils, Clara rose from her chair. Crossing the room, she snatched up a web-silk shawl thrown carelessly over the back of a three-seat. Folding it, she came back to the table, and dropping it over both objects, scooped them into a bundle, before unceremoniously dumping them back into the bone white casket, while she snatched the remaining box out.

Black - the colour of the void. Wings of obsidian drooping over her hand, hard and cold to the touch, revealed nothing more than an area of darkest coloured material, its luxuriant pile tinged with iridescence. On it, a tiny tassel of soft silken thread lay. She pulled it gently. The cover raised, and there, sunk deep into more of the same cloth, and no bigger than half a playing card, a square tablet formed from an emerald with a glowing spark at its heart, reminding her of the colour of Atrament's eyes, was the speak-cube. She prised it out. Amazed by its fragile thinness, she held it to the breaking light to see it was almost translucent, suspecting it could never hold all the information promised, and wondering, if Atrament had been truthful with her.

For a time, she let it rest on the palm of her hand, thinking its heat would make it spring open, as the others had done, then held it between cupped hands, yet the little box remained shut. Frustrated, she carefully inspected its smooth surfaces and edges, but could detect no hinges.

By the powers, how am I to hear Atrament, if I cannot discover how to make the contraption work? There must be a way...

But there was no time for lengthy investigation, or experiment. Morning was almost full-fledged. The soft tread of servants moving through spacious halls, and corridors, was quickly being replaced by the tramp, and thud, of more careless traffic on marbled floors. Doors opening. Doors slamming. The voices of the living were beginning to ride high above the susurration of the faded. No time for anything now, save to prepare for duties the Kingdom State, and her schedule demanded.

Resolving to destroy the casket, and its contents at some later time, she shoved it into the bottom of a cupboard and locked the door. The speak-cube placed into a pouch, and hung upon a lengthy chain, Clara fastened it around her neck, and wore it beneath her clothing, where none would see it.

Chapter 4.

Wondrous and varied, the true aspect of the Disobedient Ones, none being like to another. This I was told. The full palette of colour draped upon them ranged through a vivid spectrum that was uncommon among the people they came to.
Not so strange, many of the offspring of the Disobedient Ones were mantled in brightling hues, as was I, while others were clothed in the washed-out shades of the humans of Lessadgh.
Not so strange, some of the offspring of the Disobedient Ones had human form, as did I, and a very few were of stunted human stature. You know of whom I speak. You know, full well, what we were, and are.
For others, a fusion of shape occurred, and talent gleamed their skin not so well. These ones had elements of both the kinds. Head of hawk, or dog, or bull upon a body, formed as is human-kind, or the uppermost part owning human form that sprang from the body of a horse, or combined with the tail of a fish. These latter ones, instead of swimming in the endless infinity of space, eventually found sanctuary, and solace in watery depths. Snaked-haired, one-eyed, and many more, you know of whom I speak, you know, full well, what they were, and are.
Many of the fused ones were hybrid. They could not reproduce. It were better, to my mind, all offspring sprung from the loins of the Disobedient Ones had been so.

In 1770, Clara Maddingley began a new life. A spinster, plain in looks, solitary by nature, no-nonsense in character, and disappointed for many reasons, she left the city behind, together with those things she preferred to forget. Taking possession of a smallholding with a ramshackle house, dilapidated barns, and a very strange reputation, she set about putting the buildings to rights, and learning all she could about agriculture. At first, she worked her land with the help of casual labour, then becoming more proficient, worked it alone.

Hard work suited her. Caring for the few animals she kept, tending her crops, and a little walled orchard, left her no time to think about what might have been.

For so small an acreage, her land was astonishingly fruitful. Whatever she planted, whatever she sowed, the harvest always exceeded anything that would normally be hoped for, giving her a more than satisfactory living.

To her neighbours, Clara was more than something of an oddity. She was a mystery. She was careful to keep it so, which proved to be easy. She rarely saw them.

* * *

By nature, Persimmony Clump was secretive. Of necessity, he was more so. It is doubtful many in the area, where he lived, knew of his existence, and of those who did, no one knew exactly where that was. One man, only, knew what he did to gain a living.

Highly acclaimed for exquisite design, and workmanship, this man was said to be the finest goldsmith and jeweller in the land. The aristocracy, the extremely wealthy, were his patrons. He refused all commissions, saying he chose to work as he wished, and not as directed, yet the pieces he produced were purchased as soon as they were presented to a chosen client.

He had never taken an apprentice. No one had ever been allowed to enter his workshop, and whether he was in, or out of it, that place was always locked.

This man was a fraud. Unable to produce anything but unimaginative, mediocre jewellery, he had barely managed to keep body and soul together, and was about to lose his premises when he met Persimmony Clump. Clump had something to sell, something of exquisite design, and workmanship. Fondling the pieces, desperately wanting to purchase the trinkets, the jeweller had no money to spend, but knew of someone who would definitely be interested. Upon a quick, successful sale, Clump said he could produce more pieces, if required. An arrangement was made between them. From that time, the man's fortune changed, and, Clump keeping his precious anonymity, made a more than satisfactory living.

They met four times a year, each of them travelling to meet the other. Clump, being overly cautious, never returned home the way he had come. It was after doing such business Clump met Clara Maddingley.

In the middle of nowhere, his horse threw a shoe, forcing him to dismount and lead it down winding country lanes, until he came upon a smallholding. A woman, well on in years, was vigorously turning soil in a field. He stopped, asked if she had a piece of iron he might purchase. She didn't question what he wanted the metal for, but directed him to a small barn saying, if he could find an unwanted piece of scrap, he was welcome to have it. He found an old mattock, rusted and broken, far beyond any use it had been designed for. Before long, his horse was shod, he was mounted and touching his forelock in thanks, he passed on.

Three months later, Persimmony Clump came past the farm again. Amongst many other things in his saddlebag, he had a small, very expensive packet of tea.

"Accept it as a token of my thanks," he said to the woman, and she, not having tasted such luxury for years, thanked him for his generosity, and invited him to take a dish with her.

Every few months he would visit. Sometimes, he would barter vegetables for costly sugar, or priceless coffee for eggs and fruit. The visits lasted longer each time. Little by little, a friendship was struck, a friendship that was slightly strained.

Clump's secrecy frustrated Clara. He would never talk of his life, or what he did, and the questions she asked about the thick leather gloves he wore, never taking them off no matter the weather, were parried by diverting her to other matters, much to her exasperation. The riddle was answered, when she lost patience with his refusal to remove them one sweltering summer's day. Reluctantly, he told her, "I be badly burnt. The flame that fired me, I feel still. Very unsightly, my hands are."

He was evasive. She knew next to nothing about him. Always getting answers to questions, which upon later reflection, were no answers at all. He pretended to have no interest in an area of common land bordering the rear of her property, yet when looking in that direction, his expression said otherwise. When she challenged him, he always countered by saying he had not been looking at it, but at her walled orchard.

At times Clump infuriated her. His accent, thick, and impossible to determine, Clara rather liked, and the way he phrased sentences amused her.

Clara irritated Clump. Her sly probing, her gentle prodding, her incessant curiosity about his life, and all that he did, when she was hardly forthcoming about her former life, he found galling. He comforted himself with the thought at some point she would leave off, finding no dent could be made in those things he held most private. She did not. He would never have admitted it, but he rather liked Clara, for all her faults, and her cooking was something to look forward to.

The seasons turned, cycle after cycle. Abrasive at worst, gentle at best, their friendship remained. It developed no further. Neither of them wished for that.

Chapter 5.

After a time the Disobedient Ones learned three things. First, their powers were much diminished. Second, to the place of their origin there would be no return, for the door, thought to be always open, was barred, and to Lessadgh, they were most surely bound. Third, sterility had struck them.
Then, did the Disobedient Ones withdraw into the worship houses the humans of Lessadgh had built for them. In the world outside those walls, their faces were not seen again, nor did the ones serving them during a period that proved to be one of extensive seclusion, set eyes upon them.
Much later, a fourth thing they would understand, that was again, much to their detriment.

For a week, night after night, the same dream. Clara rose from her bed more tired than when she had laid down. During the day, snatches of the dream pursued her, mental images jumped into her mind, disjointed, and for an instant, realistic. An impression of wild speed, or the motion of a rider bent low over the neck of a nightmarish mount, or a cloak billowing madly in wind, or covering the head to shade the face, a hood spread wide as a sail. Once, for a long moment, her mind's eye fixed upon what jolted and bounced by the rider's knee, and having seen, veered in repugnance away from severed heads, hung by their hair to the pommel of the saddle.

Snippets, flicked at her in the light of day, joined together, and played at length while she slept.

* * *

She woke with a start, sweat-slicked, and shaking. Groping for the vesta on the bed-stand beside her, she found it, flipped the lid, took a match, and striking it on the ribbed edge, lit the candle stub. Draughts playing with the flame made shadows move. Clearly, her mind was far too active, if it could not only conjure up such nonsense, it retained it. If she closed her eyes again, drifted back to sleep, those dreadful images would surely return. Throwing the covers from her, Clara got up. Though still dark, it was better to be busy.

At first light, she went outside. The tiniest frill of cold rippling through the air told her winter already tested the boundaries of autumn. Her routine was the same every morning. Chickens let out of the coop to scratch in the crude pen she had made. Later, she would scatter seed, and corn for them, and collect their eggs while they were occupied. Goats milked next. Today, she would lead them both to her walled orchard. They could gorge on any wind-fallen fruit, crop grass and weeds close, as she inspected the ripeness of apples, pears and plums, and if any fruit were deemed ready for picking, she would come back with a ladder. That was her intention.

On opening the gate, she saw a length of material shimmering in the early light. Tied to the lowest bough of a nearby tree, it formed a rough hammock. There was something in it. Not small, but not large, curled inside. Hesitant, not knowing quite what to make of it, Clara approached slowly. Her goats, necks outstretched, nibbled at it. She shooed them away. Tentative, she touched it. Firm and warm. Whatever it was, it was living. Cradling it in one arm, she reached up with the other, and undid the knot that had been tied, and staggered. She had not expected whatever it was to weigh so much. Balance recovered, she parted folds of material to look inside. The very last thing she had thought to find, was a child, sleeping and naked as the day of its birth.

Shocked, Clara looked around the orchard. She went further into it, walking from wall to wall among the trees, thinking the child's mother might still be nearby. There was no one.

"Some poor girl not wanting to live with her shame has left you," she said, going out of the gate. "But never fear little one, I will take good care of you, till your mother regains her senses."

In the weeks that followed, no one came to ask how the boy fared, and no one claimed him. Clara named the child William. Knowing little of children, or their development, she judged him to be about two years old, and overlooked his strangeness, convinced there was reason for it, and also, an obvious remedy. His skin had a coppery luminosity. The dewiness of the very young doubtless accounted for it. His eyes, blue to the point of middling purple, showed no white. He had some childish ailment unknown to her that he would surely grow out of. His hair, crimson streaked with brightest orange, would doubtless grow dull to become a more subdued colour, as he grew older. His height, she put down to very tall parents, and thought no more of it. These things were trivialities, insignificant differences, nothing more. In all other ways, except for the gibberish he spoke, he was a healthy, happy, normal child. And she loved him. With all her heart…Clara loved him.

* * *

In Persimmony Clump's saddlebags, salt-fish wrapped in greased paper and thick calico. In sacks, finest milled flour for bread making. In small earthen pots, best clover honey. He knew, throughout the winter months ahead these purchases would add variety to the food she grew, and that Clara would not accept them as gifts. She never had. Approaching the farm, he wondered if he should barter them for a nice fat chicken, or two, and a supply of eggs. She had said, she would pickle this season's cherries in the brandy he had traded with her back in the spring, perhaps he would ask for some in the bargaining.

    The two small fields at the front of the house were empty. Riding through them, he could see she had been busy planting since he had last seen her six, or seven weeks ago. Putting his horse in the barn, throwing the bulging saddlebags over each shoulder, he made his way to the back, certain she would be harvesting fruit in the walled orchard. He saw her immediately. In the distance, at the very edge of her property, Clara was picking the last of the blackberries from bushes fringing the common land, but she was not alone.

Chapter 6.

Locked away in splendid isolation, the Disobedient Ones saw not how their offspring grew. Unexplained to us their absence. Untutored, were we in talent to come at puberty. Undisciplined our actions, save those imposed by each one's self according to character, and nature, and the efforts of our human guardians, and relations. When the firstborn left childhood behind to enter adolescence, the Disobedient Ones were still distant from us.

"Put him back where you found him, Clara," Clump said.

"Don't be ridiculous. Even were I willing to do that, which I most certainly am not, he would die of exposure. The nights grow cold."

"Heat and cold will not affect him. He will take no ill from weather."

"You are mad! Ignoring that madness for just a moment, tell me this," sweeping the child up into her arms, she set him on her hip, "having left him, never once calling to enquire how he does, let alone claim him, who would come looking for him now?"

"They will come. You must put him back. Just as you found him, wrapped in the material, you must put him back."

"Who will come? You make no sense. Why would I put him back?"

"Very well, I see I must make you understand. At the bottom of your gardens..."

"My gardens?" she cried. "What have they to do with anything?"

"Everything. There is a sally port in the blackberry bushes bordering the common land."

"A sally port?"

"A doorway, a portal, an entrance to another place."

Clara laughed incredulous. "Where eldritch creatures dwell, no doubt?" she scoffed. "You will be telling me next, I have fairies at the bottom of my garden. Really, Clump? Can it be possible; you have truly lost your mind? These things do not exist, save in tales, or in the heads of those who are gullible, or severely confused."

"Do they not? Explain, then, how I came to pass through it? You may poke fun at me, but I know of what I speak. See here," he drew off his gloves, holding out his hands for her inspection, "see the tips of my fingers glowing? See the palms glimmer with incandescent light?"

Holding the child close, she bent forward for a closer look. Her face screwed with astonishment, she moved away from him, and sitting down, placed the boy on her lap.

"That be talent, Clara," he continued. "That be how I earn my bread.

Metals, hard to work in the hottest fire, bend and twist at my caress. Under my hand, precious metals willingly stretch to form any design of my choosing, no matter how thin, no matter how intricate. At my touch, all metals accept gems I care to set, and hold them tight and imperceptible."

"No," she shook her head, "that cannot be done."

"I can hold nothing back from you now. I am more than ten times your age. Old, by this world's reckoning, and young at the same time, if the weight of days is counted according to those of Noor. And who are those of Noor? I hear you say it, Clara. Without speech, I hear you say it. We are Faienya. Do not seek a fight with the Faienya. You cannot win. Know this, they do not give their offspring up, nor do they abandon them. This child was left with good reason. Next week, next month, mayhap, even years from now, he will be claimed, and you…you will you let him go at the first asking? I think not. I tell you now, save yourself that pain, for he will be taken. I urge you, Clara, put him back where you found him, as you found him."

"It is hard to take all this in." The child in her arms pulled at a stray strand of her hair, winding it round chubby fingers that went on to softly explore her face. "To me," she said, gently taking the boy's hand from her mouth, "to me, you are, Clump. To find you are something entirely other, my mind can scarce encompass it. Tell me, is it possible, my boy was left for me to find?"

"It be possible," he admitted, "but I think unlikely."

Shaken, she turned away, trying to collect scattered thought.

"Clara…"

"No! You mentioned it could be years before the, whatever you called them, reclaimed my boy. Is that correct?"

"Days also were mentioned."

"I would have those days, or those years, and right gladly pay the cost."

"You be a fool, Clara. Having given best advice, I take my leave."

Much later, she found the provisions he had brought, laid out on the step by the back door.

Two days later, Clump returned. On rope leads two dogs, nearly the size of small ponies and of indeterminate breed, loped obediently by his side.

"I have given the matter more thought," he said, without preamble. "It be possible, the boy be left for you to find. If so, why? The only answer I could discover be this, to keep him out of harm's way. If some harm seeks him, it will surely seek you, too. The dogs are for you. Keep them well. They are your best chance, if harm seeks you out. At very least, they will alert you. Leave them outside. Let them roam your property. Never bring them into the house, and do not let the boy near them. Never. You understand?"

Clara nodded. She, too, had given the matter much more thought.

"If you," she began, choosing her words carefully. "If you truly believe us threatened... If you came through the sally port thing you spoke of, if you are so certain my boy is in danger, can you not go back through it? You could find out."

"I? Go back through the sally port again? Not willingly. I have jeopardy of my own, and will not run that risk. Clara, choices you had. The wrong choice you made. I give you some small comfort, and protection, in the gift of the dogs. Be sure to keep the boy well away from them. They will forage for themselves. I tell you again, never let the beasts into your house."

"I see," Clara said, not seeing at all.

Chapter 7.

Adolescence, is it not a time of confusion for all beings? It was a time when life force flowed faster, and urges never felt before, became apparent. Puberty, awakening talent that had been sleeping, we came into our own. We came into our inheritance. All the offspring of the Disobedient Ones had talent. To one degree, or another, we had it. A few had talent of a kind most special. I was such a one. Instinctive, the words to use were known to us, the sounds, the intonation, the cadence, the rhythms to create a making, and more beside. The marks of talent patterned our bodies in their entirety.
In the long ago, we were called by many names. Gibborim: the giant heroes. Zamzummin: the achievers of deep thought and great deeds of invention. Anakim Grigor: the long-necked watchers, recording the events of the planets, masters of measurement, and building. This, I believe. This, I know. I witnessed all.
In more recent times we were collectively called Nephilim until a new name was given to us. Faienya.

    The speak-cube remained silent. Every method she could think of, Clara used, trying to get it to dispense the knowledge she had been told it had.

    No hinges apparent, or visible, she trailed the tips of her fingernails slowly over every part of it, believing no workmanship, however slyly executed, would not leave some minuscule gap that would yield with a little leverage. There was no gap. No two pieces of the surface came into contact with each other. The emerald speak-cube was whole, in and of itself. She was certain of that.

    Pressed, squeezed, stroked, tapped, warmed between her hands for long periods, produced the same result. Nothing she did induced Atrament to speak.

    "Damn your eyes," she said, her anger directed at the glow lying deep within the heart of the green tablet, and shoving it back into its pouch, she let it fall between her breasts.

Chapter 8.

Before the Disobedient Ones came down to them, the humans of Lessadgh were quarrelsome. Over land, and riches, they had fought many great battles. Sometime, I was told, over women, and sometime for the joy of it. That I learned. That I experienced.
For a time, the warring ceased, for they, believing the gods to be among them, opted for peace. But avarice, and jealousy simmered, as did spite, and old grievances. Even before the Disobedient Ones went into self-imposed exile, skirmishes were fought. The red blood of the humans of Lessadgh ran always hot, and ran hotter still after the Disobedient Ones withdrew.
One of the holy books of Lessadgh has a saying, as flint sharpens flint, so the face of one man sharpens the face of another.
So, in this manner, are wars begun.

Clara carried him, riding on her hip, to meet the dogs the next morning. Opening the back door, she said, "You will like them, William. If you do not pull their ears, or tails, if you are gentle with them, they will like you, too, and be playmates for you."

Going over the threshold, she stopped, uncertain if the noise the dogs made was threat or greeting. Getting to their feet, hackles up, tails tucked tight between hind legs, they dropped into stalking gait. Moving in tandem, they slunk toward her, bellies almost scraping the ground, their heads low between raised shoulders. Growling, and snarling, they came on.

She backed into the house. The dogs were up in an instant, powering over a distance of only yards. She slammed the door shut, wedging her whole weight against it, frightened the animals would splinter the wood, and tear both she and her boy limb from limb. William laughed, patted her cheeks with his chubby little hands, and put his head on her shoulder.

"It was no game," she said, clasping him tight. "That was no game," and silently cursed Clump with every foul word her mind could grasp.

Much later, carrying a stout piece of firewood, she ventured out alone. The dogs, laying a little way off, raised their heads, eyed her, sniffed the air and disinterested, rested their muzzles back on the ground. Evidently, the animals Clump had given her, did not like her boy, but were prepared to tolerate her.

She shut them in the barn during the day, letting them out to roam as they pleased at night to bring down rabbits, or anything else that might lurk nearby.

* * *

"Did I not tell you to keep the boy well away from them?" Persimmony Clump shouted, in answer to the tongue-lashing he had just received. "They are trained to recognize the scent of any Faienya, not my own, and attack."

"Trained to attack?" she repeated, confused.

"Of course. Did I not say, I had jeopardy of my own? What did you expect?"

"You did not say."

"Must you have every little thing spelled out for you, woman? Had you heeded my advice, this would not have happened. Since you and the boy suffered no hurt…"

"No hurt!" she raged. "By the grace of all things holy, we did not, and no thanks to you, Clump."

"Well, you know the measure of the animals now," he said, quiet, stunned by the fierceness of her anger. "Or be it your wish, I take the gift given to guard you, back into my keeping?"

"They guarded you?"

"Did I not say so?" he growled.

"I had not realized, they were your protection," Clara said.

"No matter. Other ways, I can find. You cannot, not with the child."

"Very well. We will put that matter from us."

"That be most gracious." Sarcasm rode on his breath. "I have given much thought to your situation. I want no involvement in the choice you made. You know this. It be yours alone, and alone, you must meet the consequences. I bring another gift that might provide, if needed, if you have time, a means of escape. I have made a little box-cart, together with harnesses for your beasts to draw it. It is a rude affair with no pretence to grace, or elegance, yet it may serve to bear you to friends, or relations. It waits outside. Shall I take it into the barn?"

"I am most grateful, Clump," Clara murmured, taken aback by his generosity.

"You must understand, I regret, I can do nothing further."

"I understand," she nodded feeling utterly alone, and very frightened. "The risk is mine, entirely mine."

"Nor be it likely we will meet again," he said. "That, too…I regret."

Chapter 9.

Combat made their blood sing out. When the steel, so prized by them connected, the length of one blade sliding against another in sparking shower, when weapons chimed and tolled at the clash, when strength and endurance was tested to its utmost to evade death, or in pursuit of victory, at no other time were they more alive. In my youth the men of Lessadgh said this.

How much more intense, how greater the stir of battle for us male and female offspring of the Disobedient Ones, the few who took up arms? And what weapons we bore. Metal we would not wear. Energy is the life force of all worlds. Metal its marrow. Rock its bones. Vegetation is its adornment and clothing. To use the marrow of Lessadgh was to show great disrespect. To use Lessadgh's bones, or raiment was our choosing. And if these bones, ancient and owning no flexibility, likely to chip, or shatter at the stroke, then with making did we imbue that which was lacking into our blades. Our crystalline shards, our woody slivers, selected, and ground, to pleasing shape as each one chose, had fragile beauty denying the lethal strength our weapons had.

Barely contained by the channels, through which it ran, life force surged. It raced, screaming its thrill. When the press was hardest, the screams of despair, or victory, loudest, who did not hear that savage hymn, and hum it ever after? And through our weapons of obsidian, jade and ebony, in softer tones the same tune echoed.

My loathing of the beings of Lessadgh, already taking shape and form, I took no side as others did. In the mayhem, I challenged as I willed, seeking out the strongest, the fastest, and did the fallen of Lessadgh honour. I took their heads. Stripped the flesh. Polished the skull. I did this that all of their body might not descend into decay complete. For even while they walk in full vigour, the bodies of the humans of Lessadgh are putrefying. These skulls were ever by me.

And when the carnage was over, some trained by it, and fattened on it, would not forget its ways. Would not live in the ways of peace. Would not stop.

The men of Lessadgh made urgent supplication in the houses of worship. Bringing great gifts for the Disobedient Ones, they pled for them to intervene. Yet the Disobedient Ones, continuing to mourn losses of their own, were deaf to the pleas of those doing them homage.

Moisture trickled over her scalp, and down her forehead to prick her eyes with saltiness that could not be wiped away. Inside the full-faced mask, and headdress, signifying continuity of the Lord of the Helm, Clara sweated. Encased in precious urilatum from head to collarbone, her skin itched. The ceremonial robe, and voluminous cloak pinioned to her shoulders, both richly embroidered with urilatum threads, and studded with gems, trailed from the Chair of Authority down the stairs of the dais. All heavy, and growing heavier, and beneath the symbols of power, beneath shift and chemise, the pouch hiding the speak-cube lay between her breasts.

Myriad fire crystals flamed in the galleries above, and suspended from the ceiling, lit the space below. The great hall blazed with light. Packed into every available space that was not reserved for the Counsel, and visiting dignitaries, the crowd waited in silence.

Small, upon the Chair of Authority in Almandine, Clara sat perfectly still. Persimmony Clump stood a little behind, and to her right, Malfroid to her left. Below the dais, bending his neck as protocol demanded, the ambassador of Spessa launched into his address the instant ancient words of formal invitation had been spoken.

"To the High Lord of Almandine, the High Lord of Spessa sends warmest greetings, and bids me say this. I regret to inform you our borders have been breached. Our watchers..."

Clara held her hand up. "We know of what you speak, sir. Before tending apology, we give explanation. It was a necessary incursion into your territory based on intelligence received."

"My Lord, what intelligence of such great import it could not wait for the correct procedures, and ignored protocol?"

"News of Atrament living still." A huge gasp, faster than scudding storm-blown clouds, blasted throughout the hall. "You know the dangers that one once posed to all Kingdom States. We had no option, but to act immediately. Delay was not tenable. The intelligence proved false. That one has faded to trouble us no more. Of that we are most certain. Seek verification, if you wish upon the field of Madricore. Almandine apologises, secure in the knowledge, our brothers of Spessa understand the need for swift action, and freely give us pardon."

"Great Lord, Spessa is most grateful for your vigilance. Be sure, I will convey all that has been said this day."

Through the eyeholes of the mask, her vision blurred by salted water, Clara watched him bow, and scrape, his way out of the cleared floor space, back into the mass below.

"Ambassadors from Tocantinae next," Clump growled, soft into her ear. "Renewal of trading rights."

"Zumacdgh medgh," she cried, issuing the formal invite louder than usual.

A slight buzzed vibration between her breasts. A soft murmuring not heard a moment ago. The speak-cube, somehow activated, had begun to spin out its knowledge. It was not leverage, pressure, warmth, or any other of the ways she had tried, but simple words. The words of formal invitation, spoken in the old language: zumacdgh medgh.

Chapter 10.

If a child be not disciplined when young, how will it know discipline when grown? Where then does fault lie, if not with the parents or guardians?
Severely limited in talent, the fused ones who had allied themselves to one faction, or another, found it hardest to give up berserker ways. Strength they had, speed, agility, and great stamina in abundance, but little intellect, or so I have come to believe. Or is it, perhaps, war itself that breeds a kind of intransigent madness?
In time of peace, crops spoiled, herds of cattle devastated, homes razed to the ground, and worse by far to the humans of Lessadgh, families killed, or maimed. In time of peace, such action could not be countenanced, the ones of Lessadgh said, redoubling their supplications.
Still, the Disobedient Ones would not hear.
Then did the men of Lessadgh, grow wild with fury. In vengeance, they rose up. Focusing all blame upon the fused ones, who they now claimed were not natural, nor the true children of the gods, but monsters, they set about destroying them.

Over the years, the dogs Clump had given, came to accept her, but never lost their hatred of her boy. When outside, she kept a good strong cudgel by her just in case they should somehow get out of the barn. She worked her land. Her boy played in the dirt beside her. For added security, so she would know exactly where William was, she fastened a length of cord around his waist that was then attached to her own. He was always with her. Inside the house, morning, or night, she made sure every door and window was locked, and even then, kept him always in her sight.

If she lived in fear, she believed it was a price that must be paid, and worth paying. William's childish prattle made her heart flutter. When he wound affectionate arms round her neck, or kissed her, happiness flooded through her. His smile filled her heart with sunshine, and she loved him. With all her heart, Clara loved her boy.

The days were always full of activity. At night, when William slept safe in bed beside her, she thought of Clump, missing his rude bluntness, his secrecy, and the luxurious gifts he had once brought. Most of all she missed Clump for himself, grieving for the loss of friendship in her own way.

The threat he had been so adamant would come about had not materialized. No one had claimed William, growing from toddler to eight-year-old infant, and perhaps, never would, but both the little box-cart in the barn gathering dust, and the dogs rampaging about the property at night, were constant reminders of his gruff kindness.

Chapter 11.

Illness does not touch us. Old age does not wrinkle us on the outside, nor shrivel us from within. Our bones do not crumble, nor do our bodies disintegrate bit by bit, as do the imperfect bodies of the humans of Lessadgh. We do not die, leaving remains to taint the air with stink while mouldering in the ground.
We, the offspring of the Disobedient Ones, slowly grow pale, and paler, with the passing of time. So slow, it is not noticeable until...one day it is apparent, and we know the weight of many spans, lying heavy upon our shoulders, begins to bear us down. Our colours losing their brightness, we fade, and fade, until we are no more.
Since we are long-lived, we did not learn of this until ages past. The men of Lessadgh remained in ignorance even longer, but in their warring, they had learned excessive loss of life force to the point of draining, would make us disappear. One of the fused ones they treated so. Another, not so grievously wounded, they took captive, incarcerating him in a labyrinth deep underground on an island far out to sea.
How the Disobedient Ones came to hear of this, I know not, but of a sudden, the offspring they had seeded were of interest. Gathering all who would go, they took the ones with dual forms into the great worship houses built to pay them homage. For safekeeping they took these ones in.

Rich, and sonorous in tone, the voice spoke the old language. The speak-cube ran, telling its knowledge in words Clara could not understand.

"Were you not faded, I would damn your heart and liver," she growled at the emerald tablet. "In giving this knowledge, I am made to work hard for it, you cunning, old bastard."

Could she ask Clump? She thought he knew the old language, though the breach between them was still not fully healed. The asking might open that wound, and ignite yet another quarrel. Did she want to risk that? The speak-cube was still running. How to stop it?

"Zumacdgh medgh," she said hoping the formal words of invitation might bring it to a halt.

Atrament continued to speak.

That settles it. What choice do I have? Clump... No wait! Malfroid may know the old language. I will ask him what words to use. If he knows, I shall sound him out to see if he is willing to translate for me.

"Lady?" Malfroid said, when she was shown into his salon. "Something urgent brings you here?"

"It is a piffling matter…"

"That had you running through the corridors of the Helm at this hour?" The brightness of his blue eye sharpened with suspicion, he leant to look her in the face. "Best tell me of it," he said, soft, and listened carefully to what she said, sorting truth from fiction as she spoke.

"A sudden interest in the old language," Malfroid said, and smiled a lazy, knowing smile. "I wonder, for what reason might that be?"

"For sparns," she lied, "I have spoken the traditional greeting without ever knowing how to tell someone to cease speaking. I thought you might have a smattering of the tongue, but if you have not, it is no loss."

"Zumacdgh needgh," Malfroid said. "Talk not, the exact opposite to talk to me." Clara repeated what he had said, stumbling over subtle twists in seemingly simple words. "I presume this has something to do with the casket you bought back from Atrament's lair?"

"Clump told you about it?"

"Why should he not, when the likelihood is, all of Noor shall hear of it soon? The security of the Helm is mine. Knowing I do duty at all times, of course he confided his opinion Atrament faded, could be as dangerous as Atrament living. I share his concern. There is definite risk. It grieves me, Clara, you made no mention to me of it."

"Will you quarrel with me also?'

"No, I merely point out you are High Lord of the Helm. A risk you run, could affect us all, throughout Almandine, and beyond."

"There is no risk, Malfroid. I am sure of it. The casket was given for another reason. One, I do not yet know, so do not ask me. I have need of a translator," she said, coming straight to the point, instead of winding her way about it. "There is a speak-cube, like a cube, but not. It is more like a tablet than anything else. Zumacdgh medgh activated it. I have no clue what is being said. I do not have time to learn the blasted language, so I have need, as I said. Zumacdgh needgh will hopefully stop its play, but my tongue slips, and is clumsy on the words."

"You require me to come to your apartments, then?"

"If you would be so good, it would be much appreciated."

"Zumacdgh needgh," Malfroid said, and the mellow voice of Atrament ceased.

Picking up the speak-cube, Clara slid it into its pouch, saying, "If you would consider translation, I would be most thankful."

"My knowledge of the old language is not good enough. I have not managed to master the complexity of it." To Clara's frowned inquiry, he answered, "Nuances that can turn a phrase upon its head, or a word meaning one thing made into something entirely different, that is the problem. A big one. If you insist on hearing Atrament speak, it is important to understand exactly what he says."

"Then, what am I to do? He has knowledge about my boy."

"Yes," Malfroid shifted uneasily. "Clump mentioned something of the sort. May I make a suggestion? Only we three know of the speak-cube, and must keep it so. Clump not only has the old language, he can speak it fluent."

"I should ask him? I had not thought of that," she lied.

"Ask him nice. Ask him pretty. Ask him with full courtesy. In the interests of Almandine, if nothing else, perhaps he will do it."

"You mean..."

"I mean, when blade touches blade, fragments from each are shorn away. Use a gentler method than your usual, Clara."

Instead of summoning Persimony Clump, she went to his apartments accompanied by Malfroid. Throughout the discussion, an agreement made, and conditions set, Clara had the feeling both of them had somehow known what her predicament would be, and had carefully rehearsed such a meeting.

What did it matter, she thought, she had her interpreter, and would get the knowledge she craved. Malfroid would be present to hear all that was said in order to make an ongoing assessment of risk, and Clump would get what he wanted, whatever that was.

Chapter 12.

The Disobedient Ones chose one worship house, and abandoning all others, took the fused ones with them to congregate beneath a single roof. In conference, they acknowledged, tasks once performed alone, they could not now achieve. Only, acting in unity, could they have enough talent to perform a great making.
Matter they drew to them to create a world they would name Noor, the place of perfect light, and painting it with vivacious colours, most pleasing to their eye, wrapped the material around Lessadgh, denying that place the full brightness of the sun. All things good to them, they called forth, and mantled Noor with mountains and valleys, seas and grasslands, and all things necessary to sustain their offspring. Content with this newest creation, the Disobedient Ones took the fused ones into it, with the exception of the fishtailed ones, who were not to be found at this time, and set up gates that all their children might follow, if they had a mind.
When the sun shone not so bright, the men of Lessadgh had no understanding why this might be, and cast about for the reason. To the house of worship they went, and girding up courage; went through that place only to discover the Disobedient Ones were gone. Dismayed, they went to the true children, the firstborn who remained, to ask what fault they had committed that they were forsaken, but got no answer. Throughout their world; the people of Lessadgh searched, but finding no trace of those they venerated as gods, beat their breasts, tore out their hair and wailed, so great was their anguish.
Statues, huge in height and breadth, they carved, and setting these up in the worship houses in their stead, paid these idols homage. Stories, they made, concerning those who had gone that soon passed into myth and legend.
The gates the Disobedient Ones had left open for their children to pass through at a time of their choosing, became known as sally ports, but some of their offspring had come to care about the humans of Lessadgh over much, and never came.
The fourth thing learnt by the Disobedient Ones was learned then. The weight of spans would no longer rest lightly upon them, but bear them down until they staggered beneath its oppressive crush, and between the millstones of shortened time, they would be ground to very dust.

"Talk not."
"Well," Clara asked expectant, "what was said, Clump?"
"He speaks of the forefathers creating Noor. Of them abandoning

Lessadgh, and taking the fused ones to the new world, together with some of their other children. The sally ports be touched on. These we know exist still, though in smaller number than before. He also talks of immortality lost as punishment."

"Nothing of William?"

Clump shook his head. "It be a potted history, in so far as I can make out, of ancient events seen from Atrament's perspective. It be likely your boy will have no mention till much further on."

"Does he make me listen to all, to hear what most concerns me, or can portions be jumped over?"

"If that were possible," Malfroid said, thoughtful, "how far to leap? How would you know? Co-ordinates of some kind would be needed, but try it, if you wish."

"William. The boy. The child. The Ins..." she could not finish those words. The speak-cube remained silent.

"To all intent and purpose, there be only one way to begin a hearing, and to end it," Clump said. "You must accept, he means the speak-cube to be heard in entirety, Clara."

"Once again, he pushes me to act upon his intent, and in a time of his choosing, gives me reward," she said, her voice harsh with anger, and disappointment, "knowing I cannot refuse because of my boy."

"How else have you been pushed?" Malfroid asked.

"Choices," Clara wiped a tear from her eye. "I am pushed to make a choice."

"Which brings me timely to..." from the corner of his eye, Clump saw Malfroid discreetly shake his head, "to take my leave. The hour be late. Until next darkling then."

"I was about to ask her," Clump said, when they had gone from Clara's apartments, and were a little way down the corridor. "Why did you advise not to?"

"She was tight wound. To make mention of the casket, of the other things we know are in it, what would have her reaction been?" Malfroid said, smooth. "I will tell you. An argument. That is what. A razor would her tongue have been, and yours a bludgeon. She would not say. You would counter by refusing to translate. Nothing moves when frozen stiff, as would the mood between you both have become. She cares nothing for the speak-cube, save what she may learn about her child. Her focus rests solely on him, where he is, and what he does that keeps him from her. For the present, the other items are forgot. If there is risk, it lies dormant. Give her time to accept, she must hear the speak-cube through, then pretty words soft spoken, may prosper us all."

Chapter 13.

Who could fathom the minds of the Disobedient Ones? I understood not why they had desired to lay with the women of Lessadgh.
That some of my siblings cared for the humans of Lessadgh, that also did I not understand, nor why some chose to stay out of Noor because of it.
By right of birth, the true children of the Disobedient Ones, for no others could claim such direct descent, these ones now bred children for themselves, and in time their progeny begat children, too. For me, who would not spill my seed into even one of my own kind, this was offence. More, it was a most grave and deep transgression.
To squander seed in the women of Lessadgh, or to open wombs to the men of Lessadgh, in my mind such acts were crimes committed. In such a way talent's purity would be diluted by these couplings, such was my thought, and the firstborn together with their offspring violated the unique gift they had inherited.
In generations yet to come, the humans of Lessadgh would wash talent away. In the redness of their watery blood, talent would drown. Such was my perception.

Her child asleep on the settle, all Clara could see of him was a tuft of crimson hair poking above the blankets, which had not dulled as expected. Unlocking the back door, opening it slightly, she picked up the basin, and went out into the night.

It would be a cold one, she noted, throwing dirty water to one side of back step. For a moment, she stood there, marvelling at the fullness of the brightest moon, and how many stars speckled the clear sky with pinpoint radiance.

One of the dogs yapped, trilling out a disjointed, excited howl. Immediately, the other took up the cry, yammering and yowling in frenzied concert. Two sleek shapes, stretched to full stride, rounded the barn, and sped down toward the walled orchard.

From its shadow, an extremely tall, two-legged figure fled out into a patch of moonlight, and stumbled as it looked back over its shoulder. Thin legs frantically pistoned feet that skimmed the ground, its arms pumped, drawing itself through air as a swimmer might water, and a long garment of some kind was spread, flapping behind it. Heading for the common land, it disappeared into the dark. Silent, now the hunt was in earnest, the dogs followed in deadly pursuit.

Transfixed, her breath frosting the night with tiny spurts of panic, Clara's mind raced. Her boy. Had someone come for her boy? Or was this a precursor of a future event?

The dogs were at bay. The growling snarls said as much with the sudden change in their tone. Disappointed whines, interjected into those sounds, signalled their quarry was lost, though they were still expectant. This message propelled her back inside the house.

"William! William, wake up," her voice trembled. "Wake up. We have to leave." She shook him. "William!" She shook him harder, but could not pull him from sleep.

Calm, calm, I must be calm. I must hurry, but hurry in a calm fashion. Think logically. Think methodically. What is needed?

Throwing her shawl about her shoulders, she snatched the lantern from the table, went outside, and slammed the door fast behind her. She crossed the open ground before the barn, slipped the latch, and slid inside. Her goats made uneasy by the commotion, moved restless.

"Bless you Clump," she said on a breath, sweeping dust, and a matted tangle of dog hair out of the back of the small cart with her hands as best she could. From the box, under the narrow seat, she took out the harnesses Clump had made, and stopped to listen. The dogs still howled the same message. Nerves on edge, their strange eyes wary, the goats backed away when she went toward them.

Useless minutes spent trying to coax unwilling beasts to wear the trappings. More useless minutes spent trying to force them. They butted, tried to bite, and kick her, each attempt made earning a more violent refusal.

What should I do?

She put the harnesses into the back of the box cart, thinking it was not so heavy, and if need be, she would draw it herself. Throwing the barn doors wide, she dragged it out, and setting the shaft down realised, wheels scrunching over light frost were the only sounds she had heard. The night was still. The dogs no longer barked, or whined.

What to do? It will not be safe to bring William out of the house, not without knowing exactly where they are, and even then, there is risk. A risk worth taking?

If the dogs caught William's scent, they would be on him in minutes, and she would not be able to fend both off. Could she locate them, lure them into the barn? Bar the doors, and let the goats fend for themselves as best they could? William, and she, would have a chance to get away, if she could do that.

She went outside, and looked down past the walled orchard to the common land. The animals were coming toward her, moonlight dappled and moving slow, with great streams of frozen breath coming from their nostrils, curling in air above them. Going to the cart, she took the harnesses back out, and stationed herself where they could see her. Unhurried, the dogs came on, went past her, caught a scent and came back to sniff the leather dangling from her hands. Running their noses along the lengths of it, recognising a scent with half-closed eyes, neither made any protest when she slipped the trappings on them, buckling it round neck, under chest, and over shoulders. Almost meek, the animals allowed her to secure them to the shaft.

William slept on. Tucking the blankets round him, Clara lifted him up. *Almost the same as our nightly ritual, save I do not carry him to a feather mattress, but a bed of a different kind.*

The dogs growled deep, and low, when she came out of her cottage. Laying him in the cart, they twisted, and bucked, trying to get free, and it pitched forward and began to roll. Clinging to the side, she was dragged along while trying to bring it to a halt. Straining against the weight of the little vehicle, claws gouging the ground, muscled haunches quivering with effort, the dogs gained momentum. She managed to climb on, to pull herself up to the narrow seat, before the animals lurched into the beginnings of speed, and found their stride. Bounced and jolted, Clara looked for the guide reins, only to find there were none.

Mile, after bruising mile, the iron-bound wheels crushed slender branches, struck small rocks, and large stones, jarred against tussocks of coarse grass, bumped into deep ruts, and out of them. The cart creaked, and groaned, as it sped along. The wind ripped at her, its coldness gnawing through clothing, and boots, until she was numb with it. Not knowing where they were, or where they were going she clung on, terrified the cart might overturn, or break up beneath them. Over fields, the dogs raced. Down winding tree-lined lanes, their pace slackened only to pick up again coming out into open space.

Pointless to remain on the seat, tossed violently from side to side, and hanging on for dear life when she had no control. Climbing into the back of the cart, she lay beside William, cushioning him with her body, and enfolding him in her arms. Telling him when he woke, startled and crying, they were having an adventure.

"What kind" he asked.

She answered, if she knew that it would not be an adventure.

They were travelling through dense woodland. Dawn, pale, pink and hesitant, showed between the lace-worked branches, and twigs of the trees. The pace was much slower, and had been for some time now. The rasping, long-drawn breaths of the dogs had relaxed into steadier intakes of air. The cart seemed to be intact, and William, bored with an adventure where nothing happened, had fallen back into sleep when she smelt smoke.

Raising herself up a little, she peered over the side, and noted, at a snails pace they were coming into a small glade. In the middle, pieces of cut turf had been placed to make a mound that steamed.

"Charcoal burning," she spoke her thought out loud, just as one of the dogs let out a keening howl. The cart stopped, and lurched when the animals sat down, making it plain they would go no further.

What to do now?

She had no idea. If charcoal burners were close by, perhaps they would spare a little food, tell her where she was, and direct her to the nearest village, or something like.

And do what? She fretted, all she had were the clothes on her back.

"You bring trouble to my door?"

She knew that voice. Knew it well. A little way off, under low hanging branches, Clump stood with his hands on his hips.

"It would appear," she answered, sharp, "you provided the means to do it. Those damned harnesses were never meant for goats as I thought, were they?"

"Goats?" Clump growled, his look, and manner, as irascible as she remembered, "what gave you that idea, woman?"

Chapter 14.

Profane abusers of precious talent. Irreverent, recipients of the precious gift. Righteous anger stirred me to act against such ones.
A making of anonymity I spoke and cloaked me in it. Through the chosen sally port, I thundered into Lessadgh. By stealth, I sought out an abuser of talent, fading the first I came on. Jade, the short stabbing sword, I punctured that one with. So great my rage, in thoughtless act, I tore his throat. With my teeth, I tore it, and swallowed the copious flood of life force gushing into my mouth.
Big with child, a woman of Lessadgh he had by him. Her, I dispatched, and did her no honour.
Reward enough to be rid of an abuser, I had not thought to look for more, yet discovered further, and greater, reward was mine. A little of the talent this one cared nothing for, my own talent now nurtured. In channels through which mine own life force ran, this new talent was coupled with it. Unlooked for reward indeed.

Dusk. A curtain of purpled grey slowly drawn to cover the green-waned sky, and yellowed wisps of high-blown clouds. Limping, still shaken by the narrow escape from the jaws of the human woman's slavering dogs, he hurried as best he could. Through deepening dark, tall white turrets gleaming with spectral beauty, came into view. Seeing the Helm was not far off, his pace quickened.

In corridors, fire crystals were beginning to spark. He moved swiftly, negotiating his way with ease through these lanes, and the milling crowds that clogged them, with his arms protecting the paunch protruding through his greatcoat. Speaking to no one, acknowledging no one, he made his way to Semyon's apartments to report a successful mission.

He could not be seen immediately. Semyon had urgent business. He must wait.

Withdrawing into the alcove opposite, he was tempted to take a seat. Certain he would be admitted soon, he resisted temptation, for if he had to wait very long fatigue would push him into sleep, and while he rested, pain would stiffen his injured leg making him appear ridiculous when trying to rise.

When fire crystals reached their fullest height, flaring with a silvery brilliance that bounced wantonly from ceilings and walls, and leapt to invade myriad alcoves lining the draughty corridor, before spilling in joyous torrents through pillared windows into the gardens, and byways beyond, he took a seat. At last, understanding the full import of the wordless insult offered, he channelled what little energy he had left into mounting anger.

He must wait. Semyon was well aware of his presence, and would give him audience, so soon as it was possible.

"Brother, no more waiting," a child-like voice piped. "Break down the door. Better still, go to the Lady Apatia."

Instinctively, his hands went to his paunch, "I dare not. Semyon would fade us both. At the first opportunity, he would do it. Be silent. Be still in your cradle a little longer," he whispered.

The crowds thinned, and disappeared, taking with them hubbub, and jostle. Occasionally, the dull thud of booted feet rose above the susurrant murmurs of the faded, the faint whisper of silken robes, and slippers, joining with them. In the distance, echoing softly, a door quietly opened, and slyly closed. Consumed with fury, he ignored these sounds, for once showing no curiosity in who came, or went, or what the nature of their business was at this late hour.

He must wait. Semyon knew he had information of great import to divulge. Matters of state took precedence over all others.

Now the lustre of fire crystals was waning. Flickering into an ever more fitful, softening glow with oncoming dawn. The dim advance of morning shadows recorded not only the hours he had spent waiting, they charted the journey, the rise and fall, of impotent rage.

Quietly, servants began to move with reverential efficiency through corridors, and halls. Low, and cautious speech, barely audible, edged gradually into more confident tones, and rose seamless through the vocal scale, finally reaching orchestral proportions of chattered sound. Footfall drummed loud on marbled floors by many feet. Doors wrenched open purposefully, slammed in reckless haste. The Helm was wide-awake.

Semyon would see him now.

"Be brief, Slubeadgh," Semyon said, noting with satisfaction how badly he limped. How muddied, and torn, his treasured greatcoat was. How fatigue coloured, and carved deep lines into the thin, much hated face of the creature he loathed.

"I have found the child as the Lady Apatia wished."

"Indeed. You are sure of it? You have seen him?"

"From a distance, sir," Slubeadgh whined.

"From a distance?" Propping his booted feet up on the desk, and lacing his voice with scorn, Semyon said, "From a distance, a tall person may seem small, and a fool, wise."

"No, no, sir, there is more. In the fullness of the brightling, I saw him plain. His hair was unmistakably Faienya. No human of Lessadgh wears such a colour. And tall, almost as tall as the woman of Lessadgh he was with. I had schemed to get a closer look, once the darkling fell, but savage dogs set upon me, and did me terrible injury."

"You were lucky to keep your miserable life, Slubeadgh?'

"Twice, I thought myself surely faded. Once by dogs, and again when I came through the sally port at such speed the force..."

"I would not care had you not come at all," Semyon smiled, and picking up an obsidian dagger twirled it between his fingers. "This then is your report? This is the important information I am to take to the Lady Apatia?"

"I am sure it is the child she seeks, sir."

"I am sure, she will make you suffer, if it is not. Wait outside."

"May I refresh myself in my room, sir?'

'Wait outside, I say. You may be needed at a moment's notice for one reason or another."

"But, sir," Slubeadgh's hands went to his paunch.

"You contest my will?"

Slubeadgh held Semyon's eyes for an instant, and taking note of the faint line of talent marks spread thin across the bridge of his nose, he hung his head. "No, sir, I do as you bid."

"Then begone, you gluttonous creature. Your belly, and its rumblings, will have to wait."

* * *

How to get the stench of the creature out of his nostrils? To keep Slubeadgh waiting throughout the night had amused him. This full-rounded stink, the price paid. As always, the creature's odour disturbed him. Underlining the base tone, faint, but most definitely there, the scent of another. Duality in one person, how could that be? These thoughts occupied Semyon, until coming near the passageway leading to her apartment he caught Apatia's scent. Her natural aroma, a sweet perfume left there hours ago, slowly dissipating in the air, but the message within it still potent. He breathed it deep, read its content, and understood its promises. Sexual excitement, abandoned pleasure, explosive fulfilment. He had drunk deep from that well, and would do so many times again. He would never have enough of her.

Straight from her bath, Apatia came into the room. Droplets of water dribbling languidly over paler than pale skin, dripped from partially dried silvery hair, and slid down breasts pushing against a robe thrown on in haste. Instantly aroused, Semyon bowed.

"You bring news?" she asked, crisp.

"Your creature has just reported. He has found the child you seek."

"Slubeadgh is sure?" Apatia questioned, aware he was helpless to prevent his eyes from roaming across her.

"He says as sure as may be. He suffered some slight misfortune that prevented him from verifying the sighting."

"A misfortune? What?"

"He claims to have been bitten by a dog, Lady."

"The nearest sally port?"

"On your own lands. By good fortune the location, where the child is to be found, bordering on it. Will you hear Slubeadgh tell it?"

"No. Make ready. Chose only those with a tight mouth to accompany us. I will not have my business chattered about in the corridors of the Helm, and in turn, every bean and leaf house in the city. You understand? Slubeadgh must guide us. Tell him, it will not go well for him, if I throw myself through the sally port for nothing. Arrange all within half a segment, Semyon, no longer, and put it about I go hunting today. It is not, after all, so very far from the truth." She moved slowly towards him, and reaching out the tips of her fingers, traced the contour of his cheek. "And, Semyon, when today's work is done, we meet in private for more pleasurable sport."

* * *

Distrusting anything with more than two legs, he had never learnt to ride. Unable to find balance, Slubeadgh slipped from side to side of the haran's back, desperately trying to avoid the barbed quills ranged along its neck, and would have fallen, but for the stirrups his feet were firmly planted in.

"No need to polish the beast's saddle with your arse, stable lads take care of the tack," Semyon sneered, skilfully making his mount rear, and dance, over the cobbles before leading the group out of the Helm.

Trailing at the back of the group, he flew up, and smacked down, wincing each time he made brutal contact with the saddle. His face sullen, Slubeadgh silently cursed his luck at having to pass through the sally port again in so short a time.

"Brother, you should fade the peacock, Semyon," a childlike voice said. "Apatia's favourite he may be, but you must find a way to bring him down. At every turn, he shows us no respect. Forever taking pains to make us a laughing stock. He shows us no pity, laughing at your injury, and I, cradled for overlong. I tell you fade him."

"Be sure I will, Galateo," Slubeadgh promised, "when I find a path that does not lead back to me."

Slow and easy, through the sally port into Lessadgh. The barrier placed over it juddering against them as they came out of a mass of tangled brushwood, and brambles, onto clearer ground. No sign of any dogs. No sign of anyone on the land, and the house in plain sight.

Apatia summoned Sludgeath forward to ask, "Who is with the child?"

"A woman. I saw her over there," he said, pointing to one of the smaller vegetable patches. "The boy was with her. She kept him by her, tied with a leash. All the brightling, I watched, and saw no other."

"Semyon, what does your talent tell you?"

Throwing back his head, he sampled the air, taking in long slow draughts through flaring nostrils.

"A human. Female. A male child. Definitely Faienya, and possibly some dogs, but," he smirked slyly at Slubeadgh, "none are here now."

"Not here?" he wailed. "They cannot be gone."

"None are here now," Semyon repeated, punctuating each word with smarting crispness. "They left some time ago, if I judge it right."

"Some time ago? Some time ago?" Slubeadgh babbled. "Lady, I swear, the fault is not mine. The whole darkling through, I waited to deliver my report. He kept me waiting. Out of spite, Semyon kept me waiting, knowing I had urgent news for you. A message bubble, had I been equipped with a message bubble, no need to wait on Semyon's malicious pleasure."

"Enough! If there is fault," Apatia said, through clenched teeth, "I will judge where it should be laid. Only ascertain they are here, or most surely gone. All of you; search the dwelling. Scour the hovel from top to bottom. If they hide, discover the hiding place. Break down the doors. Rip up the floor. Tear the walls apart, if need be. Do it. Do it, now."

Dropping from her haran, she strode back and forth, trampling rage into the ground. A shambles. A fiasco. Her time wasted. Nothing accomplished, and nothing to show. And fault? Most definitely, there was fault. Her fingers, toying with the little quiver hanging from her girdle, eased the darts in and out of their stays one, by one. The search was useless. Semyon's talent had never proved wrong. Where to lay blame, and how to deal with it? Her eyes, fixing on the house, narrowed. They were making their way back to the sally port, Semyon leading, his guards following and, Slubeadgh slinking behind, kept close to the orchard wall.

"We found nothing, Lady" Semyon said. "Do you wish further search of the grounds?"

Apatia shook her head. "We both know it would be fruitless."

Sauntering further onto the human woman's land, she beckoned him to keep pace with her.

"It is possible they may return."

"Do not play the fool, Semyon. It is plain enough. The woman and child have fled. Some warning they must have received."

"The woman's dogs?"

"I think so, do you not? In such isolation, a woman living alone would be wise to have such as they. Especially caring for a young child, whom she must know, is like to her own kind, yet very obviously not."

"Slubeadgh blundered upon them. His clumsiness is to blame for lack of success."

"Perhaps." Apatia stopped her slow walk, and turned to him. Yellow eyes blazing in the almost phosphorescent colourlessness of her face, she said, "But then, Semyon, you kept him waiting. Through the watches of the darkling, and beyond, you kept Slubeadgh waiting."

"The creature lied. I..."

The point of one of her darts pressed against his throat, the pressure hard enough to make its sharpness known, but not enough to break skin.

"Do not trouble me with lies. Slubeadgh told true. Being more in fear of me, than of you, he could do nothing else. I know the enmity you bear him. That were he not in my favour, under my protection, you would fade him, and laugh while doing it. I hold him accountable. And you, Semyon, you also."

Slubeadgh slowed, and crept nearer to the orchard wall. Something was happening. He recognized the signal given off by Apatia's languid walk. She beckoned Semyon, drawing him away from the others. They spoke. She turned, brought her face close, so very close to his. Light glinting briefly on metal in her hand, now bloomed in a single flash as it was held to his throat. It could only be one of her famous darts she threatened him with. Between Apatia, and the peacock, something momentous was happening.

Fault. That is it. Apatia rightly lays fault at Semyon's door!

Hugging the wall, believing he watched the peacock's rapid fall from the High Lord's good grace, Slubeadgh crept nearer to see him brought low, if not faded.

"You will find this woman and child." Her weapon scratched his neck. Resting the full length of her body against his, Apatia put her lips to the welling life force, and licked the trembling droplet. "Find them for me, Semyon. Hunt them down. Call when they are found. Remember, if Slubeadgh has my favour, you have more. Much more. And there is understanding of a different kind between us, yes?"

"Lady, there is. I shall not fail you."

"No," in one fluid movement, she twisted away from him, launched her dart, and watched it find its mark, "I know you will not."

In the shelter of the wall, Slubeadgh screeched, fell to the ground, and rolled in agony.

"In company with my creature, whom you will not harm to fading, such punishment is for placing your needs above mine for scant amusement. His punishment, he earned for daring to criticize me. This, I will not tolerate. Tell him so, and Semyon, retrieve my dart. Return it when we two next meet."

Chapter 15.

Truth, even to my detriment, I speak it. Arrogance ever went hand in hand with lack of caution. Eschewing the darkling, I went forth in the broadness of the brightling time. Far from the sally port previously gone through, I went again into Lessadgh, where the second one I took, near brought about my downfall.

If physical beauty could have swayed me from my chosen course, hers it would have been. Luscious the sheen of blue-black, velvet skin, made more so by talent marks scattered over it. Well proportioned, tall as I, and very proud, this next generation abuser of talent would have no quiet fading. Jade in both hands, she rose, and came to greet me. Great her ferocity, brilliant her skill in the dance, more than once her blades opened me. And all the while, in the fury of this last fight, she cried desperate to her men and children, 'flee.'

From her, I drank deep. All those with her, I chased down. Her children, I faded. Her men, I slew. To honour this one I took their heads. By their hair, I hung them from my saddle, and rode at speed back through the sally port, with the hood of my cloak wide as a sail.

As remembrance to the courage of this beauty, a great chamber of amethyst I created very deep below the ground, and in this place, kept this one's honour there.

Adamantine, the fangs I caused to come into being, long and sharp-pointed. These I used thereafter. I had no pleasure in the beautiful one's attempts to resist, while my teeth sought firm hold on her neck. Better it were done quick, and clean.

In the full light of the brightling orb, I went no more into Lessadgh, nor again did I issue challenge. When the darkling brought down the brightling orb, and held it by its heels, till it could come again, then I went to my work using stealth.

In such a way the beginning of terror was begun.

"He cared for nothing, but talent," Clara said, putting the speak-cube back into its pouch. "I saw the skulls he speaks of. Did I tell you of that?"

"No," Clump answered, "you have told us little, and we, not pushed you to it."

"I had no understanding of what significance he attached to them. There were so many, so many skulls lining the ledges on all walls. Amethyst crystals had been placed in the eye sockets, thinking, he did those whom he faded honour," Clara said shaking her head, "how can that be?"

"Who knows? In strange ways, does the mind oft time work, and very different were the ancient spans." Malfroid glanced sideways at Clump.

"You saw him. What did he look like?"

"He had a beauty, both strange, and terrible. A loincloth wrapped about his hips, displayed talent marks racing over every part his body. Never had I seen so much talent in one person before. Even as I looked at him, I knew it was not Atrament in the flesh, but a replica of some kind, he had created. Pride, I think, would not let him be seen maimed, and likely close to fading. In physical appearance, he was as different to you as the Faienya are to me. His colours deeper, richer, more vibrantly striking, and his talent, no mean glow, or glimmer, shone like flame."

"The fangs he speaks of," Malfroid said, tentative, to no one in particular, "they would have been something he cared much about. It is possible, he would not have destroyed them, since fashioned for a specific purpose they were? What think you, he did with them?"

"Plain, and blunt, an end to slow jigging about," Clump said. "It is my belief they be one of the artefacts you bought away in the casket, Clara. Do you deny it?"

"No. No, I deny it not." She sat quietly picking her fingers, twisting the emerald ring she always wore, twisting it once, twisting it twice, and stroking the table of the gem. "It is not beyond the bounds of probability," she said, when the silence had become unbearable, "you wish to see them, Malfroid." Without waiting for an answer, she got up, rummaged for some minutes in the bottom of a cupboard. "It is here," she drew the casket out. "Come to the table. Assess all you please," a trace of sarcasm trickled through her voice, "what risk they may present, though I tell you, I cannot see how the foul things could threaten this Kingdom State, or any other."

Throwing open the lid of the casket, she took the bundle out, laid it on the wooden surface, and gesturing to it with a small bow, walked away.

Carefully, Malfroid found a corner of the shawl, peeled the cloth gently to one side, and began the same process on another in a slow, cautious reveal. A scintillating flash of roped green-gold, and the dull, subtle gleam of coppered-silver winked from a piece of a small basket woven from urilatum. Next to him, Clump gasped and reeled, and steadied himself by grasping the lip of the table.

"What troubles you?" Clara asked.

"The little quiver Apatia always wore slung on her girdle," Malfroid said, gentle, pulling the last of the cloth away.

"It was a thing accursed," Clump growled, "that once belonged to the Anathema. In contravention to the ancient code, the she-bitch Lingaradgh wore its likeness. But that," his eyes starting from his head, his face blanched of all colour, he pointed at it as he stumbled away, "that, by all the powers I swear, be not my work."

"Your work?"

"You have kept your secrets close. I keep mine a while yet, Clara," he shouted, and flung out of the room.

Chapter 16.

Where did I not go in Lessadgh to continue work begun? I tell you, all parts, and in all places I found the firstborn of the Disobedient Ones, who had remained in Lessadgh, were multiplying. So also were their children, and children's children.
As water spilled from a goblet, rushes out to soak whole swathes of the cloth it stands upon, these ones were spreading out over lands, where none had ever walked before.
And what of precious talent? In virulent fashion it was drowning in the red water of human blood. In proof of this catastrophe, the women of Lessadgh died not in the birthing as in former times.
Through every sally port, and there were very many in those brightling times of which I speak, I passed again, and again. Fading some with violence, while they slept. Charming some with a seductive making, who in response, willingly offered necks for draining. Behind me, a trail of corpses with head intact, or without, as circumstance dictated. Talent I took where I could, and shone the better for it.
Soon, few there were, who did not know what waited in the shadows of the darkling. Terror went before me. Death-stalker, the humans of Lessadgh called me then. Vampyre, they call me now. None knew, who I truly was, though many have since imitated me.
And small compensation there was. Leaving human mates behind, a few of the Faienya went into Noor, and taking their children with them, came never into Lessadgh again.
I would, all had done so.

The boy hid behind Clara, his head buried in her skirts, and shawl.

"What need is there to be afraid?" she said, gentle. "Persimmony Clump is a friend, one not seen in a long time, but a friend nevertheless. Will you not greet him?" The boy pressed closer, sunk his head deeper. "I am sorry, Clump, we are not used to company. We have kept to ourselves, have we not, William?"

"Leave him be. Force not the boy to good manners. He does well to be wary of strangers, and likely this be very confusing for him."

"Yes," she said, not knowing what else to say, "adventures can be."

"We will talk of adventures, and what may come of adventuring, later. What be needed at present be warmth, and food. Follow me."

Leading them away from the glade, Clump wound through the trees until reaching an area thick with undergrowth, he stopped. Telling them to stand back, he squatted, groped among a mass of dried roots, and snarled ivy, then grunting satisfaction, slowly straightened. Earth-darkened, a length of thick rope emerged from the greenery, scattering a detritus of withered leaves, dried twigs, and clotted soil, as it was raised, and becoming taut, shivered in mid air as he began to lift a hidden trap door.

Wooden steps led down to a corridor, its ceiling, walls, and floor, shored up and lined by well-fitted planks, and beams. Placed at intervals all along, candles lit in lanterns, chased away the gloom. A short walk, the thump of their footsteps reverberant on the boards, they went into a large open area with a wood-stove burning.

"Well come to my home," Clump said. "There be porridge simmering on the hot plate. Eat, if you will. Tea there be, and coffee also, in cupboards over here. If you have need of them, for added warmth, blankets be in the sleeping area over there. This place," he pointed to a curtained alcove, "you may not go into. This be my work space, and private. Now, leaving you to your own devices, I go to see to the dogs, and draw the box-cart out of view. Make yourselves comfortable as best you may."

* * *

The sound of jade tinkling on harnesses, the soft whickering of the harans, and their tread, crisp on frosted grass, was gone. Gone through the sally port with Apatia, and with her, the ceremonial guard he commanded. Semyon did not watch them go. Humiliating enough to be left behind. Left in the drab world of Lessadgh in a situation he had not foreseen, and in hateful company, without witnessing confirmation of it.

By the walled orchard, Slubeadgh writhed in agony. His groans of pain were intermittently entwined with improbable whining argument.

The foul creature is disordered. Fit only for carrion. Would I could make him so, Semyon thought trudging over to where he rolled, and thrashed. "Hush your mewling," he said, bending to extract Apatia's dart. "For the present, it seems, I must forget you have brought me to this, you vile snake. Rise to your feet. There is work to be done."

"I cannot. I cannot. The dust in Apatia's dart doubtless fades me.

I feel its fatal presence in life force streaming."

"Dust may be rollicking in your soup, but not the fatal kind, fool."

"No?"

"Some other penance she exacts, but not a fading."

"No?" Slubeadgh stopped pummelling the ground with his arms, and legs, and lay still. "No, I see it clear, shock brought me to that belief, but...but now, I think more clearly," he sat up, and sobbing relief, sank his face into his hands. "How could she fade me, her most faithful servant? She could not, for by doing so she would dim her eyes and ears."

"On your feet, I say. The child she craves is yet to be found."

"We two, yes, we two will find him. In this we are equal."

Semyon fell to his knees, grabbed a hank of Slubeadgh's hair, and twisted the thin face to look into his own. Smiling pleasantly, he said, "Do not, for one moment, think we are alike, you and I. Equal, we have never been, you excremental dollop, you worthless, sniffling streak of rat's piss. Equal, we never shall be, in favour, or out. Coward, you are marked. Forever running here, and there, gathering tales embellished in the retelling to bring your betters to ruin. A festering sore, a continual blight you are, and always shall be. You see the difference between our stations?" Releasing him, Semyon wiped his hand on his jacket, and strode away. "Be sure your contribution will be told!" he cried, without a backward glance.

"He named you fool, and rightly. Did I not tell you to bridle your tongue, brother?" a childlike voice hissed. "Your outburst earned Apatia's dart in payment. The dust it contained yet to be known, the result affects us. Do you work hard to fade us both, or am I your target yet again? In our mother's womb, you consumed me, brother, but could not digest the whole. I am what your embryonic self made of me. Growing with you, part of you, I am. More than you can know. Have a care with me, with us. On your feet! To the peacock's face, show yourself servile. Be acquiescent to all his commands. I will look for opportunity to fade him, after the child has been found, and tell you when to strike."

"You are right, Galateo," Slubeadgh scrambled to his feet. "As ever, you are in the right."

* * *

A deep breath taken, slowly released. The process repeated again, and again. Apatia, with one palm flat against the door, breathed to calm fluttering nerves, and hammering heart. Her voice low, she rounded vowels to utmost fullness, and compressed consonants to near oblivion, chanting words she had been taught to unlock the door, and open it.

Off bounds, held secure by high walls, and a devious making, the garden she went into was sprawled, and overgrown. The path she must take, meandering through willodgh trees, chilled her before stepping onto it. Many times, she had trodden the beaten road of latticed grass, and always sped along its distance. Ears blocked to voices stirring the fronds of the willodghs, not wanting, not willing to hear what they said of treachery, and a life lived in limbo, she still caught fragments of the stories they told. It would be no different today. Today, there would be another frantic dash to the round summerhouse with its pillars, domed roof, and spire of crystal, her mother's retreat, at the very centre of this place.

Gathering the folds of her cloak close, Apatia breathed deep again, readying herself for the fast trot, and the sprint that would follow.

"Mother?" Her voice echoing from walls, bounded with drunken, percussive vigour up the stairwell. "Mother?" Apatia called again, wiping sweat from her face with her hands, while semblances of her voice sped to announce her presence. Nervous, her mouth dry with the effort just made, and the audience to come, she smoothed cobweb fine hair that floated on every random draught.

"Come," a chiming resonance that could only be her mother drifted down. "Bring your news to me."

Climbing the spiral stair, she thought how best to tell it. How to tell of a catch unwittingly warned, and stupidly lost, and the measures taken to seize hold of the child her mother most fervently wanted. Hovering in the doorway, seeing the washed out shade of talent spangling her mother's face, and the hard lines of frowning concentration drawn upon it, she blurted out, "They were gone. When we arrived to take the child from the woman of Lessadgh, both were gone.'"

Lingaradgh looked up from books, and charts, strewn across the tabletop.

"And?"

"I have sent Semyon, and Slubeadgh, to find them."

"Apatia," Lingaradgh stalked out from behind the table. "Delay is a thing I cannot afford. See me? See how colour, once vibrant, goes from me?"

"They will not fail, Mother."

"They will not fail? Understand, girl, if they fail, their failure is yours and mine." Taking her arm, Lingaradgh led her to the window. "Sweet, daughter, foolish child of mine, do you imagine it costs me nothing to keep your Kingdom pristine? Its tall spires shining, its turrets gleaming, its bridges delicately arched from one wondrous building to another, its avenues broad and straight, its many gardens smelling sweet?"

"I know it costs you much, Mother."

"That is so. The making goes ever round in my head. Darkling and brightling it spins without end, or beginning, burning energy from me at every turn. This is the price I pay. The price to deceive all eyes with marvels, with illusions of grandeur, and beauty, and more energy is lost by the tariff I pay to fend off the probes sent by the Guardians to detect walkers on the Way of Atrament. And the Way, in velvet whispers says, in a voice both loud, and clear, the child is the key. The child is the key to unlock all things. The child is the beginning of knowledge without end, and undreamt power." Lingaradgh's fingers dug into Apatia's arm. "And, if I fade before my time, go down into oblivion that is the void, what of you, daughter? The scales that blind all eyes will disappear. As summer mist, my making will go, and truth be revealed.

"Will you rule then? Rule what? With what, and how will you rule? You, whose talent is spread so thin it cannot raise a breath's puff in high-wind. Apatia, all our plans come to nothing without this child." The pressure of her fingers screwed deeper into her daughter's flesh, her sonorous voice now dripping acid, "And you tell me...all now rests in the hands of the rod you ride so frequent, and the malformed twins with but one head and one set of limbs between them? Know this, if failure come, daughter mine, I will strike you down, myself. Now get you hence."

Shaken, Apatia made her way outside, and rested her forehead against one of the marble pillars, hoping its coldness would ease pressure built up inside it.

"I rule," she moaned, "I am Lord of the Helm, and that is real. That is all that really matters."

Even as she spoke, she knew words spoken to reassure were hollow, and had less substance than a shadow. She was the visible source of power, she sat in the Chair of Authority, wore the mask, the headgear, robes of office, and the quiver, an ancient mark of high status, slung always on her girdle. But, Lingaradgh's talent drove the kingdom. Her artistry held it in place. Her own talent, so lacking no cultivation could further it, cemented them together. Dependant, she was, and could never break free. Come good or ill, it was so.

* * *

"Come. Sit down. Leave the dishes, and pans, they can be washed later."

"It will not take long, and the water will grow cold, if left."

"'Clara, now the boy sleeps, some talk we must have of the next move."

"The next move, Clump?" frowning, wiping her hands dry on a cloth, she came to the table, and sat down. "I do not understand."

"If there be a kinder way to say what must be said, I do not know it. You cannot remain here for any length of time. They will be looking for you."

"How can we be found? We are directly under a charcoal burner's mound. Who would think to look here? Besides, to all intent and purpose, William and I have disappeared. No one saw us leave, nor where we went, your dogs saw to that."

"It is my belief, the dogs saw off someone gathering intelligence. The Faienya do not sap energy by coming through the sally port for nothing. Confirmation was likely needed. Yesterday, you and the boy were outside?"

"Yes," she nodded, "not a day passes when we are not working the land. The vegetable patches at the back of the cottage had our attention."

"Then, the sighting be made. Talent be how they will find you and your boy, Clara. Make no mistake of it." He held out his hands, turned the glowing palms uppermost. "You have no understanding of talent, and why should you? Were I to cut myself, my blood, which Faienya call life force, would flow green...not red like yours. You humans call talent, skill. A natural aptitude, you say, when one of your people performs an act exceptionally well.

"For the Faienya, talent be magnified, exceeding your people's skill many, many times over. Through life force, talent runs invisible till receptors, stimulated by puberty, bring it forth to shine beneath our skin. Accelerated power, physical, or mental, to do a certain thing be the gift of talent, in some cases a number of things. For me, it be manifested in just one place, my hands. The strength, or weakness, of talent be made evident by the glow, high shine, or dull, and how liberally we are sprinkled with it, little or much."

Sceptical, Clara said, "Show me your talent at work."

"Very well, if you wish it." Getting up from the table, Clump went to the curtain screening his workplace, and drew it aside. "Enter. Here, you will see to best account. All things on the bench, and shelves, be made by me."

Cups, plates, bowls, badges, jewellery, anything that could be made with metal, anything that could be set with gems, both common, and rare, were crammed into the small space.

"Look close, so there be no doubt in your mind," he said, taking a small ingot of gold between thumb, and forefinger. Under slight pressure the metal spread. Clump pinched it in half. Laying aside one piece, he stroked the metal, shaping it into a broad strip. Caressing the strip, he coaxed it to form a band, joining the ends seamlessly together to make a ring. Taking a small wooden box from a drawer in the bench, he carelessly scattered gemstones on its surface, and selected a large emerald. His fingers teased the metal, drawing up four elegant prongs. Gently rubbing the gold over his palms, he polished it to brightness. Between the prongs, he positioned the stone, and fluidly closed the claws over to hold the emerald secure.

"Take it," he said, holding the finished piece out, "for all it is a crude thing, it is the best that can be done in minutes."

"It is warm!" Clara said.

"It be yours. Green be the colour of life for the Faienya. Green the skies, green the water, and green the life force of Noor. I chose it for you, Clara, in hope long life hangs heavy from your shoulders, yet the weight be unfelt. Try it on. You will find it be a good fit."

"If I had not seen you make this with my own eyes, Clump, I should never have believed it."

"You will accept a small gift, given with good heart without argument? Wear it always. Let it be evidence, should you forget, more things exist in this world, and others, than you could possibly know. Take the ring, Clara, in the spirit it was made and given."

"I know not what to say."

"Then, say nothing."

"Very well, I give you thanks," she said, slipping it onto her finger, "for your help, and also for giving me understanding of how great talent is. The question now is; how shall we be found?"

"There be many methods, but I favour smell. Your scent, and that of the boy, will linger, especially on cold air. It be easy for one with certain talent marks to snatch it from the chill. Intelligence gathered will, no doubt, have been quickly reported to agents waiting close by. Yes, to my mind, smell be the quickest way to locate you."

Her face rimed with worry, she asked, "How long do you think before this comes to pass?"

Clump shrugged, "Hard to say, a day, or two...three at most. The dogs have rested. I will turn them loose to run through the woods, so they may give warning, if need there is. You must be on the move again by tomorrow morning at the very latest. Sleep, if you can."

Chapter 17.

As the waves of the sea gently ripple the shore, so had begun the abandonment of hateful Lessadgh. The campaign went on. Terror increased. Terror, the spur used to turn a trickle into a flood. I made it so, by deliberate violence done to humans held dear by the true children of the Disobedient Ones, and their children's children. With calculated savagery, dismembering those slain, leaving Lessadgh corpses to rot, but son occasion I left one alive to carry the tale. These humans, gibbering of atrocity, my unwitting allies were. By fang and seduction those careless of talent, I faded.
Pity did not then abide in me, nor in truth, does it now. As an onrushing tide, so was the exodus from Lessadgh into Noor.
The true children of the Disobedient Ones, and their children, ten generations on, came, bringing their possessions with them, leaving all else behind, or so I thought then.
Pestilent is humanity, its virulence ferocious, and implacable. Its infections oft time hid deep, its imperfections buried beneath seeming outward perfection.
Human traits, customs and language easy to detect, but corrosive in and of their own nature, could not be ousted, but intermingled with the ancient customs and tongue of the Faienya. Once richly layered and subtle, by inferior simplistic words laced with poverty-stricken meaning, so was our language forever changed.
Not so apparent, faulty human genes that in the seeded womb sprang out of latent state to form abnormalities. And worse of all things abhorrent, the ninth and tenth generations, lately passed through the sally ports to Noor, found on coming into their own, the fullness of talent washed down to the dregs.
Sex, in our history, played no trifling role. And I? I had what I had wished for, and in having it, found that which I sought to preserve almost spent. I had nothing.

"Imperfect humans subverted perfect Faienya?" Clara smiled. "Improbable, don't you think?"

"I have no wish to debate the subject," Clump said, getting to his feet. "Translation I have carried out this darkling, as be the agreement, and be on my way."

"Take no notice of Clump," Malfroid said, as the door closed, "he has not yet got over his little outburst, and vehemently declines to explain why sight of the quiver distressed him so."

"You believe this?" Clara waggled the speak-cube at him before sliding it into its pouch.

"I truly believe a lesser thing can bring one greater down. Also, it answers for the wide variety of colours we Faienya wear, together with the absence of white in some eyes, and its presence in others. Why some look very much like you, as does Clump, and others for the most part, as I. Height, too, it explains. You, and Clump, are practically of the same stature, and I, taller by far. Hence, in Faienya eyes, you are both Stunted Ones, as are those who live beyond the Drusy Sea. He speaks of abnormalities. A curious thing, this is, that I know nothing of. What can you tell me of it?"

"It is not common in Lessadgh, but it is known. Those unfortunate enough to be born this way often lead lives that are as full as those who are not. It is a matter of perception."

"Clara, what do you intend to do with the quiver and fangs?"

"I had thought to destroy them."

"Yet you have not?" Malfroid smiled his crooked smile. "I am of the opinion they are linked in some way, and have purpose, other than that to be seen, or which we know of. They were given for a reason. A specific reason."

"I am glad to hear you say it. Your opinion matches my own."

"Good. Lay these artefacts aside. In time, all things become clear."

"And Clump?" She twisted her emerald ring. Round once. Round twice. "What if he urges me to be rid of them?"

"A small deception?" Malfroid's brilliantly blue eye took on a darker hue. "For peaceful existence, in this instance, I think it necessary, Clara. Tell him the deed is done."

* * *

The warm, milky smell of the human woman, the slight lavender scent of the Faienya child, residues of both hung heavy on the layered air of morning. No need to take account of tracks etched in frost. The only story of interest they had to tell, the carriage they rode in had been pulled by dogs. Semyon laughed. Beneath a slate-grey sky, blocking the path of an insipid sun, he swaggered away in the direction the woman and child had taken, still laughing.

Rubbing his head, cursing the strutting peacock beneath his breath, Slubeagh supported his paunched belly with his arms to ease the bite of straps digging into his shoulders, and followed, carefully keeping a respectable distance between them.

Barely a mile gone, and his feet hurt. Through the soles of his boots, something stabbed. He sat down, pulled them off and investigated. No stone had sliced through the sole, and no thorn invaded, the leather was complete and intact. Shaking his head, he put the boots back on. A few steps more and he hobbled, the pain so intense it felt as though he walked over a bed of sharp-pointed crystal shards in his bare feet.

"The Lady's dart, brother," Galateo's piping voice said. "Now we feel the results of dust. Grit your teeth. Show fortitude. Press on. We must continue, else the peacock tells your part. He wins. You lose. We lose."

Turning the collar of his greatcoat up, Slubeadgh struggled onward. Trying to ignore mounting pain, he focused only on the back of the peacock striding ahead, hating the elaborate show each time the air was tested, the smug nod, the swinging hair sweeping broad shoulders. Both these deliberate actions saying in concert the quarry was, of course, detected with consummate ease.

"Think of pleasure, brother," Galateo piped, when fiery arrows harpooning through his ankles began to carve a way through calve and thigh muscles, "concentrate on no quick end for Semyon. Imagine a skilful plucking of the peacock's brilliant plumage. How you will do it? How it will feel, little by little, to destroy his handsome arrogance. To strip him of all Apatia thinks fine. Imagine, brother. Imagine, how sly we will be to bring the peacock to nothing more than a speck of dust, and none knowing. Rise above pain. Turn it to pleasure."

Slow and laborious, each step taken by will, slowly eroded by suffering, Slubeadgh fell further and further behind. Galateo all the while, pleading, cajoling, setting out the best scenario, laying out dire consequence, screaming distance had half-swallowed Semyon, while his twin faltered, lurched from side to side and stumbled onward.

In the middle of a narrow track, overhung with branches and withering rust-coloured leaves, he came to a stop. Pain no longer journeyed, but coalesced in a concentrated swirl at the base of his spine and he could not ignore the vortex of agony gathered there. He fell to his knees, clawing the earth, his whole body racked by wave after wave of tremors.

"Get up! On your feet, brother, if you would not bring us to ruin."

"I cannot," he panted. "A little rest for pity's sake, and cease your clack."

"Brother," moderating his tone, Galateo asked, "how goes it?"

With the sleeve of his coat, Slubeadgh wiped sweat cascading from his brow and said, "The pain is not so severe. I think it is subsiding. I no longer shake."

"That I know. Can you stand?"

"A moment longer. Let me stay only a moment longer."

"No longer. We do not dare, brother. The peacock is completely lost from sight. I fear we lose him altogether."

Groaning, he tried to get up. Fingers splayed in leaf mould and loam, his back humped, and knees bent in the act of standing, the muscles in upper thighs and calves refused to carry him erect. Instead, his feet scrabbled the ground, propelling him forward so rapidly he sprawled flat.

"Have a care!" Galateo cried.

Slubeadgh rolled onto his side, gasping for air knocked out of him.

"Now, we see how you are punished," Galateo said, mournful. "Did I not tell you to go to the Lady Apatia and give report? But no, oh, no, you would not, saying Semyon would fade us if you did. The darkling through, you waited on the peacock. Because of his malice, because of your perennial cowardice, we are come to this."

"It is but a momentary weakness," he replied, trying once again to stand upright. "The effects of her dart will presently be gone."

"You cannot do it, can you, brother? Your feet paw the earth. I fear, if at some point movement should return to you, upon all fours you will go."

"She would not be so cruel."

"Would she not? Unpredictable and malicious she has always been. For her amusement, what would the Lady not do? If you cannot stand, brother, you must crawl. Semyon must not locate the child without us. If we are to worm our way back into the good grace of the Lady, we must be present when he is found. If we are not, will she be inclined to lift the blight placed so cruelly upon you? Likely not."

Groaning, Slubeadgh heaved himself onto hands and knees saying, "I am wearied to the bone. All energy is gone from me."

"If I could change places with you, brother, or alleviate exhaustion, I would. But, I am cradled, pickling in your salt sweat, and can do nothing. Summon up strength. Continue. You must continue. There is no other option for us now."

Drawing air through his nostrils, filtering out scents that were of no interest, Semyon held what remained deep in his lungs for as long as possible before exhaling slowly through his mouth. Two lines of the same two scents. One was a little stronger, fresher and farther away than the one floating around him.

They doubled back! Some distance on, they came off this track, made a wide hairpin curve to take another path parallel to this.

Pushing aside a mass of interwoven branches and twigged shrubbery spangled with frost, Semyon eased himself into the undergrowth. Stepping lightly, he wound between slender trunked saplings, and with his long-bladed obsidian dagger, hacked a crude path through sinewy brambles, desiccated bracken, high-shot grass, brown-mossed humps of earth, and jumbled roots, until he broke through onto the expected path.

He sniffed the air. Breathed it in through his nose and exhaled it slowly through his mouth, letting odours trickle over his palate and across his tongue. A moment later, he set off again, the scent of the Lessadgh woman and the Faienya child pulling him in their wake.

Along either side of this new and narrower water-dripped track, tips of freshly broken branches swung forlorn from pliant strips of bark, and tussocks with half-sheared heads and cleaved sides slowly crumbled. A set of deep, sliced ruts, claw-gouged scratches, and paw-pads, heavily imprinted in the frost-hardened ground, all signs marking where they had passed at great speed.

A new smell detected, insinuated into the other scents. Growing in potency, it confidently rode the currents. Twisting, mingling with closeted woodland warmth, it came on. Crispness, tinged with sure and certain grassy winter sourness, together with the faint yeasty mustiness of turned soil. It could only be a large open space. Soon, he knew, the trammelled track he strode swiftly upon would give out onto this place.

At the edge of the fields, Semyon paused. Beyond, open grassland cowered beneath a graphite sky and the sun, no more than a blurred smudge of limpid brightness. Further off, trees mimicking the rise and fall of the landscape, stretched in an endless line. From where he stood, furrows created by the wheels of the cart and clods of earth thrown piecemeal from them, were clearly visible. The path they had taken seemingly invited pursuit into the woods.

Too easy. There is trickery here. If once they doubled back, why not twice?

He did not cross the field, but turned away from the opening he had come out of, and tramped along the angled thickets of hedges bordering it. Testing the air every ten paces, he analysed scents for the slightest trace that would set him upon a new path, in a new direction. Furlongs on, he found what he looked for. Laughing at the Lessadgh woman's duplicitous cunning, Semyon travelled quickly after her and the child.

Dimming light brought frustration with it. The day almost spent, and patience with it. Zigzags and tight hairpin bends, wide arching curves, long straight stretches before sharp-angled turns. All she could do to evade any pursuer, the Lessadgh woman had skilfully done. Cutting across routes already taken, time and time again, she had created a web, a network of odours crafted to deceive and confound. The chase had brought him to this. A jumbled, far flung ball of confused scents. The strongest and newest lines merging with the oldest and weakest, dancing elegant pirouettes on airless currents, only to disperse in graceful curling spirals before returning like drifting smoke, one to overlay the other, and once again, impregnate strength with faintness, failing smells with vigour.

"Where to start?" Semyon moaned, noting part of the infuriating bundle climbed restless on his own breath. *How to separate? Which thread to pull, when stale curdles with fresh?*

Silently cursing, he began the laborious task of tracing each one back to its untainted state.

Through falling night's most sombre pigments, he worked, trying to order chaotic smells. Trampling the ground until it was bald of grass and tenacious weeds, back and forth he went. Identifying one false lead, a second, a third and many after. His determination, he swore, would be a match for the woman's artfulness. Steaming the hours with deep breathed breath and fruitless concentration, he slowly tumbled towards lurking despair.

Cracking the stillness of the night, a throaty song, long-drawn and rising to a higher pitch. Semyon swung round. Instinct dropped him to a crouch as he listened, fixing the position of possible attack exactly. Too far away to pose immediate threat, a joyful duet was now being sung. Smiling, certain his luck had changed, he rose to his feet.

"Hundghs! The woman's hundghs," he whooped exultant.

Stripping his jacket off, holding the sleeves, one in each hand, he raised it high above his head and began to run. The improvised canopy splayed out, and flapping, spread his scent over as wide an area as possible, and a laggard breeze at his back carried it before him. Carried it to the noses of the dogs.

* * *

Throughout the dismal day, urged on by his brother's insistent goading, Slubeadgh crawled, hoping some fluke would lead him to the peacock, Semyon. Afraid to be caught in the open by Lessadgh beings, he kept to the undergrowth, where he might see, but not be seen. Fingernails broken, hands scratched and bleeding, the knees of his breeches in tatters, his greatcoat and boots muddied and scarred beyond redemption, past hope and past caring, he came at last to a fast running rill. Ignoring the outraged shrieks in his head, he stopped.

"We will not find the peacock now," he said, angry.

"We must. You know we must."

"No. You will listen to me now, Galateo. You have bellowed and raged until my head is full of the beat you drum with just one stick. I can stand it no longer. I, and, I alone, make the physical effort. I, and not you, am half way to fading with exhaustion. Mine is the hunger and thirst. Your sustenance is taken from me and you feed well. Mine alone is the hunger. I can do nothing to assuage it for the present. Mine alone is the thirst. This I can, and will, quench."

He stooped low to cup a few drops of water in his hand, and drank.

"You are right, brother. Drink your fill, then we continue our search for the peacock."

"No," Slubeadgh cried. "He is not to be found. We have wandered the whole of this span with nothing to show. We are completely lost. Where the sally port may be, I have no idea, and the darkling is coming down. We must resign ourselves to these facts."

"I think only of you when I push hard. When you are watered, you will see your little rebellion serves you nothing. What of the Lady Apatia?"

"She may go hang."

"An understandable sentiment, though not practical, I fear…"

"Be silent a moment. Be still. Heard you that?"

"I heard nothing."

"I thought...I thought I heard a hundgh bark. Far off, but too near for any comfort."

Dipping his hand into the water, Slubeadgh drank a few more drops then cocked his head.

"Do you smell that, brother?" Galateo said.

"Wood smoke and damp grass?"

"It is. Lessadgh beings must be close by."

"They have hundghs?" In answer, a long drawn out howl, joined quickly by another, pierced him as surely as the teeth that had sunk into his leg the night before. Shuddering, completely panicked, he scampered away from the rill, heading for the nearest tree and relative safety.

For many minutes after, he did not register, the excited yip-yap barking of dogs full-stretched for the hunt, was heading away from and not towards him.

* * *

Soot-blued the night. Dense, black clouds, blown by a slothful breeze, swathed a reluctant moon and graced star-shine with the same impenetrable stain. All noises, usually made in the darkness; gone to silence, palpable and complete over wood and open countryside. The hoot and swoop of owl, the quietly scurrying feet of rat, mouse and vole, the nervous hip-hop of wary rabbit, and unhurried stealth of soft-pawed fox, all gone away, gone to ground. Gone too, the menacing cry of intended hunt. Now it had begun in earnest, the dogs were in full throat.

The Lessadgh woman's dogs, he smelt them. Musty and musky, hard-working, lean-muscled bodies, their pelts soiled by dirt, stale water, acrid urine, and minuscule pieces of rotting meat lodged firm between tight-packed teeth. The pungency becoming stronger, Semyon gauged how far off they were, and slowed his gait to a purposeful walk until he found a copse of beech, the young trees growing very near to one another. Without hesitation, he went inside and was barred all around by living wood.

This place will do as well as any, he thought, rubbing his jacket over sweat-slicked hair and face. Lifting his shirt to wipe under both arms and across his chest, he then laid it in the space a few yards away from the tree with the widest girth.

He could hear the dogs now, frenzied with excitement. Their pace erratic, they came on, muscular shoulders barging through brushwood, shredding bracken and scattering leaf-mould with dashing paws and slashing claws.

His mind cool and clear, he went behind the tree, drew his blade, adjusted his grip on the hilt, and stilled his breath in readiness.

Luminescent eyes glazed with night shine. Flanks quivering, tongues lolling from gaping jaws, the dogs raced into the copse at full speed and fell upon his jacket. Gripping it with drool-dripped teeth, they yanked it this way and that between them, tearing, and destroying.

His blade slashed through the neck of the nearest dog, severing its spinal cord with one blow, drenching all with a spurting fountain of blood. The other animal yelped alarm, and jumped awkwardly away, then tried to manoeuvre in the tight space, made smaller by the nerve-twitched corpse of its companion. Snarling, and cautious, it moved its sinuous body into position, gathering its haunches for a killing leap to head or throat.

Standing perfectly still, his eyes locked on the dog's, his peripheral vision acutely aware of the animal's changing stance, he challenged it to make that leap. It sprang, but could not find the height needed. He stepped forward to meet it, moved aside with fluid grace when the thrust of his blade ripped into its soft belly, and held firm, despite the jarring impact and sudden weight on wrist and arm.

Taken in mid air, impaled on the long-bladed dagger, yelping and squealing it writhed frantic with pain, as gravity pulled its body down, and the Faienya blade sliced upward. Lashing out with claws and teeth, shredding his shirt and the skin beneath, the animal sank slowly to the ground, and lay convulsing upon a heap of its own intestines.

He slit the creature's throat to make sure it would trouble him no more, and wiped his dagger clean on its furry back. Only then did he allow himself to concentrate on a scent the animals had brought with them. Faienya. Adult male. Slubeadgh? No, never his. Not that hated, confusing stench of duality. This scent was whole. Single. Complete.

* * *

"Of a sudden, your dogs are quiet," Clara said.

"Likely they have found prey and are busy making a meal of it," Clump said. "They be back soon enough to do what they were trained to."

"Yes. I suppose that is the right of it. They used to make a great din when I let them out of the barn each night, but never quite like this evening's rumpus."

"Excitable creatures they be, and hunting on their own territory again could make them more so. Nothing to worry about, I shouldn't think."

"Clump?"

"Yes."

"You do not have to come with William and I. You have done more than enough already."

"Clara, if I am right, and I know I am, the Faienya are coming for the boy. If it makes you feel better, my bridges were burnt long since."

* * *

"See, brother? It is mind over matter. Despite a crooked back, you shinned up into this tree as fast as any able-bodied Faienya."

"I believed we were in imminent danger."

"No hundghs now. No barking, no snarling, no nothing. We should continue our search for the peacock."

"Without searching," Slubeadgh said, "I may have found something far better than that feculent turd has found for all the effort he puts in. See? Over there?" he pointed, "in that mass of clinging foliage and roots? Something illuminates a thin strip of leaves. It is not the light of the darkling orb. There is hardly a glimmer of its shine. And the strange line of dull light gleams slender and weedy, in just one place. That is not normal."

"No brother, it is not. Shall we investigate? Just a little? Knowing with what alacrity you can climb back to roost, if need be. I believe we should."

"Yes, I think, I must. I really think, Galateo, I must."

* * *

He bound his wounds with the remaining sleeve of his shirt. Regretting the loss of his jacket, made from finest spun web-silk and past any repair, he slung the remnants over one shoulder, and casually sauntered from the scene of battle, out of the copse to follow the scent of the dogs and the intriguing smells intermingled with them.

"To think, for just a moment, that noxious, misshapen pustule on legs had found the woman and boy before I," he said, grinning at the stupidity of such a thought. "Ludicrous, inconceivable when the slinking cadaver, that pathetic excuse for anything remotely resembling Faienya, could not find his own arse in a blackout. For all her cunning and cleverness, the Lessadgh woman's own dogs lead me straight to her. The animals she thought would keep her from me, have betrayed her."

The irony of it brought a smile to Semyon's lips.

* * *

"Hist! Someone comes," Slubeadgh craned his neck trying to catch a glimpse through the branches and withering leaves. "Treading light, they come this way."

"They creep, brother."

"They breathe very deep. Hear it? And again."

"Only one I know draws breath so," Galateo said, and stifled a giggle. "It is Semyon. We have found the peacock without even looking. Mind your tongue, brother, if you do not wish a good pummelling."

"Hush, he is almost beneath us. Hush."

Beneath the tree, dappled in night's shade, Semyon filtered out the loathsome scent of duality rippling down from above. Swallowing the last vestiges of overwhelming disappointment, combined with white-hot anger that had accompanied him, together with the stench stinking out his nostrils for the last half mile, he focused on a miserably weak glow highlighting the underside of a single strip of ivy among a tumbled mass, saying, "What is it you do, hiding in the branches, you clinker on the arse of a whipped cur?"

"Sir," Slubeadgh whispered, ignoring wild laughter sounding in his head, "is that truly you?" Semyon looked up. Looked past the dangling feet, and into the pinched face framed between them. "Sir, I see the day has not gone well with you, besmirched from crown to toe in filth, and your wondrous jacket no more than rags."

"You scabrous bag of bile," Semyon growled, "did I not say your contribution would be told?"

"Great sir, indeed you did, and I most grateful for it. I have found them. In the undergrowth, just over there, you will find a stout rope hidden and more beside. A trap door, I have discovered; though did not dare raise it. For hours, sir, I have waited to share the good news, never thinking you would be so sorely tried by unfortunate delay."

"You found one entrance, and knowing they were underground, never thought to look for others?"

"Sir, I am badly afflicted. The lady's dart has disabled me. There are hundghs. Hundghs that have already tasted me, and I would not risk that jeopardy again."

"Would they have torn your pus ridden hide to pieces, you vilest, of all things most vile. The hundghs are no more. The other entrances I have found while you loiter and lounge in wilting leafiness, risking little in the Lady Apatia's service. Out, I say. Out, you walking cesspit."

Catching hold of one of Slubeadgh's ankles, Semyon yanked him down.

"Sir," he whined, rolling onto hands and knees. "You see my circumstance for yourself. Not being able to walk, trot or run; I could do no more than I have done. Sir, you see me in pitiful state."

"That was always your condition," Semyon smiled. "Now go. Go far from me. Take your putrid stench with you. If you wish to come again to Noor, or even wander this dismal, dreary place a little longer, trouble me no further this darkling."

He watched Slubeadgh drag himself away before taking a small envelope of pressed flax-paper from a pocket in his breeches. Opening it carefully, a tiny nebulous sphere rolled onto the palm of his hand. Raising it to his lips, he spoke gently to it. Absorbing words to summon the Lady Apatia it grew bigger, and when he had finished speaking, Semyon let the message bubble fly.

Chapter 18.

From the sanctuary of their island in the middle of the Trapiche Emeral, the vast river that floods violent through the land known as Hessonii, and which they had taken solely for themselves, the Disobedient Ones roused themselves once more. From the Great Houses they had erected there, they came from self-imposed isolation, and for a time, walked the land of Noor. Their purpose, easy to divine.
Ownership of land, the reason for squabbles that had broken out. He who had little challenged he who had much. Many skirmishes were fought. Every aggressor, believing might of arms would prove their claim in combat, as did their supporters. Alliances constantly made, to further this end, were fractured when gain was perceived not to be what it should have been. Round and round, shifting loyalties and betrayals commonplace. Raids and pitched battles won and lost. The many voices of those faded whispered on a continual flurry of ill-begotten breezes until none knowing whom to trust, chaos reigned and full-scale war threatened.
In this madness, I took no part. None contested my right, nor my might, for that which I owned, for only the greatest fool would not know little fruit could be gained from that exercise.
The Disobedient Ones let it be known, they and they alone, were the power in Noor and Lordship was held in their hands. The division of the world they had created, theirs alone to determine. If the Faienya would not govern themselves, and live in peace, rulers would be placed over them. Throughout Noor, the Disobedient Ones appeared. Calling together great assemblies, they parcelled out the land. Their true children, the first of their line, though few in number now, were allocated to reign, and on through the second, and third generations, until no more land was there to give.
In a great book, these judgments were recorded and many copies made. The original, the Disobedient Ones took with them when they departed. To the stewards of Noor, copies were given, each one setting out their portion to hold in perpetuity.
One last thing, the Disobedient Ones did. Across the sally ports, a barrier they placed. Faienya might pass through into Lessadgh, if the desire should take them, or, if those still remaining in that dismal place desired to come into Noor, but no Lessadgh being could ever stray into the place of perfect light.
And when it was done, all submitting to restored peace, the Disobedient Ones returned to the vast river Trapiche Emeral. Returned to their lonely island, to their Houses where isolation reigned supreme, and in secret, continued the same work carried out through past ages.

Into my hands Spessa was given. This being a larger portion than that held, or hoped for, my lands were now bounded by six other states. Tsavoe, Almandine, Demantae, Tocantinae, Bekily and Andradia.

"I have work to do. Papers to finalise," Clump said, rising to his feet. "You well know, the trade delegation from Bekily wish to negotiate new terms for passage through our sally port into Lessadgh. You be prepared for the meeting tomorrow, Clara?"

"I am. The ceremonial robes are laid out ready to be fitted, though why we continue with these silly charades, I do not understand, when all the Kingdom States we deal with know, a woman of Lessadgh stands as High Lord of the Helm in Almandine."

"Tradition. Protocol. You must suffer them, unless it is your wish to insult not only our closest trading partners, but also your own subjects."

"No. That is not my wish. Forgive me, Clump, I am a little out of temper this darkling."

"Then our business be concluded for the time being, I take my leave. Malfroid?"

"Malfroid must remain," she said. "It is my wish to learn from my Spymaster what useful information our agents in Bekily have recently unearthed that may aid me in the negotiations on the morrow."

"Though your presence be mandatory, no one expects you to make an active contribution, Clara."

"Boredom and ignorance is to continue to be my allotted role? While you haggle back and forth, and I all but drown in my own sweat, suffocating from such heat it is difficult not to fall into a stupor? I believe more involvement would alleviate this problem, and I should not want to look the fool by interrupting to ask a question that insults the envoys. No, Malfroid must remain."

"As you wish," Clump answered. "Until next brightling."

"That lie dripped smooth from your tongue," Malfroid said.

"There is truth in it. For all of Clump's competence, and that of my ministers, I have long wished to know and understand the minutiae of diplomatic language employed during these meetings. Imagine, if I should fall into sleep? Imagine, if I should snore? Beside, I truly want to know what secrets, if any, Bekily would prefer to keep close."

Malfroid smiled his crooked smile, "Your iron will would not let you slip into slumber. Much though you may despise prescribed protocol; you would not breach it. Now tell me, Clara, what is it you really wish of me?"

"To be blunt? I desire to learn the old language. Find me one well versed in it."

"You wish to hear the speak-cube alone? Is that it?"

"We listen to a fast gallop through history that cannot be passed over. Who can tell how long the ride we are on? Clump's time is valuable, as is yours, and I eat into the little free time you both have."

"It is for our benefit you wish to learn? Come, Clara, you have always made free with our time and thought nothing of it."

"You deny me? You will not find someone to tutor me?"

"It would be my privilege," he said, choosing his words carefully. "Also, if it became known, you study the old language, I am sure it would please many that you seek to immerse yourself so thoroughly in Faienya history and culture. As for reports received...."

* * *

In his own apartment, Malfroid considered Clara's request. If Clump's free time and his own was sorely limited, hers was even more so. Protocol demanded much. As for flouting it, she as High Lord of the Helm, could do nothing but obey, unless she wanted to create a schism in the regimented codes governing Faienya society. She would not advocate divisions.

On the face of it, the reason she had given for learning the old language was rational, perhaps desirable, but it was not the truth. Opportunity in plenty she had had to learn the ancient tongue and never taken it. Every avenue of thought he wandered down took him to one place only. His immediate and instinctive reaction, she wanted to listen to the speak-cube alone. Why? The only obvious answer, Atrament would later speak of things she did not wish either he, or Clump, to know of. The question scalding his mind was, what?

* * *

Red as Lessadgh's blood, and accentuating her extraordinary pallor, gems large as a coobir's egg, and shaped in like manner. Each precious stone, lavishly encased in urilatum, added to the weight of the necklet draped around her long, slender throat. Wayward, floating hair, tamed by whipped egg white, was twisted into sleek curls and adamantine nuggets, fixed to artful pins, held them in place high upon her head. Worn low on her brow, the urilatum circlet of authority. Decked in palatial finery, Apatia was seated at table on the dais, smiling, gracious and serene.

Languidly toying with the quiver slung on her girdle, she listened with half an ear to droning compliments spilled by the head of the visiting delegation from Spessa, and with the other, to more interesting conversation further down the table.

Yellow eyes restlessly darting about the hall, she noted who spoke openly to whom now the banquet was over, now dishes and cutlery were cleared away, and tables and chairs moved back to make a space for entertainment shortly to begin, and the dancing to follow.

Now wine flowed more freely, she noted who drew whom aside to whisper, or with heads clustered together stood in small serious groups.

Who flirted, who rejected, who too readily acquiesced and laughing demure, slyly disappeared to reappear a short while later in a somewhat dishevelled state.

Through rising chatter at the end of the short play, and raucous laughter in the dance, she noted everything and everybody, but did not see the message bubble, in arrowing flight, speed through a half-closed window. Soaring high, beyond the glare of flaming fire crystals, it circled the frescoed gilt ceiling to hover above the dais before making a slow descent. Its smooth iridescence grazed Apatia's cheek with the texture of a brief, wet kiss and popping, delivered the message contained within.

Come now, Lady. What you desired to find has been found.

"Ambassador," her slender fingers lay light on his arm, "unexpected affairs of state call, and I must take my leave. You will forgive this untimely absence?"

"Always Lady. Tomorrow, we will talk further?"

"We will," she promised, making her escape.

* * *

Fingers tight wrapped in the haran's reins, Apatia urged it on with whip and spur. Crashing through the sally port at break-neck speed, the barrier hit her with such force she was nearly thrown from the saddle. Never slackening the pace, steadying herself with clenching thighs, and feet thrust hard down in the stirrups, she shot out of brushwood and brambles at the bottom of the Lessadgh woman's garden and charged on.

Focused on her task, she did not hear the winded grunts and muffled cries of alarm from those following behind, when the unseen barrier smashed against them in the struggle to keep up with the headlong dash. Ferocious, icy wind blasted her, snatching at her cloak, lifting it on streams of roistering air to cast it flying wild behind, and needling her face with sharp, pinpointed coldness, tore away gems twisted in her sleek-dressed hair, scattering them to fall unnoticed from the fine, fibrous strands bound in lacquer, and blowing freely through it, loosed and tossed them into an unruly, ever moving cloud.

Her arm rose and fell, whipping the haran onward. Onward, to where Semyon waited. Onward. Her mother's expectation drove her. Whipping her haran until greening bruises sullied the iridescence of its scaled skin. Onwards. Spread toes and claws pounding, ripped the ground. Faster. Faster. Ever faster. Eating up the miles. The countryside a frost-cracked blur, Apatia thundered reckless through the night to claim the means to make all ambition possible. Onward: to claim the child.

* * *

She came out of the chamber beneath the crystal spire, and ghosted down the winding stairs. Soft as a whisper, she trod across the marbled atrium, out through the ornate entrance to pass through colonnaded pillars and onto the latticed grass path. Lingaradgh paused, to taste and savour the freshness of the air, and the anxious rustle of leaves that stirred without the aid of wind or breeze.

"Did you think I had forgot you?" she asked, beginning the unhurried walk amongst the swaying fronds and creaking branches of the willodghs. "Never would I neglect my most constant companions. The stepping-stones to all I have, and hope to attain? Never, would I abandon you. Not for one darkling, would I do that. You are meat and drink for me. Sustenance you are, for both my flesh and talent flowing through life force. Husband," her hand caressed a gnarled trunk, tracing deep cracks in the bark with teasing fingers, "how do you fare? I see, you rot slow and quiet and perfect in your living tomb of wood. Will you not speak in your scratch-whispered voice of foul deeds carried out, injustice done and usurpation? Or, having too much time, to think in drifting thought, do you regret trust stupidly placed in me, and for your error, sulk? What? No words of recrimination? Another darkling, perhaps...we will have freer talk."

She passed on, going from one tree to another, addressing each by name and title, listening to laments for lives curtailed, yet living still. Listening to desperate pleas to end torment for crimes unknown, entreaties begging clemency for offences given, and mindless requests in mournful tones for restoration that would never come. Always, they gave her pleasure, broadened the smile hovering at the corners of her mouth, and softened the hardness in her silver eyes. Hearing passionate, if not lively petitions, voiced in tired sighs through the fronds, to cut down entrapping wood and give the most final of releases, elated her.

She would never let them go. How could she? Political opponents, outspoken critics, adversaries who thought they worked in secret, her own husband, and many more beside, were dungeoned in her garden. Their rotting flesh rich nourishment for the ancient willodgh's. Their constant misery: a joyful invigoration that never failed to lift her from darkest moods. No. She never would, never could allow them to go.

On completing a full circuit, lighter of mind, and in high spirits, Lingaradgh went back into the summerhouse to prepare for her first visitor in centuries. He would be the most welcome of well come arrivals.

* * *

"We are agreed," Galateo said, "he will summon the Lady Apatia. We are agreed, there is no doubt she will come without delay. Then why do you linger? Two other entrances the peacock claimed to have found. You also must find them, brother."

"If they are found, why must I find them again?"

"You discover them for yourself. In doing so, the peacock cannot claim sole right to the finding. You see? Further, knowing where the other entrances are, acts as surety for us. Someone goes uninvited into one of them, it is certain sure the woman and child flee from another. Simple logic."

Slubeadgh nodded, "But tell me this," he said, thinking the matter through, "which entrance will the Lady Apatia choose? Not knowing, how can we be there?"

"Semyon will choose the easiest route for her. We will not be present, brother. Remember, he banished you earlier with dark threat, and likely would not tolerate us when about to seize the child. The credit for that action, he seeks for himself alone."

"True. What then must we do?"

"Our challenge is to guess which exit the Lessadgh woman will choose. That is where we wait in hiding. We, not the peacock, will effect the capture and thereby, complete his disgrace."

"I like that. Your cunning does you credit," Slubeadgh said, mulling over the possibility. "It is a good plan, but...there is risk. What if our choice is incorrect?"

"The entrances cannot be widespread. We wait in hiding between them. At the first hint of noise, and there will be much to my mind, we can position ourselves, brother."

"What if the Lady brings others with her? Stations them outside. What then?"

"Our wits combined could make a diversion. Draw the guards away, perhaps? Or, better still; silence them for a time. A good thwack with a stout log across the pate should suffice. You could do that?"

"I could," Slubeadgh agreed.

"Then, brother, we must first find the other two entrances."

* * *

Slowed to a walk, Apatia turned to see how many still followed. Four of the six guards, originally chosen by Semyon, remained in their saddles, blowing as hard as their mounts heaving sides.

In half-light heralding dawn, she signalled her intention to turn into the wood. Throwing the reins over the panting haran's neck, she guided it through the trees using only the pressure of her knees. Minutes later, a figure stepped out of shadows. Taking hold of her bridle, he looked up into her eyes.

"Well met, Lady," Semyon saluted her quietly.

"They are close?" she whispered, sliding from the saddle into his arms. "You are sure of it?"

"Yes, to both questions."

Taking his face in her hands, she drew him close, and closer still, saying, "Then a small token of reward to come, you must have now, Semyon," and took his breath away, yet again, with the sweet violence of her mouth.

* * *

Snuggled against William on the narrow bed, Clara hovered between sleep and waking. She could hear his faint, bee-buzzed snore and the odd gurgling sound he made in the back of his throat. Those sounds were comforting and normal. Clump moving quietly about, creaking the boards with his tread, filled her with anxiety, and if she were truthful, dread.

While cupboards opened and closed, she thought, *he is collecting supplies we shall need.* And while paper gently rustled and material softly flapped, *he is packing things in hessian sacks.* And when a few dull thuds were tagged onto the percussion his feet made, *he puts the sacks by one of the doors, ready to be loaded into the box-cart when morning comes. When morning comes, where shall we go? Where shall we go?* The question repeated, beat in time with his steps, *where shall we go?*

Clump stopped. In her mind's eye, she could see him, head up, ears straining, eyes traversing the beamed ceiling as if to squint through it, to pierce through the layers of earth and roots growing in it, and through the leaves to look at the world above.

"What is it?" she asked

"No chorus. Almost dawn, yet no bird sings in territorial challenge. Best you wake the boy, Clara."

"You think we are discovered?" she gasped.

"Perhaps. I must go outside to load the cart. If we have company, I will meet it soon enough. Meantime, you and he must hide. Beneath my workbench, at the back, there be a wooden panel fitted to look part of the wall. Push the left side with firmness. The panel will angle on its pivot. There will be space enough, though it be small, for the pair of you to squeeze into. Stay hid till I say it be safe to come out, and not before. You understand?"

"Yes. But what of your dogs, Clump? Surely they cannot have failed you."

"Not willingly. It may be, I act too cautious. Mayhap, nothing be amiss save the birds leave roost late this morning. All the same, better be safe than sorry."

* * *

"Lead on."

"Others are with you?"

"Four of the guards you selected for the first fiasco, Semyon. They follow not long behind."

"Then we must wait for them, unless you will risk another such. Three entrances, I have located. We will need to set guard over them. One thing more, a Faienya is with them. Who, I cannot say. His scent is unknown to me, and though I have fought one battle this darkling, it is probable there may be another to be had."

"The boy must not be harmed," Apatia said, fondling the quiver hanging from her girdle. "At all cost, he must not be harmed. What is done to those with him, I care not."

"I have had enough of shedding life force this span. If possible, I would harm none, Lady."

"As you will. Though much good may your tender heart do you. Only get me this child."

"You have not said why he is of such great import."

"Is it not enough, a child of the Faienya has been left in this drab place? No. I see it is not. Then truth you shall have..." Apatia began.

"There is no time for pretty lies," Semyon said. "What remains of my chosen guard are come. I have but to set them in place, and the boy is in your hand."

* * *

"Be, prepared I said, brother. A stout log, not so large that you may not wield it, nor so weedy thin it break at the first crack."

Slubeadgh dropped the shattered piece of wood and crawled a few yards more. "Over there," he said. "I see a likely looking stave poking from the skirt of that bush."

"Be quick. Be fast. There is still much to do, if our plan is to succeed."

Slubeadgh grabbed hold of the smooth length of wood. Yanked it hard to free it from brushwood, and not expecting it to move so easily, fell onto his side covered with freshly cut branches tasselled with spruce needles.

"What have we here, brother?"

"Unless I am mistaken, it is the little cart the Lessadgh woman used, Galateo. What is it to us, except evidence she lurks close by?"

"You do not think clear, brother. This may be the end to scrabbling about in search for the last entrance. The Lessadgh woman will come to this place. She cannot know her dogs met their destruction, can she? Whatever exit she chooses to fly from, she must come here bringing the boy with her, in hope her animals will carry them fast away. And what will she find, brother?"

"She will find us. Triumphant us."

* * *

"Why do we hide in the little hole?" William asked.

"We play a trick on Clump."

"It is a game, Clara? Like one of those we play?"

"Yes. We have to be so very quiet. Not make the tiniest sound. And when Clump returns, he will think we have gone away."

"Won't he try to find us?"

"He will. But he must not, not easily. We must make him work hard to come across us. No jumping out to scare him, William. That is the difference between this game and the one we play. Now we are well and truly squashed in, let me try to close the panel."

"Do we have to? It will be very, very dark. I don't like the dark, Clara."

"We aren't frightened of the dark are we, my darling? I am here to look after you. Here is my arm holding you close, keeping you safe and warm. Here is my hand to squeeze tight when you do not feel so brave. We will do well enough, William. It is only a game. A good game. You will see. Shush now," she whispered, "no more talking. I believe he comes back."

Too quiet. Too quiet by far Clump thought moving swiftly along the narrow corridor to the door at its end. Opening it, he looked through the woven screen disguising the entrance. *And where be my dogs? Dawn almost takes hold and still they be not back. This has a very bad feel to it.*

Dropping the sacks of supplies, he pushed the screen open a little, and edged through the gap.

"Hit him now, brother!" Galateo screeched.

A few yards away, Clump saw the box-cart had almost been dragged clear of its covering.

"Strike him! Strike him," Galateo shrieked again.

"It is already done," Slubeath grinned. "Did you not see how quick I sprang? How I laid him out before he knew I was there?"

"I did, brother. It was well done. Now you must drag him behind the cart. Then we wait for the Lessadgh woman. It will not be long."

Semyon lifted the trap door.

So strong, it was almost concentrated, the warmed scents of the child, the Lessadgh woman, and that of the Faienya accompanying them, burst out from the stairwell. At the bottom of the steps, he turned, and held out his hand to help her down. Waving him away, Apatia, nimble and quick, joined him. Stooping, the ceiling brushing his back, the walls of the corridor scraping against his shoulders, he went along its short length and out into the living area.

"They live in worse condition than my gostles," Apatia sneered, fingering the quiver. "Where are they, Semyon? Never say they are gone."

"Patience, Lady," he said, laying his tattered coat neatly over the back of a chair. "The Faienya male is somewhere close by. We will not trouble ourselves with that one till he makes his play. Lessadgh and the child are most surely here."

"Smell them out. Find where they hide."

Drawing a series of deep breaths in quick succession, sampling the air from every direction, he nodded confirmation.

"There" he said, pointing to the curtain across Clump's workspace. Drawing it back, he knelt to look under the workbench. "Behind the panel."

"Smash it in."

"You would risk damage to the child?"

"No! No, find another way."

Pushing against the wood a small crack appeared that was quickly closed.

In the dark, sound was magnified, and fear heightened all senses, Clara told herself.

The heavy thud, shaking vibrations through the ground could not be the trap door falling. Could it? Footsteps! For pity's sake let it be Clump. Let it be Clump. More footsteps. More than one person! Not Clump then. Not Clump.

What should she do? She could not alarm William. No sign of concern, no sign of fright, and no trembling, though her body inclined to those spasms.

Musical voices, speaking a language she did not know, one imperious and demanding, the other confident and calm. Beside her, William stiffened, his hand squeezing hers with a strength she did not know he had. In response, she kissed his cheek, a long lingering kiss filled with all the tenderness and love she would not now be able to give him. They had come to take him from her, just as Clump had predicted when she had found her boy and let him into her heart six years ago.

They have come for my boy, my William, her mind wailed as warmth trickled down her cheeks. *I will not give him up without a fight. No, even if it is the death of me, I will not give him up.*

Planting her feet firmly against the board, wedging her back more tightly against the wall, Clara straightened her legs, as much as she could just a moment too late. A small gap appeared, and light cracked through it. She slammed it out.

"Lessadgh resists, Lady," Semyon laughed. "It would seem I must dig them out."

"Do it," Apatia said. "Be quick about it, else first brightling wastes into full."

Taking his obsidian dagger from its sheath, fitting the point to the seasoned wood, he hammered it with the heel of his hand, then twisting the blade in the slit made, splintered a strip away. Through the opening, he could hear the child crying quietly, the woman speaking soft and urgent. He put the blade to the wood again, chipped away another piece just large enough for his fingers to fit through and grip, and prised half of the panel free. On his knees, he bent to look inside, and saw them.

"I have you now, Lessadgh," he said. "There can only be one outcome. Will you not come quiet? No harm will be done to you, or the boy."

A crouching figure blocked out the light and looked into the hole it had made. Showing no white at all, impossibly luminescent, impossibly blue and unblinking eyes stared at her from a shadow-cast face, and from one sculptured cheekbone to the other, a thin band of bright marks flowed across the bridge of the nose.

The coaxing, sincere sounds it made, arrogant and offensive to her ears, Clara spat, spraying the face with spittle. It drew back, banging its head on the underside of Clump's workbench, and said something in its strange language that could be nothing other than a curse, then tried to lay hold of her skirts, her ankles, and legs. She kicked out, pummelling its hand and arm with the heels of her boots. In response, it tore off the rest of the wooden panel taking the upright pivot with it. Again, the face briefly appeared, eyes now narrowed and determined, mouth curved in threatening promise, it noted the exact position of her boy.

A large hand, fingers spread wide, shot out and with perfect aim, seized William's shirt. Terrified, he screamed and tried to beat it off with his fist, clinging to her tighter than ever, his other arm around her neck in an almost throttling embrace. Clara bared her teeth and sank them into the flesh of their attacker, broke through the skin and bit harder still. Tasting the salted copper of blood seep into her mouth, she shook her head as if trying to tear flesh from bone.

"Lessadgh has bitten me!" Semyon snarled, letting go of the child.

"Enough of this charade. The space is too confined for your large frame. Lessadgh is mad enough, or desperate enough, to harm the child. I will not risk that. Get away from the opening, Semyon," Apatia said, selecting darts from the quiver. "Make room. Let me have true aim."

* * *

"We did not think of guards," Slubeath's voice scraped the depths of misery.

"I did. You, dear, brother, did not keep to the plan. Diversion. Remember? You were to create one, and lead the guards away from this place to give us a clear field. You will doubtless plead exhaustion as the reason for our monumental undoing."

"Yes, I plead that. Two spans without sleep. Thrice through the sally port in that time, sapping the best part of energy I had. Sorely afflicted by the Lady's dart, am I. And through all those segments, you have bawled, screamed, yelled, squawked and shouted, so I cannot hear my own thoughts. I am not exhausted, Galateo, near to collapse, I am. How then could I challenge two guards? Skip away to lead them on a merry chase when I can barely move my bones? And I am so thirsty. I am so hungry, and knowing this, you still feed off me."

"You ate me first, brother. But come. Let us not quarrel. The child is lost to us. Semyon, the loathsome peacock, came out first in this bout. We must accept the unpalatable fact and swallow it down whole, secure in the knowledge, you will fade him on another day."

"The one I banged over the head stirs," Slubeath moaned, getting to his knees. "I shall not be here when he comes into full wakefulness."

"To the rill then, brother. Drink reviving water, sooth yourself with its coolness. When you are rested, we must review our situation to see what can be done to reinstate ourselves in the Lady's good grace."

Chapter 19.

In peace that followed, a great house I raised. Less than a league from the Field of Madricore, I raised its tall, thick walls. Graced with elegance they were, and tupped with tiled roofs, many and stately. A marvel to behold, the balconies hung from all its façades, and a high terrace with many steps leading up to its broadness, scoped into the frontage. Very fine, the trellisworked windows of intricate design. The floors of pictured marble, the interior decorated with mosaic work, most pleasing to the eye. In the midst of this splendour, a courtyard with myriad pillars, where fountains played and water splashed the brightling and darkling through, sounding pretty to my ear, and soothing the turbulence of my heart.

Gardens I caused to be. The black lily, the colour of the void, renowned for venom held within its most secret heart of petals, I chased down, and creating an enclosure to keep it, and it alone, put these blooms in pride of place. Of all flowers to be found in Noor, they alone are stained with colour. Lethal they are, but of extraordinary beauty. This wondrous lily reminded me of the beauteous one vanquished long since. I delighted in its heady perfume; shed only when the orb of the darkling span rode high and its grip on the brightling past was held fast.

Throughout Noor, I searched for other rare and fragrant blooms, adding them to an ever-growing collection, for it seems, though I saw it not then, collecting was an especial pleasure to me.

Each seven span, I sat to hear complaints, and gave judgment on their worth, together with getting satisfaction from the making of new law to benefit my people.

I took my tithes, in fairness a tenth part. For those, who most lamentably lacked talent, I found gainful employ that their spans might be occupied. In those times, to be a good steward, to husband my lands and those on it, was my determined aim.

These activities did nothing to abate the emptiness I found to be consuming me. With another collection, I next tried to fill this void. For artefacts of merit, both of age and contemporary, I began a search.

"Clump is still on edge with you?" Malfroid asked.

"He is ever on edge with me," she said, finishing the last of her wine. "I scratch him. He needles me. It is an abrasive relationship, has been so since first we met and will likely continue to sprint in the same vein. We are used to it and in time, always forgive, but never, perhaps, forget."

"There lies your problem."

"Enough of Clump. What of my tutor? You have found me someone?"

"I have, Clara. Fluent in the old tongue and patient as circumstance allows."

"I see something concerns you on this matter. Spit it out. Speak plain."

"I have told you of the intricate nature of the language. How subtle changes of inflexion, intonation and pronunciation can have great bearing on the meaning of what is spoken. My concern is this. Your temper of late is shorter than formerly. I would not have you quarrel with the learned gentleman who will teach you, guide you through the difficulties to make you competent in both understanding and speech."

"I, quarrelsome?"

"You asked me to speak plain, Clara."

"Then I give you solemn promise to mind my temper and my tongue. I will remember, in this gentleman's company, he is the master, I, the most humble of students."

Malfroid laughed saying, "If only you would."

"You think, I cannot?"

"Let us say, I have doubt."

"Then," she said, squaring her shoulders, "I will prove you utterly wrong. What is this person's name, and what arrangements have you made on my behalf?"

"His name is Persimmony Clump, a gentleman of vast knowledge, complete in discretion and irascible of temperament, especially with students slow to learn their lessons. Be mindful of your promise, Clara."

"Touche`," she said, stony-faced. "I salute the perfect ambush."

* * *

Subtle green, the dawn sky rising, spliced by varied hues of palest yellow and gauzy clouds of limpid purple. The child, a precious cargo, soft and warm, held fast in slumber-dusted dream and the circle of her arms. Apatia smiling, her yellow eyes blazed with success. Her mind moving between how her mother's vaunting ambition would soon be met, and lust for Lessadgh bloodied Semyon.

Riding a little in front, he led Apatia by her haran's reins, his thoughts occupied by his belief, the well-known secret of their union would certainly be made public very soon, and hottest desire for her pale, pale body.

"We go through the gate into my private courtyard," she said, breaking the silence, when the tall crystalline turrets and spires of her Kingdom City could be seen through the trees.

"The longest route?"

"What need of haste is there now, Semyon?"

"Every haste, Lady, I burn."

"Then you must roast a while longer yet. Your appearance would excite much comment, were we to travel through the city. The mongers of gossip, concocting outlandish stories to fit the gore you wear, would doubtless have us at odds with our neighbours within the hour, and bring the Guardians down upon us."

"The longest route," he said, disappointed. "You are right, better we make our way with quiet discretion through early brightling. Tell me, why treat Lessadgh so when you dragged her out of the hiding place?"

"For the trouble she caused. Why else? And, but for your tender heart, I would have served her far worse. My will is not to be denied. Do you still burn?"

"I do, Lady. For you, always I am afire."

"Later, Semyon," she said, lowering her voice, "I will serve you also, as you deserve. Together we shall melt in a furnace of our own making."

* * *

Clump groaned. Nausea tickled his throat. Somehow, light seemed to be scorching his eyeballs through closed lids and pounding lively on one particular spot on top of his head. Rolling to one side, trying to get away from the relentless light, he smelt pinesap. Cracking open his eyes, through oddly wavering sight saw he was lying on a heap of cut spruce. He sat up, instantly regretting the move, and vomited over the tail end of the box-cart.

Wiping his mouth with the back of his hand, he thought, *how did I come to be outside? Where be my dogs?* He rested his forehead against the cart. *I was going to see... What was I going to see? By all the powers, Clara!*

His legs buckled beneath him when he first tried to stand, and sagged and bowed while he took shaky steps toward the woven screen only to betray him in the darkened corridor, throwing him down to meet the floor with a crash.

"Clara! Clara!" he called, wincing at sounds ricocheting through his skull.

Using the walls to prop himself up, Clump staggered toward flickering light shed by guttering candles, and the steady red glow cast out from the stove in the living area. The curtain across his workspace had been torn down. Pieces of the wood panelling beneath his bench lay scattered over the floor, and the space was empty.

"Clara!"

His heart thudding in his chest, banged against his ribs on seeing a ragged cluster of long white hair, spattered with globs of green life force, on the floorboards. His stomach lurched on seeing two sketchy lines of black, indicating something had been dragged. Calming himself a little, he followed them and found her lying slumped across his narrow bed, a red mark blooming violent over one eye and cheek.

"Clara!" He shook her. She flopped limp and lifeless. Putting his ear to her mouth, relieved to find she still breathed, Clump gently eased her onto the mattress and covered her with a blanket. Of the boy there was no trace.

* * *

Onto a tray of urilatum, Lindgaradgh deftly sprinkled a measure of fine-textured, white powder from the small ruby bottle, screwed the cap tight, and let it fall to hang from the chain at her waist. A haran's quill, gilded with urilatum, taken from its holder, she coaxed the Trooh into two straight lines, and bent to follow them, inhaling first with one nostril and then the other. Wiping trace remains away with her fingers, she waited for it to strike.

The blow was palpable, almost rocking her from her feet. Steadying herself against the table, she waited for the aftermath. The slow-grown euphoria, matched by the steady pump of life force, ratcheting to a quicker speed until it went trilling so urgently through her veins it threatened to burst the constraint of fleshy canals, rejuvenating talent as it went and bringing clarity of mind in its wake.

Trooh never fails, but my need of the stimulant becomes more frequent. Worryingly frequent, and for what?

The answer surrounded her. From the crystal spire of the summerhouse, she could see it all.

"My kingdom," Lingaradgh breathed, misting the crystal pane she now gazed through. "In dreams I saw you. From imagination dragged you forth. With talent created you."

Wherever she looked, reaching high to spear the clouds, iridescent spires of pearly lustre gleamed in the early morning light. Beneath them, breathtaking in design, shapely onion-domed turrets rose above gold-veined marble walls of dazzling whiteness. Exquisite, the intricate crystalline delicacy of lace-like bridges that arched over broad avenues to link one structure to another. The public gardens and leisure parks, based on those fabled to have been created by the Anathema, Atrament, if the chronicles in her archives told true, all blazing perfect colour and pristine form.

How tall, how straight your walls. Your whiteness, dazzling the eye, rivals the brightling orb in brilliance during the second trichotomy's prime. My Kingdom City. Perfect the conception. Bold the execution. Wondrous, in form, and symmetry. Your architecture, the marvel and envy of the Faienya world, your beauty and fame known throughout all Noor, you are a sight I never tire of. My contrivance...and so very, very...rash.

"Mother?" Apatia called, breathless from the dash along the latticed path.

"Come. I am above you," Lingaradgh chimed in answer, adding in lower tone, "and always shall be, daughter."

"Mother, I have such news that will delight you," Apatia said, on reaching the last stair.

"The child is taken?"

"And in my custody."

"He is unharmed? No scratch, no blemish, other than those that are his own must he have."

"Unharmed, Mother, save for the dart's prick."

"You darted him?" Lingaradgh's tone soured. "You perforated his skin?"

"It was necessary, Mother," Apatia cried. "The Lessadgh woman fought, kicking and biting like some wild and savage thing. She would not be subdued, and the child, the child followed her example. Some further damage would have been caused had I not darted the pair of them."

"With what did you dart him?"

"Slumber-dust, Mother. Only slumber-dust."

"Of adult dosage!" Lingaradgh turned to face her daughter. "He is small, a child, and you fill him with adult dosage? Fool! Fool, thrice times over. Talentless and mindless you are, Apatia. Well may you move away, girl, fearing I will strike you. My hand itches to perform that act, for you have set me back. Once again, delay is the block you set before me to stumble over."

"But he will soon wake, Mother. Surely, all you need to do can be done then?"

"Eventually. Eventually he will wake, and what then? Contaminating dust travels in the purity of his life force," her voice now soft and menacing had lost its musicality. "How long for that corruption to clear his system? How much more delay?"

"I do not know," Apatia stammered.

"How long for punctured skin to heal? Not long, not long, mother, I hear you say it in your mind, Apatia, as clear as you had spoken the very words in piteous, wheedling tones."

"Forgive me, Mother. I did what I thought best to avoid further injury to his body."

"Forgive you? I will forgive, when your mind does not turn constant on sexual pleasure. I will forgive, when you learn to take no note of the heated urging of your groin. You do nothing to control lascivious nature, spreading your legs for all and sundry when the mood takes you. And it takes you very often, does it not, Apatia? Who, among your guard has not discreetly, but, oh, so thoroughly ploughed your furrow? You believed, I did not know? I know all. Unlike that strutting piece of arrogance with whom you doubtless think to celebrate flawed success this night, cavorting on his rod erect?"

Rage-shaken Lingaradgh shouted, "Girl, I tell you, you will not. The child you will keep in complete seclusion. Under lock and key, you will keep him. And tend him over-well. To the exclusion of all else, and all others, your attention will be given to the child. Until he regain his senses, until his flesh is whole; no other one, no other thing exists for you. For such a time as that may be; you will curb that which is carnal in you. Understand, girl, cross me in this, and I will blast you to dust. You have my word on that, daughter, and believe me, you may trust it most truly. Now go. Do exactly as you are bid."

* * *

He couldn't bear it. Clara's long drawn howls of deepest despair gave way to keening wails of anguish, dragged from the very heart of her. Mad with grief, she ransacked his home looking for the child, and not finding him there, went outside shouting his name over and over again. Running aimless through the woods, yelling desperation, searching for William as if by some miracle he would be found close by. Persimmony Clump followed her, picked her up when she collapsed exhausted to the ground, and carried her uncomplaining, back to his home.

He put her on his bed, covered her with a blanket, but did not know what else he could do. What comfort could he give, when there was none she would accept?

"My boy is gone," she whimpered, burying her head in the pillow. "My boy is gone."

"I will make some tea, Clara," he said. "You will feel a little better with warmth in you."

"Stupid man, I will never feel better again," she said, between hiccoughing sobs.

He made the tea anyway. Hour after hour, unable to leave her, Clump listened to her heart breaking. And somehow, those sobs seemed to have permeated his mind, so that when at last, she found respite in sleep for a short while, he could still hear her crying, still see her tears dropping from the undamaged eye, and trickling from the slit in the painfully swollen, sunset-coloured flesh of the other.

"I want to go home," she said, when he took her a bowl of fresh made broth.

"If you think to pass through the sally port," he said, gentle as he could, knowing gruffness was in his nature and not easily overcome, "to go after your boy, you cannot. There be a barrier across it that allows passage to none, but the Faienya. You are human, Clara, a woman of Lessadgh, the barrier would physically repel you."

"It could be, they will bring him back to me? What could they want with such a little boy, after so long a time? Perhaps they will bring him back."

"I think not," Clump answered, not wanting to give her false hope.

Tears streaming silently down her face, she pushed away the broth he offered saying, "Sometimes, false hope is better than none. I will go home, Persimmony."

"Your mind be made up?"

"It is."

He sighed, knowing her will was iron and he could not shake her from a chosen path.

"Then," he said, "I will take you."

Chapter 20.

Many artefacts, I collected. To tell of these marvels is wasted breath. They are gone. Destroyed, or carried away, save for the quiver.
It is a thing of rare beauty. In concept most excellent, a masterpiece of design and manufacture. These qualities alone could not have drawn me to seek it out. At great cost, acquire it. More enticing, by far to me, was its history. Tempting, to try myself against the potent curse laid upon it, for all who had owned it previously had it not in their possession over long.
Its history in short, is this. A binding gift it was to have been. A token of love, but love, subverted from its course, became obsession in the making of the gift that left little thought for ought else. Of that, which at first was hoped for, all was lost. With a curse the master-crafter, Baldur of Zoiss, blighted the quiver. In despair, to the heights bordering the Sanrosa Tourmal he went. The quiver thrown into its waters, he leapt after it, and dashed upon rocks below, faded.
Of the madness of love, what do I know, who never knew, or felt it? Never was it a weapon I ever used, though some use it with abandon. It is my firm belief; only the most cowardly choose that option from their arsenal.
In the archives of the Guardians verification you may find for what has, in brief been told.
In my possession for sparns, too, numerous to count, the quiver stayed, worn slung on a belt across my chest, a symbol of talent and power...before calamity struck.

Silence, long-stretched and pregnant with expectation.

Clump finally cleared his throat, opened his mouth to speak, and said nothing.

"What?" Clara said.

"What, indeed," Malfroid said, his tone dry, "in so far as I can make out, there is talk of the quiver."

"Ah, I see," beneath one of the folds of her skirts, Clara twisted her emerald ring, round once, round twice and stroked the table of the gem, "and you struggle with incandescent rage, Clump?"

"Malfroid be right. He talks of its history, of his interest in it. Directs you to find truth, for what he says, in the archives of the Guardians, doubtless knowing you will not ask for sight of them, and if you did, they would not give access."

"Is that all that was said?"

"He speaks of a curse laid upon it by the master-crafter, who devised the wretched thing, and who faded himself shortly after. He would have you believe, it was initially a love-token."

"A love-token?" Malfroid said. "He speaks of love?"

"No, he admits knowing nothing of that emotion. In that there be most definitely truth. A binding gift would be more precise, made before a couple be bound."

"And that is all?"

"That be the gist of it. I see no better time than now to ask you what you did with them, Clara?"

"Them?"

"Do not make sport of me. You know full well, I mean those bastard baubles in that bastard casket. What did you do with them?"

"I had them sent to the Guardians," she lied. "Together with a written explanation how they came into my possession, and the threat Atrament once posed is now most certainly obsolete. What else could I do, when Spessa knew of our incursion, and the reason for it told before all?"

His blue eye alight with mischief as she told the lie, Malfroid asked, "You could not have mentioned it earlier?"

"It slipped my mind. There has been so much to do of late. However, it was an unforgivable omission, for which I apologise."

"You did the right thing, Clara. I feel easier in body and mind, knowing those bastard things be no longer housed within these walls."

"And your temper, Clump? It will improve?"

"It may," he shrugged, as Malfroid sent her a sly grin.

* * *

"Did it not occur to you, seeking confirmation, Clump may approach the Guardians?" Malfroid whispered, to her later.

"It did," Clara smiled, radiating confidence, "and he will not. I am sure of it. He would never want it known the High Lord of Almandine is a liar. Not even for himself would he want to know it. And supposing, just for a moment, he did seek confirmation. Having alerted the Guardians, would they not swoop down and seize the artefacts? Almandine would be disgraced. Under no circumstance would Clump bring that upon us. You and I, Malfroid, must continue our little conspiracy. Conceal our necessary little deception, in much the same way Clump and your good self conspire in small ways against me."

* * *

On either side of the ditch where he lay, winter leeching the last of the summered toughness from wiry stalks of fern had garnished the criss-crossed, subsiding arcs with brittle fragility. Almost blocking out light, the remains of feathery fronds hung in desiccated, brown tatters above them.

"Filling my belly with water has done nothing to curb hunger," Slubeadgh moaned. "How soon before I am reduced to eating grass?"

"Brother, we have discussed this at length. We are lost. Where the sally port is located you do not know. And you, you are not prepared to wander through this colourless place in the brightling part of the span, hence we wait for the darkling orb to rise. In short, hunger must play second fiddle to safety. At least we have shelter of sorts, and are well hidden from prying...what was that?"

"By the powers, a howl! A pack of dogs! Have I not been bit enough?" Panicking, he sat up, struggling to turn in the tight space and get onto all fours. "The beginnings of a hue and cry? Never say we are discovered!"

"I think not, brother. More like the sound of an animal in great pain," Galateo piped. "Raise your head above this trench, do it sly, and see if some kind of hunt is in progress."

Cautiously peering through the bracken, Slubeadgh said, "Lessadgh beings are crazed. It is the woman who makes the noise. Crying out in the strange language they use, she runs through the woods to no purpose, and the one I levelled gives chase."

"In belief she is the one who cracked his pate, brother?"

"Rather he think it of her: than know it was I."

"Lessadgh does not know of your existence, brother. Providing they do not change direction and inadvertently make straight for us, we must continue to make this ditch our refuge and stay here a while yet. Take rest."

"Rest with the infernal screeching the woman makes?" he hissed. "How can I rest, when my nerves are as frayed as this sorry foliage? How can I rest, knowing at any moment we may be detected, and I, on all fours like a beast of the field, must expend remaining energy to speedily carry us away to safety?"

"Brother, calm yourself. The woman's cries grow faint and fainter. Think, while those two are away from the underground dwelling, what could you do? Most likely, food is within it. Inferior in quality, as are all things in this dismal place, but good enough to quiet the rumble of your belly."

"No," shaking his head, Slubeadgh slid back down into the ditch, "inviting though it may be, that risk I will not take. To court possible confrontation when my body already suffers affliction in plenty? I will not do it."

"Then go hungry, brother."

"While you still dine and sup at my expense. Parasite."

"You are too harsh, brother. Look upon it with this view. In the womb, all capital unfairly stripped from me was invested in you. In fairness, I do but take a small part of the interest due."

* * *

Semyon dropped the fire crystal into the sconce on the palm of his hand, and pressing the button, disguised as part of the wall's decoration, waited. With barely a hushed sigh, the hidden panel slid smoothly back on its runners, revealing a passageway. Rushing from the dark interior, mingling with damp stale air and eddying dust motes, the slightest hint of Apatia's scent. Nostrils flaring, he stepped inside. Ignoring myriad passageways branching away from the one he trod, he went along the upwardly winding path following her strengthening fragrance, anticipating the eager reception he would receive and the sweat-drenched furnace of passion they would shortly burn in.

Nearing her apartment, he caught a new note. Souring the sweetness of the other strands, it wove restless and acrid between them. For an instant, confidently rising to the surface to overlay explicit promises and voracious need for sexual fulfilment, it fell back into obscure slightness only to return with greater intensity.

It smells of fear, he thought, standing outside the panel that would give him access to her, *what does she have to be afraid of?*

He knocked gently, and waited patient for her to admit him. No response. His ear put to the panel, Semyon listened. Water gliding smoothly over pebbles in the basin of the clock measured out the minutes of an hour, and the swish of silk robes quickly stilled. He took a deep breath, filtered out all other smells to concentrate on hers only. The strength and freshness of the notes confirmed, Apatia stood only inches away on the other side.

"Lady," he said, his voice thick with lust, "if it is your intention to heighten pleasure by at first withholding favour, there is no need to play a teasing game. Only admit me, and throughout the rest of this span, I will slake all possible thirsts and all impossible hungers."

No answer, other than the bitterness of the rogue note he had identified. It had risen to the fore in seconds, and now rode roughshod over all others encapsulated in her scent.

Confused, Semyon leaned his head against the panel.

"Lady," he said quietly, "I will not beg when you are not willing. If some breach has come between us, know this, it is of your making and not of mine. Should my service be later required, you have but to summon your obedient servant."

Footsteps in the passageway, Semyon come to be served as he deserved, and she could not. She could not. Foolish to think, she would be able to send him away with kind words, when just the sound of his feet on the flagstones sent the thought of carnal delights, she had thought under control, spiralling with volcanic intensity. Knowing she could not resist him, Apatia sprang out of the two-seat and fled into the adjoining chamber.

Insistent need urged her back, pulled her through the doorway and resolutely across silken rugs scattered on the floor. A soft rap on the panel. Desire, already thick-knotted, frustration tied it tighter in her stomach and groin, and drew her to where Semyon waited for admittance. He spoke, his voice curdled with lust to match her own, offering pleasure beyond all bounds and the ecstasy of release from the aching need girdling both her body and mind.

Crushing the carded tissue of web-silks she wore, Apatia leaned against the panel, pressing her body close, and closer still against it. Of its own volition, her hand moved slowly towards the button and hovered over it, while need manically yammered and howled, demanding she only admit him for the briefest period to tame its sharpest edges.

Metallic eyes, all silvered hardness and without expression, flashed before her. Unemotional, without pity, her mother's bell-like voice tolling menace struck her ears with strident softness, *'cross me in this and I will blast you to dust.'*

Semyon, there is no breach between us, she longed to cry out, but the words froze in her throat, and heavier than stone, her hand fell away from the button.

Wetness pooled the gilded yellow of her eyes, trembled silently on the brink and finally spilling in runnels down her paler than pale cheeks, Apatia listened to him walk away.

* * *

"I was right to remain alert," Slubeadgh whispered. "The one I levelled obviously caught the woman, for he carries her in his arms, and she lies there uncomplaining. What does it mean?"

"To make sense of lunacy is to make no sense at all, brother."

"Now he takes her into the dwelling."

"He would not have brought the woman back only to dump her on the doorstep," Galateo scoffed. "What would be the point in that?"

"I cannot answer, but one thing I do know. Lessadgh beings are highly unpredictable. Their behaviour erratic, their motives unfathomable, their mental agility, most questionable."

"Brother, if you wish to debate the sanity of Lessadgh and its beings, I can only assume fatigue and hunger have bettered you. After expending much effort in capturing the woman, it is unlikely the one with the cracked pate will stir for the rest of the span. Come. Sit down and un-cradle me."

"No. Have I not told you, over and over again? Given our circumstance, it is too risky. At a more opportune moment, I will gladly give you to the air. For the present, I keep watch and you must give me respite, so hush your clack."

* * *

Apatia drew back hangings of fine web-silks. Small in the wide expanse of the bed, his crimson hair flaming against pearl-sheened pillows and coverings, the child lay motionless, fast gripped in slumber-dusted dream.

"Child, in robbing me of necessary sport, the greatest fear you have bought down upon me. That is no fair trade." Bending to put her face close to his, she said, "More than half a span, and still you are sunk deep in unnatural lethargy.

"Yet I have heard tell, in the deepest reaches of unconsciousness, some semblance of the faculty to hear is retained. If this is true, hear me now. Wake. Rise up from the prison of soporific drowse. Awaken. Shake off the false shackles of dust induced abstraction and come, fully waking into reality and know your true destiny." Raising her voice she shouted into his ear, "Wake, wake up, and all will be well. I tell you, boy, all will be righted. You have only to wake."

Studying his face, noting his eyes rolling lazily beneath their lids, and the pallor lying just beneath his coppery skin, Apatia took these as signs he heard her.

* * *

Wandering through dense, bewildering clouds that ebbed and flowed in billowing confusion, but never parted long enough to see where he was going, William finally came to a small dark space, and without knowing how he knew there was nothing to fear, crawled into it. This darkness, absolute and like no other, softly embraced him. In its comforting safe depths, though he understood she was not there, he could feel the pressure of Clara arms wrapped loosely around him, holding him gently, rocking him smoothly back and forth.

"Clara will come and take me home," William told the darkness.

"I do not doubt it," the dark silently agreed. "Are you not her boy? Her dearest boy? Of course she will come, but first, she must find the way."

"What if those eyes come to find me?" he asked.

"The ones of startling blue luminosity that frightened you? They may look, but never see you, not here."

From very, very far away a voice called to him. The roiling sweep of continuous thickened cloud absorbed the words and their meanings, but could not prevent indistinct sound from penetrating their heaving masses.

"Be cautious," the dark advised. "It may not be Clara who calls. I can offer no security once you have left my sanctuary, William."

"I must go and see, but if it is not Clara, how will I find a way back?"

"I will draw you to me as I did before."

Cautious, he went out into the tumescent clouds obscuring all vision. Feather-light, he rose hesitant through many levels of opaque and confusing density. Passing into a thinner variety of fog-bound vapour and nearing the surface, he found clarity trailing in wisp-strung mist.

A harsh voice, soaked in bitterness and anger, speaking a language he did not know, shouted words that meant nothing to him.

Not Clara. Never Clara. Clara's voice was never harsh. Clara was never angry, or bitter. Clara never shouted at him when he did the wrong thing, but patiently explained why he should not.

Consciousness scraped against him as he dived away and plummeted back the way he had come, back to the welcoming darkness.

"It was not Clara," he whispered to the dark. "I will stay here and shall not stir again until I hear her voice, loud and clear, call me by my name."

* * *

Slowly parting a batch of dilapidated stalks of battered fern to see better, Slubeadgh whispered, "You were wrong, Galateo, and I right to mount a watch, for here is further lunacy. Not only does the Lessadgh man stir, it would seem he makes preparation for a journey, though the brightest part of the span is near gone. Two sacks, he has already placed into the woman's cart and now, strangest of all…he carries her, swaddled in blankets and puts her in it too!"

"Not such curious behaviour, brother. Likely he has arrived at the opinion the woman is more trouble than she is worth. It is possible he intends to cut his losses. Perhaps abandon her at some remote place, or use her as merchandise and get gain in that manner."

"Hist. The man of Lessadgh has taken up the piece of wood I thought a stout cudgel, and with much effort drags the whole contraption away."

"He draws it as a gostle would? Truly, his mind is greatly disturbed, brother."

"I know not." Slubeadgh slid back down into the sheltering ditch. "I can scarce think straight for hunger. Nor have I care to spend on what becomes of either of them."

"Now, here is good opportunity for you, brother. Fortune smiles a little on you at last."

"That whore? Never has she dangled a thing before my nose without snatching it away the very instant I reached to grasp it."

"The furnishings of this ditch," the piping voice goaded, "must have charm I know nothing of, brother. The way is now clear for you to forage in the dwelling for sustenance, yet you hesitate to take advantage?"

"Sarcasm is wasted on me," Slubeadgh said. "I merely exercise caution."

"Brother," Galateo sneered, "ever you mistake cowardice for caution. The pair touched by lunacy, are long gone."

Climbing warily out of the ditch, he crouched at its edge for a few moments and scanned the woods, cocking his head from side to side to listen.

"I am certain of that now," he sniffed, "but knew it not earlier. Make mock all you wish, yet I would remind you, it is my physical prowess and cunning that keeps us both safe."

Wary still, he sidled over frost-rimed grass to the ivy-festooned screen and opening it, pushed at the door.

"It will not open. Lessadgh has locked it."

"Then put your shoulder to it, brother. Put all your weight behind it, and by sole dint of your extraordinary physical prowess, deal such a blow to break it in."

Launching himself at the door, Slubeadgh burst it open. Momentum propelled him forward and sent him sprawling. Ricocheting smartly off the wood-lined walls of the passage, the door cracked its edge hard against his shin, and behind him, the screen slammed shut.

"Have a care, brother. On your side, you squash me flat."

Gasping, he heaved himself up, and squinted along the darkened length of the narrow passage at a feeble, red glow, fluttering nervously at its end.

"I must retreat, go back to our former lodgings," he said, barely able to squeeze fear out of his voice. "Lessadgh may have left this place, but something, or someone, remains here."

"I hear nothing, brother. Your forceful entry caused enough noise to excite the interest of any who might linger, yet no one comes to investigate. Besides, how will you turn around in the confines of this space? Nail what little courage you can muster to the sticking place. If you would appease hunger go forward, or not, as it please you for I shall take nourishment whatever decision is come to."

"You feed while I starve!"

"You have a life," Galateo hissed. "After taking the best part of mine, you live a life. Destitute of all bravery you are, brother. Am I to forfeit the little I have to succour a thing that trembles, whey-faced and panicked, at the first sight of imagined danger, a thing so base as will not lift a hand to help itself? I think not. I help myself, so long as I am able. Go forward. Better to meet our end here, and now, than allow creeping starvation to take us both. Go forward, I say. Go forward."

With his twin's childlike voice scornfully whipping him on, Slubeadgh eased through the covering canopy of darkness. Slower into the smudged beginnings of dusky, rose light, tinged with faltering grey that in the shortest distance, bloomed into transient shadows of deepest purple playing in a ruddy background. At the end of the passage, he stopped. Peering anxiously into the large space of Persimmony Clump's living area, he saw the stove and in the potbelly of its basket, the last blushes of a lustre cast from the dying embers of a fire.

"No one is here, save for that device standing guard in the corner," he said. "Yet it makes no move to challenge me."

"Nor will it. If I remember right, we have heard something of this, brother."

"I have no recollection of it."

"Having little else to do, naturally I am the repository for all information you choose to discard, am I not? It is a fire. If I am not much mistaken, it will do you no harm unless you touch it, or the metal it burns in. Remember, brother, neither heat nor cold may touch you, yet touching heat, or cold, you feel its effects to the full."

"I have more pressing need than a lecture on Lessadgh's primitive devices," Slubeadgh said, moving confidently into the open.

"Then it can be of no interest to you, brother, the fire will fail before long, and light in this hovel with it. Blundering about in the dark, how will you find food, if the fire is not fed?"

"What does it eat?"

"Is it not obvious? The receptacle by the stove is full of cut wood for the purpose, brother. Cast a small piece into the red glow. Wait for it to catch flame before throwing more on."

The far recesses of Clump's living area remained swathed in darkness that flowed swift to melt the subtle haze, ringing the soft halo thrown out from the flaring stove. In the middle of this puddled pool, he saw a table and on it, an earthenware pot. Lifting it, Slubeadgh sniffed the remains of the broth Clump had made, grimaced and drained it.

"A vile concoction of vegetable pottage," he said, scooping out the last few dregs with his fingers, "but more would not go amiss."

Against one wall of the room, a dresser stood. Wiping his mouth on the sleeve of his great coat, he opened cupboards at the bottom, dragged out the contents and rummaged through them trying to find something else to eat. Half a jar of honey. A few dried apricots in a twist of paper. Stale cheese, ripe with mould. A crust of bread, harder than a kiln-fired brick. In a bowl, raw carrots, turnips, onions and two wilted leeks. All found a way down his gullet. Clump's small packages of expensive tea and coffee beans, he spat out, declaring them to be, "Vicious herbs of no discernible merit."

In one of the drawers above, he pawed through wooden cooking utensils, cutlery, and tiny squares of crude linen. In the other, among a batch of paper, a bundle of candles tied with string. Prising one away from the rest, he bit into it, chewed and gagged and spattered the floor with partly ground pieces of tallow mingled with saliva.

"Foul grease, and rancid with it," he muttered, throwing the rest of the candle into the stove's basket.

"Brother, do your legs tingle?"

"The effect of the Lady's dart bends me double, and for the last span they have pained me almost past bearing. Whoa! Do you see that? The grease-stick I threw into the fire, flames and burns with a steady glow."

Taking another candle from the bundle he thrust it into the fire, nearly dropping it when the end nearest his hand flared up.

"It is the fuzzy end that catches," he crowed. "For all your knowledge, you did not know that! Now I have portable light and may search where I please."

"Un-cradle me, brother. I baste in noxious moisture given off by your body. Give me to fresh washed air. You have eaten sufficient."

"Eaten sufficient?' Slubeadgh lit more candles and arranged them in a long-handled pan, found by the side of the stove. "So say you, who has feasted well, to me who must make up the deficit? Before ever I take off this cursed harness and un-cradle you to take the air, I will eat my fill of what can be found, and make sure we are secure."

Lifting the flaming pan high, he thrust it to arms length, and sent its light bludgeoning through crowding darkness into areas of Clump's living space not yet seen, or foraged in. "Use the only weapon at your disposal, Galateo. Batter my ears with shrill-piped voice. Cudgel them further with wordy assault and raise such verbal storm as you may muster, but from this stance, I will by no means budge."

"We shall see," Galateo said, calm. "Your word is a pie-crust, made to crumble at first touch. Murderer. Eater of my flesh. Liver of my life. Destroyer of your kin. Foul coward and liar. All Semyon has said of you is nothing but truth. Worthless creature; hated and mocked by all, with good reason. Creeping toad, tittle-tattler, embroiderer of lies."

"Yes, yes," Slubeath shouted, to drown out the rising din, "and so much more beside is my villainy."

"Only wait a while for all your misdeeds to be recounted, brother. I do but limber up, and have barely begun to get into full stride."

Chapter 21.

The child, hearing her command, had briefly struggled to obey. Of that, Apatia was sure.

Why, then, did you fall back into the dust's clutches? Or, is it possible, even at your gentle age, little one, you have cunning enough to feign deepest slumber?

Taking hold of the front of his shirt, she pulled him up from the undulating waves of rumpled web-silk and lace, and shaking him, watched close for a reaction. No matter how vigorously his head snapped back and forth, no wrinkle of discomfort appeared above the bridge of his nose, or under his eyes, to change the serene expression of deep, peaceful sleep fixed on his face. She let him go, let him slump back onto the pillows, knowing the dust had him still.

Water, continuously trickling over the pebbles, slid them around the basin before gliding through the tiny sluice-gate, where it funnelled down to a series of valves that would force it to rise through a set of decorative, crystalline pipes and begin the controlled discharge once more. Each circuit it made, measured out an hour, and moved the hands of the clock to keep pace with the progression of its journey.

Two segments on. No muscle has the boy twitched, nor a carmine eyelash stirred. This cannot be right? The dosage may have been great, but even a child should have shaken off the effects of the dust long since. Yet he does not come out of this state, but seems to go ever deeper into it.

Seeing a thin slick of moisture coating his brow, she laid the palm of her hand upon his chest and felt heat coming off him. Alarm leapfrogged anxiety, sending cold shivers of dread up her spine.

Some other agency works here! A disease carried from Lessadgh must ail him. But no, no it cannot be. He is Faienya. None of the illnesses that scourge Lessadgh's weak flesh can make any inroad to infect him. What then? An answer there must be and I must find it.

Prising one of his eyelids up with the ball of her thumb, she gasped disbelief. Crazed with myriad, green filament veins, intensely yellowed ochre had replaced the middling purple, shot with golden flecks about the pupil, she had expected to see filling the socket.

It is the back of his orb! Front is back and back is front. By the horns of power, what manner of strangeness is this to make his eyes roll back into his skull? What is the cause? Dust does not do this. Dust cannot do this.

Ripping his shirt open, she immediately saw a livid discolouration high on his right breast. At its centre, a pinpricked speckle of hardened green showed where her dart had punctured him, and radiating outward from the tiny wound, many tendrils of a necrotic darkness leeched into the unnatural pallor lurking just beneath his skin.

"Lickspittle child," Apatia moaned, burying her head in her hands, "what sentence have you contrived to pass on me? For this, my mother will fade me. By the powers above and below, by powers unseen and unknown, you thwart all her hopes for greatness, and by so doing, condemn me to dust."

* * *

Unmoved by his twin's ongoing venomous tirade, Slubeadgh pulled half-filled sacks from a corner, and spilling the contents on to the floor, wondered what they might be as they rolled away. Their colours were unlike any he had seen before, though their shapes were not far different from vegetables found in Noor.

His belly rumbling thunderous sound, he scooped some of them up and crammed them into the large earthenware pot he had eaten slops from, then set about finding liquid to cook them in. Rummaging through cupboards, he found a bottle of liquid. The cork pulled, a smell, reminiscent of apples wafted out and was immediately added to the pot. He put it on the stove. While it boiled, he carried out a systematic search to see what other finds the lighted pan would reveal.

A good supply of candles found, he crawled away from the kitchen area, with Galateo still screeching abuse, and to his piping voice added his own complaint about twinges, busily travelling up and down his legs, riddling him with untold agony. In the far reaches of flickering light, he noted an overturned chair with a bundle of rags tumbled beneath it. Paying these no attention, he came to an archway, and cautious as ever, thrust the flaming pan out to see what was illumined. Certain this was the third exit Semyon had spoken of, he followed its course to the outside world, made sure the door was locked and bolted, then backed slowly out into the living area.

Further on, another archway. His light revealed a sparse chamber containing a narrow bed with a large, wooden chest pressed up against the footboard. By its side, a chair with a partly burned candle in its holder was placed on the seat, and a rug made of what looked like rags, spread on the floor. The next opening, he knew of already. It was the passageway he had used to come into Clump's home and led to the door disguised by ivy clambering over the screen. He went to its end, wondering how he could secure it, since he had burst it open so violently, only to discover the lock still intact and the bolts had not been thrown.

In full flood, his piping voice raised to ear splitting pitch Galateo left off his diatribe, and burst into raucous laughter.

"Moronic king of fools," he jeered, "idiotic pimple on the sphincter of all the powers. Your, so-called, physical prowess has not the capacity to break lock or bolt. Nor could Lessadgh have thrown a bolt whilst being outside, nor slipped the lock, which has no key, lest he was inside this hovel. The door was merely stiff, you mindless manifestation of vanity. I did not tell you so, for fear of wounding your all encompassing, all too fragile ego, you slack-brained blockhead."

Wilting beneath his brother's scorn, he made no answer, but worked his way back, sliding the lighted pan along the floor by its handle, knowing the entrance with the trap door would not present a solution for his safety so easily.

Determined to continue following the wall, he emerged from the passage, manoeuvred himself into position and pushed his light across the worn floorboards. Some distance away, opposite to where he crouched, tinges of brightness falteringly touched deep shadows draping the far walls, but could not penetrate a darker field lying behind. From this seemingly impenetrable gloom, a momentary flash of dulled brilliance burst out. Catching the corner of Slubeadgh's eye, it stopped him in his tracks.

"Urilatum's precious gleam," he breathed, while his twin's ranting and raving sped onward. "I saw it's luscious spangle, but no, it could not be. Not in this meanest of places. My eyes play tricks, or my mind is addled."

Moving his make-shift torch away from the wall and pushing it further out into the space, he saw high up, hanging in midnight shade, a tantalising glint. A wink of seductive coppered-silver flickered, jumped boldly from one spot to another and glistening full-rounded, but dull, disappeared. Rising up, never noticing his back was erect, he lifted the pan and held it at arms length, understanding why he had thought darkness hid behind a layer of deepest gloom.

Burgeoning brightness began to shine into a recess with many shelves lining its walls, where resplendent beauty, coyly revealed, slid back into obscurity as his arm wavered. Nearer still, edging slowly towards the vision, his breath rasped short with growing excitement. The pan trembling in his grip, priceless wealth was finally and fully disclosed. Packed tight in jumbled profusion on all the shelves, pieces wrought from fabulous urilatum and much sought after gold.

Stunned by the revelation, he did not hear his twin's malicious torrent come to an abrupt halt. Rooted to the spot, in silence he gawked, not quite believing what he saw, but unable to take his eyes away from the alcove and its contents.

"Brother," smooth as silk the piping voice now. "That whore we spoke of? It would appear she has grown tired of spiteful tease. She now lies before you with legs wide spread and begs you take her in whatever manner you will."

"She does."

"Yes, indeed she does. Another thing, brother."

"What?"

"Look to the vile mess you so carefully threw into a pot. It shrivels and burns on Lessadgh's fire."

* * *

Light failing, the verdant green sky and remnant clouds were scarified by a mixed palette of brilliant orange hues that soon bloomed to full-blown scarlet and purple, before taking on the subdued mantle of night.

Beneath the spire of the summerhouse, Lingaradgh flicked the image shown in her scrying bowl, dissipating it with the tips of her fingers. Angry, she paced restless round the circumference of the small room and then stared out over her Kingdom City.

Round and round, ever round and round, day after day, and every miniscule part of measured time a day contained, the words sung in her head. The cadence never varying one whit, the long-stretched vowels drawn out to perfection, the short-snapped consonants cut with precision. Had it not been so, all would have crumbled, all would have collapsed, and before the eyes of all, stark reality made plain.

I am tired, she thought looking through the crystal panes as she reached for the ruby bottle hanging at her waist. *Span by span, I see myself grow paler, and though regretting the energy it pulls from me, cannot cease to sing the roundelay. To do so, would expose the truth, and bring the Guardians down upon me in a flash. To lose this illusion, to lose this city when it has been my life's work? To fade in ignominy? To be remembered with derision that lasts ever after? Never. Never can I allow it to happen. What then? Then, I must do what I must to preserve what I have created, and be damned to any who, not seeing the peril, wander into my path. By whatever means possible, this illusion must stand, and I will do it.*

Reaffirming both iron purpose and ruthless determination, she prepared a message bubble. Speaking briefly into it, she opened a window, and launched it with vigour. Without waiting to see that it flew on course, she closed the casement and hurried to inhale this hour's quota of Trooh.

Rainbow shimmered, travelling swift over soft-blown currents of air, her message bubble lost speed approaching the windows of Apatia's apartment. Drawn to the place where its recipient sat with head in hands, it bobbed, tapping gently but insistent for admittance, and sensing it would soon be given access, drawing away, spun fierce on its axis.

Hearing it, Apatia dragged herself up from beside the bed. With lagging feet, she covered the distance. Heartsick with apprehension, she threw the window wide and stretched out her hand to receive it. In the same moment, the message bubbled hurled itself forward, and striking her forcibly on the forehead, popped.

"Asinine daughter," her mother's doleful voice chimed, "I see all you do. Nothing can be hid from me. Cover the boy with cloths soused in coolest water, tend him well with your own hand. Let no other come near him, Apatia. Throughout the period the pale orb rides, you will do this. No scurrilous ailment of Lessadgh afflicts him, but rather this mystery, instigated by your incompetence, is of his own doing. He must be shaken from it. I have the means to do it. Come, fetch it from me when the brightling orb first cracks the shell of this darkling part of the old span."

* * *

"Smell it now, brother?"

"I have no care if it burn to nothing," Slubeadgh answered, sharp.

"Brother, you must eat. For what seems an age, you complained starvation knocked and would soon fade you.'"

"What I see before me, sustains me better than any food power-forsaken Lessadgh has to offer."

"That is as may be, but this treasure cannot walk by itself from the shelves, brother. And if it is your intention to claim it, your body must have strength to do it. How will you carry it off, if weakness is your only ally? Come, tear yourself away for only the shortest while and take nourishment." No answer. "Well then, brother, let the meal you no longer hunger for burn. However, the pot made of sticky earth is not impervious to heat. What if it smash to smithereens? What if the shards ignite to make a bonfire of this hovel? What if the hoard, your eyes are so fixed upon, is captured by this conflagration and in the ensuing furnace, melted to molten liquid is then burnt to ash? But no, I run ahead. Being roasted, you and I, by the same flame long before that happened, we would not be here to mourn the loss."

"The pot could do all that?"

"It is possible, brother," Galateo lied. "I merely present you with a possibility. A likely, unlikely possibility."

"You tie me in knots," Slubeadgh grumbled, and getting to his feet tottered into the kitchen area.

On the top plate of the stove a few drops of juice bubbled upon a thick layer of burnt syrup, crisped to cinders at the outer edges. In the middle, the earthenware pot was charred and cracked through, its fractures bonded together by a confection of indistinguishable vegetables reduced to glutinous slurry.

"By the powers, split from base to belly. I am come not a moment too soon. You were right to open my eyes to this possibility."

"I think only of your welfare, brother. Remember, it will be hot. Touch it not with your hands."

Using the skirt of his greatcoat, Slubeadgh managed to prise the pot away, and shuffling quick, went back to the alcove.

Galateo un-cradled. Dappled red in the fire's ruddy glow on one side, and striped by the candles guttering blaze on the other, his peach-soft skin was well nourished, but appeared to have the consistency of dense jelly, lacking colour or finish.

Slightly bigger than a newborn child, he joined with Slubeadgh at the waist. Too large for the rest of his incomplete body, his head rolled uncontrollably on a short, thin neck incapable of carrying its weight. Tiny rounded shoulders were brushed with the back of his skull one moment and his thin concaved chest, grazed by his chin the next. Stumpy arms and hands, waving with uncoordinated movements through the air, were barely formed, as was his face. Puffy flesh covered eyes that would never see. His nose, a spread stub, would never smell. His lips, almost non-existent on either side of a gash of a mouth that would never speak, eat or drink.

Living a life vicariously through his brother, all sensation was shared in a delayed, secondary manner, save for the sanctum, where thought was birthed and nurtured. Into this territory, neither of the conjoined twins could trespass, and while conversing mind to mind, each one's thought remained separate, its process and produce entirely his own.

Slubeadgh sat with his back propped against the wall by the alcove, his knees drawn up and his thighs supporting his brother's half-weight. The harness to bear him, unstrapped and unbuckled, had been laid carefully aside, together with his ruined greatcoat. The fiery ache in his shoulders gradually easing, the deep indentations carved in his muscles were slowly smoothing as the flesh rose to meet skin calloused with ridges.

Spread around him, taken down from the shelves, and lovingly laid out the treasure trove he had stumbled upon. Delicate handles of doves in flight, lifelike in form and motion, were the only decoration applied to a set of hammered urilatum drinking cups and the large tray they were placed on. Undecorated goblets, satin smooth and polished to a high sheen, with long slender stems terminating in clawed feet. An octagonal bowl, poised on an elegant column leading down to a similarly shaped foot, its simple design repudiated by the size of emeralds snared at its rim, and heaped inside, trinkets studded with all manner of gemstones. A looking glass, sculpted in the shape of a scalloped shell, the handle a mermaid with each tiny scale of her tail in bold relief. Lidded pots, enamelled with flowers of both Noor and Lessadgh. A set of crystal flagons of extraordinary fineness, fitted with twists and spirals of drawn urilatum meshed over each one, and many boxes large and small, of every shape, texture and exquisite design.

Absent in Noor, buttery yellow gold echoed designs made from the superior metal urilatum, yet attention paid to detail as great, the craftsmanship superb, the quantity and weight more than he had ever seen in all his life.

From the drawers of Persimmony Clump's workbench, he had taken great nuggets of refined gold, coiled golden wire of all gauges, and gems of all kinds found in wooden boxes. Pieces made from silver had been cast back into the alcove as having little to no value.

Luxuriating in as much freedom as he would ever have, Galateo waved his arms through the air and said, "You are a perfect fool, brother, not to have realized the dust was wearing off. Yet, not bothering to exert any effort to try your legs and see if they would bear you, you still went on all fours much longer than was needed."

"If I am a fool," Slubeadgh replied, picking up the scalloped-shell mirror to fondle the mermaid's breasts and tail again, "I am a very wealthy one. Any foolishness will be excused…no…completely pardoned, because of that one factor. Many and many a time, I have seen riches pave a path to over-ride transgressions great and small."

"We, brother, we are wealthy," Galateo corrected, "but only for so long as Lessadgh does not return."

"I had forgot Lessadgh."

"Consider Lessadgh most urgently, brother. If this wealth is to make a transfer of ownership, best the transaction be completed sooner than later."

"What must I do? Where," he wondered, "should I carry this wealth to? My mind is numb at the very thought of the loss of even the smallest part," he groaned. "I could hide it away, but, where?"

"Eat what remains of your glorious stew, brother. Give me a little time to work through this conundrum of difficulty. To secure our future in all its totality, you will need strength of mind, purpose, and that of your body."

"It should be buried," Slubeadgh announced, scraping the bottom of the pot.

"We are of like mind," Galateo piped, "and some thought on the location of this most precious of burials, I have given, brother. Throughout Noor it is well known Lessadgh beings are cunning, their guile knowing no bounds. How could they be otherwise, suffering as they do from a severe deficit of moral decency?"

"True. Very true."

"It follows, does it not, brother, Lessadgh beings would not hesitate to take our wealth from us? In a blink of an eye they would steal it, and laugh at the taking."

"By the breath of all the powers, that is what any Lessadgh being would do."

"Then, brother, cunning must be turned against Lessadgh, for who can say how this one came to be in possession of such wealth? By no honest means, that much we may safely know. Under Lessadgh's nose, we bury wealth justly confiscated."

"Under Lessadgh's nose you say? Ha! He would not seek to find it there and the very place, I know it. Where we found the woman's cart. The soil is soft and loamy, covered by needling pine and rotting leaf mould. What think you of this?"

"Brother, you grow in wisdom, or perhaps you have trespassed into the one place you may not go, for you speak my thought exact."

Slubeadgh reached for the harness, saying, "There is much to be done. You must be cradled, else you are damaged in the frantic activity to follow."

"How you value me, brother," his twin piped sarcasm. "I was about to ask to return to the security of my cradle and the comfort of your belly."

Drawn to one side of the alcove, a thick curtain. Slubeadgh pulled it down from pole and moorings, and spread it flat on the floorboards. Blankets ripped from the narrow bed, torn in rough pieces and wrapped carefully around the larger items of precious urilatum. Afraid the owner might come back and confront him, he worked with speed. From time to time, he turned up the edges of the flattened material, testing the weight put in it was one he could lift and comfortably bear off.

Corners knotted tight, the unwieldy bundle ready to be spirited away, he slung it on his back, and grunting with effort made his way along the passage. Stopping just short of the screened door, he lowered it to the ground in readiness to be taken outside.

A pair of rough cotton sheets, thin with wear, and pillowcases in no better condition, he took from the bed. Both sheets laid down, one on top of the other, he worried about the layers being able to withstand the heaviness he intended to load in them. He doubled them over; then remembering the sacks he had found the vegetables in, rushed to spill the rest of their contents out. Sheeting and pillow cases, he tore up, and wrapped the urilatum boxes in the coarse linen, carefully fitting each package according to size and shape, into the hessian bags.

More wrappings needed for the gold objects. He prowled about the living space. Threw more wood into the stove. Stuck more lighted candles into the pan. Looked for anything that might serve. Back in the bedchamber again, he rediscovered the wooden chest at the foot of the bed. Wrenching the lid up, through parted lips he huffed disappointment at neatly folded clothes lying inside.

"I must make do," he muttered, taking a woollen shirt out and holding it up. "Once the arms are pulled off, the body is serviceable. Sleeves tied at one end may pouch a drinking vessel or box. Best scoop the garments out, and be not so lavish with the padding I wind around my treasure, allocating size of material to each gold item for best usage."

Thrusting his hands deep inside, a hard-edged object struck his knuckles a painful blow. Cursing, he pulled out, examined skin shaved from raw flesh and sucked away tiny beads of green life force.

"Lessadgh has hidden something?" Galateo ventured, his childlike voice calm and sly. "Something of value. Something prized. Else why hide it, brother? With utmost care, unless you would risk further injury, excavate the fabric to find that which is concealed within these covering folds."

Heavy gauged for winter wear, shirts and vests, breeches and stockings, all textured thick and scratchy, and beneath, articles made of lighter material for the warmer months.

Piece by piece, Slubeadgh drew Persimmony Clump's every day wardrobe from the chest. Half way down, a full-length cloak of fine spun, high-quality cloth, covered a satin waistcoat, intricately embroidered with silk flowers, and peeking from beneath its buttonholed edge, the tiniest sliver of coppered-silver gleamed, dull and plain, against the set of bright silver filigree buttons just inches away.

Almost reverential, he touched the cold metal lightly. Bit by bit, he gently pushed the garment away from the corner with his fingertips, slowly exposing its lustrous gleam. The subtle glint of its hammered surface fluidly pursued the receding satin that paused briefly, before passing smoothly over a large, raised oval lozenge, enamelled with opalescent blues and greens, and rushed onward to fall shortly after from the far edge of the revealed box. Rectangular in shape, no eye could deny the graceful proportion and design encompassed in the majesty of simple perfection.

"Fortune, at this moment truly loves us, brother."

"I named her whore," Slubeadgh whispered, taking the box out of the chest with trembling hands. "By the powers, I regret, I was so hasty."

"Let us hope she remembers it was you, who blackened her character, not I, brother. Mayhap it is, I, misshapen and destitute of all most take for granted, whom she showers her kindness upon. Or, mayhap, she enjoyed the vehemence of the abuse you gave her so freely. What does it matter, when we are endowed with such riches?"

Closing the lid of the chest, he set the box upon it and carefully opened it. Facing him, settled in a recess carved out expressly to meet its dimensions, a feather. The bottom of the quill pierced, and fed through the piercing, a plaited ring with a tassel, constructed of finely drawn urilatum threads suspended, from it. From the quill, a shaft elegantly extended, with barbs exquisitely aligned all along its length that on reaching the uppermost level was cut brutally straight. He touched it, for a moment believing it to be real, and that a slight breeze could ruffle through its component parts, but it was solid and without movement.

The feather out of its box, many others identical in every detail and no longer trapped in the confines of a niche, smoothly slid out from behind it to form a semi-circle.

"It is a fan!"

He worked it. With gentle movements of his wrist, he arced it through the air, angling it to catch the light and flutter. With flicks, opened and folded it.

"Of all wondrous things to behold, none could better this. None could even rival this. It is the epitome of artistry, with a beauty that tugs at my heart, and makes tears well with elated emotion. Its value must be vast. It is unique. Never can there have been anything like it, yet you say nothing. Do words fail you? No matter, I have words enough for us both."

"Lingaradgh," Galateo said, dark and quiet, "did we not once hear it whispered through the halls of the Helm, she commissioned such a thing, brother? If memory serve, both a trinket and weapon, it was to be."

"Lingaradgh? Why talk of that bitch. She faded. Without number, sparns have passed since she faded, and the Lady Apatia now sits upon the seat where she had sat. Lingaradgh can have no association with this object of great worth."

"A Stunted One," Galateo continued, as if he had not heard, "of high repute, and extraordinary skill, had travelled over the Drusy Sea from Zoiss to seek his fortune and earned much praise. His reputation reaching Lingaradgh's ears, she desired him to carry out work for her, and scandal…? Yes, scandal there was, quickly quashed."

"Well," Slubeadgh snapped the fan shut, "there is much to be done and little time to waste on reminiscences of what is long past, or suppositions of what might have been. The box, I will reluctantly hide with the rest, to collect at my leisure, but this magnificence shall go where I go. I will not be parted from it."

"Do as you wish, brother, though instinct warns me you will get little good from it."

"Ha! Now you play the prophet? Already the fan does me good, it gladdens my eye and enraptures my heart. With such a thing as this, together with the wealth I own, what might I not achieve now?"

"You mean to break fealty with the Lady Apatia, brother?"

"Perhaps."

"Further speech on this we must have, brother."

"Not now. There is more pressing need. My riches parcelled and temporarily lodged in Lessadgh's cold soil, is of greatest concern."

"Our riches, brother," Galateo piped soft. "Our riches."

Chapter 22.

Fool, and thrice a fool was I, to think beauty would fill the emptiness within, when in my heart, I knew it never could.
Can beauty retain its grace and charm? I tell you, no. A thing of beauty, too oft looked upon, loses much in the looking. Gradually, its power to enthral wanes into delight, and continues through all degrees to ordinariness. Place beauty among other things of beauty, and it is lost, for the object being no better than those it keeps company with, is devalued and becomes merely commonplace and of little interest.
All things must change. That law alone stands immutable. This lesson I learned, and the empty space within me expanding, threatened to consume me utterly.
In thought, I spent my days, my mind returning ever to the perennial question all must ask at some point, what is my purpose? To the House of the Disobedient Ones, I determined to go. To break into their solitude, bearing the full brunt of their wrath if necessary, to lay this question before them and remain until answer was given, or I was no more.
In Hessonii, a vast tract of land reserved by the Disobedient Ones for themselves alone, and where none may safely enter unless expressly bidden to come, the Trapiche Emeral surges untamed from its underground lair. At its height, the brightling orb smites its face, but cannot penetrate its depths. Nor can its warmth calm the cold rage travelling across its far reached broadness, nor along its whole length. Green upon green, so green its waters appear black, the Trapiche Emeral reaches up to lash the air, spitting foam-sprayed defiance at clouds above, and crashing down, batters translucent rocks standing tall and proud from its uneasy surface. In the midst of this fury, the island of the Disobedient Ones is to be found, and on it, the great Houses they had built.
To this place, I journeyed. Striding upon roads made by friendly winds, I went there, and came to the ravaged banks the river gnaws at constant. A portion of the steep incline selected, I drifted down lighter than thistled fluff. Upon the tips of ragged waves I rode. On bubble-frothed spume I trod. And coming to the shore, felt curious pebbles, shorn from host crystal and patterned with the likeness of wheel-spokes inside, tumble and roll treacherous beneath my feet.
Long ago, before Noor wrapped Lessadgh in its skin, and dulled the radiance shed upon that place, men covered their heads to show humility before entering the worship houses. This I had seen. This I did. On gaining firmer ground, I, who knew not how to be humble, covered my head in marked respect with the fringes of my cloak. To the great terrace spread

before the great House of the Disobedient Ones, I went, and climbing many steps, stood upon its edge and bent my knee. With hands outstretched in supplication I cried, I was of the first born, a true son, who came to beg for the enlightenment of their wisdom. Again and again, I cried out and for answer, received none.

To the middle of the terrace I crept, and squatting there in full and certain view, stared at the tall windows, one by one, in hope of catching a glimpse that might tell me, someone came to give welcome into my father's House. Blank the windows, devoid of all life, save for the slow passage of the span mirrored in their panes. I stayed there, counselling myself to patience when the hot beat of anger began to drum in my breast.

And I thought, what father hearing their child cry for admittance would not welcome that child into his house?

And I thought, not knowing which of the Disobedient Ones had sired me, perhaps, unwittingly some offence I had given.

And I thought, what father would not make himself known to his child, and tell of offence given, before seeking to correct the situation by instruction, or punishment?

And I thought, what father does not nurture his child, or does not cherish his offspring, if only as a reflection of himself? And with discipline, school his child with knowledge that should be known?

And I thought of the long perished beings in Lessadgh, who motherless from the time of my birth, cared for me, a child of the gods, with adoration, but not I think, affection. More from those ones, I had, than was ever given by my sire. From the Disobedient Ones all I had earned, together with every child of theirs, was abandonment save for the pitifully few occasions mentioned.

And I thought, when the Disobedient Ones took action on our behalf, was it truly for their children, or to their own ends? These thoughts, and many more of similar nature, flogged patience till it fled, and in its place, hurt pierced me with many pains for on these things I had not dwelt so deep before.

The darkling part of the span gave out. Its obstinate grasp failed and diminished. The brightling orb above me, I rose up. Rose up with cracking knee and aching thigh. The fringes of my cloak, I tore from my head, and drawing breath deep into my lungs, bellowed with all my might.

'For those disrespectful, be they sire or dam, there can be no respect. Be you flesh of my flesh, or no. Be you gods, or some aberrant manifestations of nature, no thing do I owe you. Nothing will I willingly give from this time onward.'

Stentorian, my voice boomed across the narrowing distance, and striking the jadeite walls of the House of the Disobedient Ones, was straightway hurled back in rejection, thrown back in final insult to bounce away over the Trapiche Emeral, over its roaring waters and into the land beyond.

Heavy the wooden doors, I had not approached out of misguided esteem, banded and studded with thick urilatum against all unlikely comers. I drew back my fist to pound its ebony smoothness to dust, and the way opened. Before ever it had felt the force of my blow, the way opened, and a weighty silence spilled out.

Into a vast anteroom, curtained with webs compacted dense, and draping from every available scrap of ceilinged space to meet the carpet of dust thick layering the floor. I stepped inside, tore the work of many spans down, and with silence and scurrying spiders my only company, through the halls on the ground level I went. Everywhere, of life, there was no sign. Before ever I set my foot upon the stair to the upper levels, I knew what there was to be found would not be any single one of those whom I had come to ask the perennial question of.

What need to tell further of halls and rooms deserted and clothed as previously told. Two rooms, alone, of special interest, there were. A library, shelves lined its walls and stood rank upon rank in the middled space between, crammed with books in ordered manner. No ordinary books these. Compiled by the Disobedient Ones, and writ in their own hand, as were coloured drawings executed with meticulous precision. Herbs and plant life, those of Noor and those of Lessadgh, the properties of each set out in detail below the painted replica, copied painstakingly from life onto flax-paper, and bound into volumes. Books filled with calculations I had no understanding of. Books: too many for me to flick through. Book upon book, enough to satisfy any with the most acute thirst for knowledge.

The second room, nine broad benches there were, arranged in circle and upon them many charts of the stars, encompassing past and future movements in the firmament we know and walk beneath. Others there were of galaxies undreamed, together with tools of measurement and those for which I knew not their purpose.

On the highest level, a garden bounded by climbing plants gone wild for lack of attention. At one end, great pots for smelting metal, each with a strange white residue clinging to bottoms and sides, the ashes beneath ossified by the extreme heat of a furnace, and pitted by weather, over many and many a sparn. At the other end, housed in large sheds, the wood eaten by the voracious appetites of wind, rain and beetles, a very large quantity of purest gold, I later came to understand, they had stripped Noor of.

In isolation, the Disobedient Ones neglected very much, but they had been very far from idle. What they worked toward was of great curiosity to me. All found in that deserted place, I claimed for my own. From the Houses of the Disobedient Ones, all that was theirs, I transferred to mine, where at leisure, I could perhaps turn scholar and in such application, unlock the paths to all their secret doings and expectations.

Carrying their possessions away, I took comfort and pleasure from this. Should the Disobedient Ones return from whence they had gone, they would have to seek me out as surely as I had once sought them, and found them not.

To my knowledge, they have not returned. Come they now, they will never find me. That, too, is comfort to me. They will be served as I was once served. Therein is some small token of justice meted out, and small amusement with it. I take from it what I can. For the shortest of times left to me, I take it.

Chapter 23.

Too much to think on. Too much to digest. Once the procession was underway, there might be a little respite to give thought to the words Atrament had spoken at length earlier in the evening.

Already jacketed in layers of soft tissue-silks to ward off bitter cold, Clara obediently held her arms up for the carded web-silk robe, resplendent with embroidered urilatum threads, to be slipped over her head and fastened. Little by little, she disappeared beneath the imagery protocol required, as each article of the regalia was fitted into place. Its weight already bearing down hard upon her, the doors of her apartments were flung wide.

Supported by the ladies of the wardrobe, she began the slow, solemn walk through long passageways to the courtyard, where the Chair of Authority waited to engulf her.

She was helped to step up onto the platform, and be seated in its depths. Ridiculously doll-like in its wide expanse, she was dwarfed by its padded back rising to tower above her. Smiling his crooked smile of reassurance, Malfroid strapped her in. Made sure she was not held too loose, or too tight, before signalling all was in readiness for the High Lord of the Helm to be hoisted onto the shoulders of the six Faienya, chosen from the ceremonial guard.

With a jerk, she was lifted from the cobbles. Swaying precariously for a sickening moment, she was borne higher, and settled on the broad shoulders of the bearers. Now she was raised up, through holes shaped like eyes in the mask, she could see Clump reining in his mount at the head of the line, and Malfroid, just about to take up position a few paces in front of his guard.

Tonight, as protocol prescribed, they would go through the North-Western gate, and over the bridge stretched across the chasm girdling the Helm, her boy, whom some called the Insane Child, had created, and out into the city to traverse its wide streets to salute the populace, and in return, receive their salutations.

Clarions blared shrill, cracking the night with wild, joyful sound. Beyond the bridge, held back from harm by decorative, balustraded barriers, the crowd waited patient. Waited for the High Lord of the Helm to come among them in living proof the line of prosperity and peace continued. Beneath the flame of a thousand fire crystals, the procession moved off, and a roar, filled with expectant excitement and approval, burst from waiting throats, competing with thrilling notes blown hard and long.

The rhythm of the bearers stride synchronised, and established, Clara knew it would not be long before the motion of the chair she rode in would produce a pleasing, almost numbing hypnotic state that made this all too frequent foray bearable.

She would never be comfortable with the ritual governing all aspects of the life she now lived. The rigid protocol the office imposed, impersonal, unemotional, completely detached and impartial, these traits reinforced by headdress, mask, neck-collar and robes that covered her completely.

Everyone, she thought, *over thirty years of age knows my look, and that a woman of Lessadgh stands as High Lord of the Helm. They know my authority is unassailable. That it cannot be repudiated, or disputed, according to law written by my boy, who once placed me here. Nor can I abdicate. That, too, my dearest William ensconced in law, more is the pity.*

And they, this alien race, adopted and now forever her own, misting the cold night air with the warm breath of good wishes and festive spirit, fearful of her boy's promised return would never attempt to usurp her, though Clara often wished they would. Never more so than now, she wished they would.

Behind the immovable urilatum mouth, she yawned. Automatic the graceful wave of her hand, the gracious incline of her head, while her mind wandered, picking through the words Atrament had spoken. Wondering how much truth was in his words, and why he told his story before broaching that which she wished to know above all else...who was instrumental in bringing about the drastic changes that overtook her boy, and why?

* * *

Promising to lift the shutters of green-mirked night, the first delicate smudge of yellowed light appeared on the horizon. At his desk, Semyon took yet another sheet of flax-paper from the drawer, and taking up his quill again began to write.

Lady, almost a span gone, and I have no word from you. Must I believe, I am banished from your favour? Can it be, the heat between us was too fierce in the burning and cold ashes, only, now remain?

Reading what he had written, he groaned, "No, no, it will not do."

Screwing the note into a ball, he let it drop to greet the growing mound of discarded paper at his feet, and taking another sheet...

Lady, I am absent from your presence too long. Understanding there was between us. If that is broken, and another now takes my place, be not cruel, but deliver the finishing blow, so that I too, may find solace in another.

"By the powers, I am no wordsmith. I all but name her faithless strumpet and, I, for my part, little better." Getting up, he kicked the chair away. "No more unwieldy words that will not shape themselves to my true intent. If she break our understanding, and with it crushes ambition long worked toward, she must do it to my face."

* * *

In the corridor, outside Apatia's apartment, a group of her ladies standing close together, whispering in conspiratorial hush, jumped apart when the door was suddenly wrenched open. For an instant, eyes wide with surprise could have portrayed innocence, if guilt flushing a bloom on the complexion of each, had not told another story.

Stress marked Apatia's paler than pale face, and tiredness had stamped dark circles beneath yellow-gold eyes accurately reading the gist of their conversation.

"You, madam, and you," she barked, pointing. "Get to your rooms straightway. Consider yourselves dungeoned in solitary confinement till I give release, unless you wish my wrath to fall a fading weight upon you. You, madam," she said, rage quivering in her voice, "being mistress of my wardrobe, what do you here at this hour?

"Do you take advantage of my coin in idle gossip, in stupid conjecture, when your time is bought to stitch my gowns? Get you hence. And, madam, if the mood take you to spend a while in foolish prattle, pin your tongue tight to the roof of your mouth, or be sure, if news of such come to my ear, I will do it right gladly for you. And, you, Ratanakiri, of you, I expected so much better."

"Lady, in all sincerity we meant no harm."

"No harm? To chatter of my business when you know not what it is I do? How long before notions, dreamed by a gaggle of empty-headed ninnies, circulates throughout the Helm, and to the streets beyond? I tell you, madam, you do me much harm."

"Lady, forgive my thoughtlessness. What must I do to earn the return of a little of your good grace?"

"Come, a small service you may perform, and part way redeem yourself." Apatia drew her through the door into her apartment. "In you, I will place some confidence."

"Lady, your trust I will not betray."

"Very well, though mind, it will go very ill with you, if you fail me once more. I have urgent business that must be attended, since it will brook no delay. For the duration of my brief absence, you must sit in the vestibule. Stir not a muscle from it."

"Lady, that is easily done, though difficulty there is should someone come to seek admittance."

"Few there are, who would tramp to my door with the brightling span barely begun. However, should any come, you must turn them away. Do not, on any account, admit them. You understand? Be they counsellor or minister, courtier or minion, none shall enter. You swear it shall be so?"

"Lady, upon all I hold dear, I swear it. But, what must I say?"

"Stupid, girl, you must say, for the present I am unavailable and you tell no lie, Ratanakari."

* * *

Deciding action must be used to resolve the situation, his first instinct was to snatch a fire crystal from its sconce and use the hidden passageways.

If she reject me a second time? I will curse myself for being such a fool as to use the byways of familiarity, when I know not how things stand. I must be formal. Measured. Letting neither jealousy, nor the premise of lost ambition, push me to rashness. I must go to the Lady's apartment, not as lover, but as her humble servant. Out of concern go. See how she fares, and if there is service I may render. In that way, if a blow is poised to strike, I may save a little face.

In the anteroom of his apartment, Semyon caught a glimpse of himself in the mirror. Shirt crumpled. Hair dishevelled, his look stale and raggedy.

By the powers, what message do I give in this condition…if not despair?'

Pride forced him back to bathe, and in hope of delivering an air of calm assurance that could not be rocked on hearing understanding was no more, to dress in sober splendour.

At the start of the day, a few bleary-eyed servants shaking off sleep, treading soft and slow to their duties, saw him come out into the broad corridor. His firm step striking sparks from granite inlaid in the patterned marble, Semyon went past the vaulted alcoves with no glance into the dew-misted gardens that lay beyond. Head erect, shoulders squared, he followed the sweeping passages not thinking where his feet carried him, but of the words he would use. Choosing them carefully, no word too intimate, or coldly distant, he picked them out and knotted them together to form a coherent string that flowed as best he could construct it, and gave thought to the tone he would say them in to the Lady Apatia.

At her door, he faltered. His aspirations, everything he had worked toward, would be decided by simply knocking upon one of the opulent panels.

Better to know where my future lies than suffer another span in doubt-ridden limbo.

"Useless to knock," a voice that did not spring easily to his mind called. "The Lady is unavailable."

Quick and deep, he drew breath through his nose. Apatia's scent came to him first, the presence of her usual, luscious invitations swamped by a sourness that left a bitter taste on his tongue, and second, a sweetness, oddly tinged by both eagerness and hesitancy limping in harmonious tandem.

"Ratanakiri? Mistress of the Lady's paint-box?"

"Yes. In that you are correct."

"It is, I. Semyon, Commander of the Ceremonial Guard, come to wait upon the Lady."

"I cannot admit you, sir."

"I do not seek admittance, nor would I press for it, if you have instruction to deny. I come only to ask how the Lady does."

The door opened a little. In the small gap, a heart-shaped face with pale blue ringlets, corkscrewing onto a broad, smooth forehead, and eyes, deeper than the darkling span, peeked curiously through long-fringed lashes to meet his.

"The Lady is not available, sir."

Lowering his voice, Semyon asked, "Is something amiss with her?"

"The Lady, being tired and anxious, has no desire for company," she answered, quiet.

"Anxious?"

"Her relation, the child bought here but yester-span does not do well."

"I am sorry to hear it, but do not understand your meaning. In what way does the child not do well?"

Ratanakiri beckoned him nearer, and standing on tiptoe, pressed full lips to his ear.

"A strange malady afflicts him. The Lady has tended him with her own hand, allowing none to aid her, save to bring cooling water and cloths."

"All energy and attention she has spent on him?"

"Since bringing the child to the Helm, she has done nothing else, sir."

"May the powers soon restore the child, and give the Lady respite of all stress."

"It is to be hoped, sir, and right speedily. The Lady's temper, short at best, is shorter by the segment," she said; then in a rush added, "I should not have spoke those words. For pity's sake, I beg you will not repeat them, sir."

Semyon bowed his head.

Apatia's cruelty and malicious spite is well known. Fostered by tales Slubeadgh, that ganglion on two legs carries to her, she sees enemies behind every wall, every pillar, and her unpredictability? Rapidly, it ferments into paranoia. Understanding between us remains intact. The burdens she staggers beneath, taken upon my shoulders to bear in her stead, others might see a different side of her nature. And here, in little Ratanakiri, might I have found a friend, who not knowing how to guard her mouth, with small effort on my part, might tell what the Lady does?

"Sir? It will go hard for me."

"Have no fear, Ratanakiri," he said. "Upon my solemn oath, all said between us will go no further. If you wish, tell the Lady, I came asking for news of her and you sent me away. Only understand, no word of this brief visit shall pass my lips."

"Yes, sir, better it were so."

A small smile confidently playing at the corners of his mouth, Semyon made his way back to his own apartment. With little effort, and from an unlikely source, all doubt had been erased. The evidence of many hours spent in useless scribble, he gathered up, shredding the flax-paper to finest scraps, that fluttering down the waste chute, littered rubbish accumulated at the bottom with a crust of unnaturally coloured dust.

Later, he would wonder why Apatia lied about her relationship to the child they had stolen away, and why she needed him. But, for the moment, shrugging into ceremonial uniform to carry out the day's duties, his mind was preoccupied in how, despite knowing patience to be his best ally, he could somehow persuade her to quickly formalise their all important understanding.

Chapter 24.

Neither one thing, nor the other, dawn's half-light hovered, blurring the definitive outlines of shape and distance with its usual veil of deception. From the crystal spire, Lingaradgh looked toward the avenue of willodghs, briefly skimming the tops of the farthest trees before looking down at the path's end and the paving it gave out onto.

Again and again, her eyes flickered back and forth, searching this small area for any sign of movement that indicated Apatia approached in her customary headlong dash.

I watch a pot boil slow. Dismissive, she turned away from the night-stained panes. *Soon enough, the little fool will come, blown of wind and panting. Crying up the stair the one word that should move me, but in any circumstance where affection ought to dwell, moves me not at all.*

"Mother?"

It is the very word.

"Mother?" Apatia cried, "are you there?"

"Idiot child, where else should I be, if not here? Come, all is in readiness."

Panic stumbled on each tread, Apatia's footstep on the stair. Breath rasped with effort and apprehension, she reached the top. Her back clinging to the wall, she edged through the open doorway and into her mother's presence. Paler than pale beneath the hood of her cloak, dismay tumbled with fear was printed on her face.

"Mother," she began, fumbling for words, "Mother, this is no easy thing to say, but the boy…he does no better."

"On that score be at peace, daughter. Have I not told you, dust could not produce this effect, nor can he be susceptible to any disease Lessadgh might try to bind him with?"

"Yet dust taints him still?"

"It does. In his life force it continues to journey, and for that, Apatia, you are most culpable. Yes," Lingaradgh's bell-like voice chimed hard and cold, "well may you hang your head. Well may your lips quiver. Save your pretty wiles for those whom it might affect. Recrimination, girl, much as a lecture on the origin and properties of the dust, will serve little at this present time. The doing has been done. Compose yourself. With utmost attention, pay heed to what I now say."

Sauntering to the table in the centre of the room, she opened a drawer and took out a little ruby bottle, similar in size to the one suspended from her waist, except for elaborate carving that had been etched deep into the gem. Below its urilatum stopper, a collar followed the graceful line of rounded shoulders from which a long chain hung.

"In this phial is the remedy to circumvent the malady the child inflicts upon himself. Wear it always about your neck for safekeeping. Four times are the contents to be administered. Measure the powder out with care. No heavy-handedness must be used here. Give too little rather than too much. One quarter of the contents give him on your immediate return. This quarter you will halve. Each half measure of the quarter prescribed, one at a time, draw up into this instrument."

Apatia took the small tube her mother handed to her.

"How shall the powder be drawn?"

"Squeeze the bulb at the end of the tube. Expel all air from it. Lower tube to powder and release the bulb, it could not be simpler. When that is done, insert the tube into one of the child's nostrils, and squeeze the bulb hard. Repeat with the powder that remains, but into the other nostril. Three times more, this must be done. At the height of the brightling span, upon its decline, and the last administered in the midst of the darkling segments. You understand?" Lingaradgh said, holding out the phial.

Nodding, Apatia took it from her.

"Now, daughter, get you gone."

"Mother? Must I continue to focus solely on him? To the exclusion of all, tend him?"

"You dare to ask? What kind of fool are you, girl? Unseemly lust you will curb, Apatia. Cavorting with the gallant Semyon, or any other for that matter, falls not within your compass."

Wilting beneath the sharp edge of her mother's voice, she said, "I did not ask for that reason. I have duties, Mother. Always, the High Lord of any Helm has duties to perform."

"Make your excuses. For the endless round of mindless ritual and protocol, let another stand in your place for just a while. What we do, takes precedence over all duties, or pleasure. From this span, and beyond, they are foreign to you. If you know nothing, you know that, do you not?"

"I do, Mother. It will be as you say. In all things, I am your obedient daughter."

Arms folded tight across her breast, Lingaradgh watched her go swiftly over the paving stones and disappear beneath the branches of the willodghs.

In the ways of flesh are her body and mind trammelled. By the powers, how came I to beget so worthless a creature as she? Yet, for the present, I am saddled with her brand of mediocrity. Being the only tool available, I must use her to best advantage knowing it will not always be so. At least she is biddable. When I am come into that which I seek, recrimination I will make and retribution I will take, disposing of all of no value to me.

* * *

Grey upon grey, its gloom blotting out the first glimmer of a pathetically feeble winter sun. Mist, rolling thick and slothful over the vegetable beds, lethargically climbed the orchard wall to water drip trees and branches. Rising to a silent crescendo, the dense fog covering the land, insolently obscured the only thing she wished to see.

At the window, her shawl drawn round hunched shoulders, Clara snapped, "I told you to leave it. To leave me."

"Leave you?" Persimmony Clump looked up from the heap of broken crockery he was sweeping into a dustpan. "In time of trouble, how could I leave you?"

"Why not?' A harsh sardonic laugh caught deep in her throat. "You have done it before easy enough."

He looked away saying quietly, "That be not fair."

"No," she turned from the window, "no, it is not. I am sorry for it. You have been more of a friend than I knew. Done more than I ever could have expected. That is true, all true, but now, in good conscience, I can ask nothing further from you, other than to leave me alone."

"This mess will not clear itself away, Clara," he said, getting to his feet.

Opening the door, he went outside, threw the broken shards onto the mound of rubbish he had already made, and came back inside.

"I care nothing for smashed pots, and pans battered out of shape. A few doors ripped from their hinges, floorboards torn up, and furniture spoiled, what are they to me?"

"Nothing. Not while your mind be numbed with grief. When your journey through that bitter, lonely place, passes into slightly better climes, these things ruined by malicious spite will have been made right for you. This, I can do for you. For your comfort and mine, too."

"I do not want you to make anything right. The things you wish to make straight have no meaning for me. The one thing, I wish you could put right, you cannot. It is beyond you. I do not want you here, skulking about playing nursemaid, Clump. Understand, I have no use for you."

"You do not mean that, Clara."

"Do I not? For goodness sake, how many times," she huffed anger, "how many ways must I find to ask you to go? To leave me alone?"

"To do what?" The dustpan clattered to the floor. He kicked it away, and thumped his fist on the table. "You do not think, I know what you be about? Once I be gone from here, I know exactly what you will do. Down to the sally port you will go and try it for yourself. Thinking to go after the child, you will try it. No," seeing the lie ready to spill from her mouth, he bellowed, "Say nothing to the contrary, for I know I be right. I see it in your eyes. In the lines set on your face, in the very way you stand. Yes, you will try it, but you cannot pass through.

"Woman, you are of Lessadgh. The sally port be charged with energy to keep all from this world out of Noor. With strong force, it will repel you. Knock you hard from your feet at very best. At worst, shrivel skin to a crisp and broil flesh from your bones, yet leave you living. Fade you, no, kill you, if fortune be kind."

"You speak of fire?" she answered, listless, having no stomach for a verbal fight. "That cannot deter me."

"See how little you know, Clara? This energy be of a kind that streaks the sky in storm."

"Lightning?"

"Similar. Invisible to all eyes, it be yoked to the sally port. Tiny discharges from that energy trickle out onto your land. It invigorates nutrients in the soil, giving you more than good harvests year after year, even when the crops of others fail."

"Yes," she said, thoughtful, "I have often felt its gentle prick. Especially when picking blackberries, where you say a sally port is placed. On many, and many, an occasion there was a sensation of pins needling my skin. I thought it no more than the gentle scratch of bramble thorns."

"Now do you see? To try the sally port be to put yourself direct in harm's way?"

"If what you say is true, Clump, I can do nothing to retrieve my boy?"

"I do not lie. Somehow, you must accept the child be gone."

"I cannot," she whispered. "To live without hope, is to die a little, day by day. That death is painful and lingering. If there is only the slightest chance to get William back, there is nothing I would not risk, no consequence too great."

"Very well, since you be stubborn, wilful and foolhardy, I know your mind cannot be swayed from a course chosen. Come. Try the sally port now. If you perish in the attempt...no banquet for crows will your carcass spread out, not if I be there to carry it away, and give burial."

In silence, they sliced through crowding mist. With long strides, quickly taken, they went down to the sally port. Crystals of frost, drummed from the grass with their heels, retaliated by embellishing the toes of their boots with droplets of moisture as they passed, and for good measure, drenched the hem of Clara's skirts.

Looming from dense, swirling whiteness, a tangled sprawl of black, long-limbed stems girthed thick with age. Coming closer, almost upon the brambles, Clara could just make out the ragged gap that had been beaten through nature's unruly lace work.

Stone still, they stood side by side. Neither of them wanting to see, or acknowledge, emotions chasing across the face of the other, they looked straight ahead.

"Do I just walk through?" she finally asked. "It is that simple?"

"Yes, but before you do, some breath I will waste. To date, no good advice of mine have you taken, this I beg you will consider. You are no moth to rush to the flame, but if destruction be your certain aim, use all haste and have done," Clump said, gruff and cold. "If not, move slow, very, very slow. In this way, you may test its perimeters and at least have small chance to withdraw, if you should wish it."

"That advice I will take."

His voice flat and hard, Clump said, "I cannot bid you fare well, for I know you will not. Your action be of your own choosing, and the results thereof."

"I know it," Clara answered. "I reproach you for nothing."

"Woman, the danger made clear, what reproach could you possibly lay upon me?"

His words stung her. With a sidelong glance at him, she drew her shawl tighter, threw back her head defiantly, and took a step forward. Now she knew of the energy emanating from this place, Clara thought she could feel it thrumming beneath the soles of her boots. Another few steps, small and hesitant, brought her within distance of the farthest reach of the bushes. Slow and careful, she negotiated a way across a mass of roughly severed branches strewn on the ground that rolled beneath her feet to trip her up, and snagged her skirts with thorns. Slow, she went towards the space, where the wildness of shrubbery had been demolished.

On the threshold of the gap, the mist thinned. Thinned enough to clearly see the carnage that had been wreaked there. Tattered roots, mashed into stringy white pulp, and smeared on soil trampled into an unleavened pathway, and not so far away, but seeming very distant, a shifting, opaque blur sealed its end.

A fraction of a step taken, and from head to toe, her body tingled.

I can bear this. Like being scrubbed hard with an abrasive cloth.

Clara shuffled forward into the beginnings of pain.

Her refusal to accept an attempt to breach the sally port was lunacy, frustrated him. Her gracious condescension to reproach him for nothing, implying there was much to reproach him with, infuriated him. The hurt in the side-ways look, she had briefly glanced at him from her swollen eye, pierced him with guilt for reasons he could not comprehend. Sifting through these emotions, he tried to bring calm and order to them, but before he had set them in their rightful proportion and place, she had stepped forward and the moment for kindness, possibly the last between them, had passed.

Watching her go, Clump was thankful to see the slow, careful movements she hesitantly made one after another. Scarcely into the gap in the brambles and she stopped. He saw her shoulders, hunched with apprehension, lower, and a small trill of alarm whistled through his mind.

Instinct urged him to go to her. Perhaps, try once again to dissuade her. Use his strength to overpower her. Pull her away. Bring her back to safety before it was too late. Reason resisted, saying she gambled with her life knowing the die was thrown, and not in her favour. Her choice. Her risk. If he interfered, she would hate him for it, and try again another time. He could do nothing to aid her.

"In so far as she be concerned, always do I battle with myself!" he breathed, anxiously watching her continue to edge further into the gap, and waited for the inevitable outcome.

He heard her cry out. A quiet sound of sudden pain, suppressed, and cut short. Still, she shuffled forward until, as if she had run headlong into a wall, came to a jerking halt. Motionless, ramrod straight, she stood for an instant before tremors, so slight he did not perceive them at first, shook her. Her shawl fell. The patterned material slid from the slope of one shoulder to drape in casual folds from the other, only to drop unnoticed to the ground behind her. Now she moved. Without leaving the spot, she moved. The hems of her skirt and petticoats swayed. Swayed a fraction, too, late to keep time with the sluggish quickstep that was being trod. Faster and faster, her feet barely leaving the ground beat out violent rhythm. Arms and body juddering uncontrollably, performing a curious string-less marionette jig, he realized the energy of the sally port had her in its deadly grip.

"No!" Clump howled, rushing into the breach.

Grabbing her waist with both hands, he snatched her away. Pulled her back. Hanging limp in his arms, he drew her out of the brambles, out into vaporous fog mobbing the entrance, and laid her down on the grass. Putting his ear to her mouth, Clump sighed with relief.

"Clara? Clara, do you hear me?"

* * *

Clothes and boots caked with a mixture of muddied loam and soil, face, hair and clothes dirt-streaked with clots of sweat and filth, Slubeadgh clambered out of the trench he had dug. Breathing hard, he threw the shovel down and moaned, "Had I known how large a hole would be needed, I would have found another way to conceal my treasure hoard, rather than use this little paddle."

"Even if there were some other way, brother," Galateo piped, "of which, I assure you there is none, to waste further time considering nonexistent options after you have spent so many segments, and so very much effort, grubbing this splendid hole in the ground, it would be a dreadful shame to waste it. Especially when the job at hand is near done. Come, all you must do now is to lay our wealth carefully inside."

"And fill it. And rake over the ground to disguise what has been done here, when I am near exhausted and starving once more."

"Then do not. Go, brother. Quick, with all haste before Lessadgh returns, make another mess of that vile pottage and seek your ease. Leave the trench open. Leave the bundles of our wealth by its side. Abandon it all."

"You are deranged!" he screeched.

"Not I, brother, it is not I who makes incessant complaint."

"It is not you who labours. Nor suffers many pains for it."

"By the powers, were I in possession of an able body, brother, I would be down upon my knees, humbly thanking fortune for the gifts she has bequeathed us with, in the sure and certain knowledge, she would not again smile upon us in such munificent fashion. Aching arms, legs, and back, cramped muscles, strained sinews, and the rumbling belly of a cloud-wracked scarecrow? What are these spasmodic twinges in comparison to the wealth that has been laid before us?

"Indeed, what is a little discomfort to make secure our future and position in life? A life of indolent ease, where every want is fulfilled, the choice is yours. Being disadvantaged in all respects, I shall have no profit from any portion of even the smallest part of it, and do not care, one way, or the other."

"Choice? There is no choice to make," Slubeadgh growled. "I abandon nothing, not one whit of it shall I give up. Time enough to eat and rest when this work is done."

Lifting the bundles, he began to align them alongside the trench and jumping down into it, began laying each one, end to end along its length.

"Brother, what of the fan?"

"You know full well," he panted. "Lying yonder, safe in the breast of my greatcoat, together with the box that houses it."

"Safe? I think not, brother. By the slenderness of its construction, the fan may easily be concealed of itself, and therefore invite no avaricious curiosity. But, the box, that treasure is too bulky to carry away with you."

"I can do nothing else. I admit, over long I kept it by me, gazing fond upon it while wrapping all other pieces in Lessadgh's garments, which were eked out in miserly allotment owing to scarcity. Nothing is left. I cannot place the box without protection into the soil."

"Brother, think on this. At present you are hardly garbed in sartorial elegance. In fact, there is a very distinct lack, jacketed with mud and nefarious grime as you are.

"How now then, if a band of cut-throats, spawned in Lessadgh, were to spy you passing? And spying you clasp something close to your breast, albeit beneath the shelter of your greatcoat, what will they say? It is nothing of value and need not concern us? No, by the very act of shelter and clasp, you proclaim to covetous Lessadgh, I hide something of great wealth. With indecent welcome you request, by the very act of shelter and clasp, catastrophic removal. Probably," Galateo paused to give his words more effect, "most violent, and with a very great outpouring of life force, if you cannot outrun them. Brother, I earnestly beseech you, reconsider."

"I have reconsidered, you bag of wind. Never saying one word when twenty can be used."

"It is my only form of interaction, brother. Surely you do not begrudge it me?"

"No. Your advice is sound. Better prudent than rueful. Better living than faded. Better think the worst, than hope for best."

Climbing out of the trench once again, he scurried back into Persimmony Clump's home, where he stoked the fire in the pot-bellied stove, lit the last of the candles, stuck them into the pan, and prowled about the rooms looking for any material of substantial size he could use as a wrapping.

"Should all else fail," Galateo volunteered, mischievous, "your greatcoat would suffice."

"No! Having much attachment to it, would I let it moulder in the ground? Make other suggestion, or hold your noisome clack."

A meticulous scouring produced nothing. Every sizeable piece of material, including the rug by the side of the bed, had been used. Even the little squares of linen found in one of the drawers, had wrapped some of the smaller items. His mood darkened at the very thought of it, Slubeadgh was gradually coming to the conclusion his greatcoat would have to be sacrificed.

"You will have no need of it, brother," his twin piped, trying to reconcile him to the loss, "not in the life that beckons. Coats of all kinds, crafted from sumptuous materials, will be easy within your grasp. Hundreds upon hundreds of them, in latest fashion, fitted to flatter your shape, if you desire it. Besides, another greatcoat could be made. The exact same in design and rough cloth as the one you commit to the ground."

"Nothing new made could be the same. No understanding do you have of these matters that you suggest a replacement. Shall the new have shared with me the dangers and intrigue the old has braved? My greatcoat is not merely a garment. It, and I, share a history beginning with a gift from a long departed friend, faded most cruelly. One who cared for me, in secrecy sheltered me from the destruction our perfect law demands. Should I cast that all aside without feeling?"

"Us, brother, always you forget us. That same lamented 'friend' bound us in fealty. In payment for his silence, put us in bondage. Unremitting servitude has been our lot. To be kicked like a mangy dog of no worth. Sent here, and there, to do a will not our own. Admitted to no society, we hover at a distance on the outskirts, always looking in. Reviled by all, with only the meanest of living to sustain us. Remember these things, brother, when sentiment threatens to override cold fact. And having come into recent possession of untold wealth, did you not so long ago, have it in mind to break that fealty?"

"We will not speak of that now. If we are to quarrel over rights and wrongs, or who owes what to whom, let me first finish what is near done without further aggravation."

Crouching, he set the pan on the floor. Not far from the dresser, four elongated shadows leapt up. Three long and straight, one stubbed and splintered. The legs of an overturned chair, angled at a slant, speared the flooding light now bathing the wall in that corner of the room.

He had seen it earlier, and taking little notice of it, had not thought to lift it to see if something lay beneath the lopsided arch, formed by its back and seat resting on the floor. Yet, something was there. Something pale wedged inside.

Intermittently, the flaming candles dragged flashes of its paleness from the inky recess of a strange cubbyhole. Getting to his feet, he crossed the room and hauled the chair away. At first glance, nothing more than a ragged heap of cloth, but cloth, with a familiar look about it. He snatched it up. Shook it out. Its colour was unmistakable. The brocaded cobweb-silk on collar and cuffs instantly recognizable, and the body of the coat was stained with great spatters of a fluid that had seeped into the fine material, and dried reddish brown.

"Semyon's jacket," he said, and looked to see what clattered at his feet.

Rolling away, the refraction of precious stones, set into the engraved barrel of the dart, sparkled. The gleam of urilatum, shyly struck from a wickedly sharp point and the delicate spines of fletches. Speechless, he watched it travel over the floorboards and come to rest in a crack.

"Now here is a thing," Galateo whispered.

"Here is a thing," Slubeadgh's laugh was wild. "What more proof can there be, fortune with her withered lips, blows kiss at me and sucks my flesh with her bony gums? Everything I could desire, she has placed in my path. Here is a thing. The sweetest gift, the ancient crone bestows, with fulsome nod and knowing wink, to bring the strutting peacock down so low, he will never rise again. The dart's return will gladden the Lady's heart, and strike the peacock's with dread despair. And here is a thing to help him most speedily to a good fading."

"Brother, be not so impetuous. Some discussion we must have on this."

"We shall, once I have wrapped my box in the peacock's finery and laid it in the cold soil. So soon as I have secured all that is mine, we will discuss all manner of topic to your liking and choosing."

Chapter 25.

Deep in the bowels of the earth, deep beneath the Field of Madricore, a great hall I caused to come into being. Here, I kept those things most dear, and those things of greatest value to me. Here, I kept the companions of my youth, doing them honour as was their due, and when need arose, took comfort and solace in their company. To this place, secret to myself alone, I brought all that I had removed from the Houses of the Disobedient Ones for safekeeping.
Beneath the watchful eyes of my silent companions, I, who never got delight from scholarly pursuit, gave myself over to the study of the books.
Patience, in my nature never had a home. Necessity was the force that drove, and with much coaxing, this quality not only found a foothold within me, but established residence. Of foremost interest, the prodigious quantity of gold, which put in gentlest terms, I had confiscated. Why amass such amounts, and more important, to what purpose? Knowing almost nothing then, one thing I knew, little did the Disobedient Ones do, that was not to their ultimate advantage.
Useless to speak of false starts, and painful stumbling in pursuit of knowledge sought. A veritable mountain of books scanned and laid aside in the search for the correct tome. With perseverance, eventually it came into my hand. Not long after, enlightenment followed.
The mystery of gold, I uncovered. Its secrets, and usage laid bare, and learning its composition in formulaic script, I, at last, had the what, the why, and the how.
Know this, too. I learned, gold carried away from the Houses of the Disobedient Ones was but a paltry amount compared to the vastness they had collected, and used, beggaring Noor with their acquisition of that metal in the process.
Experimentation, I made as the next step. With extreme heat, under a smelting pot, a small nugget of gold boiled past its fluid state and burned down to its raw constituents, a fine-grained white powder was obtained. Following the recipe exact, I blended the resultant powder together with...no! The nature, or name of this last ingredient, I shall not tell. That secret remains to this day, solely in my knowing, and goes into the nothingness that is the fate of all who are the progeny of the Disobedient Ones.
When it was done, so the script claimed, the elixir produced not only boosted existing talent, it extended life and ability far beyond the realm of what is natural. If taken at regular interval, the wondrous mixture could do this and shine talent to further brightness.
When first I took it, how my hand trembled. Onto my knees, its potent blast

took me. Throughout my system it keened with sharpened edge and clarity. And I, who had been talent's greatest champion, the sole advocate for its preservation, possessed the means to go on forever, perhaps, in healthful vigour of body, mind and power. Too much, I took at that first taking, and modified the quantity thereafter.

All claims set out in the text proved true.

Am I not the last of the firstborn? The last of the offspring spawned by the Disobedient Ones? How long has my life journeyed? I know not, nor can any other, who began at the beginning when the Disobedient Ones broke faith and walked among the humans of Lessadgh, for these ones faded long since. Many a time, upon many, I availed myself of the secret, and to this very day, would walk the fairness of Noor, had I not set a sequence of events in chain.

Few in number, copies of the text I made, faithful save for the omission I spoke of. Thinking to bestow complete incompleteness as a gift to those considered worthy, I made them, but into my mind a new thought crept that allowed no competitor to interfere with this scheme, and these copies did I hold back. My mind later changed with regard to this gifting, though no gift of one of these copies by my hand was ever given.

To bring the Kingdom States round about me under my jurisdiction, that was the primary aim. And second, introduce a means to preserve and conserve talent. Perhaps, by careful management, raise levels running in likely candidates, but never so high as mine own.

At first, I thought to bring this about by cunning. By promising much in pseudo alliance, I would give little. Such is the way of diplomacy and politics. Such is the way of gainful commerce. Of long wind, that tortuous way. Lengthy dialogue, posturing speech prating empty words, left the door to resistance, or outright refusal, too far open for my liking, or tolerance. And trickery sat ill with me, who had always been direct. And why should I tread an underhand path, when more than any other, was not talent and power with it, configured in me? To go cap in hand, ask gentle and polite for these Kingdom States willingly to pass their territories over? I could not do it.

Couched in strongest terms, I sent word to rulers nearest me, their lands I would take for my own. To Bekily, Tocantinae, Almandine, Tsavoe, Demantae and Andradia I sent word, under my hand, or under my heel, they must come. They had only to choose how the taking was done. That choice, I gave them saying, owing fealty to me, their position remained unchanged. Further, hostage to good behaviour, the eldest of each one's offspring they must send into my keeping, and I would keep them well, in a manner befitting their high station. If they came not, with dire threat of force and destruction of all they held dear, I would most surely take all that was theirs. Such drastic action was not my wish, but take it I would to accomplish what must be done.

Awaiting answer to my demands, into Hessonii, onto the island that stands *in the middle of the Trapiche Emeral, I sent stewards to reside in the abandoned Houses of the Disobedient Ones. These stewards, with little, or no talent, were trustworthy and loyal, for who would dare play the cheat, or go against my will, and incur my certain wrath? Walking on friendly breezes, made solid by my command, such servants as were needed, I also sent. Instruction given, simplicity itself, clean the Houses, clear the gardens, make all habitable and pleasingly straight, and prepare to receive honoured guests of all ages, and with utmost civility, serve these ones with courtesy.*

Later, after all had come like sheep into my fold, I learned rulers of the Kingdom States had made joint supplication against my action. Not knowing of the absence of the Disobedient Ones, to them they made it. Receiving in answer something wholly unexpected. Amthyst, of the firstborn, is High Lord of Hessonii. Amthyst holds sway over all within the boundaries of these lands.

Unbeknownst to me, the steward of my household spoke these words; mistakenly assuming it was by consent of the Disobedient Ones that they were there. How could he, or these rulers know one way, or the other?

Thus: did fortune play her part. Ever she loves conspiracy, which sits second best to her favourite game, namely deception.

Much thought was given how best to devise tests to determine potential talent. Who should be schooled in the ways of its secrets, and at what early age? How best to provide Houses of Learning, and where to situate these places? Copious notes I made, and knowing, even before it was begun, this scheme would soon come to fruition, I cast my eye further. Onto Pyrope, Grossul, Rhodal, and Uvar I cast it, and far beyond.

My mind wreathed with many plans, the possibility of peaceful conquest and conservation of what little talent still ran in the life force of the Faienya, what thought gave I to rebellion? None. That thought loitered not in my compass. I perceived myself no tyrant and saw not danger threatening.

Ambition oft time clouds judgment and befogs sight. Does not fortune encourage vaunting ambition to even greater heights?

Yea, I took her hand in tight clasp, and for it...paid a fearsome price.

"All he has said be tantamount to heresy," Clump said, breaking the silence. "Destroy the speak-cube, Clara. Do it now, and have done with this foolishness. The ravings of a twisted mind, nothing more does it contain."

"Outrageous claims are made," Malfroid nodded. "If we are to believe him, the Guardians took up where he left off. Hessonii is chief among their strongholds. Tests for talent? At very early age are those carried out by the Guardians, and schools, those too, they brought into being and manage. The cream of the best students they skim, and centralize talent to themselves."

"You would give him credence?" Clump gasped, astonished. "Cannot you see, madness runs rampant through this one's brain. What does he seek to do, if not subvert the work of the Guardians? Nothing the Order does be done out of sight, or shrouded in secrecy. All be laid out plain, for any with so much as half an eye to see. And these facts, spewed out with consummate calm and glib tongue, be well known to all. Mark my words, for a surety this information he has latched onto, and throws out hoping to create division. Not for nothing is he called Atrament Emim."

Her hands in her lap, Clara twisted her ring round once, round twice and stroked the table of the emerald, saying, "Nonsense, Clump. What division could he possibly cause and to what purpose? He has faded. There can be no benefit to him now. The Guardians do nothing in secret, you say? Ask for admittance to their archives. Ask to have access and sight of ancient papers stored within their hallowed halls. I wager you will not get leave to do so. The Guardians have secrets and jealously protect them."

"If, for one moment, we were to assume all that has been said to date is truth..." Malfroid began.

"Which we cannot, and more fool be you, twice over, to dwell upon such nonsense."

"Hear him out, Clump," Clara said. "At present we can only use conjecture. There is no proof on which to base any certainty. Continue, Malfroid."

"No, I will go along another tack. Into being, the Guardians came very shortly after the dark one fell. An alliance, the Kingdom States had with Atrament, quite separate from the new one made. From each State was drawn the nucleus of the Order, talent being the only requirement for entry, though not of the piffling variety..."

"This we all know," Clump interrupted. "What be your point?"

"My point is this, collectively their talent increased. How did that come about? It is a question I have pondered often over. And the power they now have throughout all of Noor's realms? That, too, is amazement to me. If the elixir, the dark one speaks of exists, might that not be an answer? And if the Guardians kept it to themselves throughout the lengthy sparns, what then?"

"If, we were not assuming, we would have something of a problem. That much be clear. However, since this be errant nonsense, the rant of a disordered mind should cause us no loss of sleep."

"Indeed, Clump?" Malfoid smiled his lazy, crooked smile. "Do we not have an Order that is ruler of all Noor, save in name only? What happens in every span of life that they do not direct? All is managed to their liking. No Kingdom State may pursue a course, without approval from the Guardians. All law comes under their aegis. No contract of binding may be arranged, unless agreed by them. All dispute adjudicated by them. Protocol, devised by them, governs us. And tribute? What of the tribute paid to them by all? Draw those lines together, Clump, and know, all power is held in the palm of the Order of the Guardians hand."

"Malfroid, among the many hats you own, using them when need arises to suit an appropriate role, do you have one with sedition writ inside its brim?'

"No, Clara. Most have forgot, how throughout the aeons we have accepted very much, now calling these things tradition, rightful for peaceful living, and correct use of talent. I merely pose questions."

"You have the means to answer one of them," Clump said, quietly. "Are you not master of intelligence gathered from other Kingdom States? Contacts, however tenuous, you must have within the stronghold of the Guardians. If no documentation can be obtained, verification these papers exist, and the gist of what be said in them, be all that be required. If the speak-cube, I stress most strongly, if…it be a creditable and reliable source, provide it. How say you, Clara? Put it to the test."

"I say, yes, if it can be done."

"I have such a one in place," Malfroid said, thoughtful, "though doubt it is possible information required may be safely obtained in the format mentioned. If you wish it, discreet enquiry I can make."

"If that way be too difficult, another we may try."

"Which is?" Clara frowned.

"He speaks of an elixir," Clump said, groping toward an idea that had come to him. "Of a recipe for its manufacture, and of one ingredient, undisclosed in copies made. Not specifying what this might be, he gives hint. Powder and herbage, no matter how finely ground, can never result in a potion. Not unless the herbage be fulsome to over-filled with sappy juices. Such herbage, I have not heard of, less it is a combination of many such. My guess? This omission be a fluid of some kind."

"That has sense in it. Your proposal, Clump?"

"Three questions, Malfroid. With answers we may steer closer to the truth of words spoken, or condemn them to elaborate fabrication. Those questions, recently sprung to mind be these.

"One, do the Guardians use a substance to heighten talent and prolong life? Two, most vital to know, if such substance exists, how do they administer it? Three. Why, using secret monopoly, do they withhold it? Especially when the few among us owning what is termed, the common lustre of sparse and pale freckled talent, and who might have benefit of it, are never chosen for Hessonii?"

"There is sense in the proposal," Malfroid nodded, "more easily obtained these answers might be than brief sight of ancient documents well hidden away. We try Clump's suggestion first? Agreed?"

"Agreed," Clara said, "another thing before you both leave. William could not have been much more than two years old when I found him in my orchard. I am now wondering, could this so-called temporary abandonment have come about because of the Guardians initial test? They do the first analysis on all children at the age of two, do they not?"

* * *

Cullinan pushed the report away. That a woman of Lessadgh stood as High Lord of Almandine was untenable, but under the protection of the Insane Child for many years, and in all probability, many more to come, nothing could be done to rectify the situation. Nor could revenge be taken for insolent insults given him from the mouth of the hateful woman's boy.

That she had gone into Spessa's territory for any reason, without first gaining permission from the High Lord of the Kingdom State, was bad enough. Worse followed. To then, in peremptory tones, sugared with ingratiating sweetness, audaciously notify the Order, in addition to receiving notice from some obscure, and still to be identified source, Atrament might be still living, she investigated. And all this, only once the deed was done. Urgency, she claimed, was the reason for haste.

The bitter taste of bile had risen in his throat the first time he had knowledge of this, and when he had seen the letter, written by her own hand and bearing the seal of Almandine, he had almost vomited. That same taste stuck in his craw each time he thought of it, and of her words, 'No evidence of Atrament living was found. Without doubt that one is most certainly faded.'

Disrespectful. Her actions, nothing more than arrogant high-handedness, cannot be tolerated. Does she really expect the Order to accept her findings? Does she think, she can slide out from under the Guardians authority? If she had truly received news of the dark one living, she should have notified the Order immediately. That was correct protocol. Is protocol so withered and toothless a thing, she thought to deviate from it without being bitten? No, she will learn the length of its teeth, the sharpness of its bite.

But then, in reality, what action can the Order take against her? To bring her to heel, and rightful ways of deferential humility, by what means? Always, the hand of the Insane Child shelters her.

What penalty for the unwarranted incursion into Spessa? Close down the sally port on Almandine's lands? No.

Much as he would have liked to, by doing so, access would also be denied to other Kingdom States, and the resultant uproar that would bring to the Guardians door, not needed.

A large fine then, and payment tendered in gold? Cullinan smiled to think of the trouble amassing a large quantity of the metal would cause her.

"Yes," he said, drawing the folder back to him. "Very much more to this, there has always been than meets the eye. This confirms it."

His eyes flicked over the preliminaries, the beginning of a very lengthy, and for the most part, boring report. The investigative team's journey to the Field of Madricore, the difficulties experienced, were of little interest to him and a waste of his precious time. Impatiently rifling through the pages of flax-paper, he found the paragraph looked for and read the crucial passage again.

Of the Field of Madricore, little remains. In its place, a large crater now exists, its depth so deep, its girth so wide, we were first of the opinion a meteor crashing into the land, destroyed all that stood upon it utterly.

However, residual signs of a powerful making hanging heavily some way above this enormous cavity were detected, dispelling initial thought. Over this area of devastation it remained all the while we stayed in the vicinity, its strength not diminishing. Of its origin, little could be ascertained. It was of a kind unknown to us.

Drawing a sheet of flax-paper from the tray on his desk, Cullinan wrote:

1. Essential to discover what truly was the spur for the Lessadgh's venture? (Her source of information?)

2. At the site, if she were not cognizant of the residue of talent, it may be others with her knew of it. (Make discreet enquiry, to establish who accompanied her?)

3. Make investigation with Spessa. Determine if the condition of the Field of Madricore, as it now exists, was known. If the answer is yea, establish when this came about and give cursory investigation to the site, identifying the source of the making, if possible. The answer being nay, very thoroughly investigate.

4. Attendant to item 3 - Consider excavation of the field. Purpose? Discover if anything of interest to the Order lies beneath.

5. Watchers we have in Almandine's Helm. Another must be found who can get closer to Lessadgh.

"Clearly," he said, thinking out loud as he slipped the list into the folder, "the woman does not know her place, if she think it permissible to interfere in any part of the Guardians business. She must presently learn it is their preserve alone."

Sucking his teeth, he steepled his fingers, and resting his chin on the tips of them, thought of alternatives, in the interest of seeming fairness, he would lay before the conclave of elders, who would inevitably do as he directed.

* * *

"A storm comes," the dark said. "A big one."

"Storms are not good," William shuddered. "I do not like storms. The sound of thunder frightens me, and when lightning flashes, I hide my head in Clara's lap, but she is not here. What shall I do?"

"Have no fear. That is exactly what you must do. Imagine we are in a little boat, cuddled up safe and warm below the deck. Outside the storm rages with high winds, and shouting and screaming, it shakes our little vessel. Buffeting and blowing very hard, it smashes great waves against our sides. Pulling and pushing us this way and that with dreadful rocking, perhaps even trying to snatch us up, and carry us away, but here is a thing."

"It will turn us over and throw us into the water?" William asked, trying to keep his voice steady.

"No, no it cannot do that. Nor can it tear us apart, or dislodge us. This storm has power, though its strength is not enough to do that."

"But how can a storm come to this place?"

"This is no ordinary storm. It is like nothing you know of. It wants two things. To bring you to your senses, William, by winkling you out of the very innermost core of yourself."

"I'm not going out, not until I hear Clara call. What else does it want?"

"To begin unwrapping the gift you have."

"A gift I have? Where is it?"

"You cannot see, or feel it yet. While you are a child, it runs silent in the green, which Clara calls your blood. On reaching the very edge of the threshold of adulthood, the gift will begin to unwrap and show itself to be a wondrous thing to have."

"But..."

"Enough now, little one. The storm is almost upon us. Clara is not here, but I am, so curl up small and neat. Rest easy in the security I offer, and I will take good care of you, William."

Chapter 26.

The chain of the ruby bottle clattered on the surface of the table by the bed when she placed it, and the pump-tube, down.

Had the boy's nostrils really twitched, after the powder had been blown up them? Had his brow furrowed in minute creases, and the long red eyelashes fluttered ever so slight? Was it her imagination, Apatia wondered, or were these tiny movements made in unconscious response?

His face was still now, the expression on it serenely unaltered, and his forehead and cheeks remained hot to her touch. On his chest, so motionless it was hard to believe he breathed, the strange markings were no less livid, their widespread dimensions un-retracted.

Anxious, she put her head to his once again, and listening, was relieved to hear his breath, although shallow, was regular and even.

I should have asked what to look for. No, mother knows I understand nothing of these matters and should have told me what to expect. If the powder has effect, or no, how am I to judge, save all on a sudden he wake? By the powers, what must I do? Keep watch, shackled with an invisible bond to his side, until the second dosage administered at the height of the brightling span comes due. Mayhap some change will come about when that is done.

* * *

Consumed in the heat of a roaring fire, the heartwood of logs crumbled, spattering molten droplets and flinty sparks, and trickling an incandescent flow of bright embers into the grey ash beneath. For hours, while Clump moved quietly about putting broken things to rights, and preparing the midday meal, she sat by the hearth. Wrapped in blankets, she watched the destruction, pale as death itself and saying nothing. But now she said, "I feel scalded inside."

"So you ought, and have many pains more beside. Long before I realized, you were held fast in the sally port's grip, and dragged you away, the force of the barrier should have killed you. To come out relatively unscathed, it would appear you have talent of your own, Clara, for living."

"You should have left me."

"Left you?" Clump vigorously stirred the chicken stew he was making, clanging the ladle hard against the sides of the pan to hide irritation. "Dangled on the sinister threads of that energy? To dance your life away with disconnected step? Do not talk nonsense, woman. To give up, give out, give in, be not your nature, nor shall it ever be."

"I am close to it, Persimmony. I tell you, very close."

"Grief speaks," he said, bringing the pan to the table. "I have come to a decision that may, in some part, alleviate the blow you have suffered. Eat a little food, Clara, and I shall tell what that be."

"It is no bargain for one with no appetite."

"In that, you are wrong. You have more to gain from my decision than I shall likely receive."

"Do as you wish with your decision," she scowled, "I care nothing for it."

"But you will, Clara," he said, sliding a bowl of stew across the table. "Very much, you will care. Come, a few spoonfuls only, chewed and swallowed. I must see you take something before I leave."

"You are leaving? I would you had done that when asked first."

"I go through the sally port."

Her head snapped round. Clump winced to see multi-coloured bruises staining the side of her face, and one eye almost hidden in swollen flesh. Heartening to see the other eye, dull and lifeless before, now had a glimmer of bright alertness in its depths.

"You said, you never would. You said, you had jeopardy of your own. Why would you do that now?" she spoke in a rush. "Go back on all you have said, and take great risk for what reason?"

"The bargain offered, holds. Eat, Clara."

Swaddled in blankets, she came to the table and sat down.

"Why, is it, I feel so cold on the outside?"

"Shock," he said, putting a spoon into her hand. "That be it. In a few days, with a little rest and an easier mind, you will feel more yourself. Do not play with the food."

She took a mouthful. Clagged sawdust greased with gravy. She forced herself to swallow it, and keep it down.

"You ask why I be prepared to run the risk, when formerly I was not. Your acid tongue, and a certain sickness for my homeland have brought me to it," he lied. "Besides, I am grown tired, forever extracting you from one situation after another with barely a breath of life left in you. Another mouthful, Clara."

He watched her eat, reluctance in every movement of her jaw. The quick jerk at the base of her throat indicating the morsel of food had properly been disposed of.

"If," he continued, "perchance on my journey I happen to learn something of your boy, or...where he might be, discover if he be with family, or what exactly be his circumstance. Should I find him in good spirit, well cared for, if not entirely happy, this information I could somehow relay. It was in my mind, acceptance he be gone might be not so hard to manage for you."

"It would be a blessing to know he has not been harmed, Persimmony. If his family has taken him, I know he would not forget me so soon. And...if he chose not come back to be with me always, maybe visit occasionally, to tell me how he does."

"I understand. The not knowing is most painful to you."

"You run this risk for me," she accused, throwing her spoon into the bowl. "I cannot let you."

"Cannot let me? Who are you, Clara, to tell me what I may, or may not do? Did you not hear my reasons? I told them plain enough. I go back through the sally port, returning to my home. If information be of no interest to you, should I come across it, I will not trouble sending it. However, we both know this subject alone be of interest to you, and pretence otherwise be a lame and hirpled thing." She nodded. "Then take up the spoon. For once, woman, do what I request."

"You are determined to do this?"

"I am. But I must be sure you do not waste away in the time it takes to get news. So you must eat, Clara. Get back your strength."

"And...if you do not return? If the jeopardy you risk...overtakes you, what then?"

"You have lost little more than you already have, and must make shift best as best can."

I will have lost much, she thought, spooning another morsel into her mouth, and forcing herself to chew it. *I will have lost not only the child of my heart, but my dearest friend, too. In effect, I will lose everything.*

"Then you must go, Clump. Of course you must."

"I will, on the morrow, that be soon enough," he said.

Nodding agreement, she swallowed another meagre portion of the meal he had made, and shuddered. How could she say things felt at that moment? Deep appreciation for all he had done for her already. Heartfelt gratitude for all he would do. And affection? Yes affection, that emotion was woven amongst the others. Not knowing how to express these feelings, to put them into every day language, which could be passed over without remark, or embarrassment, Clara said nothing.

Strong emotion. The atmosphere was suddenly charged with it. It made him uncomfortable, especially now. Feelings, he could not deal with them. To speak openly of the way he felt, to make himself so vulnerable, to offer himself up for sharp rebuff? He could not do it. Clump coughed, took up his spoon, and in an effort to defuse the situation, began to talk about his home and his life, the life led before coming to Lessadgh.

And Clara encouraged him by eating what he had set in front of her.

"I am of the Tenadadgh, commonly called in derogatory manner a Stunted One. My kind have long been looked down upon by all other Faienya for our close resemblance to Lessadgh beings.

"Before ever Noor, the place of perfect light, came into being, my forebears had removed themselves, and living in what isolation they could find, kept separate. Not for them the wars that continuously shook Lessadgh in former times. When such tiding came to their ears, they took no part, having no delight in such brutal pastime, nor in acquiring that which was not their own, but the certain property of others.

"Our talent lies not in lofty things of the mind, or the ability to create curious makings of power to shake and grind. It lies most often in our hands, as you have seen, and gilds most bodies and faces, too. Peaceful trade has ever been our living. Master-craftsmen, without dispute, we be. With metals in the main, though threads woven, and glass of intricate and most delicate design are traded. Throughout Noor, the quality of our manufacture is now revered. In Lessadgh, do we trade that which the Faienya would consider crude, but the people of this place seize upon our goods avidly, saying of finest quality it is, never knowing from whence it has truly come to them.

"Trade, we must in Lessadgh for gold. More than any other Kingdom State, great taxes do the Guardians levy from us. Our fame, well known, be not always to our good. Well enough, and to my cost I found that out, though it be another history than that I tell at this present time.

"When sickening wrangles flared up, regarding ownership of fertile lands shortly after coming into Noor, my forebears, abandoning the hills they had settled upon, journeyed far. Over the Drusy Sea they went to a place where salt-water and the shore be in constant debate. Set back a little from argumentative coastlines, the knobbed spines of the Ammolian Mountains range across a vast tract, and here they stayed.

"How shall I describe the home of my birth? If Noor is a place of perfect light, the scape where I was born is full of exquisite wonder. Everywhere, colour lies waiting to assault with vicious charm. It scrapes the eye, and with sumptuous loveliness, makes feverish the creative mind.

"Imagine, if you can, the Drusy Sea, its depths drenched in many hued sallow greens, and flirting across its sparkling waves, a purple sequinned flash drawn from them, slaps the sprayed foam on their crests. Imagine: if you can, the Ammolian Mountains, tall and vast. Red and blue and green, those are the towering colours that circulate, mingling with iridescent oranges and yellows that switch and twist upon the face of their spiralled ridges and chasms, with every flickering change of light. The sky hangs green above, wreathing the crown of these giants with pastel clouds, that on a time, grow dark with vibrant stunning colour, and the air, twanged with saline, is fresh and sweet smelling. In this place I first drew breath...

* * *

No spit, crackle, or satisfying whoomph of flame steadily searing through fuel thrown into it, for the fire in the pot-bellied stove had gone out, and residual ash had long settled into resolute stillness. No sibilant hiss of waxy fat sizzling. The candles in the pan were spent, the remnants congealed, opaquely glazed the bottom with a thin layer of burnt grease. Even the creak and soft clicks of wood-lined walls and floors expanding in the heat, or contracting in subsequent coolness, had stopped.

No indistinct whispers of the faded tickled his ears with rustling murmur. And Galateo, normally garrulous in the extreme, was not expounding opinionated theory, or garnishing Slubeadgh with his usual tactic of querulous tantrum to obtain what he wanted, or thought best. Opposition and protest to the decision his brother had made, and would not move away from, he lodged in a petition involving no speech.

Silence. Complete and unnerving.

Unused to such abnormal quiet, Slubeadgh was deafened by it. The sound grated loud in his ears, particularly since it followed a night of heated discussion, where tempers had flared. Screaming and shouting, viewpoints had been shredded, only to be resurrected offering new slants, and differing angles.

Worse, in only a short time, silence had taken on an eerie presence that was almost physical, raising hairs on the back of his neck. Sitting in the dark, he could feel it pressing in, threatening to stifle him with growing pressure.

"If it is your intention," he said, at last, "to bludgeon me to your way of thinking by ceasing all jibber jabber, you are much mistaken. Your need for clacking speech, is more than mine to hear it." He paused, thankful his voice fragmented the silence, and seemed to push it further away with every word spoken. "Before, acting upon your advice, I would have gone. Taking recently acquired treasure with me, I would have gone to a place, where none knew anything of me and begun a new life. Wealthy and indolent, played the landed lord gratifying every whim. I might even have had some contentment of it, though my mind would, from time to time, undoubtedly have dwelt upon regret for work unfinished.

"The finding of the lady's dart did not change much. It changed all. Other roads, the dart flung open and laid them out in front of me, chief among them, vengeance on Semyon the peacock. No longer do I see advantage in a future life lived in a place, where none can see how high I have risen above the mire. All who have shunned me with haughty ways, reviled me for being a thing lesser than shit on the sole of their shoes, will see how I shine. That is a brilliant thing to happen, is it not?

"Throughout the darkling, these things, these aspirations, you have stubbornly opposed, citing risk. I say, go hang the minuscule risk you bleat about. Achievement within clear sight of all, and Semyon faded by Apatia's will, if not her hand. Can you not taste the pleasure of these accomplishments as I do? Already their sweetness rolls with hard-boiled stickiness round my mouth.

"My decision made, I stand by it. Neither by squawking fit, nor wordless sulk, can you sway me from this, my chosen avenue, and since the only set of legs between us just so happen to be mine, I bear you where I wish at such time of my choosing. The oppressive void of quiet you thought to moat me in with?

"Pshaw, I have filled to overflowing and now, on tidal waters of lengthy spoken wordage, float away. Revenge awaits, and configured by my good friend fortune, destiny, too."

Getting to his feet, Slubeadgh stretched, un-cricked his back and legs, and sensing unnatural quiet about to come flooding back, hurried through black-tarred light from Persimmony Clump's home without a backward look, out into the dim shadowed glow of earliest morning.

Ragged mist, juicy with moisture, draped the trees with tattered threads and spread a watery carpet over the grass.

"By the powers," he grumbled, blinking in the sudden change of light, "this place grows ever bleaker. I swear; some blight afflicts the brightling orb. Never once has it beamed with strong concentration in any meaningful way. A rare astigmatism it must have, if focus prove too much for it."

Squelching over the grass, he checked the site where his treasure was buried. Certain the disguise scattered over it looked convincing and his hoard was safe, he began to search for any marks left by the wheels of the cart Lessadgh had dragged away.

"It may be," he reasoned with himself, "Lessadgh took the woman back to where I first saw her and the boy. If so, the sally port lies close by, and the way to fragrant Noor, a few steps further on."

* * *

"You are early," Clara said, when Clump came into the room.

"Yes," he said, laying a bundle of papers on her writing desk. "If there be no objection, I thought a little business we might dispose of before hearing the speak-cube this darkling?"

"What business?"

"The transfer of your farm and lands once again."

"So soon?" she said, reaching for a quill, "I can scarce credit it is time to do it again."

"Time rolls," he shrugged.

"It does," she agreed, watching him use the inkwell to batten down one end of the scroll of heavy parchment Lessadgh used for legal documents, and the other with his gloved, blunt-fingered hand. "Who does it go to this time?"

"Tristram Makepeace. This be his will for your perusal. He leaves all to his son. It lacks only your approval."

"Thomas served us well. You are certain his son, Tristram, will do the same?"

"Why would he not? In payment for small service rendered, the acreage you owned, distinct and apart from the strip-land of great interest to us, by way of the sally port, went into his father's hands. A wealthy family, they now be and shall continue, providing the sally port be off bounds to all comers, save at our discretion, or when trade is made through it. The advantages be well known and enjoyed. Fine harvests, flocks and herds increased without problem, these be no small things. The penalty for reneging on the agreement, resultant devastation and penury, completely understood."

Reading through the legalized jargon, which she knew Clump had already scrutinized, Clara nodded acceptance all was correct.

"Your signature be needed on the agreement," he said, rolling up the will and testament, "which be the first paper of the bundle. Your initials by Tristram Makepeace's name, made by his own hand, confirm you have witnessed it. That be right, just above it, and if you would, sign with your mark on the line allocated."

"Is there any other business?" she asked, while her pen scratched its way over the paper.

"I think not," he answered, blotting the ink and placing the document with the other papers. "All to my mind be accomplished for the present. We wait for Malfroid now."

Chapter 27.

Rebellion? How begins it? With discontent and quiet whimper, does it germinate underground? With whispers, passed to and fro, is it watered? With secret alliance and subterfuge, is it nurtured, to bring forth the first leaf, or bud? And with pledged resolve, does it grow and is pruned into shape? Yea, in this manner does rebellion begin and in a while flourish into full-bloomed maturity.
No more than a pinprick, life force taken from hostages held in Hessonii for testing the potential for talent. No secret this. All I did, and hoped to do, was laid before the rulers of the Kingdom States under dominion that was mine.
Did some say, in reality, this was a cloak to feed unnatural craving? Mayhap, that was the way of it. I know not. This, I know. Little by little, attached to my name and gaining prevalence, the resurrection of the word 'vampyre.' I, who rarely cracked a smile, laughed outright to hear report of such stupidity, though in my younger age that name I well earned.
And shortly after, there appeared a more concerning slander. Having found audience for the former calumny, did some go on to say, the flesh of children was my delight? No merriment spaced itself upon my mouth at that hearing. This, I asked of myself, who would place belief in stories fit only to frighten those of feeble brain, or titillate those of most prurient tendency? No, or so I told myself, these ill-conceived tales would soon find exhaustion and perish, even in the very act of being told.
Busy in the work of furthering talent throughout the whole of Noor, I knew not how rumour flew back and forth, growing with each telling into vaster and more terrible shape. But this, I know, though came too it late. Adorned with a new title was I, having done nothing to earn it, that of 'cannibal.'
What to do? Such nonsense, forcefully suppressed, would in some minds confirmation be. Nothing do? The same result in the minds of some. I, decisive in all things going before, dithered. Bending my mind to all manner of action, each solution discarded so soon as it presented, for none would serve me well and therefore not to my liking.
Unlooked for, answer there was to this dilemma. To my ear, word came of rebellion fully fermented. From the Kingdom States, drawn a faction of malcontents, who in greatest secrecy, having banded together a force of some thousands, were now in readiness to march against me. I let them come, collecting others of like conviction along the way. Seeing opportunity to show to all those, who in future time and for other reason might construe to contend authority with me, without impediment I let them come, that I might show the true extent of talent that was mine.
At the height of the warmest season, the second trichotomy of the sparn,

when the orb was at its fiercest, and foliage on every tree and bush at their most luxuriant shade of variant blue. When grasses stood tall, their stalks ripe with sap and bladed with luscious cyan and mauves, and soil, clutched in the roots of growing things, a rich reddish orange, then did we come together. On the Field of Madricore we met. They ranked in thousands. I...alone.

No pitched battle this, though many might tell it so. As a thick cloth is vigorously shaken to tease out folds and creases, so I shook the field in the brightling part of that span. Yea, I took the ground from beneath the feet of rebels, cast them down into cracks wide opened, and sealed them safely in to their destruction. Thus, were these ones faded. It was a work of short duration.

Came then envoys of the rulers of the Kingdom States. Full of humility and deep contrition they came, saying these words.

Great one, know this. In observance of fealty owed, and by our word combined, was warning given. Know also, most offensive to us, is all mendacious and vile speech spoken in secret against you. Evil tongues spreading vicious falsities have been stilled. Great one; penalty you must draw from us in punishment to annul all grievance that must now exist within your breast, and to allay shame that has been dealt us by miscreants, who in their turn, were rightly served for egregious criminal action.

My response? No foot of mine would rest upon their necks. Under my hand was shelter and protection against wrongdoers. No penalty would I impose other than this. To conference they must come, that I might lay out sites chosen for Houses of Learning within their realms, where the furtherance and enhancement of that most precious gift of talent was to find a home, to the betterment of all.

Away, back to their homelands these envoys went, after offering many assurances all would be done according to my will.

Should alarum have clamoured at such easy acquiescence? Mayhap, some appearance it should have put in to disturb my mind with warning knell. It came not, and for this reason. Ever beyond my grasp, contentment now dwelt. Never filled, the gaping emptiness within me, for the first time in remembrance, true satisfaction stirred. Talent no longer squandered, but recognized and cultivated, was that not the goal I had always worked toward? Heady, the feeling of imminent success, that was heavily embellished with the shining prospect of much more to come.

At the time appointed, the rulers of the Kingdom States came for conference, though in a way most unexpected.

In mighty cavalcade they came. Workers, on the furthest reaches of my lands, espied them from afar and rushed from their labours to tell the steward of my house. And he, in turn, went forth in haste to ascertain the validity of what he had heard, and more speedily returned to advise me of it.

How shall I describe dust raised by the passage of this cavalcade? Dust, thrown up by its progression, stirred by trampling foot, hoof, and claw, rose high into the air. In ever more dense clouds it rose over fields of wheat, corn and barley and hung suspended over those, where herds and flocks grazed, long after this elegant carnival had passed.

Noise accompanying the passage of this procession is more difficult to convey. Imagine the sound of myriad jade horns blowing. Drums beating. Urilatum cymbals clashing. Crystalline bells ringing. Countless number of pipes fluting. And amid this cacophony of sound, the churning wheels of flat-bedded wagons and chariots and carriages travelling on gravelled roads, and the scree of lesser paths. The trumpeting of harans, the snort, neigh and croak, of many beasts in the hundreds, if not thousands. Deafening the noise, without beginning to account for the voices of Faienya melded in this aural mix. The buzz of ordinary conversation, mute in the roar of shout and song, and all lost in the confusion of organised chaos that wracked the air with loud vibrations spilled from many throats.

From immense distance could be seen the cloud kicked up. From afar, I heard the cavalcade coming. Once again, my steward went forth to welcome all, and show where they might come to rest. In a short while, bright-coloured, silk pavilions were pitched about my house. Yea, a tented city spread even to the perimeter of the Field of Madricore, and above these pavilions, banners flew.

In my house panic reigned. The kitchens in tumult, chefs barking orders, or screeching lament, what provision could be made in shortest time for the uninvited multitude that had descended upon them? Similar enquiry, in exact tone, the master of my cellars made. I kept from it. These places were not my preserve, but that of my steward and those who did his bidding.

Good tea and sweetmeats I always had by me. With these meagre refreshments, and in such circumstance did our conference, straightway begin. Rolled out was my scheme, the where, and the why, explained in simple terms that none might twist my words to suit an aim wholly of their own, or with cunning try to fit them against an agenda not mine. And when it was done, he who spoke for the rulers of the Kingdoms rose to his feet, saying, 'Great Lord, with all you have said, we are in accordance. No one among us dissents, for who can deny, talent is now at best a golden ticket lying latent in the gene pool all bear? A sorry condition we are come to. Beneath your caring hand, halted shall be this sad decline, and in some measure talent be restored. To this end we are, and shall be, most earnestly committed. In proof, we offer stringent action against all, who coming to our attention, harbour even slight desire to bring this, the work of your life, to ruin. This pledge do we give, upon the rocks of no hope shall these ones founder.'

What need to disbelieve words sweet to my ear? I saw not the taint of duplicity etched on their faces, nor noticed insincerity in collective voice and manner. No, I saw no thing that might have caused concern in this meeting, or in the congregation assembled beyond my doors, save this.

Out onto the balcony I went, so soon as the conference was done, and saw Tepauni, wandering amid the throng. Unmistakable, the swan neck holding her head aloft, the skull of elongated shape at the back and devoid of hair. Bare-breasted, to display bright flecks of talent scattered in profusion across the scales of lilac skin, and silvered web-silk tied round her waist for modesty, as was her preferred attire, in mockery, or imitation of me, I cared not. Her, I knew of old, and if trust I now invested in the rulers of the Kingdoms, none did I place at her door.

On me, seduction she had tried and failing miserably, next employed blustering friendship laid thick atop wily craft, all in hope of gaining knowledge I held only to myself. And finding secrets could not be torn from me with gentle touch, or rough, she departed with not a little acrimony.

Her progress, I watched with interest, noting how, with easy charm she hailed this one and that going on her way, until coming to a group, she stopped to have conversation.

Ophrir, spiky blossoms garlanding her brow to arrest the path of hair, that floating cobweb fine and black as the colour of nothingness, was formless as the void. Hykei, his sloping face and long jutted jaw, surely modelled on the features of a dog, gave her too friendly welcome that told much. Of this group, these two, I knew, the others not. Plain to see, more than the sparse measures common to this time, talent stained them all.

Even then, alarm did not blow chill. Curiosity, alone, I felt.

Once again, the steward of my house went forth to learn the reason why these ones came with the company, receiving in answer, to honour me a night of celebration was planned. Music, singing, and dancing there would be, and brought to perform a wondrous entertainment, these most talented ones.

Came those colours of darkening green, overlaid with purpled greys, signifying the darkling span's stranglehold tightened on the brightling part of the span. Out onto the raised terrace, overlooking lawns and gardens, a chair was placed, so that I might see all, and by all, be seen. A great cheer went upon my appearance. Talent marks, close packed and shining bright, chasing across every particle of my skin. The quiver, symbol of my power and authority, slung across my chest, and covering my loins, a simple cloth made lambent by the play of moving light beneath.

A round of formalities, carried out before the performance could begin, of timely tribute laid before my feet, together with an exchange of lavish gifts, though copies made revealing the secret mysteries of gold, I held back, intending to present these to the Kingdoms so soon as festivities came to an end, and flowery speeches made at length together with many promises given.

At every opportunity, the crowd crying my name out loud, elevated their voices to higher and higher pitch, and in recognition of what I had done, made obeisance, lauding me with all manner of blessing for what I would do. A frenzied tone did their cries take on, much akin to worship

experienced in Lessadgh, thus was my vanity massaged. To my shame, and most disgraceful, these verbal offerings were not only accepted...in such praise, I revelled.
Above the heads of the seated rulers, above the head of the mass swarming close to glimpse performances beginning, did I note Tepauni and her following? In plain sight, did I see them ordering themselves in preordained formation, upon a knoll? Mayhap. Warmed by the reception, basking in its afterglow, I gave little thought to her, to them, believing I knew their purpose at this gathering.
Memory should have served me better. Should have whispered, that which one cannot achieve alone, in union with others achievement has better chance to come. Memory should have nudged me to remembrance of the Disobedient Ones and the creation of Noor. Through combined effort and pooling of their talent, only in this way was that feat accomplished.
To my cost, distracted by recent accolade, buoyed up that all I wished for was certain to come about, evident unity on that distant mound was lost on me. I saw not the power coalesced in the early stages of a making, nor the shapes their mouths made in concert, nor the sounds issued forth, nor the actions their hands wove to send their weapon against me. None of this I saw. Not until the air-formed disc spinning upon its side, with blade invisible and wickedly thin, cleaved the space before me with its sharpness, did I see the danger.
Seen too soon for it to send me to destruction. Seen too late to avoid completely...it struck me...and in the striking...

"What? He lapses into silence. Having previously said, he will tell all truthfully, he declines to tell this part?" Clump spluttered indignant.

"Truth?" Malfroid smiled his crooked smile. "Does he speak it? You for one, my friend, are yet to be convinced. This, you have made plain on many occasion, so what matter if he break off at this juncture?"

"Ah, but this portion of his long-winded saga be..."

"Have a little patience, Clump," Clara said. "His voice trembled. Did you not hear it? Likely he is most distressed by this event, even after so long, and will continue once he has composed himself."

"The hour grows very late," Malfroid yawned, "perhaps it is better we leave..."

...and in the striking, cruelly severed an arm and part shoulder from my left side. Crude the method. Most effective its result. Life force spouting a fountain from the wound, I comprehended not the physical injury, even on seeing my arm with twitching nerves, contracting muscles and fingers, upon the ground. In copious amount of gore, precious talent was jetting away. All, too, well I comprehended that.
On the back of horrified silence there came rising notes, bold and brash, a warbled ululation of triumph.

How soon may an amiable crowd turn into rioting mob? A heartbeat.

"Graphic enough for you, Clump?" Clara said, placing the speak-cube into its pouch and drawing the strings tight. "It would appear, contrary to expectation, he leaves nothing out."

"Apparently not," he answered, gruff. "Though his tale be far-fetched to my mind."

"On what score?"

"A disc formed by air alone, Malfroid. That be what…travelling at great speed and honed to perfect sharpness, this was the cause of such an injury, and with just one blow?"

"You doubt it?" Malfroid uncrossed his long legs and got to his feet. "Better placed is doubt in the kindly power the Guardians hold. If Tepauni, founder of the Order, with far less talent than the one brought low, devised such dread weapon, what might the Guardians keep in a secret arsenal of making?"

"With the darkling almost done," Clara said, "you give us no good thought to take with us to our beds."

Chapter 28.

The small quantity of white powder used. Puffed into the boy's nostrils by the pump-tube throughout the day, exactly as her mother had said should be done. Slumber dust still had him, and would not let go. Nothing had changed, except for one thing. Though the strange marks on his chest remained, and the deep colour of taint no less, they had grown no larger.

Whatever it was she bade me administer, Apatia thought moving away from the bed, *worked in part, though not near so effective as was anticipated. It did not drag him forth, and will not now, I think. And for my pains, worn to a frazzle by constant attendance and another span with no sleep, once again, I must relay failure to mother.*

* * *

Fine grains of white powder clinging to her upper lip and the edge of her nostrils, Lingaradgh angrily slapped the surface of water in her scrying bowl. The image of the child lying quiet and still in Apatia's enormous bed, immediately breaking into pieces, scattered in all directions to the edges of the shallow dish and gradually disappeared.

Inhaling deep, the last vestiges of that hour's dosage of Trooh scraped into her system, she hissed, "He resists the irresistible. Even in diluted form, cut down to weakest strength with common chalk, in ordinary circumstance should have pulled him forth."

Her mind worked quickly, thinking it through. Annoyance, experienced only moments ago, was replaced by a soft laugh, chiming satisfaction. If confirmation was needed to expel any doubt, the child taken from Lessadgh was indeed the one of great potential, complete assurance had been given. By this most recent failure, it had been most surely given. No ordinary circumstance then for this extraordinary boy.

If dust continues to taint his life force still, she mused, taking up habitual pacing, *what then? Wait longer? How long? The Guardians search for him, too. As a babe, barely out of swaddling, was he snatched from under their noses and hidden most cunning. And snatched again by Apatia, but for the present those vultures know it not.*

She paused to stare out over her Kingdom city, through crystal panes that were still dark with night's fingerprints pressed on them. *How long might it take the Order to finally sniff a way to my door? The penalty those hyenas would impose cannot be countenanced. The back of the city would be broken by the demands they would make in restitution.*

She shuddered, thinking of the wealth they would force from her.

And worse, by far, finally discovering the making I wove, and continue to weave, what penalty for that crime, if not fading for wrongful use of talent?

Agitated, she began pacing again, working towards a decision.

There is little choice. Time is a commodity I cannot influence, and if the Order draws near... No, dust-tainted, or not, it must begin. His talent must be stimulated to come to full force long before its time, so that I may take it to myself and improving talents shine, extend my life beyond natural limits.

From the deep recesses of her sleeve, she brought out a flat packaged message bubble. Teasing it onto the palm of one hand, she plumped it out with brief speech and sent it on its way to call her daughter to her.

* * *

"Is it over?" William asked.

"For the time being only, I think," the dark said. "Getting no response from you, it is possible they will try again."

"They? The ones who stole me away from Clara?"

"Who else?"

"They must want my gift very much to be so wicked."

"Yes, I told you it was precious. William," the dark said, thoughtful. "I do not wish to upset you, or frighten you in any way, but it is only right you know what is in my mind. If another storm comes against us, it will blow harder and stronger. You must prepare yourself."

"I know. The gift has already begun to unwrap. I feel it tingling inside me, and it is whispering."

"What does it whisper?"

"The same thing you said about the storm, except it likes the storm and wants it to come back."

"Has the gift said anything more, William?"

"It has and does. It whispers, saying it has only just begun to wake up and soon, despite the strength the storm brings with it, I need have no fear of anything because all things will fear me and clear the road in front of me. I am not sure that is a good thing. I don't want Clara to be frightened of me."

"It is better to have the gift than have no gift at all. With it, you may do many great things."

"I just want Clara to come. Could the gift bring her?"

"Perhaps."

"I would like that. I miss Clara. I miss her a lot."

"William, is it possible you could ask the gift not to become unwrapped, too quickly?"

"I can, if you want, but I don't think it will listen. It's too excited."

* * *

Every facial expression that might betray emotion, caged and locked away. Their tongues buttoned tight, for those traitors, if left unattended could work to their own device, and plucking unwanted words from the sanctuary of the hidden mind, mischievously spew them out to the embarrassment of both.

"Well," Clump said, "I be off then."

"So I see." Wrapping her shawl more closely around herself, Clara said, "You have everything needed for the journey?"

"Maybe. What I do not have, I can find along the way."

"Yes," speech seemed thick in her mouth, "I suppose you can."

He opened the door and went outside. She trailed after him into the frozen rawness of early morning.

"Best you do not linger," he said, squeezing words past an enormous lump that had grown in his throat.

"I thought," she fiddled with the fringes of her shawl. "I thought...I might come down to the sally port."

"Be sure I really go?"

"Not at all," she snapped. "Nothing was further from my mind. Go back into Noor, that place of perfect light, or not. Do as it pleases you."

For a moment, he fumbled awkwardly with the strap of the bag he carried, then slung it over one of his shoulders, and snapped back, "Right. We all know where we stand."

"We most certainly do."

She watched him walk briskly away, regretting she had been so sharp for such little reason. Trying to unloose her tongue, unbend cold reserve and call after him saying words of kindness and gratitude, or failing that, simply good speed, safe journey. The struggle, too great to be done in the short time it took for him to begin to disappear in white-clouded fog, was won too late.

He turned, just before he was swallowed by mist that for the past few days, had enveloped the countryside with persistent obstinacy.

"Just you be sure not to perish before news comes," Clump bawled, and went quickly on his way, not knowing he had brought her to tears.

* * *

Beneath the bared breasts of Tepauni, within the shelter of her outstretched arms, Cullinan, seated on the junction of her kneeling thighs and stomach, glimmered in the shadow of her towering statue. Talent speckled him from shaved head to naked toe, and lambent light faintly showed through the only article of clothing he wore, a simple cloth, decorously swathing him from hip to hip.

Steps, carved into Tepauni's bent knees, led down to the theatre where chairs to seat the Nine, second highest in the echelon of the Order's hierarchy, were ranged around a large circular table. Set completely apart from the lower ranks, they were distinguished by a tuft of hair, starched and oiled to stand up straight, and covering only the crowns of their heads, to symbolize Cullianan alone, stood above them in this world. Their dark, emerald-green robes, the accepted colour of life, were tied with broad sashes of Hessonii's colour, a deep and brilliant orange.

A great distance away from the table, row upon row of seats were arranged in tiers, rising in a sharp slope to meet the walls on three sides of the great hall. The benches on the lowest part of the incline, known as the stalls, were reserved for seasoned members of the Order, who having given long and faithful service, were most trusted in the duties and offices appointed to them. They were the Headmasters of departments; administrative, quisitorial, treasury, tutors, overseers, and archive keepers, and blocks of seats allocated to them had to be taken at such time as they were called to hear judgment given, and no other. A thin strip of hair, standing upright, ran from brow to nape over the top of their otherwise bald heads, which defined their grade and ranking, and was endorsed by robes of a lighter green, tied with Hessonii's colour.

In the galleries above, one side was reserved for the lower ranks working in the various departments. Their hair was shaved from the front and sides, the back left to grow long, which indicated the longevity of their service. On the other side, also working in the various departments, but not owning such length of service, hair shaved from the front of their heads, lengthened their brows to indicate this fact. Both of these rankings wore pale-green robes together with the colour of Hessonii.

From all of Noor, selected for extraordinary potential in the ways of talent, were the students. A wide strip of hair, shaved from the left side of their heads, just above the ear, indicated their noviciate had ended, which they lauded over novices of one to two years learning, their low rank shown by full heads of hair. Both of these ranks, clothed in the same shapeless robes of palest green, and sashed by the colour of Hessonii, were relegated to the highest galleries.

No Mendicant had ever attended an assembly. The eyes and ears of the Order would never cross the raging waters of the Trapiche Emeral, or be allowed to gain a toehold on the island that was once the home of the Disobedient Ones. Nor, would any one of them ever hear the Doge, revered Cullinan, utter a single word.

Long ago the Guardians found a use for those with little, or no talent, but with excessive passion to live a life in the service of the Order, however hard, or peripheral. Taking advantage of this brand of zealotry, the Guardians dressed them in robes of Hessoni's orange, boldly striped with green. Equipping them with begging bowls and sistens, peculiar to their rank alone, they were instantly recognizable as the Order's servants.

Into all of Noor they were sent, and constantly on the move, travelled from Kingdom State to Kingdom State playing their strange music, crying out the blessings of the Blessed Lady, and those of her Doge, as they journeyed, subsisting on alms voluntarily given. Appearing innocuous, they served a more sinister purpose, the gathering of information. Conversations overheard, rumours, possible unlicensed use of talent, and anything that might be detrimental to the Guardians, and of advantage to their coffers, was collected and relayed. Through a series of networks strung between the Houses of Learning, the Mendicants findings were passed on and sifted, until it came into the office of the Quisitors. There it was decided if further, more stringent investigation should be made, and if penalty was payable.

Eight of the Nine were seated at the circular table in the vast expanse of the theatre, while Malachor stalked about the floor space. An untidy bundle of flax-papers clenched in his hand, was dramatically shaken at the stalls and galleries as he passed them.

"Contained in these documents," he said, listening to his own voice resonate throughout the great hall, "and in plainest language, is Almandine's crime laid out. What need for advocacy, when the High Lord of that realm, in her own hand, willingly admits incursion into Spessa's territory? Almandine's crime is twofold. The first already mentioned, the second a more serious matter, though not worthy of debate, for guilt is clear. Almandine ignored protocol." A low growl of disapproval rumbled through the hall. "And all the more heinous, the ludicrous pretext given for it, which, if truth for one moment clung to the High Lord's claim, would concern the safety and sanctity of Noor, our precious place of perfect light. Among you, there may be some who wonder why Almandine was not called to stand before the Headmaster of the House of Learning...'

Does the ancient windbag intend to go through all points to be considered again, Cullinan thought, *when he knows full well the outcome decided upon? Or...is he so enamoured with the grinding rattle of his own voice, we must suffer further delay for his pleasure?*

"...again, I say, no need," Malachor thundered. "By her very own hand, the High Lord condemns Almandine's action."

Now we get to it, Cullinan thought, poised to get to his feet and pronounce judgment.

"All here assembled," Cullinan slouched back into the carved granite seat, his eyes rolling with impatience, "bear witness, no bias has been used in this, our discourse, nor have the charges against Almandine been represented in unfair manner. Alleged wrong-doing has most finely been dissected, and discussed to the full..."

By the powers, he drones on, Cullinan, propping his chin upon his hand, a sure sign of aching boredom, turned his mind to the selection of a suitable candidate, and how the one chosen could be discreetly insinuated into Lessadgh's household.

His eyes meandered over the stalls, passing quickly over faces rapt with attention, and those too obviously following the path of wordy speech without knowing where it would lead. Up in the galleries, where students and novices were crammed, one face caught his eye, an expression of rapidly diminishing interest and controlled annoyance playing over its features.

She knows the outcome, and is eager for its arrival, as am I.

"Elder, Malachor," Agatadgh interrupted his flow, bringing Cullinan's attention back into the theatre. "The charges have been read. Proof we have. To go round and round, treading a path already trod serves no good purpose when other cases have yet to be presented. I propose, time enough has been spent on this matter, and all that now remains is for our revered Doge to pass judgement. What say you all?"

The Eight seated round the table murmured agreement.

"The case being put with all fairness possible, was my only aim," Malachor said, in quick defence. "Gladly, I relinquish the floor and having heard all deliberation, ask our revered, friend, the Doge, to pass judgment."

At last! Rising to his feet Cullinan cleared his throat and said, "My judgment, given with heavy heart, can only work one way. Long discourse there has been on a matter, which from the first was of most straightforward outcome. Has not Almandine admitted such incursion? It has. My judgment is this. Gold, to match the weight of the High Lord exact, is correct penalty in recompense for wrong doing."

Once again, the face he had lingered on moments before caught Cullinan's eye. A knowing smirk, turning the corners of the mouth upward a little, indicated deep satisfaction, unless he was very mistaken. Resuming his seat to hear other cases involving minor misdemeanours that would feed the Order's hunger for gold, he made a mental list.

Find the name to fit that face. Her file must be brought to me, and discreet enquiry had with her tutors. If all goes well, the owner of that face could be very useful. And Malachor, he thought, irritated his time had been wasted by egotistical waffle and bluster, *what of him? His colours grow very pale. Almost a breathing spectre, he is. Before too long, on grounds one of the Nine has sadly faded, an election to appoint a new one? Yes, yes, I really think so.*

* * *

In the cellars of the summerhouse, Lingaradgh heard it. Magnified by the emptiness in the anteroom, bouncing off walls and pillars and repeated by echoes, Apatia's panting breath. Those panicky sounds, hoarse and rasping as air was sucked in and let out on a rush, grated on her, set teeth on edge and each new gasp her daughter took, fired her with irritation.

"Mother?"

That word, pathetically bleated, was comparable to nails dragged over the face of sanded crystal, to her.

"Mother, shall I come up?"

"No. In the anteroom wait, till I come," she called back, trying to inject a little pleasantry in the ringing chime.

Her face grimed with soot from the smelting flame, dulled talent's shine. Her hands blistered from touching its heat, she finished packaging the last of the batch of Trooh. Slipping on her robe, she girdled her waist with the chain and the ruby bottle hung from it. Dusting particles of ash and powder from her hair, she went up to meet her daughter.

"Un-hunch your shoulders, girl," she said, closing the door to the cellar behind her, "their proper place is not up by your ears, and loose your tight-wrapped cloak. There is no need to tell of failure. In this instance, I have suffered none."

"I am much relieved to hear it, Mother."

"Better news, yet," she said, beginning to climb the stairs to the spire. "'In resisting medication, the child confirms his potential. Not a thing, I should imagine, he will shortly wish to have done, but that need not concern you."

"Am I to come up with you, Mother?"

"Would you have me lean over the banister and bawl at you in screeching conversation?" Lingaradgh flared. "Ridiculous, child, use the little brain inside that stupid head, or very soon you will have no means to prevent the vacancy that appears to wish to take up residency there."

Lifting her skirts, Apatia hurried after her.

"You bought the ruby bottle with you?"

"I did." She slipped the chain over her head, laid it gently on the table, and watched her mother unscrew the lid of the bottle, fit a tiny funnel into its neck and begin to fill it with more of the white powder.

"If neither slumber dust, nor the strange illnesses of Lessadgh threaten the child not, why administer more medication?"

"It has purpose, more than you imagine. Unseen it does the work I wish, daughter."

"Mother," she said, when a few moments had passed, "must I continue to watch over him? Solitariness is not in my nature. It is hard to have no company. Of late, not only do I talk to myself, I answer also."

"What prattle do you speak now?" Lingaradgh looked up, her expression sharp, "more than ever, you must tend him. In company with him, alone, you must do this and watch very close, closer than before. Have patience. Find resolve. Harden the fabric of your weak flesh and its desires. From feeble aspect, forge determination, and do what must be done. Wander only a little from my bidding, Apatia, and it is more than possible, you cast all I have worked toward into destruction, and you and I with it, unless I send you there before that ever happen."

Shuddering, she hung her head and whispered, "To our benefit you work, Mother. Resolve, I will find and continue obedient to your will."

"Know this, the medication I give now is of more potent mix than the former. Its effect more easily noted, when the child comes into the beginnings of waking state. Since he resists that condition, no other option do I have. For that reason did I chide you to keep close watch.

"Pay good attention, enough for the length of two spans does the ruby in your keeping now contain. Measure it out exact with this." From the recess inside her sleeve, she took out a tiny spoon. "Level the powder to lie flat against its edges and use the pump-tube in the same manner as before."

"What must I look for?"

"The markings on his breast, observe if they become less apparent. If so, then will you know, the workings of the medication are to our good. If the markings grow, expand and become of darker hue, then do you know more of the powder is be given in further dosage. You understand?

"Very likely his body will twitch, perhaps convulse from time to time. If that happen, be not alarmed, but bind him down, so he may not cause harm to himself. I would rather it were done gently. Little by little, if it were in my choosing, I would draw it out of him," she went on, seemingly forgetting her daughter was still with her, "though choice he has taken in opposition, leaving only the selection of force. So be it. Now begins a tussle he can never win."

"Take what, Mother? Never have you told me what it is you wish from him?"

"Why, Apatia," Lingaradgh said, through a radiant smile, "only everything."

Chapter 29.

Every moment of his life had been filled with a sliding scale of persistent noise. In the background there had always been the muted murmuring of the faded. In the forefront, Galateo's constant chatter as he spilled advice, opinion, jokes, remarked on the rights and wrongs of his actions, scolded with as much regularity as a water clock ticked, and sometimes, pummelled him with vitriolic tantrum. Lying somewhere in between, there had been the bustling rumpus inside the Helm, the raucous clamour of the city, together with infrequent conversation.

Discordant, the occasional cry of a solitary crow. Except for this harsh-throated expletive, the sound of silence was loud. Slubeadgh could not bear it. For him, the quiet was absolute. Eerie. Completely alien. In its unnatural blast, his skin pimpled, hair prickled, sweat trickled, and more worrying, he had a nagging feeling, in the hush, some indeterminate thing waited and watched. Misting fog, hiding everything more than a few feet away from view, was surely its accomplice.

If a slight breeze had blown, stirring twiggy branches and ruffling winter deadened foliage, he might have been able to tell himself the faded murmured. Galateo's speechless protest continued, much to his amazement, and since he had not the smallest intention of changing his decision, Slubeadgh's pride dictated no attempt should be made that might result in another bout of useless argument. One option was open to him. He did his best to ignore his twin's wordless absence, muttering to himself to crowd out the threatening presence of oppressive quiet.

In Persimmony Clump's darkened house the monologue began, and once outside, it raced away in running commentary. All hopeful progress made toward the sally port was remarked on, especially the depth of tram-lined tracks left in the frosted grass. Signs, clearly visible at first, became less and less distinct. He bent down to see them better, followed them slowly and carefully through varying degrees of disappearing faintness, until eventually, there was nothing to track. Alarmed, he squatted, trying to see if the direction had somehow changed, if he had missed some vital thing, murmuring to himself all the while.

"It made perfect sense. To follow the tracks of Lessadgh's cart, a simple plan with much merit. And what has Lessadgh done to spite me? Drawn me on with well-made marks that were, in the beginning, easily discernible. What became of them? Where did they go?

"By the powers, I see what he has done to my undoing. Gradually, cunning Lessadgh, most reprehensible and despicable villain that he is, travelled on paths that would not take an imprint of the wheels he dragged.

Petered out to nothing, they have become. My only guideline back to the sally port and wondrous Noor, through no fault of mine, vanished before my eyes." He paused for a few moments, suffering quiet that came flooding into the empty space his mumbling had left, wondering if Galateo would call off his protest, and break his long silence by offering much needed helpful advice. "Our predicament," he said, trying to hold down rising panic, "in all bluntness, is this. We are lost. More than ever, we are lost. And our treasure hoard, how are we to locate that now? What grief. How soon does fortune bare her scurvy arse in mock? How soon that raddled, poxy whore turns hope upon its head, and plunges us into the shitty midden of despair? Better to fade, than remain in this loathsome place. Better to fade, than starve. Did you not say, Galateo," he cried, forgetting they were not speaking, "the fan a weapon was. Yes, so you said."

Drawing it from his greatcoat, he flicked the struts into a semi-circle. "Let me try the sharpness of its curved edge against my throat, and we avoid the misery awaiting us. One swipe, aimed precise, and it is done."

"Brother," unheard for many hours, Galateo piped. "A very great fool you are."

"You would bandy insults at such a time?"

"No. I merely point out the obvious, brother."

"Obvious? What obvious?"

"Legs being in your sole possession, you may bear me where you will, for ill, or good, save your will has no sense of direction, nor is sense common to it."

"You toy with me. Speaking in riddle, and I distraught." Angling his head to one side, Slubeadgh exposed his grimy throat and held the edge of the fan lightly against the jugular vein. "No more, I end it here."

"Hold!" Galateo shrieked. "You misjudge me, brother. The way ahead is plain. Lessadgh continued in the exact same direction. He has not the wit to try evading tactics, and even had he, was not aware of our presence."

"Say, you, follow the path?" Slubeath said, lowering the fan.

"I do, brother."

"By and by, we come to the sally port?"

"Close, I am sure of it. To recover our treasure, brother, reverse our step at such time as is appropriate. Nothing could be easier."

He spoke with such confidence, Slubeadgh snapped the fan shut and placed it back inside his greatcoat.

"If your advice prove correct, at first opportunity, in a sheltered place, where none may see us, I will un-cradle you, Galateo, and let you have the air for so long as it pleases you."

"To that promise, I will hold you, brother. One more thing. Your decision, the one we quarrelled over? I fear things will not go so well with us, if you continue in it."

* * *

"The storm comes again," the dark said. "It will reach us soon."

"I know. The gift said so."

"It will be more powerful and violent than last time, I think."

"It whispered that, too."

"William, did you ask the gift if it could unwrap more slowly?"

"Yes. It said even if it wanted to, it cannot because the storm rips at the layers covering it, tearing bits away. It said it is being woken long before it should. There is nothing it can do to stop this when the storm strikes again, especially as it is hungry for what it brings."

"The gift cannot help you?"

"I asked that. It said, it will make sure the part of me that is not here with you, and I, will not get hurt. That is good?"

"Yes, William, I suppose it is. Hold fast now, in the distance I hear wind howl. It will not be long before the gale is upon us."

* * *

A blur, the long bladed jade. Humming the air with deadly song, it stopped short, a hairs-breadth from her neck.

"You are faded, Reboia," Semyon said.

"Not so faded," she grinned, lowering her weapon, "since I live to fight another day, sir."

Filmed with sweat, breathing hard with exertion, Semyon inclined his head as courtesy demanded, and slid his weapon into its sheath.

"Training went well," he said, wiping his face. "Your play with the sword improves with each span. Your technique is good. With practice it will become even better. Excellent your balance, but still, you do not use the blade as an extension of your arm. Plan no step. Let instinct serve you, and fluidity most needed to perform the perfect dance, it will provide."

"Skilled enough, to be considered for promotion to the Ceremonial Guard, sir?"

"We will speak of that another time. Meanwhile, we practice again on the morrow?"

"If it is your pleasure, sir."

Outside the small barracks, the air was very warm with a snap of crispness running through it. Slinging his jacket over his shoulder, Semyon breathed deep. From the gardens and walkways many scents flooded into his nostrils and with them, hers. Its faintness telling him, she was distant.

Earlier, messages screamed in the natural perfume of her body had been spiked with sourness. Explicit with sexual lust in all its forms, those promises that had driven him wild just a few spans ago were now in shreds. Far more pronounced than he remembered, almost honed to fatal sharpness, the rancid stench of fear he smelt. He took another breath trying to locate exactly where Apatia walked, and believing he had fixed on the direction, began to run.

Leaping over the knee-high, boxed hedges of the formal gardens surrounding the barracks, on through gardens of kitchen herbs and vegetables, he went with her much changed smell growing stronger. Into gardens of roses and tall grown moss, manicured into abstract shapes. Through loggias draped with pendulous fruits, and archways of clement honeysuckle artistically framing statuary. He sped on, past the beds of dormant, rare lilies, skirting fountains of ornamental grasses, and jogging around the boating lake, came out onto the sweep of wide lawns. At their furthest edge, where few rarely came, Semyon saw her. He stopped, shocked by the intensity of panic keening among the other scents coming to him.

Cloaked and hooded, she was at the edge of the copse, slumped against one of the trees, but before he could call to attract her attention, she was off, scurrying helter-skelter like a frightened rabbit back to the Helm. He watched her go, wondering what she could have been doing so early and what could have provoked such strange behaviour.

Ahead, rising above ancient trees, the morning sun was teasing prismatic colour from the crystal spire with its shine.

The memorial garden, constructed to honour her faded mother? Apatia came here?

With a thousand questions in his mind, Semyon strode over the grass and down the incline to the copse, where mushroomed yeast stuffed his nose with noxious spice. Healthy trees grew on the edge of the wood, further in it was a different story. Old trees of stunted growth, all in differing stages of rampant decay and through their midst, rambling untamed in spaces left by fallen trees, sickly looking saplings went right to the wall encircling the garden.

He found the door, but could find no way to open it, and strangely, no matter how hard he drew breath, slowly trickling it down nasal passages and over his tongue, no scent at all came from the garden. Not even the smell of willodghs, whose fronded leaves he could see above the height of the wall.

Come to the path Apatia had obviously trodden many times, if layers of her scent and packed loamy soil, bare of any growth, was anything to go by. Deep in thought, he slowly followed it back out into cleaner air.

Clearly, Apatia kept many more things secret from him than he had ever imagined.

* * *

Elbows and shoulders used to push roughly through crowded corridors. His face reddened by the effort to contain incandescent fury, the heat of its bubbling fizz began to slide out from the tight rein he had put on it as he neared the door of her apartments. Knowing he was about to explode,

Clump barged in. No need to search the warren of rooms for her. At this time of the day, with no official function scheduled, there was only one place she, and the ladies who waited upon her, could be. Scowling rage, he marched to the dining room. Seeing his mood, servants quietly carrying out their duties turned away, offering no greeting.

Double-doors thrown open with force, crashed back against the wall. Bantering gossip and light-hearted giggles were instantly cut short, as the clattered ring of cutlery, dropped in shocked surprise, struck fine porcelain.

"Clump?" Lowering the forkful of food she was about to put into her mouth, Clara said, "As you see, we are at the mid-brightling repast."

"Best tell your companions to pick up their plates and get out," he growled, almost dancing on the spot. "I be in no mood for niceties."

A raised eyebrow briefly considered Clump's demand, followed by a curt nod of agreement, and with a weak smile of apology, she dismissed her ladies. Like a flock of twittering birds, they rose from the table in a flurry of brocaded silks and lace. Slippers quickly skimmed carpets to edge past him, heads bowed, or eyes narrowed in speculative curiosity, they escaped from the field of battle.

In silence, he waited for the room to be cleared, for the doors to be closed with a sharp click, before launching his attack.

"See this here?" he shouted, waving a sheet of flax-paper at her. "This be the direct result of selfish action. Your selfish action."

"How am I supposed to know what it is, if I cannot see it?" she asked, calm.

"No need. Can you not see the seal on it? The seal of the Guardians?"

"Oh," Clara said, completely at a loss, "what do those unscrupulous rogues want that could bring you near to apoplexy?"

"Your weight in gold," he screamed. "Penalty for Almandine's incursion into Spessa, that be what. That jaunt you insisted on going on, against my express wishes. Did I not tell you plain enough, this would happen? Did you not see it coming, woman?"

"Yes," she said, folding her napkin and dropping it onto the tabletop, "I insisted, overriding all advice contrary to my will. Yes, you made all clear enough. Yes, I knew there would be financial punishment," she faltered, "but not near so much as they seek to extract."

"Then tell me, High Lord, so tall and mighty in your ways, you will listen to no good, or rational reasoning, how am I to find the amount demanded? Tell me. How?"

"I understand, you are angry," she began.

"It be evident, you understand nothing, save the urging of your want. A period of thirty spans there be to give payment. If payment be not made, those with talent in your court, working for the good of Almandine and under license by the Order, will be withdrawn."

"Did I suggest not paying?"

"It be the kind of foolish solution you would offer," he bellowed, incensed by her calm. "I merely pluck the words from your mouth before you utter them, and throw them on the scrap heap of further stupidity."

"My weight in gold?"

"Did you not hear me? Were you not listening? How can it be paid? With what shall it be paid?"

"It is excessive."

"Woman, your jaunt was in excess of Almandine's requirement," he fumed. "Unnecessary, to no purpose for Almandine's good."

"What of our coffers? Surely, there is gold enough."

"That be not the point, Lady. Strip Almandine for your folly? No, I will not!"

"Will you not?" she asked, suddenly cold. "When to all intent and purpose, I - AM - ALMANDINE."

Outraged, Clump threw the Guardians' notice of penalty at her, and saying nothing further, turned on his heel and left, slamming the door hard behind him.

* * *

Galateo, chattering cheerful gabble about this and that, never veering toward any subject that might spark a renewal of bad feeling, or drill into the exposed nerve of a decision strongly disagreed. Galateo, jabbering, healing the split between them, and somehow, miraculously in possession of a mysterious charm that made misting fog slink away faster than a whipped dog, murdered creeping silence. With his childlike, piping voice, churning words in an endless stream, he strangled abominable quiet with a thick ligature of boundless garrulity.

Content to settle back in the rhythm of normality, Slubeadgh made no mention of aches and pains, of his beloved greatcoat, tattered and muddied, hanging in ruins from him, or of the sole on one boot, freed from its upper, slapping the path with each step taken. The urilatum fan safe against his breast, nestling alongside the Lady Apatia's dart, he trudged the rest of the day away without complaint, into a future that was surely his.

Light, gradually going, hesitant star-shine specked the sky, while a coy sickle-moon rising, hid behind denuded branches, and shadows were lengthened into grotesque parodies of reality. A darkened house, with one window shallow lit, and a little way distant, a large wooden structure. Onto this stage, Slubeadgh came and recognized the scenery immediately.

A few steps away, the walled orchard he would have to pass before coming to the sally port, and going through it, return to Noor, the place of perfect light.

"You promised," Galateo said. "At the first sheltered place, with no eye to see us, you would give me to the air. Have you forgot, or do you go back on your word, brother?"

"No, I forget not the words spoken," Slubeadgh ceded, "and with good heart hold true to them. In the walled place we will rest, where you may play unfettered through this darkling part of the span."

* * *

No room for doubt. Not this time. The child's response to the white powder almost immediate, he shivered from head to toe. Muscles behind coppery skin toyed with fleeting spasms. Eyelids fluttered, and the fullness of his mouth, rapidly drawn into a straight line.

Is he in pain? Does he wake? Apatia wondered.

In answer, the trembled movements his small body made subsided, and once again, he lay motionless. Baring his chest Apatia studied the marks intently. "Neither to good, nor ill, no change do I see," she sighed, placing her hand on his forehead. *And over hot, he remains. If he were in waking state, what different effect would the powder have? Better, mother said.* Climbing on to the bed, she rested beside the child, closing her eyes to examine an idea, based on her certainty the boy had reacted to her voice earlier.

What if, hearing my speech and in belief the woman of Lessadgh called, the bonds of slumber-dusted dream he tried to break? Were those bindings too tight? Too strongly was he held, and could not escape? Or...yes, other far-fetched possibility there is. Discovering it was not she, he turned away at the very point of waking? What if Lessadgh truly called? What if, providing the force of the sally port did not destroy her, she was brought to him? What chance Lessadgh could draw him forth? What harm to try? Where is there any harm in trying, when no injury touches me? And, if such trying should find success, I gain the rarest of all things. Credit in my mother's eye.

Getting up, Apatia strode through her apartment to the anteroom, where Ratanakiri sat, ready to send packing with polite firmness, anyone who came knocking at the Lord of the Helm's door.

"Lady, no one has called."

"I care not if the powers themselves had sought admission," she snapped. "An errand I have for you. Run straight to Semyon. If in his chambers he is not, find him. Bid him come to me at once. I have need of him."

"I will, Lady, but who will stand doorkeeper for you?"

"Small worry, it is, Ratanakiri, that troubles me not at all. Now, go quick."

* * *

Stepping out of the bathing pool, Semyon wrapped a cloth about his waist and dripping water in his wake, padded barefoot to the reception room, where Ratanakiri waited. Blushing, her head hung so low, her eyes saw only the floor she managed to deliver the message.

"I am to come at once? You are sure?"

"Yes, sir," Ratanakiri said. "The Lady has need of you. Those were her very words. What the Lady wishes, I know not. She did not say, though she was much agitated."

Believing he knew exactly what Apatia required, Semyon grinned and said, "No matter what her need. I am the Lady's faithful servant and do her bidding. Run ahead, having clothed myself, presently I shall catch up."

Hands, travelling silently around the face of the water clock with small jolting movements, telling time passed. Apatia took no notice. Semyon forgotten for the moment, her mind preoccupied, she pushed against a question. How to get Lessadgh through the sally port unharmed? That problem was the spoiler. If it could be overcome, a solution found, her idea would not only work, it would bear fruit. She was convinced of it.

Pacing, she looked for an answer that remained stubbornly elusive.

The wrong way do I go at this, she thought.

Checking the child for sudden change and finding there was none, she went to her dressing table and sitting, looked into the mirror. Cupping her chin with the palm of one hand, she said to her reflection, "To get answer to the problem, another question I should first ask. To ensure Lessadgh's safety, what is most needed?

"Negate the striking force of the sally port, or drastically lessen it."

With talent it could be done, mayhap. No, that path is shut tight. To place confidence in one licensed by the Guardians would be to court certain disaster. Lessadgh must be protected, shielded against its power. Yes, a shield! Deflect the sally port's force with a shield? What kind? With Faienya, who may come and go at will? Possibility, there is, the bodies of Semyon's guard could lessen the striking force, but not negate it. A casket of wood? Encase her complete? Better. Better chance she suffer no harm. Such must be my hope, she is brought safe into Noor.'

Pleased with this solution, pleased with her cleverness, Apatia watched a triumphant smile crawl over her lips, then seeing a glint of urilatum at the edge of the silvered glass, she turned to see what shone. On the tall stand, next to the door, lay the quiver. Taken from her girdle when she brought the child to this chamber, and shortly after, with dire threat charged to his care, it had been forgotten.

Crossing the room, she picked it up, noting its lustre was dimmed by a fine layer of dust, more important and with probable dreadful consequence, one of its darts was missing.

"Lady," Ratanakiri called, through the door, "Semyon has come in answer to your summons."

"Tell him wait," she answered, and looked at the boy for change once again. "I have an errand for you."

The same sour odour smelt in the gardens. Fear, anxiety and panic mingled, and for some reason he could not guess, anger. Knowing Apatia approached the reception chamber, scrubbed and perfumed for bed duty, he got to his feet not knowing quite what to expect now.

Throwing the doors wide, she entered, her white hair a cloud of cobweb fine strands flying on the breeze created. Great dark circles underlined her golden eyes, which in the paleness of her pale, pale face were feverish.

"I have a task for you," she said, without preamble.

"Lady, you have but to name it."

"The woman of Lessadgh. You are to bring her to me."

"Lessadgh? The woman, brought here?" Semyon asked, incredulous. "The sally port will damage her to destruction."

"If my instruction be closely followed, I think not. In a casket made of wood, you will imprison her, Semyon, and with the bodies of your guard, you will shield her. From all hurt the sally port seeks to inflict, you will keep her."

"That may be effective," he nodded. "To what purpose am I to bring her?"

"My own," she said, "and no concern of yours."

"How does your...relation?" he dared to ask.

"Full of questions you are this darkling span, Semyon. Now hear one of mine. Where is my dart?"

"Your dart?"

"Must you repeat all that is said, when you know full well it is the object that skewered Slubeadgh?" she said, with venom in her voice, and cold began to sink into him. "The very object you were to retrieve and return into my hand. That is what I speak of. Where is it?"

"Lady, a moment to think."

Confusion jumbled his mind. He tried to go back, to run through events from the time he had pulled it from her creature's flesh through to...

"The underground dwelling. The place from where we took the boy. In my jacket it was, placed over a seat and forgotten in the heat of the skirmish that ensued."

"Like as not, Lessadgh remained with the unknown Faienya whose scent you noted. Fortune is with you, Semyon. With one strike, you may take two birds, my dart and Lessadgh both. If she is not found there, go next to the place Slubeadgh located. Go as soon as may be."

"Lady, time it will take to assemble those among my guard, possessing the tight mouth demanded when first this was begun."

"All must be done by the morrow's darkling span. Order it how you will, I care not, only return property that is mine, and bring what I desire. The casket of which we spoke, you will find delivered already to your rooms."

Chapter 30.

"I wondered," Clara scowled, "how long it would be before you came to scold me, Malfroid."

"Scold you, for quarrelling with Clump, again? Would, I had the balls to dare attempt it. No, I come not to play the nagging harridan, nor flying his colours to do battle on his behalf."

"He drives me to distraction, that is the truth of it. With Clump, there is no room for compromise. All must be done his way, or not at all. Irascible, short-tempered, unbending, he is set in his ways to the point of being mortared to them, and so very difficult. Am I to blame, if he rubs me the wrong way?"

"It is a picture drawn with briefest line," Malfroid said, "had I not known you described Clump, the likeness of that sketch I would have put to you, Clara."

"I? Difficult? Nonsense!"

"To that recent and incomplete sketch, I would also add, wilful, headstrong, cut-tongue, and ungrateful, with rapid strokes of the verbal brush." Seeing she steeled herself for another fight, he said, "Always you are too blunt with him. Clump is a sensitive flower, who wilts beneath the acid rain you pour. His precious treasury, depleted in such fashion, for a cause he struggled from the first to understand? Knowing this, how can you take umbrage when he rants and roars at its outcome?"

Clara shrugged, "Put in that way, Malfroid, perhaps I could have done better. I did not know the penalty imposed would be so great."

"Had you known, would your actions have been any different?"

"No, I think not."

"And would he, if the penalty were not so costly, do different?"

"Perhaps not."

"The problem is laid bare. Two sides of the same coin you both are. What you lack, Clara, he possesses. What he lacks, you own. When next he huffs and puffs, think on all he does for Almandine's good. Within the maze that is his mind, at every twist and turn, and blind alley...there you are. If this is too much to countenance, at least give him leeway, and think hard on how diligent he works for you."

"I, too, work constant," she bristled.

"You forget, Clara, to your flame I do not flare as would he."

"It may be...perhaps...perhaps, I was too harsh. Small redress, I will make, to put things right when next we meet."

"For that, I thank you. Well, you know, I cannot bear bad atmosphere of any kind."

"Malfroid?' she said, as he opened the door to leave. "Did you say, you had not the balls to scold me, yet chastised I stand."

"My balls? They are not with me, Clara. Never would I bring them at such time as they may suffer damage, but leave them where I might find them safe. Of a certainty, fitted back into place, very shortly they will be."

She burst out laughing and wondered when he had gone, how he managed to manipulate her to his way every time.

"I hear you quarrelled with Clara, again," Malfroid said, to the top of Clump's head.

"Where did you hear it?" he answered, without looking up.

"The news flies round the Helm at break-neck speed. To throw her ladies out before the meal was eaten, is best cause for gossip I ever knew."

"Then you know the reason for it?"

"I do. That, too, circulates with wings attached. You work on accounts? Tell me, how do Almandine's coffers fare?"

"Well enough." Clump threw down his quill. "Trade be good, and revenue from the sally port, higher than it ever was."

"And we may pass through it at will in collection of Lessadgh's gold, the sally port being on our lands?"

"You know it for a fact, Malfroid."

"I do. Payment to the Guardians can be made without bankruptcy ensuing?"

"I suppose, though it break my heart to do it. Hard enough, to learn the cost of penalty, it was the tone of language used to tell it that drove me to further rage. And Clara, her manner nonchalant, said most emphatic, she be Almandine!"

"Is she not? By the will of her boy, the Insane Child, was she not placed in foremost position over our lands? And think on this, Clump, her hand is light in Almandine's affairs, compared to other Kingdom States we know of. Curiosity was the goad that drove her in the matter of penalty. When next it rears, her judgement will be better, knowing now the price that must be paid."

"My temper needs a shorter rein," Clump admitted. "But confess, Malfroid, do you not find at times she be impossible? How then can I be blamed, if she send me spiralling into dyspeptic frenzy?"

"I fear it was too much on this occasion."

"It might have been. You think she might be amenable to small apology when next we meet?"

"It would not hurt. Now tell me," Malfroid asked casually, "how go the lessons?"

"Slow. And not by design, as we two agreed. In her haste to master the language, Clara stumbles badly. Her tongue has yet to find the method to produce the needed sibilance and my patience, spurred by her ineptitude, staggers."

"Your patience, Clump, must find the will to endure without complaint. We remain like-minded in this matter?"

"Yes, more than ever, I believe...no, I know, something comes on the speak-cube she does not wish us to hear."

"Have you caught some inkling of what it might be?"

"None, other than it concern her boy, and that we already knew. Always, it be her boy. There be no room in her heart for aught else, be my thinking."

Chapter 31.

Shall I speak of shock, or pain, or trauma suffered? If empathy resides within the smallest part of you, some understanding of these things is known. Suffice it to say, my mind in turmoil, I did not instantly focus on a making to staunch the copious amount of life force gushing from the savage wound of mutilation.

Pandemonium had broke out, and in its breaking, I remained in full view of all, stunned to mindless inactivity. Into my house was I taken, dragged from the terrace by my steward, a trail of gore left behind me. There, where the shriek of rioting fight was not so loud, and screaming shout to 'fade the tyrant' not so harsh, instinct to survive came forth and found a footing. Into my mind, even as assault upon my house began in earnest, words for a making to seal the wound sprang unbidden.

Then, did I bid my faithful steward look to his own safety. With thanks for loyal service I fared him well, and taking to secret ways none would find, effected my escape.

Fear, a thing most foreign, I had not known till then. Yet fear now gripped me so strong, the security of old makings was in doubt, peril to the point of fading being uppermost in my mind. The little energy still remaining at my command, I used in making a double lock. And this done, collapsed senseless. Great loss of life force, and the makings performed shortly after, took their toll for never was a making made, however great or small, without huge cost of energy to the maker.

I know not how long I lay prone, but coming back into consciousness, had not the strength to drag myself away from the ground. Listening to the rampage above, the hue and cry in full throat, as they searched for me, I listened to the sacking of my house.

Thus was my downfall accomplished, and falling, fell so low, never walked upon Noor's beauteous lands during the brightling part of the span again.

All that was mine, of lands, property, and goods was stolen away. The pain of mutilation? So quick it was done, so sharp the blade, I never felt it. Pain, after such vicious maiming, like none I ever knew. The loss of flesh and bone severed from me, the loss of lands, home and possessions? These losses mourned for deeply, over time, I learned to accept. Loss of talent spouted away in life force? Grievous: that utter desolation, the mourning of it so long in duration, acceptance never came.

Time turned. Spans rolled away. Gradually, strength returned to me, and energy with it, though never so much as had been before, and never would it ever again. In body crippled. Much handicapped in talent owned. Solitary, save for the companions of my youth, such was the existence allotted and endured. Within me, hatred and bitterness grew, hard and cold

and unremitting. From it, a seed was spawned, dragging me from the single dimension of mere existence into life. How bright, that invigorating seed called vengeance, burned. Purpose and meaning, yea, those things did it give back to me.
A new scrying bowl made and used, a watcher I became. No need to choose whom first to watch from among so many. There was no choice. Tepauni, she of the swan neck, it had to be. Fluid deftly quartered in the bowl. Upon the surface of the water, her name writ. The making thought and voiceless spoke. For an instant, smooth calmness trembled and returning to unruffled state, presently there did her image appear. She was not alone. Ophrir and Hykei were by her, together with others of the union, nine in number. All those I saw, that fateful day, upon the mound. Together they were grouped, and if the scrying bowl had not the means to replicate speech, no need of it, had I. What held such rapt attention? What they did, I knew, by that which Tepauni held in her hand, a copy of my formula. Never knowing, incomplete it was, they soon put into production the means to obtain Trooh. Through the good office of the scrying bowl, watching over many spans, I saw all these ones did.
A frantic search for gold, and finding none in Noor, the nine sent straightway into Lessadgh, thus was trade begun, where there had formerly been none.
Gold obtained and smelted and burned to its raw state, smelted and burned again, by such practice was the white powder obtained. Trooh taken; sniffed up by the nose. I got much amusement on seeing it. The inferior result these ones acquired, pleased them to the point of exultation, despite their brains being rocked violent within their pans. Their ignorance and ongoing error, from that, I got some enjoyment.
Other papers, wherein plans conceived had been brought to completeness, and in readiness awaited implementation, whilst some, rough projections only. These things, these ideas, once were mine, did Tepauni now possess. Always in conference, by their scrutiny of these writings, the nine pillaged the thought of my mind and the hope of my heart.
 And in Tepauni's hand, gripped firm, the lead reins of authority. She, at its head, the Order into shape came gradually. Taking to themselves a name, with agenda all their own, the Guardians of talent began the walk to power. Far beyond the reach of mine intent, did the Guardians progress.
Look you, for illness and disease that long ago were carried into Noor, by those afflicted with Lessadgh's watery, red blood and faulty genes. Look, too, for bodily malformation that once was present by reason of the same. I tell you, no trace you will find. By process of eradication, that work in greatest secrecy, the Guardians carried out. The methods employed, well within your compass, not difficult to guess at. If confirmation you would have, look to the birthing houses, where you shall get an answer.
 Truth only, do I speak. Though many are those who have said, when first I set foot upon the soil of Noor, truth fled from the contact. Such is the way of

propaganda.
Believe, or not. The choice is yours.

"Well," Malfroid broke the uneasy silence, "that was unexpected. He did not rage as I had thought. In matter of fact tone, many things he hangs from the shoulders of the Guardians. What are we to think?"

"He speaks of distressing events, I doubt, time has lessened," Clara said. "What good would passion do him in the telling, but scrape a wound unhealed? To my mind, his voice was controlled and there is a ring of truth in what he spoke. Ruthless, we know the Guardians to be. What do you think, Clump?" she asked, trying to draw him out of the last vestiges of sulk he clung to.

"My opinion? Living, he played one tune. That tune be talent. Faded, he again plays one tune. That be to vilify the Guardians."

"The Order thinks talent is worth preserving. They go to great lengths to do it, as did he. I wonder, are they more or less obsessive about talent than he? Admitted, he went about it entirely the wrong way, and it is strange, is it not, in failing to achieve what he wished, in roundabout way he succeeded?"

"My thought ran along similar lines, Clara," Malfroid said, "but could not order words to express it so succinctly. Is it possible the Guardians, too, have done many things they prefer never to see the light of day? Many are the signs to say that is true, if one cares to look. I, like Clump, advise caution until proof one way, or the other, may be obtained."

"Which brings the subject of your enquiries to the fore," Clara said. "Have you received answer yet from your contact, Malfroid?"

"No. In reality, it is difficult to know if any answer will come. Matters of this nature are most delicate, and dangerous. Careful handling is required, and time, such work always takes."

"Does not everything?" Clump growled.

* * *

One after another, a succession of storms thrown against him. No sooner had one done its worse, battering and smashing at him, another came with increased violence. The dark reassured him, held him tighter, somehow resembling comforting arms that smelled strangely of Clara, cold air and starch.

"The storms are getting stronger and stronger," William said, during a brief lull, "lasting longer and longer. When will they stop?"

"When they get what they want," the dark replied, "and you know what that is."

"Yes, I do. They can't have it. If Clara was here, I might give it up."

"William, I do not think the storm wants the gift until it is unwrapped completely. Besides, how could you give it? It is not a package to be handed over."

"I had not thought of it in that way. How then...can it ever be given to someone else, or be taken from me? So, why do the storms keep coming? I do not understand."

"Best not to concern ourselves with how, or why, at the moment. We have enough to contend with, and answers to questions will surely be made clear."

"Did you notice, we were not rocked, or thrown about so much during the last storm? Do you know why that is?"

"I am not sure, William, but I think the last storm might have lifted us up and swung us. It was very, very strong. Have you asked the gift?"

"I have, but it did not answer. It is too busy eating what the storms bring to it, and I am not sure, but I think the winds might have brought me something, too."

"Really? What is it?"

"At the back of my head, a far away buzzing noise that sounds like the tiniest, tiniest bee. It wasn't there until the storm went, and I can only just hear it. Or, maybe it is because I am so tired."

"Perhaps that is it, William," said the dark, holding him tighter than ever.

* * *

Walking down to the sally port, he could feel Clara's eyes pinned to his back. Even when swirling fog shrouded him from her sight, he could still feel them.

In the gaping breach made in the brambles, just in front of the sally port, Clump cursed himself roundly for a fool. What is it about her, he wondered, that got him doing exactly what he did not want to do? Saying things he did not want to say and wishing a moment after, he had cut his tongue out before saying them? Doing things for her, never to his benefit?

Here, he was, every trace of bravado evaporated, with a feeling of dread slicking his back under rough homespun clothes, longing to retrace his steps. But he could not. He cared too much what she would think of him.

"There be nothing for it," he sighed, hoisting his bag more firmly onto his shoulder, "She did not ask it of me. Idiocy spoke in my stead, offering to do this. The powers will decide my fate."

One step took him into the place of his birth, never to return to Lessadgh again, or so he thought.

To speak of Noor and all its colours was one thing, to experience them, quite another. Memory had not served Clump well. Over the centuries memory, once so strong, had been beaten down and modified by the washed-out shades of Lessadgh. And these drab shades were wrong. A blue sky? Green grass and foliage? Four divisions in a year? Wrong, all wrong.

Then there was the repetition of grey on grey that appeared to drench the spirit in slow-ground misery, during the cold seasons of ice and snow. Monotonous pastels during warmer months, when flowers, contrary to the law of nature he knew, dotted the landscape with all different colours, none of which sizzled, or punched, with any vigour. Only when harvest time rolled round, was there a splash of glory that amounted to a quick spasm, too, soon over.

Lessadgh's seasons? Wrong. Lessadgh's dreary palette? Wrong, very wrong, and it had taken him time to adjust, to get used to the world he was about to leave. Having come to terms with Lessadgh's deficiencies with reluctant acceptance, and its shortcomings now unnoticed, he was completely unprepared for the place of perfect light.

He stepped through the sally port, and Noor struck him a physical blow, piercing his eye with vivid brightness. Sky and tree and grass attacked with whiplash hues, the impact driving breath from his body, unbalancing him so completely, he staggered beneath its scourging stroke, and crouched, his forearm shielding his face from Noor's colours singing a strident song.

Swayed by the breeze in passing, purpled-pink seed-heads atop the long stalked grass gently parted, to flash blades of palest blue. Swingeing, pinging, variant shades, blue leaves fluttered on every tree. And low on the horizon of a land painted with hostile colour, seductive by virtue of its sheer extravagance, implacable and glorious, the radiant burn of the sun and the brilliancy of rays shed.

Clump shaded his eyes, keeping them fixed on the ground, where the intense light was not so blinding, and crawled away from the sally port to find a little shade, if he could, dragging his bag behind him.

"Well," he said, noticing wild flowers growing beneath his feet, "white, and white only, as they bloody should be. I am come home."

* * *

Hearing voices, Slubeadgh leapt to the wall, carefully peered over it and quickly dropped down.

"It is him," he said, panicking. "By the powers, it is the one whose pate I cracked, the one who worked as a beast may do."

"Where that one is, brother, the woman is also, less he has disposed of her."

"It was to her, he called before going down toward the sally port?"

"To the sally port? To what purpose, brother?"

"To view the scenery for all I know. We suffer a set back," he groaned, "Lessadgh sends our plans awry. Whilst he is abroad, here we must stay, or suffer the consequences."

"Too easily are you agitated," Galateo hissed, "doubtless, he will soon return. We have only to keep watch, see without being seen."

"Impatience to be gone, kept me from that truth," Slubeadgh said, and bounding back to the wall, clung there with his head raised just enough to see over it.

"No sign do I see yet. Am I to waste the span away clinging to this wretched thing, when having clung here for so long, the brickwork bites into my hand and gives my arms to aching nag?"

"You exaggerate, brother. Less than half a segment has passed."

"No matter how long I have been here. It is my hand that takes the injury, my arms that are wracked."

"Is it possible, you were mistaken on Lessadgh's destination, brother?" Galateo wondered. "What business could that one ever have with the sally port? It may be, he set out in that direction and shortly after, changed his route."

"Where Lessadgh is concerned," Slubeadgh hoisted himself further up the wall, twisted to one side to avoid crushing his twin and leaned over, "much is possible. With our own eyes, we have witnessed that. I see nothing of remark, save the white mist that came back whilst you washed yourself in air. Nothing moves through it."

"It is in my mind, Lessadgh did as I spoke, brother. If that is so, we do indeed waste time. What of the woman?"

"Sheltered in her hovel, for all I know."

"Then what say you? With all due caution, we glide through covering cloud and come to the sally port undetected, brother?"

For answer, Slubeadgh lifted his legs over the wall and jumped onto the grass below. Keeping close to its shelter, he went swiftly down the stretch of grass. Upon reaching the brambles, confident no danger lurked and no challenge would be issued, he walked through the gap into Noor, and appalled by what he saw stopped short, his mouth hanging open in disbelief.

In full view of the sally port, trying to adjust to the devastating assault of dazzling colour, Persimmony Clump was sitting beneath a vibrant bush of deepest blue, with his hands over his eyes.

"Lessadgh!" he shrieked, internally.

"Certainly, he is no Lessadgh being, and he knows you not," Galateo shrieked back. "This we have discussed at length, though more clear than ever it is to me, logic for you is a muddy pool. Besides, he sees nothing, brother. If his presence troubles you, creep up to him. Strike him. Clear our way."

"And have him strike me back? Not I."

Turning tail, Slubeadgh fled back through the sally port to seek the sanctuary of the walled orchard.

"Coward!" Galateo's voice reverberated in his head. "Always, when it comes to it, cowardice gets in the way."

"It is a perennial illness that afflicts me," he agreed, without remorse. "Deep lodged it is, nor can it be shifted, there being no cure. Knowing that, what am I to do?"

* * *

Fresh straw and hay, sweet-filled with sap, and blended with fragrant herbs. Musk scented urine, acridly pungent, and dung newly dropped, its warm piquancy not unpleasant.

Those smells, permeating the air over and around the stables, had infused the wood and invaded the stone of the buildings during the course of many years. Had he no talent to lead him, Semyon could have found his way there blindfolded.

Grim-faced, he came to the courtyard to find the troop mounted, waiting for his arrival. Beneath the flare of ebbing fire crystals, impatient harans waited, tossing their heads to rattle the quilled barbs along the length of arched necks, their haunches bunched with quivering muscle, while three-toed feet stamped and pawed, and horned talons struck sparks from the paving in the yard. Saddle fringes dancing, jade accoutrements on bridles and reins tinkling, orchestrated the harans eagerness for the fast gallop, or pacing canter to begin.

Nodding swift greeting, he took the stirrup, and up on the broad back, settling his feet in the stirrups, said, "The casket is securely bound? Make sure. We must not lose it, vital to this task it is, and I ride hard."

Beneath him, the haran, sensing it would be given its head very soon, shuffled a restless side-step while the check was made, then willingly allowed itself to be manoeuvred to the entrance. With spurs lightly touched to its sides, it thundered through the opened gates, out into the countryside, where the dark green sky, conceding to the rapid advance of first light, softly grazed the tops of trees with tender fingertips in mute farewell, and the lustre of myriad stars, stretching a splintered roadway across the heights, waned fast before its touch.

His body at one with the haran's stride, Semyon's thoughts circled, as they had in all the time it had taken those of his guard, who were not on leave of duty, to locate the chosen ones of the troop he now led, and summon them. His mind had not revolved around his men, though he had cursed time wasted while a search was made in every alehouse and brothel on the outskirts of the city. Instead, his thought had been focused on Apatia's dart, as it was now. Beyond careless to have forgotten the sigil of the Lady's house, the symbol of her power and right to rule. A priceless heirloom, she had once told him, passed down throughout the ages and...he had carelessly left it in Lessadgh.

This was cause enough to break understanding between them, and worse, much worse, if it was not where he had left it? What would she do, if it were truly lost? He could not bring himself to frame the answer to that question.

Chapter 32.

The windows opened, Apatia stepped out onto the balcony. Regretting first-light had begun to bleach the green-dark sky, she breathed into the air, "Smooth as soft-piled velvet it is, and as luscious, but for all its star decorated vastness, it has not the power to make me feel small and insignificant, as does my mother do that work."

Soon, she thought, *Semyon will ride out. With good fortune at his side, he will bring Lessadgh through the sally port, whole and undamaged. And the woman, calling to the child, shall stir him to wakefulness by the power of her voice. Of this, I am certain.*

Semyon? What of him? His body, what he did with it to give me pleasure has not come to mind in spans. For good, or ill, fear cast memory out, and those wild, unmanageable cravings for his touch that stirred madness in me, give no trouble now. Nor shall they ever, if he hand me not the dart...if it be lost? Fault for that error will doubtless be laid at my door, should mother come to hear of it, though I make sure her fury is directed at him, before penalty she can extract from me. No! I cannot think on it, nor shall I, till it is certain gone.

Light comes flooding. Grown milky, the glow of stars, which flee from an imminent and much stronger shine, but even in flight, prepare to come again. It is time.

White powder her mother had given her, carefully measured and blown into the child's nostrils. Instantly, his body arced from the bed and hovered, shivering above it. The pump-tube still in her hand, Apatia jumped away in fright.

He crashed back down, the force of his weight billowing the coverlet around him. His head thrashed madly from side to side on the pillows, his heels drummed the mattress, and his hands ploughed wrinkled troughs into the sheets and lace. His lips drew back from his clenched teeth, before his mouth parted slightly, and from somewhere deep inside of him, dragged up and out on a gush of breath...pain, despair, and curious elation, all were present in the heavy groan he sighed. Then he was motionless, his face relaxing back into serenity.

Warily approaching the bed, Apatia said, "If the powder torture him, I know not to what profit."

She prodded him, and quickly stepped away, waiting for a reaction. Encouraged by his stillness, she ventured back, and kneeling, dared to bare his chest.

"By the powers! It has begun." Excited, she leaned in to inspect the strange marks more closely. "Not only do they recede, their colour is less vivid. Does the powder somehow push them back and force strange illness to do its bidding? Is that why he groaned a groan, as would break the heart of one more tender than I? No matter, all goes as mother predicted. If the next application produces more violent throes, bindings will be needed. Ratanakiri must fetch them for me."

* * *

A generous offer impetuously made and acted on. Caught up in the moment, Persimmony Clump had not considered a vital fact. The sally port he had just come through was not the same one he had used so long ago to pass into Lessadgh. Huddled beneath the bush, this realisation came to him.

Irritated by the perpetual whispers of the faded, and annoyed with himself for lack of thought, he cursed his rashness, lowered his hands and slowly got to his feet. Squinting, in an attempt to shade out the glaring light and colour, he studied the landscape. Grassland as far as the eye could see, dotted with trees and low-lying shrubs.

"A fine start to the search for Clara's boy, I have made," he growled. "With nothing to indicate where I be. No hamlet, or village in view, where I might make enquiry. What direction do I take? In such circumstance, one way be as good as another."

Slinging his bag over one shoulder, and with the sally port at his back, he began the long trudge over what seemed to be unending meadowland.

* * *

Leagues eaten by the long stride of the harans. Standing in the stirrups, knees flexed, body lying close to the back of the animal and slightly to one side, with his face avoiding the rattling quills, almost resting on its scaly neck, Semyon urged it to greater speed. Nearing the sally port, he slowed the pace and coming to it, halted. Raising his voice, to be heard above the heaving pant of the harans, he cried to the chosen guard, "We are come to bring the Lessadgh woman into Noor."

"Never living, sir," one of the number said.

"The Lady demands it, and we obey. Into the casket brought with us, Lessadgh is to go. With your bodies packed tight about the mount that bears it, to act as a fleshy shield against the force that bars her kind from it, there may be some success."

"And the taking of her? How is it to be achieved, sir?" Reboia asked.

"That concern is mine. Sole purpose for you here, is one of cartage. The cost of the sally port paid by the casket, and your immunity. Understood?"

As one, they eased themselves through, and once in the gap they had previously made in the blackberry bushes, went into Lessadgh, where misting fog swirled over the brambles and beyond.

* * *

She twisted the ring Clump had given her, round once, round twice and stroked the table of the gem with the tip of her finger.

Hours since, he went to get news, good or bad, of my boy. I must rouse myself, keep to my end of the bargain and not wallow into slow decline. The start of industry, bank the fire, it has almost gone out. Yes, rouse yourself, Clara. Let industry occupy you to the point of exhaustion. Spend a little of your anger on logs for burning, then might your mind be distracted from grief at night.

With effort, she levered herself out of the chair and swayed on legs that felt nothing like her own. As heavy as if bags of sand were tied to her ankles to weigh her down, she moved slow across the floorboards to the door, and went outside to the woodpile by the side of the house.

The unwieldy languor was gradually thrown off as her body remembered the rhythm. Automatic action. With one hand snatch a log, place it upright on the block, with the other, swing the hatchet, cleave the wood and feel the judder of contact through wrist and arm. She worked steadily, finding some satisfaction in the violence of heft and strike. Imagining what she could have done to prevent William being taken, if the hatchet had been in her hand that morning, and took pleasure in the resistance the sharp blade met before slicing through, rendering large lumps of fruitwood into kindling. There was pleasure in the smell of sap, locked for a year inside branches pruned from trees in the orchard, and now fresh on the air. Caught in a loop of destruction, she chopped far more than was needed.

Breathless and sweating, strands of hair worked loose from carelessly tied bonds, she crouched to collect pieces of wood scattered on the mud-patched grass, for binding into bundles, before they were stacked on top of the existing mound. On hearing strange sounds, instinctively taking hold of the hatchet, she got up and cautiously peered over the top of the woodpile.

Thick mist confused all definition. Through its eddying haze, she could just make out huge shapes moving in unison, casually gliding along the strip of land lying alongside her walled orchard.

Jade tinkling on bridles, reins and saddles, and hot breath snorted through quivering nostrils, combined with the steady thud of the harans feet on icy grass. On the approach, sullying the wrapper of moisture everything was clothed in, a hated stench.

"Slubeadgh," Semyon murmured. "What does that festering maggot do here? Him, I will deal with in a manner that will, for all time, erase his vile stink from the reservoir of scents I carry, so soon as Lessdagh is taken."

He rode on with confident ease, giving no sign to the rest of the troop his focus had, for a moment, been distracted from the work in hand, and on ground just in front of the woman's cottage, dismounted.

The troop rapidly disappearing into the enveloping mist, Slubeadgh riddled Semyon's back with dagger looks.

"What does the peacock do here?" he wondered, dropping down from the wall. "Come to find the Lady's mislaid dart?"

"Does he have an inkling the artefact, at present, rests next to your breast? If that were known, would he not have come straightway, brother, to take it from you? No, other business does he have. Climb back up, see what he does."

"Not I. With all haste, I make for the sally port."

"Legs you have to outrun a haran at full tilt? I think not, brother. To run will surely give him cause for suspicion, and for a little sport, may he not hunt us down to taste of his venom? Stay, see what he does."

"I like it not," he hissed.

"In the cleft of a metaphorical stick are we stuck, do you not agree, brother?"

"Most certainly. If I run, wrath and suspicion I draw to me. To remain, no better prospect. And, if he find the dart on me, who will keep his hand from dealing many blows upon my body?"

"Brother, in that circumstance, and before one of his fingers touches you, lie. Tell the peacock, but for his swift passage past this place, into his hand you would have given it. Besides, brother, fortune has been generous to you and I, and it may be, if we stay and watch for development, she may serve us to our benefit again. Go quick. Up on the wall nearest to Lessadgh's hovel, go on, raise yourself a little over it that we may have clearest view."

Monstrous, four-legged creatures materialized out of the mist, with beings of proportionate stature mounted upon their backs.

Behind the woodpile, saliva dried in her mouth. Her heart pounding with a heaving thump, Clara watched their progress, certain they were of Noor, but uncertain what their purpose could be. On the ground before her cottage, the strange group stopped. One of their number dismounting, said something in the strange language she had heard before to the others, then began to make his way towards her home.

On the short approach to Lessadgh's dwelling, Semyon decided no force would be used unless absolutely necessary. She would not understand his words, but the conciliatory tone they were spoken in, and the gentle language of his body, would be recognized, he hoped.

"Woman," he called, "no harm do we intend. With uncalled for violence we took the child from you. For that, I offer sincere apology. And for hurt inflicted upon your person, I am most truly sorry. In friendlier way, this time, are we come that we may bring you to the child we took. Come with us. Respect, we will show. Come with us, and soon you two will be reunited."

He moved nearer, thinking she could not hear him, and drawing breath to begin the speech again, found a fresher milky smell than that emanating from Lessadgh's home. A half turn, and his eyes roaming over the woodpile, he stretched out his hand and went to her.

Clara saw him clearly. Recognized luminescent eyes of startling blue, their long-lashed shape a perfect match for those seared indelibly in her mind. Unmistakable those eyes, filled with mocking self-assurance, remorselessly chasing her through the day and throughout the night, taunting her helplessness with pitiless expression. She recognized the handsome, arrogant face of the Faienya who had stolen the child of her heart, her William, from her.

Here he was, a few short yards away, no dream induced incarnation, but in the flesh. Her boy's abductor advancing confidently toward her, speaking soft with arm outstretched.

No thought, only the weight of the hatchet in her hand. No plan, only William's cries of terror ringing in her ears, she judged his towering height, and the distance between them, unaware of the careful assessment made. The heaviness that lingered in her body and mind vanished, as euphoric lightness took its place. With a single bound, she was on top of the woodpile, skirt and petticoats flaring about her legs. Balanced on the logs for a split second, she leapt at him, the hatchet raised, and swinging...found its mark.

"Lessadgh has struck the peacock a blow!" Slubeadgh gloated, raising himself higher on the wall to see better, "He staggers. By the powers, life force streams down his face from the wound she has given him. Ha! Not near so pretty will he be as once he was."

"For a time only, brother," Galateo piped. "All trace of injury will be easily wiped away, so hold not that thought overlong."

Semyon bent down. Snatching the weapon from Clara's hand, he lifted her by the wrist. Raising her up, level with his face, he looked long and hard at her. Blinking blood from his eyes, he said between gritted teeth, "For this work, I would dispatch you, Lessadgh, leaving your body for the attention of unlovely birds. This, I would do, did not the Lady crave your presence."

She spat at him, and tried to rake his face with her fingernails. He let her fall.

"She has given you injury?" Reboia shouted, jumping from her mount and running to him.

"A scratch, nothing more," he answered, wiping his face with the edge of his cloak.

"Sir, more than a scratch the woman has served you. It is a wicked gash that has laid one side of your face open to the bone. Urgent attention it needs."

"A scratch, it is," Semyon growled. "Take hold of Lessadgh. Into your care I give her, Reboia. Take her into Noor in the exact manner you were told. By the indirect route you know of, to the Lady's private courtyard you are to go."

"You come not with us?"

"Other business I have in this place. Go now. Do all as I have commanded, as is your duty. And Reboia, give Lessadgh respect; mistreat her not. If she threaten violence, do only what is necessary to restrain her, no more."

Shock-shaken and in great pain, pride kept him on his feet. Biting the inside of his lip to stop from crying out, with one eye Semyon watched his troop bundle the woman, clawing and kicking into a cloak, and binding her fast, put her inside the casket. The lid closed, and locked, he fought to keep his footing, determined to show no weakness while supervising the end of his part in the task. His vision, half obscured and unsteady, he watched Reboia, whom he had put in charge of the troop, mount her haran and sit gracefully in the saddle. On the verge of fainting, he heard her curse at the others, shouting if the box was not properly secured, if it came loose, or fell, she would have their balls for earrings. He managed a brief nod in response to her salute, and stood erect while they slipped into the mist and disappeared from sight.

Once they had gone, half-blinded by gore, and gritting his teeth against throbbing agony, he kicked open the door of the woman's home and staggered inside.

Panting ineffectual fury, Clara gave up futile struggle against her bonds and lay still. No chink of light came through the scented wood she was entombed in, though she could hear a woman's voice shouting orders. Moments later, the casket she was confined in, was hoisted up, hearing what she thought were curses as it was strapped to one of the ferocious animals they rode.

I should be dead. In his eyes, I saw he wished to kill me, yet he did not. Something held him back. And now, they bear me away. Where to? Do they take me to the sally port? Is that how I am to die? At least, I have the satisfaction of knowing I have hurt him, even if it is not near so much as the damage he has done me. And Clump, if he returns, will never know what became of me. Nor will he know how dear he was to me. For that, and nothing else, I am sorry.

Slubeadgh got down from the wall.

"The peacock's guard has carried Lessadgh away," he said. "There is but one place they can take her, through the sally port, though why they should attempt such a thing is baffling."

"What concern is it of ours, when its force will fry her gizzards, brother?"

"None. Now has my chance come, never will I have a better. Alone and weak from loss of life force the peacock is. Did you not see him staggering? All fight surely gone out of him."

"You will fade him?"

"With the dart, I shall do it," he nodded. "With the very thing he perhaps now searches for."

"Be very careful, brother," Galateo piped. "That one will not be easily overcome, even injured as he is."

"You change your tune!" he spat angrily.

"Not I, brother. Ripe he is for a good fading. It is the method I like not."

"What better than with the dart, the very thing he lost? There is irony in it. Imagine, Semyon faded, with none to know how, or where. Imagine the Lady's gratitude at receiving her possession laid safe in her hand, put into it, by me. Or, imagine not putting it in the Lady's hand. What stories, at my instigation, might circulate throughout the Helm and beyond, of the peacock's treachery and theft? To bring his name down into dust, where indeed, before long he will loiter, and forever reviled? To do this is my pleasure."

"You go too fast, brother. Get you into Noor, and receiving the Lady's favour, bask in its light a little while. The peacock's name by this action alone, tarnished will be, and beyond any redemption."

"And let him breathe a while yet? No. I cannot."

"Ha! What of pervading cowardice, brother? That is the stop to your go. It ever is."

"What self-confessed coward, worth his salt, would pass over a chance such as this? None. My mind is made up. The deed all but done, and my satisfaction, Galateo, assured."

"You have the legs, brother," the childlike voice piped acid.

"Have no fear, with due caution will I do it."

* * *

The Trapiche Emeral, green water gone to white, its turbulent surface whipped to thick foam, and a savage symphony of musical percussion played by the surging rage of its flow.

Behind him, windows opened wide to breezes coming off the river below, Cullinan, bent over the file on his desk barely heard its rant and roar. Raising his head from the text, he glanced at the water clock. Noting the appointed time had arrived, he sat back in his chair and moments later, the expected sharp rap was made on the door.

"Come," he cried, closing the file and sliding it into a drawer.

Fresh-faced, the novice entered the room. A full head of hair, but for a strip shaved just above her left ear, immediately identified, she was in the third year of tutelage. Closing the door, she stood respectfully by it waiting for traditional greeting to be given.

"Well come, friend, Caryadgh. The blessings of the Blessed Lady be upon you."

"And you also, friend, Doge," she answered, with a clear voice full of humility, "may the Blessed Lady make your face radiant."

He nodded, sucking his teeth in approval, and said, "Come forward, friend. Be seated, if it please you." He waited until she had taken a place on a bench, noting her movements and expression betrayed no sense of nervousness. "It may be, there is a task you can perform to the benefit of the illustrious Order, wherein sacrifice is required of you, namely delay in your projected advancement."

"I live to serve, friend, Doge."

"From your file, I note, to gain a little experience, briefly you have worked in various offices of the Order. Aptitude in the Quisitorial you showed. Preference, there is, to join this department once your noviciate is ended?"

"It is, friend, Doge."

"Why should that be?"

"May I speak freely, friend, Doge?" He nodded assent. "Hard, it is, to believe the Guardians have enemies, but true. To protect the Order, to uphold the perfect rightness of its tenets and prescribed protocol, and bring to grief all who would subvert, or attempt deviation from the Blessed Lady's teachings, is the reason for it."

Cullinan steepled his fingers, and rested his chin upon the tips, thinking her answer lacked for nothing. Sucking his teeth, he wondered if the traits of a zealot lurked beneath cool reserve and control. These qualities could be most useful, but was self-possession her nature, or a mask worn to hide the heat of true character?

"Zealotry is the preserve of the Mendicants. It has no place within any other part of the Order, and cannot be countenanced within these walls. I wonder, friend, if it may be," he said, drawing his words out to test her, "you are tainted by it?"

"I am grieved you think it may be so, friend, Doge," she said, unruffled by the suggestion. "Not for all of Noor, would I wish to be afflicted by irrational fervour, or extreme behaviour. The preservation of talent, and all the goodness the Blessed Lady brought into being, is my only concern. If that is zealotry, or not, you alone must judge and I must submit to your judgment."

"In that, you are quite correct," he answered, smiling inwardly at her allusion to his power. "Tell me, friend, your name, does Caryadgh not mean beloved?"

"My parents named me so in hope I would be much loved by the Blessed Lady, friend, Doge."

"May it be so," he sighed, hiding he was well pleased with the way the short interview had gone. "One more thing, friend, you are of Almandine?"

"That is so, friend, Doge."

"Your father is placed high in the Lord of that Helm's service?"
"He is," she answered, adding harshly, "and much put upon."
"Thank you, friend, you may leave now."

* * *

"The storm is at its height," the dark said, holding William tight, "block out its screeching moan, and do not tremble so. No longer does it smash and batter against us, but rocks us smooth and slow. Feel it? Like swinging on the rope Clara threw over a bough of one of the trees in the orchard for your amusement? Soon the storm will lose its strength, and blowing itself out, give a period of calm before it comes again. William? William, can you hear me?"

"Just. The buzzing in my head has got louder. It was not tiny bees buzzing at all, but many far-away voices calling to me. Jumbled into one, they are, and strange. I have been listening very hard, but cannot make out the words they speak."

"Are you frightened by them, William?"

"No. It is part of the gift getting more unwrapped."

Chapter 33.

Rage? Once, filled to the brim with rage, was I. By the circumstance of my birth, part god, or so some thought, and part Lessadgh being. These two parts made not a whole, for the one I ever loved, and the other, hated. For a time, a relentless war was waged and fiercely fought within me. I own that fault was mine, though long enough it took me to accept. And in coming to the knowledge, the part I wished to erase was indelibly and forever with me, I called truce and raged no more.
In rage there is madness; blind to reason it is. Long ago, this I learnt. Therefore rage came not, when mourning grief abated in some measure. Beside, what room for rage, when vengeance burned hot?
To the Guardians, once again I must return.
Were they not daring to take Hessonii for their own? Not from me, nor any papers of mine, did they learn the Disobedient Ones had long ago departed. Perhaps they did not care, who can say? I know not.
Never forget; the Guardians had good cause to believe me faded. Remember, the High Lords of many Helms had good cause to place much faith in the Guardians, by virtue of a deed well done, as was the opinion of most. That thought was further encouraged by talent, strangely blooming upon the skin of the nine, and on her, my bane, Tepauni.
Throughout Kingdom States, released from a tyrant's sway, a force to be reckoned with, the Guardians now were. To their words, grateful High Lords listened. Seeing opportunity to increase and extend power, they took it, and to raise the newly formed Order's status beyond question, the Way of Atrament did the Guardians devise.
First, was I proclaimed, Anathema, the source from whence all evil, supposedly came.
None baulked at this proclamation, but with it, in complete agreement were. A second proclamation did the Guardians make. Outlawed was talent used for self-gain, whether of property, or to hold another down, and the sole adjudicator of talent rightly used, the Order of the Guardians. Accepting this edict, little did the Lords of many Helms dream, how power of their own would soon be curtailed for this acceptance. Under my hand, or under my heel, these Lords had reluctantly come. Under the robe of the Guardians did they most willingly go, and promptly, were they sat upon.
Talent licensed, punishment and penalty, candidates for the giving and taking of binding vows, and all manner of decisions, once theirs to make, were transferred from them to the Order, for their approval. With these tools, and very many more, the stranglehold of the Guardians began to take firm hold. And the Way of Atrament, with subtle, artful craft, the bones of this tale was conceived. With dexterous skill was flesh laid upon them. By

devious and diverse methods did the Guardians cunningly put it about, how the Way whispers with a silken voice, promising many things to the walker, who daring to set foot upon the broadness of its velvet path, a rich reward may reap by foul demonic means.
Yet none thought to ask this question. How came the Order by knowledge: unknown till then?
Thus did fear of the Guardians' probes, in pretence search for these walkers, elevate the Order to the highest echelon of power and cement them in it. Shortly after, was their power extended throughout Noor? Yea. Even at this calumny, I did not rage, and infamy settled round me. The Way of Atrament, a name conjured that bore no semblance of my given name, that often spoke would not soon be forgot. Faded to all intent and purpose, yet in the mouths of the Guardians and their subjects, if not in body, in spirit, I lived on. Is that not irony?

Interpretation finished for that evening, Clump said, "Some sense of his words, you must have had whilst they be spoken, Clara?"

"Yes," she answered truthfully, and promptly lied, "a little. If his speech were slower, I might have had a better chance to understand more of what was said, though I have my doubts. It is a hard language to master."

"It is not like you to admit difficulty," Malfroid said.

"What point in denial, when my failings are well known by my tutor? I fear, Clump, your patience is sorely stretched."

"No more than is usual," he growled.

"Did I mention, secret word I have received from Spessa?" Malfroid said to divert the beginnings of possible argument. "The Guardians investigate the Field of Madricore."

"They will find that door bolted," Clara answered.

"Quite. By a large crater, suddenly appeared. So information received tells me, they grub in the rubble."

"Let us hope they find nothing of note, Malfroid," Clump frowned. "Almandine could not withstand another penalty such as the one be recently paid."

"Nor shall they," Clara assured him. "Of that I am certain."

* * *

Before entering the sally port, Reboia paused to bring the rest of the company and their haran's even closer together. Nose to tail, flank to flank, the beast carrying the casket hemmed in as tightly as possible on all sides to finally complete the shield that would hopefully, deflect the force barring any from Lessadgh entering Noor. As one, they gently coaxed the harans forward, felt resistance judder and push gently against them while they passed through.

"Wait! The box smokes. No piece of cooked, or decaying Lessadgh meat will I carry with us," Reboia cried, urging her haran back with reins and knees, and circling the casket, thumped it with her fist, and grinned.

"Lessadgh's squeal tells me she has not perished."

"If she had, what then?"

"What could be done," Reboia shrugged, "but throw her back through?"

* * *

He staggered into the woman's home with nausea waltzing in his stomach. A curiously cold numbness, he attributed to the wound, was spreading from his eyebrow up into his hairline and down into his chin.

A cloth lying on the kitchen table, he snatched up, and pressed it hard against the wicked gash, in hope of stemming the rapid flow of blood. Within moments it was soaked. Moments more, blood oozing through his fingers, drizzled among fine hairs on the back of his hand, and slowly ran in sticky paths along to his wrist.

"Take hold of yourself," Semyon groaned. "Do not fall into senseless drowse. Shake off light-headedness and attend the wound. Cleaned and sewn it must be."

Lurching about the room, holding onto furniture to steady himself, he looked through cupboards and drawers searching for instruments to draw the edges of the wound together. Near the hearth, he found a lidded basket made of rushes, with needles, thread and buttons stored inside. A large silvered tray, a jug of water and a large basin on a stand. Cloths of differing sizes, hanging from a rack. These things discovered, and laid onto the table, he sank exhausted into a chair he could barely fit on, and arranged what he needed in the order he would use them.

Propping the tray up to serve as a mirror, he prepared himself to look at the injury the woman had inflicted.

"He will smell you, brother. Long before you are within striking distance. His talent will sniff you out and warn of your coming."

"That thought has already occurred," Slugbeadgh said. "If the normal reaction to me is invoked, the usual abusive language and the like, I shall stand my ground. If he looks as if strength remains to do me slightest hurt, you have my solemn word I shall away. Faster than the swiftest wind, will I go through the sally port, while he galumphs after, with no chance of getting close enough to catch hold of me. Small risk there is, I admit, but worth the taking, so let us not quarrel on this score."

Cautious, he opened the orchard gate, cringing at the squeaks the hinges made, and peered through the mist. Certain no one was outside to see, he kept to the wall, and began to sidle along its length to the house.

His image distorted and blurred by the imperfect surface of the tray, with the eye she had not blinded, he could see the woman had done him irreparable damage. Gore wiped from his face revealed a cruel gash, exposing white bone and a jellied mass sliding from the injured socket. The wound, extending in a slant from just above his left eyebrow, slashed across the bridge of his nose and ended just below his right cheek.

Trying not to think of what she had taken from him, Semyon concentrated on getting the task in hand over as quickly as possible, and not on skin where freckled light no longer shone, nor on receptors severed, and talent, irrevocably lost.

A needle threaded, he pierced his skin to make the first stitch. Mewling in pain, he pushed it through his flesh, dragging the thread behind. Drawing the needle out, he howled in anguish. With shaking fingers, he drew the thread tight, and with a clumsy knot tied, dabbed at blood welling in preparation for the next stitch.

"If Lessadgh thought to take sight," he wept, "she is foiled, for such an injury there is certain repair, for lose of talent…there is none."

"You see?" Slubeadgh said, poised for flight on approaching the barn. "My advance goes unnoticed."

"Use utmost caution, brother. For the peacock in a rage, you are no match. Or at any other time, so memory reminds me."

"What sound is that?" he said, panicking. "Not his haran. The creature crops the bush it is tethered to."

"It comes from Lessadgh's house, and has much of the peacock's tone about it, unless I am much mistaken, brother. It seems the Lady's favourite warbles a pretty tune. Agony is surely in its composition."

"If all go well, a tune of mine he will presently screech the words to."

Edging to the corner of the barn, he considered the distance to the corner of the house. Whether it was better to glide slow, or flit fast over the ground. Making his mind up, he was over the ground in a flash and hugging the brickwork. Crouched low, he made his way to the first window, and waited for his breathing to calm before trying to sneak a look through glass panes into the room.

"Curtains," Galateo sneered. "Did you not see the window masked? Is it possible, brother, you can see through material hung to fend off prying eyes?"

"Right enough, I saw. The lightening dash confused me. Haste driving out of mind what my eyes had seen, and the peacock's merry song is a distraction."

"Go forward. Finish what has been started, brother, unless your mind is changed."

"No! No change. No dithering. At my own pace, I will go, heedless of your chiding. A certain delicacy has this work and stealth, which always is challenging. Determining the correct time to do what must be done, flexible."

"The peacock has other trouble than thought of you, brother. Listen to the songster trilling so loud it might be heard in Noor."

His confidence rising, he crept forward. All of his courage stuck to the sticking point, he peeked through the open door and seeing little, flashed across the opening to crouch beneath the other window. Cautiously, keeping to one side of the frame, he rose to take a quick glance through it.

"Better and better," he bobbed back down. "With his back to us, does the peacock sit, and in so doing dispels any qualms a face to face meeting would provoke."

"Brother, so full of valour you are," Galateo gurgled.

"Sarcasm will profit us nothing at such a time. A perfect target does his back present. The way is clear. Unseen, I will go in, take him by the neck and plunging the dart full into his throat, rip him further with the weapon. If regret, I have, it is that in an instant shall it be done."

"Talk, brother, never did the deed. Whilst we fritter away time with pleasant chatter it may be the peacock changed position, and now faces you."

Another hurried look through the window confirmed Semyon had not moved. Drawing the dart from his great coat, Slubeadgh crept to the doorway and went into the cottage.

Cleaning the area around the badly closed wound, Semyon thought his needlework left much to be desired. Unevenly spaced, the stitches were of differing lengths and untidy angles, and between the tufty-headed knots, he had tied, beads of blood were growing larger. He did not attempt to wipe them away. Unconcerned at the hash he had made of the temporary measure, he threw the cloth back into the bowl and leaning back, relieved the painful task was completed, noticed a wavering reflection in the blur of his makeshift mirror that had not been there before.

"If he smell you not, he has seen you!" Galateo screamed. "Go to, use your weapon. Deliver the fading stroke."

"In that primitive excuse for a looking-glass," Slubeadgh sneered, raising his arm to strike, "he can see nothing."

"It is enough he see's your mass, brother. I tell you, stick him, stab him, or flee before it is too late and now...by the powers, now the dart betrays you!"

A soft sheen glinted, brilliant and yet subtle, moving on the surface of the tray. From the reflected quaver of zig-zagging dark shapelessness, a slender form detaching, moved a sliver of coppered-silver upward.

Urilatum!

"Slubeadgh," Semyon said, getting leisurely to his feet, "other than foul murder, what do you do here?"

Eyes, bulged in terror, he opened his mouth to speak. His mind a complete blank, his tongue a lump of useless gristle, he stared into the glare of a luminous blue eye. Gulping air, he instinctively backed slowly away.

"Lower your arm, incompetent fool," his twin shrieked. "Flee despicable coward, or give the peacock the dart before he strike us."

Shaking, Slubeadgh obediently held the dart out. Semyon took it. Twirling the barrel appreciatively between his fingers for a moment before putting it in his pocket, he said, soft, "You rancid stink on legs. You thought to fade me with the Lady's trinket, when my back was to you? Are you not a creeping piece of malignancy, biding in a sack of shit? Accept my thanks for the return of the Lady's property, and with it, your just desserts."

His hand shot out, seized Slubeadgh's throat, and in seconds he had and dragged him outside.

"By horns of power!" Galateo screeched, "he means to make a duet of the song of agony we heard him trill, and we are to yowl the second part!"

"You will have noted," he said pleasantly, "injury I have been dealt, and more than injurious, the loss of talent. Doubtless, understanding you will have of my need to express disappointment at this unfortunate turn of events. And here you are, bedecked in the glory of all vileness, my failed assassin. A most worthy object to vent fury upon."

"Speak!" Galateo cried, frantic. "Wriggle free. Be something, other than a quaking heap, brother. In great peril of our lives, we surely are."

"Great sir," he whined, finding his voice. "No assassin am I, you mistook the situation, mistook my design and motive."

Semyon nodded sympathetically, "As much as you mistake what is now to occur, did I mistake your actions."

Throwing Slubeadgh to the ground, he kicked out.

Chapter 34.

The windows and doors of the Doge's office, closed against all distractions, could not keep the muted roar of the Trapiche Emeral's rage from breaking the silence. The Eight, seated on benches ranged about his desk, looked expectantly at Cullinan. Wearing his most solemn look, his eyes travelled from one face to another, and reaching the last, fell briefly to inspect his own hands clasped on the desk. Sucking his teeth, he looked up, and said, "Friends, saddest reason there is for this assembly of incomplete Nine. Unexpected, and far too soon, our good, friend, Malachor's fading."

Clean-shaven, except for a small circular tuft of hair on top of their heads, signifying none stood above them, save the Doge, the Eight expressed heartfelt agreement by slowly nodding.

"Did not our Blessed Lady tell us," Cullinan sighed, "Eight is an imperfect number?"

"You speak truth," they answered in unison.

"Can imperfection be tolerated among the highest echelon of the Order, the wearers of the deepest colour of life? The mainstay of wisdom, advice, check, balance and power, personified by the Nine, can it be relegated to imperfection? No, nor will it be allowed to continue. In an imperfect state you find yourselves, friends. Eight, of you there are. To your number, another must be added, for nine symbolizes perfection.

"This, our Blessed Lady also told us, gathering to her nine of like mind and power at the founding of the Order. There can be no indecent haste to bring perfection back into the bosom of the Order, the very heartbeat at its centre, to that end are we assembled. Malachor faded, a cause for much grief, is of secondary import. Mourning rites, in due course, carried out for our revered and missed, friend, there shall be. Let us trouble ourselves no more on that issue, but concentrate on the matter at hand.

"To elect another to complete incompleteness, is our true business here," tufted heads went down, folders opened, flax-paper rustled in preparation, "and doubtless, each one of you has proposals to make, candidates to put forward, as do I, but," holding up his hand, Cullinan smiled apology. "There is a small matter, best got out of our path, before immersing ourselves in serious conference. I speak of the placement of an informant into the household of Lessadgh, the woman who stands as High Lord of Almandine, whom I now name Sphalerite. A treacherous rock, I believe her to be, and careful watch must be kept on all of her actions. Your agreement, I seek for this action."

* * *

Certain, if he kept on going toward low lying hills in the distance he must eventually come to a village or small hamlet, Persimmony Clump, footsore and thirsty, shrugged the bag off his shoulder and sat down in long grass. No longer quite so vicious, the colours of Noor's lessening glare now pricked his eyes with an aching nag. Closing them, he leant back and rested on his elbows.

Gently warm, with ribboned coolness layered through it, the air was sweetly tinged by smells of perfumed flowers and sap-filled grass, whose heavily podded seed-heads nodding, bumped and rubbed together in a continuous rustle and mild clap. Hypnotically peaceful, the sound of crickets industriously sawing hind legs, the whirring buzz of wings and insect hum, and the low whispering of the faded. And wafting on the lazy breeze, a faint vibration barely heard, which he thought might be bells tinkling.

"Mendicants?" Clump sat up, straining his ears for the subtle chimes, and hearing repetition in divergent currents, got to his knees. Shading his eyes, he scanned the countryside trying to locate where they were, what direction he should go to catch them and ask a simple question, where am I?

* * *

"The voices are getting louder," William said, to the dark.

"What do they say?"

"I do not know. They do not speak like Clara, you and I. They say a lot, an awful lot, but I do not understand them at all. The gift says the voices are a part of what is given to me. They tell me many things of great importance, but if I do not understand, it is useless. The gift says, I must not worry, it has the power to bring me understanding, so that when I come into my own, I may know and understand everything the voices have said, and will say. I will have knowledge of the mother tongue, unpolluted by Lessadgh's gab."

"When will you come into your own?"

"I do not know that either. I just know, it will be much, much sooner than I should."

"What does the gift say about that, William?' the dark asked.

"It says, it cannot be helped, the timing has not been of its choosing, or doing. The storms have called to it, drawn it out, and now there can be no stopping it coming, because the power they feed to it is getting stronger all the time. And that is strange. I thought the storms were not so bad as they were. What do you think?"

"I think," the dark said, slowly, "the winds don't howl and snap in violent bursts as they did. You know, beginning and lasting for a while, going away and coming back again. I think we are caught up in one huge storm that constantly blows, and we are becoming used to the noises it makes."

"But we are not rocked about anymore. Why is that?"

"I think...we are moving so fast now it is almost like standing still. Does that make sense?"

"Not really."

"Never mind. It doesn't matter. Curl up neat and snug. As long as we two are together, there is no need to worry."

"That is strange, too," William said, burrowing more deeply into the dark's warm arms, "because part of me, the part that is not with us, feels really stretched out."

* * *

Gone, white powder all used up. Gone too, the marks on the child's chest. The pallor blanching his skin, the heated sweat, the weirdly crazed veins and discolouration at the back of his eyes, all gone.

"If he were not tied hand and foot to the bedposts, stretched as if on a rack, his look would be no different from a child sleeping," Apatia said, and picking up the ruby bottle from the coverlet, where she had thrown it, placed it on the bedside table.

Some speech I must have with mother on matters of concern, lest she be of the opinion I have been lax in my care of him, she thought moving away from the bed. *He has taken no food, or drink, nor passed any waste, which must surely be detrimental. No twitch, nor shift, has his body made since he thrashed the bed, and his stillness belies the reason why he was bound.*

And I? Sliding onto her dressing table stool, she stared into the mirror and grimaced at her reflection. *Look at yourself, Apatia; proud Lord of the Helm, talentless daughter of a talent-blessed demon. Are you not bound much as he? With invisible ties, you are bound secure, never to be loosed. Emphasized by the imminent prospect of another visit, another breathless dash through that hated garden, in but a little while.*

How unkempt and haggard is your look. Dark circles, dug by exhaustion, lie buried beneath your eyes. And skin? Once pearled perfection, its fabric is drabbed by the same affliction. Comparable to a tatty bale of hay, has your hair become. In shortest time, Apatia, where is your beauty gone? Its lustre hides in the deepest depths of matriarchal fear, and over weaning tiredness.

"No," she said, attempting to throw off melancholic sloth, "to bathe in scented waters shall be a revival, a recovery of depressed spirit. If the child rests easy, some semblance of beauty that was mine may be coaxed forth with application of the paint-box and a little grooming.

"These things shall I do, and earn back a little of lost self-esteem, so mother may pluck it from me with ease again? What matter? To feel myself, as I once was, if only for a little while, is enough. Time there is, if I am quick."

* * *

The making sung effortlessly in her head. The vowels, massaged and oiled by vocal chords in a virtual throat, stroked and caressed by a virtual tongue, stretched out to exquisite length and perfect thinness, were linked by consonants snapped short. Second nature to her now, the song sung without thought, or stumble, its tones mellow and subtle, its rhythm sweetly lilting, polished by the ages she had been singing the constant loop that could have no beginning and no end.

"No end?" Lingaradgh chimed, "an end there must shortly be. So pale, am I, the fabric of my being is near translucent and spectral. An end there will be. In no fatal crash, shall it come, nor the illusion of my kingdom city be destroyed. Not now. No, not now. The means to set all right lies sleeping in Apatia's bed. Within his puny body does power coalesce, that come to full fruition, shortly will be mine, I have but to coax it to the limit."

"Mother? Mother?"

"Come. Late you are, and stand at the bottom of the stair bleating, 'mother', when you know I wait for you? Come!"

"Mother," Apatia said, on reaching the top of the winding stair, "a plan I have devised, which if successful..."

"I have no care for anything of your devising, Apatia, nor time to waste on hair-brained schemes dreamt up by a ninny," Lingaradgh's voice clanked impatience. "My devising is the only way we will win through. Pay most careful attention. A stronger, more potent mix, I now provide. The method is as before, save eight dosages must now be given. Evenly spaced, the times of ministration must be. Keep close watch on your water clock, and monitor the child with ever more vigilance and regularity. Changes you will see, if things go as I design. A soft glow beneath his skin should appear and gradually strengthen into brightness."

"You give the brat talent!" Apatia cried. "And gave me not the means to acquire it."

"Little fool," shaking with fiery temper, Lingaradgh rounded on her, spiking her with the blaze in silver eyes. "I give him nothing. Talent cannot be made, nor given by any hand. Nor can it be drawn from one, such as you, who having a deficiency at the first shall ever suffer the lack.

"Not so the boy. Great potential, does he have, and you will see it shine brilliant. Since Atrament faded, its like will never have been seen. You do me much wrong, Apatia," she said, with sudden softness, "to drive me to anger, when at such time, imperilled are we both, and much needed energy is wasted. If talent were mine to give, think you, I would not give it?"

"Forgive me, Mother."

"Do I not always? Now the bottle, give it to me that I may fill it."

"The bottle?" Apatia stammered, seeing it in her mind's eye on the table by her bed.

"Never tell me," Lingaradgh chimed, sweet, "that in your haste to bathe and preen and scent vanity, it is forgot? No, do not shake with sudden terror…its forgetting is a small matter with easy remedy."

From a cupboard, she took a small flask of clearest crystal, and into it, carefully poured the Trooh she had prepared.

"Mother…"

"There is no need for tearful apology. Go now, child of mine. Take what I have prepared, and doing as I bid, all will be well with us."

Soon, Lingaradgh thought, listening to the rapidly receding footsteps of her daughter, *when I have no need of such an imbecile as she, my hand will not be stayed, but strike with devastating force that not even the Guardians will be able to withstand it. If…if talent the child possesses can be harvested, as is my belief.*

* * *

Not knowing where she was being taken, or what would happen to her, was frightening, Clara finally admitted, but she would deal with that fear in good time, since a more pressing one concerned her, that of vomiting. To bring up the contents of her stomach, humiliating. Having to wallow in the acrid mess and stench, revolting. Each time sickness jumped, she pushed it down, the bitter acidic taste left in her throat and mouth a promise, no matter how hard she fought, it would come again. The motion of the beast she was tied to, endlessly bouncing and jouncing, made this threat a reality. The heat inside the confines of the scented box already stifling…and growing hotter, confirmed it.

Her mouth watering again, she abandoned any dignity she had hoped to maintain, and at the top of her lungs cried out.

"Hold," Reboia shouted, "something is wrong with Lessadgh. If she perish with fright, we are not served well. Take her out."

The guards trotting ahead of her wheeled their animals round, and dismounting, ran to take their captive in the casket down from the haran bearing her.

The lid unlocked and thrust open, bindings cut, and the cloak pulled roughly away, soaked with sweat, hair plastered to her face, and gasping for air, Clara sprawled into Noor's brilliant light and colour.

"I had forgot," Reboia said, looking down at her, "Lessadgh feels heat and cold that touches her, and that which does not."

* * *

Each time Clump thought he knew the direction to follow, breezes carrying the faint tinkling of tiny bells confused him by changing direction, or dying away altogether. Frustrated, he wandered aimlessly back and forth, intersecting ground he had already trodden until wandering further, quite by chance, he stumbled onto a wide meandering pathway. Stretching across the huge expanse of the plain, he knew at once, grass and flowers beaten to smash, could only have been created by the uncoordinated step danced by Mendicants.

He paused to calm himself and listen. There were only two directions he could go now. A slight breeze rushed, sighing past, and in its wake the sounds listened for. Shifting his bag into a more comfortable position, Clump set off thinking, when he knew where he was, the search for Clara's boy could begin in earnest.

* * *

"Best, I am blunt." Cullinan sucked his teeth thoughtfully. "The proposal I shall put to you, friend, Caryadgh, is not without an element of danger. You are, of course, at liberty to refuse this service to the Blessed Lady and her servants, the Guardians. However, before laying such proposal out, I must be sure of your discretion, both in the acceptance of the task, or if it is your inclination, its refusal. Once given, I will hold you most surely to it. Think carefully, friend, for you may say in all honesty, Doge, discretion I cannot give. Saying these words, you are free to leave with no lose of regard."

"Friend, Doge, is not my life held in the palms of the Blessed Lady? Can distrust in her loving care be viewed in any light, other than that of faithlessness? If danger finds me, it is by the Blessed Lady's will. Discretion is given, together with any service I can perform to the good of the Blessed Lady, and her gracious servants, the Guardians."

Sucking his teeth hard, Cullinan nodded.

Zealotry's clammy hand rubs her shoulder in preparation for a full embrace. Can I use her, and having used, discard her?

"Very well, friend," he said, "unusual, it is, for one with so little training to embark on such a task, involving secrecy and intrigue. Be aware, great faith and trust is placed in you. The proposal is this, a simple matter on the face of it. Into the Helm of the High Lord of Almandine you shall go."

"I must return to the domain of Lessadgh, friend Doge?" Caryadgh's face wrinkled slightly in distaste.

"You like Lessadgh not?" Cullinan probed.

"Dislike comes not into the equation, friend, Doge. Surely, the taint of possible heretic rebellion must rest on one who disrespects, who flagrantly disregards protocol set out by the Guardians?" she asked humbly.

She understands the nub of the matter without any prompting. This one will do well enough, if... if she hold righteous indignation in check.

"Yes, the possibility is present that Lessadgh, having no talent, still seeks to walk upon the Way of Atrament. It is the Order's solemn duty to be vigilant for walkers upon that heinous path, and therein is your task. Listen well, friend. The Helm of Almandine has not the structure of other

Helms, as you must know. All ranks may freely wander its corridors, even to approaching its High Lord with petition, or complaint, without preamble. Is that not so?"

"To my remembrance it is, friend, Doge."

"Most irregular," he said, shaking his head in reproach. "Family, others who are dear, and acquaintances you surely have there. Thus, is some ease given for what you, friend, Caryadgh, must do.

"With the innocent amiability of youth, you will engage with those closest to the High Lord. With your connections, this will be an easy task, but it must be done carefully to invoke no suspicion. With chatter and gossip, draw from them secrets not readily known outside the Helm, and in particular..." Cullinan sucked hard on his teeth. Steepling his fingers, resting his chin on the tips, he said, "In particular, discover what compelled the High Lord to go into Spessa, and of utmost import, if she carried anything away from the Field of Madricore."

"Friend, Doge," she said, bowing her head to hide tears welling in her eyes. "You do me great honour. I accept the task, and with all my heart, thank you for opportunity to show, commitment to the Guardians is total."

"Carry the task out well, and reward shall find you earlier than could be hoped for."

"What is to be found, I will find, friend, Doge."

"Hidden beneath your hair, friend, talent sparks on your scalp, does it not? With enhancement, upon successful completion of the task," he said, and smiled a tight smile, "with patience and time, greatness could be yours."

"I am much in your debt, friend, Doge."

"It is obvious your return will raise remark. You must say the Order found you unworthy and would not countenance your presence any further in Hessonii. You may use a story of your choosing for expulsion. It sits well with you?"

"I am equal to sniping comments that must surely come the way of one discarded by the Guardians. From me, their acid will glide away as does rainwater, friend, Doge."

"Good. Good," he said. "Yet you do not ask, friend, Caryadgh, a vital question."

"Friend, Doge, I thought it impertinence to question how you would collect information gathered."

"Perhaps," he answered. "You may leave now, friend."

"May the Blessed Lady make your face shine, friend, Doge," she said, rising from the bench, bowed obeisance and left his office.

Opening windows, the Trapiche Emeral's roaring rant crashed into his office, its turbulent sounds battering his ears, and strong breezes thrown up by raging waters blasting against him, went unnoticed.

Is, friend, Caryadgh right for the task? Cullinan thought, momentarily doubting his own judgment. *Knowing the Helm so intimate, she is perfect, or so she seems.* For all her self-possession, away from Hessonii and the sacred halls of the Guardians, might not that icy calm fracture? It is possible. Among the decadent opulence of Almandine's Helm, might she be seduced by pleasure? Unsuitable friendships renewed, could she forget her purpose there? It is possible. Friend, Caryadgh, is very young. For all her knowing ways and strong intellect, the young are very often foolish. That is true. Suppose...suppose, in the exchange of one juicy nugget of gossip for another she lets something slip? Pshaw! I plague myself with useless thought. In the event, she is incautious and found out, is not the option ours to disown her?

For a certainty it is. And small is the effort to concoct a tale to place us outside the compass of her espionage. Already, those seeds of repudiation are sown, if she tells the reason for her return as was outlined. Others, more experienced in the ways of cunning and guile, there are of our Order already ensconced in Almandine's Helm, if she comes to grief.

Going back to his desk, Cullinan prepared instructions to raise the bridge of air Caryadgh would pass over later that day, once all things belonging to the Guardians had been stripped from her, and suitable clothing found for a return to her home that would have no lustre clinging to it.

* * *

Hard to think clearly, when Noor's sizzling colours skittered with rapid pulse against the back of her skull. Through the double-bound folds of the flimsy cloth wound around her head and over her eyes, Clara could still see them, their vibrancy muted to something more manageable, but still potent.

No ice-laden frost ironed the ground hard with bitter coldness. No misting fog suffocated the land, lacing all it touched with dampness carried in its curling tentacles. Only sweet-smelling air, alive with the scent of white flowers, whose perfume, released from the meadowland by the trampling feet of sleek-scaled beasts, floated on warm breezes. And riding the layers of slight current, adding to the strangeness of a world never dreamed, or imagined, something she was struggling to comprehend. Disembodied, the language indiscernible, susurrant and wistful, sibilant and persistent and endlessly all about, were rustling whispers that were not leaves, but clearly murmuring voices.

Hard to think clearly, when spiked quills, huge and shaking on the beast's arched neck, clattered and clanked with every loping stride, were so wickedly near. She leaned back against the rider, who had carried her through the sally port, and whose arm effortlessly held her in place.

Hard to think of anything, but one thought.

They are taking me to William.

Chapter 35.

Ever was vengeance uppermost in my mind. How to achieve it, a constant thought. Yet a creeping thing, I had become, that not daring to show its face in brightest light scurried through covering dark, and from fields round about, stole sustenance. To such a state was I reduced, and more, as shall I presently confess, for lack of talent.

Small makings with the scrying bowl, leeched energy from me at an alarming rate, and in the process, curtailed continuous making, which in turn, impeded careful watch.

Talent, ravenous was I for its replenishment, and to old ways returned. Unused for aeons, adamantine teeth were again employed. Faded without pity, those unfortunates who came wandering into my path. What little talent was theirs, I took to be mine own. And from this beginning, did a scheme present, wherein vengeance I sought might, in time rolling, be accomplished. To the Guardians Houses of Learning, I looked, and bent all focus on the testing booths, seeking for those with extraordinary potential, which must surely make itself evident through the chance of genes drawn from a former time. Sure, it must be so, where better to find such a one?

To take knowledge from the Guardians, to steal it away from that hateful tribe, as they had once stolen it from me, I thought most excellent repayment.

To find a thing, of consummate rarity, is no easy task. This I knew. Time would roll and roll, before I came upon such a one, if ever. The testing booths, I scanned, reading results more accurately than the Guardians ever could, for was not this process of my devising?

Time rolled. And in its rolling turn, many things came about. Tepauni faded, and not by natural cause. Spans allotted to me grew short, the means to lengthen them shorter. For this reason, alone, though my heart rejoiced at a good deed done, on this most pleasurable occurrence, I shall not elaborate, but neither will I gloss over it complete. In brief, the tale is this. Excluding the Nine, all power Tepauni thought to hold solely to herself. For her perfidy and betrayal was she faded, and in the act of fading, so was immortality of a sort given to her, when she could do nothing with it. Thus, was the myth of the Blessed Lady brought into being, and I, who rarely cracked a smile, laughed long and hard at this...the best of jests.

Shall I speak of false starts, despair, and hopes? I think not. In the testing booths of Tsavoe, during tests carried out on babes with two sparns of life, a likely candidate did I stumble upon. A boy from the venerable house of Aldridgh, with whom, even before it was begun, I lost all chance. At the age of nine, was his potential confirmed, and taken straightway into the Guardian's lair on the isle that once was owned by the Disobedient Ones in

Hessonii.
No puppet for the Guardians use, this one, but a foil that would not bend to their will, causing that hateful tribe much frustration. Ideas he had, and interests too, that ran not in similar vein to the Order's, and they, in hope to sway the boy to their cause, gave him Trooh even as he was approaching puberty and making plans of his own.
The healing of scars, to form new limbs, to remedy all manner of mutilation, together with the creation of beauty in flesh thought plain, this discipline held his interest and delight. For power, other than this, Barr of Aldridgh cared nothing.
A lesson learned, for both the Guardians and I.
Talent practiced under license, was their learning from this incident, to recoup a little of time and gold invested in this one, and thus get profit from all others coming after him. For this, and fearing the power he would turn against them, should they dispute his leaving, they raised a bridge of air, and let him depart in peace.
To tutor mind to mind at an early age, when next a candidate presented, was my learning.

"It is my belief," Malfroid spoke soft, "Clara, in playing the dullard, understands more of the old language than she would have you believe."

"Your reason, other than she holds many secrets to herself?"

"Your interpretation, must of necessity, lag behind the words Atrament speaks, is that not so?" Clump nodded. "You did not note the expression on her face, when the boy, Barr of Aldridgh was mentioned?"

"No, I be concentrating on keeping up with a flood of words as best as may be. Her expression, what of it?"

"Her face lighting up, on hearing the word 'boy', quickly dimmed when he went on to tell of testing at the age of nine. She knew, before you could translate a word, what had been spoken. Of that I am sure."

"But her speech is clumsy, her tongue stumbles to twist and push against the length of vowels and consonants. If acting a part she be, Clara is most excellent at it."

"I do not mention speech, Clump. To read, and reading, understand the content of the text without ability to formulate the written word into speech is possible, is it not?"

"I would say, yes, but not in this instance. We talk of a complex language, and Clara, ever quick to learn...ah, I see now what you be getting at. Language be learnt in most cases by listening, as are our lessons based on, in the main."

"Watch her most close, Clump, as will I, and further talk on this we will have."

"We will. Another thing, Barr Aldridgh, is it likely he be living still?"

"What is in your mind?"

"If your contact fail, Malfroid, it may be this Barr Aldridgh can lay hold of answers we seek regarding the Guardians, and also shed light on the authenticity of the speak-cube. What think you on this?"

"Worth some effort. Wheels, I will set in motion, and advise what is churned up."

* * *

"No reaction?" she said, aloud. "Why does his body not jump and twitch? Why does he not strain against his bonds? A more potent mix this is, and should surely provoke some response from him? A half measure given, and no movement he makes. Patience. Patience," Apatia counselled herself, "with the other half, he will perhaps stir."

Inserting the tube into one of the boy's nostrils, white powder sucked up and waiting for release, pumped out when she squeezed the bulb. Quickly laying the tube aside, she made careful note of the time shown on the face of the water clock, and waited.

"Lady," Ratanakiri rapped on the door.

"What is it that you disturb me?"

"Lady, forgive me for troubling you. Reboia, one of Commander Semyon's guards, is in the corridor. She said to tell, what you desired, is brought safe and well. What must I do, Lady? Bid her go away and leave you in peace, or admit her?"

"Get you back to the vestibule, Ratanakiri," Apatia called. "Tell the guard, wait. I shall be there presently to take delivery of her cargo."

It would appear...I am not near so useless as my mother believes. Success is mine, Lessadgh is come, now shall we see what power is in her voice.

In a flurry of cobweb silks, her eyes narrowed and speculative, her face a mask of exhaustion and triumph, Apatia came into the vestibule. Ratanakiri, eyes wide and alive with curiosity, jumped up to open the door.

Her expression inscrutable, the guard in the corridor snapped to attention, smartly clicking her heels as protocol demanded. Beside her, held by one arm, the woman. Long strands of white hair, worked loose from pins, tumbled around her face and over her shoulders. Insolent and hard, the expression of the face upturned to hers, one eye of murked colour and unnaturally ringed with white, the other, almost closed by swollen flesh, livid with storm-cloud bruising, a memento of their last meeting.

Lessadgh barely controls her rage, Apatia thought, staring back, *wild, and scowling her expression. Lined with age, she is, as is the peculiar affliction of her kind. How she longs to strike out at me, yet knowing it would be futile, will not. In her eye, hiding behind hatred, I see hope glimmers.*

"Semyon is not with you?" she asked, taking hold of Clara's arm and pulling her into the vestibule.

"He is not, Lady. Other business, the Commander said he had."

"And so he does," she said, and signalled Ratanakiri should close the door.

"Lady, he has taken injury," Reboia said. "No trifling scratch, but grievous harm."

"Trouble me not with rigors dared in my service," Apatia said, cold, and kicked the door shut with her foot. "You, Ratanakiri, lift up your chin from the carpeting. Is sight of a Stunted One so strange, you must gawk amazed?"

"No, Lady," she whispered.

"Resume your seat in the vestibule, and remember, into my confidence I have taken you. Speak any word of what passes here, punishment of severest kind I will visit upon you."

Her first instinct was to break free from the grip of the woman towering over her, and run through the rooms beyond the antechamber searching for William.

What then? Clara thought. *Hothead will get me little. I must be calm, be docile, and I shall be taken to him. This bitch is in a position of authority. By her tone, she engenders no loyalty, but uses threat. Such behaviour may be to my advantage, later.*

Submissive, she allowed Apatia to lead her through room after room, where tall windows, paned with shimmering crystal, lit crowded, organically shaped furniture, and teased blazing colour from the wall hangings. Over thick-piled carpets and rugs, past clocks driven by water, beneath lights suspended from high ceilings, and set into walls, and all the paraphernalia of wealth and privilege. Dwarfed by size and scale, she had no interest in the strangeness around her. At a pair of elaborately carved double-doors, Apatia stopped.

"Lessadgh," she said, to get the woman's full attention, then using signs, she attempted to indicate what was required of her.

* * *

"You have been very quiet, William," the dark said. "Are you listening to the voices?"

"No, not any more. They got louder and louder, as if that would make what they said clear, but I still did not understand, so I stopped listening a long time ago."

"The gift said it would give you understanding, perhaps it is best to wait until it does."

"I think that might be a long time. The gift has other things to do at the moment. It says it is full to bursting, but the power it is being fed just keeps coming, and it has to eat it all up."

"Surely the gift could stop if it wanted too?"

"No, it cannot. It said, it is a bit like when Clara says I must eat everything on a plate put in front of me, otherwise, I will not grow to be big and strong, and she gets cross when I do not want to."

"Who will get cross with the gift?"

"It said it would be angry with itself, if it was less than it could be."

"William, if have not been listening to the voices...why have you been so quiet? Were you sleeping?"

"I was watching the pictures."

"Pictures?"

"Yes, they keep flashing into my head."

"What kind of pictures, William?"

"All sorts. I have been shown things I am too young to know about. Wars, I have seen, and the stupid reasons why they are fought. Greed seems to begin them and those fighting, think glory comes to them, but that isn't true. Killing and rape and destruction, how can there be glory in those things? It made me very sad to see them. And because no one ever learned how terrible war is, the same things were done again and again, which made me sadder still.

"I did not know about the things some people hide inside themselves, where no one can see how bad they really are. Spite and malice and deceit are just some of the things I have seen. Bad things that hurt others, and sometimes, even the ones that walk in these ways. I know what men and women do, how babies are begun, how they grow in the mother's stomach and are born. I don't think Clara ever did what I saw, because she never had a child. And..."

"William," the dark interrupted, "what does the gift say about the pictures and where they come from?"

"It sent them. It told me the names of the things it showed. It says, I have to know about everything, so I can choose which path I want to walk on, because there are some who will try to bend me to their ways. It says, if I did not know the difference between good and bad, I could make wrong choices, and it would be too late to be sorry afterwards."

"I see," said the dark quietly.

"You remember saying, you thought we were going so fast it seems we stand still? I see what you meant now. The wind's howl has gone to one long whine, and I can feel air whooshing past, while we stay exactly where we are. And another thing, Clara is here."

"Clara? Here?"

"The gift told me. The one who is feeding it power has brought her. She thinks I am asleep. She wants Clara to wake me."

"Is that good?"

"It says it is not. It says, if we two are parted, before it has become all it can be, we may be separated forever."

"That would be a very bad thing, William."

"Yes, I know. Hold me tighter, please."

Chapter 36.

A soggy bundle of muddied rags, balled on frost trampled grass. Semyon, panting out the last shreds of fury, prowled around it, his hands clenched into fists.

"Worthless creature, riddled with all that is foul," he screamed, "failed murderer, inept assassin, but for the Lady's admonition, I would fade you. Her word, alone, stays my hand, else with purest delight, putrescent maggot, would I send you to join the dust you grovel in, to contaminate Lessadgh's dirt with a single speck for all time. If you hear me…" he said, drawing away, smoothing hair back from his forehead, straightening neckwear, and the lapels of his frock coat, "…know this. In compliance with the Lady's wish, I leave you breathing, but dare come within a spit of distance to me again, and by the powers, I swear, before I am finished, not only will you wish I had faded you at this time, you will beg that I do it."

Turning on his heel, he marched to his haran and mounting, rode away into the misting fog.

* * *

Clara nodded. Putting both hands flat together, she raised them to one cheek and closed her eyes, showing she understood her boy slept.

"And then?" Apatia touched her mouth and rolled her hands.

Understanding she was expected to talk to William and wake him up, Clara frowned and said, "Why can you not wake him? He cannot be in such a deep…ah, that dart you stuck us with. Some drug was in it to make us sleep, and now, you cannot bring him from the slumber you induced."

Frowning back, Apatia shook her head at incomprehensible speech. Signalling toward the double-doors, she took hold of Clara's arm, and pushed them open.

A huge room filled with light, airy except for a faint smell of yeast and mushrooms drifting on the breeze coming in through the windows. At the far end, a scene depicting fantastic birds, and harans, stretched to full gallop, had been woven into a silk panelled screen elegantly cordoning an area off. Eager to see William, to hold him, talk to, and with him, Clara ran, matching Apatia's quick stride over the carpets.

Rounding one end of the partition, she saw an opulent swathe of drapery hung suspended from the ceiling over a large bed. On it, almost swamped in waving folds of the crumpled coverlet, William lay. His little body splayed out by cords, attached to wrists and ankles, and tied to the four corners of the bed. Stunned at the sight, Clara approached, and kneeling at its side, began to untie the nearest knot, hissing, "What is it, you do?"

"No," Apatia knocked her hands away. "Call to him, wake him. For that sole purpose were you carried here. Stupid, Lessadgh, does not understand," she said, and exasperated, made signs Clara should talk to the boy.

"You torture my child, you bitch," she said, between gritted teeth, her fingers busy on the knot once more, "and expect me to bring him into wakefulness that you may enjoy his agony? Is that it?"

"No!" terrified, if loosed from his bonds he might harm himself, Apatia knocked her hands away, again.

Leaping to her feet, Clara struck back.

In the vestibule, Ratanakiri heard her mistress cry out. For a moment, she wondered what she should do. Hearing furniture crash, and glass shatter, she left her post. Running through rooms to give assistance if needed, she was just in time to see Apatia hauling the woman by the scruff of her neck to one of the small side chambers.

"You treat your responsibilities lightly," Apatia stormed catching sight of her.

"No, Lady," she answered, "alarmed by sounds of a struggle, I thought to come to your aid."

"You may aid me by fetching the key to this room," she answered, throwing Clara inside.

* * *

Groaning, Slubeadgh regained consciousness.

"Brother, you have returned!" Galateo piped relief, mingled with concern. "I feared you teetered on the brink of fading, about to fall into the abyss of nothingness and become matter of the smallest kind, a piffling speck of dirt. And what could I then do, but shortly follow to join with you? For the longest time, I called to no avail, in hope of raising you from insensibility, and just when darkest thought troubled me, you answer with a moan and make all right."

Slowly unfolding from the protective ball he had curled into, Slubeadgh spat congealed blood from his mouth and groaned again.

"I suffer agonies," he whimpered. "No part of me there is that does not ache, or throb, and in my chest a fire rages."

"Cracked ribs, brother, courtesy of the peacock's boot. Have a care how you move."

"If ever I move again, I can do nothing, but take care. The slightest movement wrongly made, or over hasty, and I feel…into little pieces I will scatter."

"Brother, if you lie overlong, will not your injuries stiffen and bring you to more grief? Some injury, I, too, have sustained, admittedly in measure not so much punishment as was served to you, but would dearly appreciate un-cradling."

"Always, you think of you."

"Indeed, brother, I do not. Always, I think of your good, for is not your good my own? Did I not advise you against this venture? Did I not warn the dart betrayed you by shining in the peacock's makeshift mirror? Did I not with wild shriek, urge you to strike while the peacock's back was still turned to you? I scarce like to chide, brother, when you are brought so low, but had you taken any piece of the most excellent advice I gave, we would not now be in the sorry condition we find ourselves."

"Give me no lecture at such a time," he winced, having made the slightest movement. "Have you no pity?"

"More pity, do I have for us, than you can know. Always, we come off worse, and for it, there is but one reason, brother."

"Have some mercy, brute," Slubeadgh whined. "No strength do I have for argument. If confession is your aim, then I own, as my arm was poised for the fading blow, my mind went blank with fear. Mine is the fault. Right was the peacock to name me a failed murderer, or words to that effect, so far as he is concerned."

"Brother, be not so hard upon yourself. With murder, you have had no little success. In former time, it is true, though you were no bolder then. Gradually, I have come to the opinion, the peacock exerts strange power with just his presence, that does make your knees to knock as the rattle of castanets, your arm to tremble as violent as a young sapling in high wind, and turns your brain to liquid jelly, fit only for a chef's mould. For this reason, above many others there surely are, he inspires the venom of your hatred."

"Insult and mockery you left out," Slubeadgh groaned.

"Brother, I spared you a lengthy monologue of wrong he does you. Come; try to raise yourself in gentle fashion. Lessadgh's house stands empty for our shelter. Water, there must be to cleanse clots from your mouth, tend lumps and bumps grown with violent colour on face and head, investigate wounds perpetrated upon your body, and with a little good fortune, food, when you are able to stomach the thought of it."

"Speak not to me of that whore named fortune," he sobbed. "I am robbed of the Lady's dart, which she, the raddled doxy, having given it into my hand, then allowed its robbery."

"Brother, in your possession the fan remains. Of greater worth is that thing of wonder than ever was the dart for all its beauty."

"The fan!" Snorting pain at the effort to reach inside his greatcoat, he found it safe in the pocket he had stowed the treasure in, and drawing it from his breast, carefully spread the feathered struts to look for damage. "A thing of perfection, it still is," he said, sighing with relief. "How does the span?"

"Throughout what laughingly passes for the time when the brightling orb holds sway in this dismal place, you have lain prone, your mind wandering through fields only you know of, for many segments. The span now advances into the darkling. Unless it is your wish to lie here through it, move you must, and try to sit up."

"By the powers," Slubeadgh wailed, "would I had faded, rather than suffer such monumental, all consuming pain."

"Brother, a little more effort," Galateo encouraged, "and shelter, where you might take your ease, is attainable."

"And un-cradle you, no doubt," he yelped.

"I will not say, brother, the thought had not occurred."

* * *

Wind-blown, its sides heaving, its arched neck drooping and with reins trailing limp from the bridle, the rider-less haran trudged through the gates and into the stable courtyard.

"The Commander's mount!" one of the lads shouted.

Reboia appeared in the stable doorway, "Semyon?"

"No sign," the lad said, leading the animal away, "but hard-ridden has the beast been. Marks of the spur are on his flanks. Concern for him may be well-founded."

"I am not anxious," she lied, leaning casually against the doorpost. "Semyon is well able to take care of himself. Give the beast an extra portion of spikenard in his ground meal, once you have washed and oiled his skin. By his look, he has earned it."

She watched until the haran had been led to its stall, then pulling her jacket from the wall, put it on as she walked. Fire crystals were beginning to flame, their shine flickering through the windows as she approached the barracks, and going in, certain she knew where Semyon would be, made for the practice rooms.

In a room, where they had never trained, or exercised, she found him huddled in a corner, with his jacket thrown over a fire crystal to dim its blossoming glow.

"You left your haran to find its own way home?" she said, closing the door behind her.

"I took him to the gate, near enough."

"And," her footsteps echoing in the empty space, she began to walk its length, "came here?"

"I desired a little peace," he growled, "that looks unlikely now."

"The wound you sustained has been attended?"

Ignoring her question, he asked, "Lessadgh was safely delivered to the Lady?"

"She was, and suffered no hurt by my hand, nor any other of the troop. All was done as you commanded."

"The Lady was pleased?"

"Pleased?" Reboia barked a laugh. "I saw no glimmer of it in the short time before the door was kicked shut in my face. Your injury has received attention?"

"It has."

"Show me." Without waiting for him to raise his head, she bent down, and cupping his chin in her hand, tilted his face to meet hers. "Sir, I tell you true, a very big mess you have made of looks some might have thought attractive. Get you to the Lady's healer straightway, and pay whatever price they ask for restoration. It is an ugly wound, made uglier by inexpert stitching."

"What talent I had is lost," he gulped, trying to keep tremors from his voice.

"I saw. That is the reason you hide away? To mourn its passing?"

"Among other things."

Reboia put her back to the wall and slid down to sit next to him.

"Other things?" she said.

"For stealing the child, Lessadgh struck me a blow, and striking, took my talent. Soft words, gently spoken, she could not understand, but in vanity I thought actions, clearly with no threat, or malicious intent hidden in them, she would see and realize our purpose."

"She saw nothing, but the child's abductor," Reboia shrugged, "and in mindless fury lashed out?"

"She did. Tell me, thought have you given to the stealing of the boy?"

"I know the child is no more a relative of the Lady's, as is commonly put about, than you, or I."

"What troubles me is this, Reboia. Are we myrmidons, who ruthlessly perform whatsoever she wishes?"

"The Lady commands and we obey. If pushed, I will admit, my heart was touched by affection clearly shown between the boy and Lessadgh. Tearing them apart so rough, was not right, and the beating given to the woman, unnecessary."

"No, none of it was right, and thus am I punished for my part. Anger at being struck by her hand, rose volcanic, though no resentment do I hold for Lessadgh now. Come then to the Lady's purpose for the child, why is it that she should desire to have him so hotly? What does she intend for Lessadgh, who never gave her any hurt?"

"Should her purpose be of concern to us?"

"Should it not?" Semyon bit his lip, thinking of what had been done. "Did we not enable her purpose, never knowing what it was? My mind, on the return, dwelt on nothing but these matters. In my head, round and round, such thought went and finding no answer, nor resolution, my mood is heavy."

"I never had you for a thinker," Reboia laughed, soft, "or does sudden gentleness blunt hard edges? Tiredness and shock are good reason for the quandary you now see yourself entangled in. Go to your apartment, bathe, make arrangement to have disfigurement removed, and then rest well. On the morrow, Semyon, these matters that concern you so, will have a different appearance."

"That foul creature, who goes by the name of Slubeadgh, I near kicked into fading," he said.

"The span has not been without benefit then," Reboia grinned.

* * *

Darkness falling. Wooding a copse, cyanic leafed trees were dappled with sombre colour, and beneath branches shading a small hollow with gloom, Mendicants, faltering in the dance after the exertions of the day, pushed themselves to the very limits of endurance with slow and sluggish steps.

Set apart, recruits yet to be admitted into the group, were busy with a small wheelbarrow they had pushed, or pulled. Alms and food, willingly given to the servants of the Blessed Lady by those seeking her favour, or in gratitude for blessings bestowed, were carted in it.

Unworthy to join the dance, wear the robes, or bear the sisten until it was proven, devotion to the Lady could be paid by the rigors and hardship of grinding poverty, theirs was the drudgery of haulage and carrying out mundane tasks. The longest serving, near to acceptance and full admission, performed the most important task the recruits were charged with. His sole responsibility was to retrieve Mendicants, who, dancing themselves into the ecstasy of exhaustion, fell to ground and would have been trampled by the stamping feet of the remaining dancers, but for his care.

While the recruits located the only fire crystal the Mendicants possessed, and prepared a meal of finely ground rice, mixed with cold water, the nine Mendicants danced. Green and orange striped robes, shapeless and slashed to the knee, allowed free expression of movement, as they kicked and stamped, shuffled and capered. Pushed back from their heads, and carelessly draped down backs, or over shoulders, hoods culminating in long points. At the very tip, accentuating the length, stringed tassels jiggled and swayed, lurched and flew, keeping unsynchronized time with the now dirge-like jangled rhythm of sistens shaking.

He had not seen even the slightest glimpse of the group, but the nearer Persimmony Clump got to them, the more the clinking chime of glass bells grated his nerves with unmusical scraping, and the raucous cries of Mendicants, showering blessings over the unpopulated landscape, verbally stippled his ears with constant rant.

Irritated, he kept reminding himself, "There be no other option," and striding doggedly in pursuit of elusive quarry, followed the path of destruction.

In failing light, indicating they were no longer on the move, sounds floating back to him were becoming louder. The path seemed to lead straight into a wooded copse some distance away. Sliding the broad strap over his head and under one arm, he shifted his bag onto his back, and quickened his pace.

Sharp eyes spotted him, a dark shape back-lit by star-shine, standing respectfully under trees at the lip of the hollow.

Dancing on the spot, a Mendicant cried, "Well come, friend, may the blessings of the Blessed Lady be poured upon you."

"May the Blessed Lady make your face shine, friend," he replied, surprised to find the Guardians words of traditional greeting sprang to his lips readily after so long a time.

"With the Blessed Lady's grace, impossible things are made possible. Do you seek to join us, friend?"

"Friend, with regret, such vocation be not mine."

"No matter, no matter, friend, all have value in the Blessed Lady's sight. We have lately finished our meal, but if hunger roils your stomach, come down, scrape out the pots."

"Friend, for your hospitality, I thank you. It is conversation, I am in most need of."

Detaching himself from the group, the Mendicant waltzed to the wheelbarrow. Snatching the fire crystal from its boards, he hopped back across the clearing and nimbly springing up the slope to where Clump waited, shuffled a dance on the spot, blessing him with the sour odour of body and clothes.

Lean, almost to the point of emaciation, his face rimed with dirt, hair and beard matted and rank with grease, and his robe ingrained with filth, he said, hopefully, with maniacal adoration lighting deep sunk eyes, "Conversation, friend? You have need of instruction in the ways of the Blessed Lady?"

"I be well versed in the blessings of the Blessed Lady, friend. From where have you come?" Clump asked, not wanting to admit he did not know where he was.

"From where the breath of the Blessed Lady blew us, friend, and hither do we go as her will takes us. All places being a continuation of another in the Blessed Lady's sight, and in much need of her blessings."

"Useless, then, to ask you of news, friend?"

"We hear many things, how can we not? What news is it you wish to know of, friend?"

"Something and nothing, friend," Clump said, choosing his words carefully. "I am lately returned from trading in Lessadgh and chanced to hear a strange story."

"Say on, friend."

"I dare say, there be no truth in it, but it told of a Faienya child, left in that place of dreary light for nurturing, and recently taken back. You have heard of it?"

"Not I, friend," the Mendicant shook his head. "A curious tale bearing the certain hallmark of fabrication. I never heard the like."

"I thought as much," Clump agreed. "Stupid to give it credence, and for such stupidity, I plead this injury," turning, he showed the lump on the back of his head, "addled what little brain I had, no doubt."

"May the Blessed Lady deal harshly with your assailant, friend. A nasty knock you have taken, and the proceeds of goods traded in Lessadgh, robbed?"

Clump shrugged, going along with an imaginary event provided by the Mendicant, "And suffered such trauma, I scarce know where I have wandered."

"By the power of the Blessed Lady, may her face shine with ever more radiance," the joyful light in the fanatic's eyes filmed with concern, "I now see, you are ill-equipped for travel. Is it not truth, in time of trouble, the Blessed Lady brought you to us? Security in number there is, friend. Journey with us, and in the company of the servants of the Blessed Lady, have all peace of mind. Where did you say you were from?"

"Hard times have befallen you, by all accounts, friend," said the youngest recruit, charged with cleaning out the bowls and packing them safely into the wheelbarrow. "It is a wicked world, is it not, when we prey on one another?"

"It be no different than it ever was," he answered. "Do they never stop?"

"Only when they fall." Duty done, he came and sat cross-legged beside Clump. "See Girasole there?" he said, in conspiratorial undertone, "always, he watches like a hawk, knowing before a Mendicant knows it, they are about to drop insensible to the ground. Near to full acceptance he is, and waits only for one of the nine to complete devoted adoration of the Blessed Lady by fading in the dance."

"It be a hard life, friend, and not one of long duration."

"There are many blessings to be found in the embrace of the Blessed Lady, or so I keep being told."

"You do not sound sure."

"If, I were honest, I would admit," the recruit leaned closer, "precious little benefit have I seen in the time I have trailed after the Mendicants. Starvation and exhaustion are no benefits, I wish to take advantage of."

"What then will you do, being bound to them?"

"I am not bound, save of my own free will, I desire it," the recruit lowered his voice. "Abandoning this life has long been on my mind and to a decision, I have finally arrived. When we are come to Spessa, it is my intention to leave the group."

"Spessa? You go to Spessa?"

"We do, and should arrive on the morrow, if we travel well. Come from Almandine we are, and before that..."

"Almandine?" Clump's heart jumped at the mention of the name, "who stands as Lord of the Helm in that place?"

"Apatia, she of gold-gilded eyes."

"For how long?"

"Friend," the recruit shot him a suspicious look, "a most serious knock to the head you must have taken to have such length of time removed from remembrance. Lingaradgh, her mother, faded in mysterious circumstance. Some say of a broken heart, after her Lord of a sudden perished. Others, in the gossip they speak, are not so kind. I see your interest is sparked by talk of beauteous Almandine. Is that where you belong, or do you have business there?"

"I am not sure," Clump answered, thinking furiously. "Memories you have stirred, where there were none and for information given, I owe you thanks."

"High prancing and shambled shuffle no longer hold allure for me. The sistens constant tinkle having lost any sweetness it once had, now grinds a way, slow but sure to madness. It may be, you will decide to go on your way before too long, friend. If thanks you would extend, extend it in this manner. Let me go with you, so I may, all the sooner preserve my sanity. I go to my rest, such as I may find, and beg you, take note of where I lay me down."

Through Almandine's sally port I have come back into Noor, Clump thought, shaking his head at the irony. *From that dreaded place, where Lingaradgh ruled with an iron fist wrapped in a urilatum glove, I once fled, and travelling far from it, went into Lessadgh by means of another, never thinking to find my way back.*

By accident, I am returned. If Lingaradgh be faded, how does jeopardy sit with me now? Full on my shoulders, or not at all? Would any remember my face? If I go not near the Helm, who is there that could link the manufacture of the quiver to me? Who link me with the partial manufacture of the fan and its disappearance? Who remember, while effecting escape, I faded two of Lingaradgh's guard, and cry me murderer? I cannot say, time rolls and rolling, dims memory, and with it, perhaps risk.

Through Almandine's sally port, the Faienya must have come to steal Clara's boy away. No other be so near to her farm, and therefore, it be not viable to assume another was used for the boy's abduction.

If Spessa were responsible, permission they would most surely have had to obtain to use neighbouring Almandine's sally port...and give good reason for it. If Spessa lied, saying trade was their reason? Almandine's border-watch would have seen they carried no goods and were in Lessadgh for too short a time for profitable trade.

Telling partial truth, if Spessa said to repatriate a Faienya child? No, by this telling too many problems there would be. Would not Almandine demand to know how and why the child was taken into Lessadgh? By the powers, they would, and that be just the first of many searching questions put. Not Spessa then, nor any other Kingdom State.

Whichever way I turn it, all roads lead to Almandine, Persimmony Clump concluded. *And, so, what can I do? I must away to that place in order to get news of Clara's boy, and face what trouble may come in the keeping of my word.*

Spiritless rhythm now, the sistens barely shaken, the silvery clink and occasional dull clank of little bells whispered exhaustion. Lost in the ecstatic embrace of the Blessed Lady, Mendicants still on their feet stepped out the dance with slow-motioned pace and stumble.

Girasole, squatting, watched intent for signs another was about to drop to the ground, and if the blessings of the Blessed Lady were showered his way, would take the fallen Mendicant into her arms for all time, and he could be raised to wear the robe, play the sisten and join the dance.

No one took any notice of Clump making his way to where the rest of the recruits lay.

"Friend," he shook the shoulder of the young man he had spoken to earlier. "Rise now, if it be your wish to accompany me."

Clear-eyed and wide-awake, he scrabbled to his feet.

Chapter 37.

Carried on the breeze, and seeming to quilt the warm layered currents with soft chatter, she had first heard the voices and paid no attention to them. Her thought, focused on hope she was being taken to William, bypassed all the strangeness she had been brought into.

In the courtyard, recognizing the destination had been reached, and hope rising expectant, she had heard them again, the persistent murmur of voices lying beneath the bustle of activity. Tinkling jade, on reins and saddles. The scraping claws of the beasts on the granite paving, while they snuffled and trumpeted, tossing their heads to make the quills on their necks rattle. Riders dismounting, quietly laughing and speaking to one another, above all this noise, somehow, she had heard them.

Still blindfolded, guided by a large hand on her arm, she had been led up a short flight of steps and into lessening glare. The voices, grown slightly louder, accompanied her and the guard, through long corridors and up wide staircases. Loud in her ears, only the rapid thump of her heart, beating, joyful and anxious, the murmuring voices were barely registered.

Outside a huge pair of elaborately carved doors, the blindfold had been torn from her eyes, and she had rushed beside the giantess, to her boy. What happened next was a blur, except for William. Fast asleep, he had been, and for some perverted reason, bound hand and foot to a huge bed. Heated with fury, she had lashed out to free him.

Now her hands, bruised from futile beating on the door of the room she was locked in, lay in her lap with the last vestiges of rage rapidly dissipating. Slumped on the floor, regret accusing her for being a hothead, stopped to draw breath, and in the brief interval, Clara heard a dry subtle rustling. Whispers, a fluid mumble of indeterminable language. No sentence, no single word distinguishable from another. Finally, taking note of the ongoing quiet hubbub, chasing all around her, she heard the voices and knew them for what they were.

The dead speak!

Suddenly afraid, she crawled into a corner and huddled there.

* * *

Saturated with voices of the faded, the wind rushed in, and tangling with panels of silk-gauzed curtains draped at the long windows, billowed them into the room before capriciously blowing them back out in fluttering confusion.

Leaning on the edge of the balcony to watch the last of the rapidly diminishing light go, Apatia thought, *Lessadgh did not perform as I had hoped. Inescapable, sight of the child's bonds maddened her, and provoked her refusal to call to him. To remove his bindings, to smooth the way for Lessadgh's compliance to my will, is to risk damage to him from sudden convulsion. If such tremor has not yet shaken him, no guarantee is there, it will not, nor is there her voice can stir him. Untenable is that risk.*

She may yet do as I wish. Time will tell, and for that reason do I, for the present, keep her intact, but time rolling is now at a premium, and upon her, I cannot rely, if ever I could.

Some other way there must be, to try and rouse the boy, that depends not on Lessadgh. If he hears, is it necessary he hear her voice? It may be, just the knowledge she is close by is enough. That path I will try before ministering to him again.

Fighting her way past floating drapery, Apatia went back into the room and straight to the bed.

"If you hear me, boy," she whispered, in William's ear "you will be pleased to know the woman of Lessadgh, she whom you clung to so tenaciously, has been brought here for you. At great length, trouble and effort, this has been done and for my kindness, she has struck me! Me, the Lord of this Helm, whom none dare raise a voice to, let alone a hand.

"For your sake, boy, I have suffered this insult, and no punishment meted out upon her person. Safe and secure, undamaged and unharmed, she waits for you in yonder room. She longs to hold you in her arms and have speech with you. Will you not wake and greet her?"

Avidly, she watched his face for any sign he heard. Sighing disappointment, she turned away to measure out the next dose of white powder, and draw it deep inside the pump-tube.

* * *

"My name is Bezel," he said, the instant they were out of the hollow, where the Mendicants still stumbled in the dance. "Almost as mad as they, was I to think the life they have chosen was one I cared to live. Doubtless, you are curious to know what drew me to them, friend? I will tell you true, it was the adventure of travel. All the wonders of Noor journeyed to, and travelled through, that prospect I saw right enough. So enthralled by it was I, nothing else did I see. The hardship Mendicants impose upon themselves went unobserved. Those rigours I learned at first hand, and liked them not at all.

"Who would blame you, friend, for wondering what kept me by them. I shall enlighten you. Far from home, with no money, or resource for a triumphant return, for such was the promise made in anger, what could I do, but stick it out? Courage, it takes to break away alone. Thought of leaving, ever in my mind, so frequently toyed with and intimately explored, I never quite summoned up the wherewithal to actually do it. And, friend, do not underestimate the hypnotic power of the sistens and the dance.

"The bells tinkle without cessation, unless all Mendicants in the group drop down in the dance. That happened not overmuch." Bezel grinned, as he trudged beside Persimmony Clump, "I swear, all of it has an effect that is both stimulating and stupefying. Over time, the bells penetrate the mind to such an extent, in my head, I hear them loud and clear, whilst knowing, few play at this moment and we, going fast beyond their range. And the dance. That, too, has a mind-numbing quality acquired by watching constant.

Then, friend, there were times, on going into a Kingdom City, crowds ran before us heralding our entrance with loud halloo. That I found most exhilarating. The masses pressing forward, hands outstretched, begging for the blessings of the Blessed Lady to be showered upon them by her servants, the Mendicants. Exciting to feel that power, the reverential respect shown, the gifts and alms given by way of thanks, nothing to be sniffed at. To be a part of that show, even in the lowliest role, I have not the words to describe that feeling, friend.

"And what, think you, the Mendicants did with gifts and alms? Coin they gave to the Houses of Learning. Once the city was left in our wake, fine food and wine discarded, tipped from the wheelbarrow as so much chaff, and we in starved condition. Madness!

"Here is confession, friend. Loitering behind, against all rule, I helped myself as opportunity allowed, and felt no guilt in the taking of it. Take Almandine, rich pickings in that city there were, and a crime to leave it to spoil and rot, such was my thinking. Beside, some reward there must be for the interminable instruction in the ways of the Blessed Lady, and more than could be believed, concerning the Way of Atrament. I never heard the like.

"They say the Way whispers with velvet voice, seducing a body to do the wrong thing. You will not credit this, friend, but the Mendicants said promises are made by the Way to the walker who treads its path, that all desire will be satisfied if they walk its length, though destruction was at its end. Can that be believed?

"Many things have I done, that I would not shout of, but to say it was the Way of Atrament, is foolish. I, myself, dared and cajoled me, into doing those things, and nothing will persuade me different. Bunkam and bosh, friend, that is what I say to the Way of Atrament, though I should be glad, if you were kind enough, not to repeat my words, which likely are heresy of one description or another.

"So I am come away from the Mendicants, and would not have you take blame for it upon your shoulders, friend. I have come to learn, sinister entrapment there is in sisten and dance, and madness produced by it, growing ever more present in Girasole's eyes. To see him crouch expectant, longing to be taken into the group as a full member, and with full rights, piffling though they are, was the final spur that sent me upon my way.

"Knowledge, I, too, in all likelihood would come to that pass, was too frightening to countenance. The truth, friend is, I like the Blessed Lady not, or not enough to give my being solely into her keeping by means of slow starvation and the exhaustion of the dance. Celibacy and abstinence of speech, the first requirement demanded from new recruits, apart from drudgery, hard enough to cope with and..."

Trudging back along the route he had previously trodden, with Bezel, the newly lapsed recruit of the Mendicants continuing his monologue, Persimmony Clump wondered if he had exchanged one kind of irritating jangle for another.

* * *

Mottled, the sky. Its darkened verdancy, hammered with deepest purple, swallowing the light shed by the roadway of stars arcing through its heights. The Trapiche Emeral in full throat, bellowing aggression, its speeding waters shredding all in its path, and high-twisted waves violently excavating the tall banks constraining its untamed flow. Angry wavelets, carrying a bounty of small, rounded stones of luminescent green, with the likeness of wheeled spokes etched inside, slammed against the shore of the island. Breezes, whipped to cooled frenzy on the river's surface, in frantic argument with brisk windy currents warmed by the land coming to meet them.

Anonymous in hood and cloak, one in Cullinan's confidence, most probably from the Quisitorial department of the Order, Caryadgh surmised, waited beside her on the terrace.

Lifting his voice above the pell-melled din of air, and water, the hooded one, breaking the silence, identified himself as male, by shouting, "How sit the clothes, friend?"

"Strangely tight," she answered, "after the freedom of the robe. Doubtless, friend, I shall get used to them."

"You have your instructions, friend?" he asked, and without waiting for an answer, "you know why you must go on foot?"

"I do, friend. My clothes are too clean. They must be convincingly dirtied by travel. My hands, too soft for the story I am to tell. For authenticity, they must be toughened by the usage of hard physical labour, where I can find it, and if not, by scraping them on rocks, or stones, before arriving at my destination as evidence the Guardians cast me out."

"In moments the bridge of air will be raised. Go swift across it, friend, and the blessings of the most gracious Blessed Lady be upon you, and bring you success."

"Thank you, friend, it is to be hoped, for in the Lady rests all confidence."

"Look, friend" he said pointing. "Behold the power of the Guardians."

At the edge of the terrace, air shimmered in the darkness. Swirled, and coalesced, and from hesitant lucidity, gained the substance of a block that locked in place with others forced into service. In sections, little by little, the bridge lengthening with ribboned elegance, traversed the destructive force of the Trapiche Emeral, and when it was complete, he said, "Go, without delay, friend."

Clutching a little food for the journey, Caryadgh made her way to the edge of the terrace, went down the stairs to the stony shore, and stepped up onto the shimmering roadway.

Chapter 38.

Once, without cause, and wholly innocent of the charge, was I named 'cannibal'. Most premature that naming: though prophetic it was.
Time rolled. Superstition rested upon the Field of Madricore for the disappearances I caused, and none now walked there once the darkling held sway. Later, not even in the full light of the brightling part of the span, would any venture to go to that place.
In pursuit of talent and food, further distance was I forced to travel, and in terror of discovery did I, creeping go, to take my prey. Cattle lowing in their pens, bleating flocks on hills and in dales, clucking birds in coops, none of these were my target as in former times. Two coobirs in a single throw, my aim.
To a small village I knew of, I went, and damn near perished there. On its out-lying reaches a sack of wine I chanced upon, wending an uncertain way home on staggered legs, his only company a crude song, sung in sweetest tone that was surely talent driven.
Hunger gnawed, yet knowing of mine own weakness no hasty assault could I plan, or launch. Did talent truly shine upon his skin? What likely outcome a swift attack at opportune time? These things I gauged in the stalking of a proposed victim, who not being in full possession of his faculties, was tempting fare.
A dolt this one. Groping in his breeches, he next patterned the air with spraying piss, crying all the while in obscene language how would he serve with rod and seed, the first to cross his path, and if that fail, give unwelcome attention to his hapless bound partner. Some aid he gave me to a decision. Seen upon his throat, bright freckled talent and whilst he tottered, striving to put away his member, I struck.
Fast and silent, my intent that counted not upon the quick reflex of defence performed by the lump of befuddlement. Shaking me from him, as easily as a raindrop is shaken from a cloak, he rained meaty fists upon my person, all the while shouting 'foul murder.' In barking concert, hundghs sounded alarum. Fire crystals flared, lighting darkness in many windows of nearby houses.
The drunkard screaming fit to bring the faded back to life, precious talent I used to get him off, and so did I escape, never to try that foolhardy method again.
Safe back in my abode, bruised and battered and hungrier than ever, then did I know I could not again be miserly with talent. In order to gain it, I must first spend. To this same one I called, and lacing his mind with bewilderment of a different kind, drew him helpless to me. Life force I took from him, though drained him not so complete that he faded. That threshold

I carefully kept him from. The carving away of a goodly portion of flesh from his body to tide me over coming days, trauma was the fatal cause that put him to dust. That platter did I lick clean.
With the very many following after, I was not so harsh. Nepenthe, the drug of forgetfulness, did I give for the easement of suffering and pain while slicing choice cuts for my consumption, and by this method, wasted nothing.
Depraved monster? Perhaps. Does not need push hard to do many things we had rather not? And sometime, does not desire push harder still? From this practice, I got no joy. In its usage, I did see only survival, and most determined was I to survive.

"You will not mind if I do not stay to discuss this narrative," Clara said, putting the speak-cube into its pouch. "I am feeling rather unwell."

* * *

Silvering the early yellow light, the dull grey of betwixt and between was gradually pushed up, and the shuttering darkness with it. Slanting rays of sun, crawling tentative through the window, sidled across floorboards, weakly illuminating cupboards, the table and chairs. Then wandering across the hearth, confidently climbed up the mantel, passing on to brighten an area on the rear wall of the room, and spreading out, lifting the corners from gloom, shone direct in Slubeadgh's face.

He rose slowly through the levels of consciousness, registering stiffened pain at the base of his skull and running the length of his back, which was propped against a cabinet. Pain went on to make its presence felt in hips and buttock, in legs splayed out, and arms hanging limp at his sides. Slitting bleary eyes against the light, he groaned, and dragging himself to a more comfortable position, listened to Galateo chattering soft in sleep.

Draped over his knees, his twin's cradle, and scattered around him, the remains of food scavenged from Clara Maddingley's winter store, together with earthenware pots and jars he had not opened. Selecting a bottle of half-eaten preserve, he began to eat, and barely chewing, complained of his injuries.

A dark bruise blemished tender skin that had the appearance of dense, white jelly. Small shoulders hunched, short neck sunk between them, and his over-large head resting on Slubeadgh's stomach, Galateo said, "You were not alone in sustaining injury. By the powers, I too suffer, brother."

"On the back only. Marked from head to toe, am I," he answered, throwing the empty jar away.

"Your sympathy is touching, brother."

"Sympathy? What benefit will you derive from that? Will it lessen the agony? Will sharp pangs and deep, dull aches be soothed with words? No, we must be grateful no bones are broken, even if teeth have been loosened and wobble in my mouth. Bruising, sliced cut, grazed lumpy bound tribulation has come upon us, served up with force by the peacock's boot, and must be borne with fortitude, there being no quick remedy to hand for its alleviation. It is strange, just a span ago, I thought I knew what hatred was, and now? Now I find, I knew it not at all. The width, breadth and depth of it unknown and unexplored till now."

"I like not that speech, brother," Galateo piped. Alarmed, he tried to push himself away from Slubeadgh with stumpy arms, saying, "Let us not dwell on heated feelings, lest they draw us into yet another calamitous happening, invoked by thoughts of that strutting piece of vanity. Rather, let us put our minds to our future, one, where if ever we come into this drear place again, it will be only to collect our wealth. Let us bend our minds to easier time and more pleasing event, a life of luxury and pleasure."

"Humiliation," he growled, " that pain stings more than any other."

"Who will know of it? We two only, brother, no one else."

"Semyon knows. What he has done to us, he knows. The ease, with which he did it, he knows. He knows, paralyzed with terror of him, I put up no defence. How his eyes will mock each time he glance in our direction. How his lip will curl, and sneering, humiliate us time and time again. Even with flaring nostrils, scorn he will show. Would, I had struck, while the striking was good. Would, I had rent to fine stranded ribbons his handsome face. Would, I..." Slubeadgh's voice cracked with emotion. "I am so riddled with, would I...I could weep."

"But you did not strike, brother. Why then plague yourself with regret? A better way there is that I now offer. Why not deprive him of the strange power he has over you, by removing us?"

"You think, he would notice my absence?"

"Brother, if I were to answer, yes, you would know it to be a lie. You may care if he see you gone, but it matters not."

"To me, it matters!" he shouted, and clutching his chest waited for the new pain to subside. "While you took rest, much thought has circled in my mind. More than one way there is to take the quills from a haran's neck, without hacking them off. With my wealth, all things are possible. To lord it over him, mock him, sneer with curling lip and, if I have not the courage to strike him down with my own hand, others I can find to do it for me. Yes, that is the thought circling, a most comforting and gratifying thought. So comforting it is, I am surprised I did not think of it earlier. Yet, for all its potential to succour it runs false."

"Leave well enough alone, brother. I beseech you, think not on these lines."

Forgetting his lips were split, Slubeadgh smiled and winced. Reaching for another pot of Clara Maddingley's preserve, he ripped waxed paper from the top, and with his finger poised to plunge into its sweetness said, "My mind can run on no other track. By my own hand must he be faded."

"Brother," Galateo wheedled, "you are obsessed with Semyon, the peacock, it is not good for your mental constitution."

"No, in that you are quite wrong. I am obsessed with fading him, and cannot be easy in body, or mind, till I have my way."

"So, brother, good advice you are prepared to once again dismiss. Am I right to understand, you intend to take us back?"

"I believe I shall. Debts there are that must be paid."

"You have forgot the Lady Apatia, brother? To her, you owe fealty. Sold and bought, you owe it. To relinquish fealty, how can this be done, if you return to her domain?"

"Wealth. Owning extraordinary wealth, what is there that I may not do? And never think to pull me from this course by use of silence. I remind you, the sally port lies not far, and beyond, voices there are whispering constant that make your clack redundant."

"Then take their company and counsel brother," Galateo said, waspish. "See where it fetch us up in quick time, and never verbally run to me, who has the brains, if not the legs of our separate duality, begging for intelligent assistance, if shit flying, find you."

* * *

Trooh blown. Beneath the child's coppery skin, faint specks of light glowing dim, faint specks of brightness moving sluggish over the contours of his face. Apatia's yellow eyes narrowed in disbelief, her hand suspended in mid air, the return of the pump-tube to the bedside table forgotten.

"His talent comes forth," she whispered, touching William's cheek, tracing talent's passage with trembling fingers, "in great amount does it come." Remembering the pump-tube, she put it in its place, and roughly pulling his shirt out from his breeches, laid his chest bare. "From shoulder to waist, here too, he is gifted!"

Thrilled at the sight of newly birthed talent, wanting to see if his whole body was similarly marked, but not daring to untie the cords binding him, she leapt to her feet and went rushing to the door. Wrenching it open, she shouted long and hard for Ratanakiri.

Dozing on her seat in the vestibule, Ratanakiri woke with a start. The far away voice shouting for her attendance no dream, she jumped up from her seat and hurrying through many rooms, wiped sleep from her eyes.

Standing in the doorway of her bedchamber, Apatia bawled, "You take your time, madam. Fetch me a dagger, the sharpest I possess. Be quick about it."

"A dagger? For such a thing, Lady, to the armoury I would have to go, and that is in the barracks. Who shall act as keeper of the door?"

"Play not the fool with me," Apatia stormed. "In my wardrobe rooms, there are my hunting daggers kept, as well you know."

"Begging your pardon gracious, Lady, mistress of your paint-box am I, and know not what is stored in the many rooms of your wardrobe, or where they might be found. Should I call the mistress, who having dominion over them, could surely set her hand with ease upon what you desire?"

"Fool!" Apatia pushed past her. "Deliberately," she called over her shoulder, "you set a stone in my path that I will not stumble on. Get back to the vestibule. I fetch it myself."

Curious, Ratanakiri peered into Apatia's chamber. Tempted to go in, to look behind the huge screen partitioning the room and hiding the bed, she decided against it, knowing the full brunt of her Lady's rage would fall, if she were found out. Raising her skirts, she scampered back to sit again in the vestibule to continue lonely vigil.

A room filled with sumptuous robes for state occasions and full regalia prescribed for the Lord of the Helm. A room crammed with robes for ordinary wear, bearing the hallmarks of her rank and status. A room filled with outerwear, headgear, slippers, shoes and boots. A room for the seamstress, and her assistants, to construct new designs for her clothing, with two walls shelved and full to bursting with bales of material.

Snorting frustration, Apatia rampaged through them, dragging clothes from hangers only to throw them on the floor. Boxes hauled out, the lids grappled with and finding nothing she wished to find inside, let fall. The doors of a large closet, containing her jewellery, was locked against her and no matter how furiously she beat it with clenched fists, it remained closed. Unable to find her daggers, she returned to where the seamstresses worked, and snatching a pair of scissors from one of the sewing tables, hurried back to her bedchamber.

Frightened of nicking the child with the blades, she worked carefully, cutting along the length of one sleeve of his shirt, noting with each cut, beneath smooth skin, dull sequins of talent trailed one after another in never-ending slow movement, decorated his arm and extended onto the palm of his hand.

"By the powers," she breathed, trying to still trembling fingers before attempting to cut the other sleeve away, "if adorned in like manner his whole body is, no equal will he have, save perhaps, for the Doge of the Guardians."

Unfastening his breeches, she took deep breaths to steady herself. Feeling a little calmer, snipping through the waistband, Apatia began to cut through material covering him to just below the knee, and that work completed, allowing herself no time to marvel, began to reveal glowed talent on the other leg.

* * *

Vengeful spirits haunting places where terrible things had happened. Apparitions suddenly appearing in horrifying form and tormenting whomever they came upon. Tales, based on these themes, told throughout Lessadgh and fit only to frighten children, not grown men and women, were no more than ridiculous superstition, nonsense and completely laughable, or so Clara had always thought.

No figment of imagination, the persistent clamour of sibilant voices, she could clearly hear. Not knowing if they menaced her with threatening intention of harm to the point of death: anything but laughable now. Oscillating between fear for William's safety, and perception of her own imminent peril, she cowered in a corner.

Through the remaining hours of light, her mind crawling through stories heard in Lessadgh, and once scoffed at, imagination alive and running riot, her eyes searched the room for the spectre, she was sure, would come for her when least expected. With the onset of darkness, and fear heightening, she experienced a brief flash of clarity. Disembodied voices circulating around the room and passing through it, had not shown, and were not showing, any interest in her presence. The whispers were exactly that and no more. They had no power of their own to hurt or aid her. Annoyed with herself for being so foolish, she left her refuge and began banging on the door again, shouting she was thirsty, hungry and needed to urinate. No one came. No one answered her. Pressing her ear to the door, she listened, hoping to hear someone pass by. Other than the subdued hum of whispering voices, there was silence.

Aching, stiffened joints, complaining at the hardness of the floor, woke her. Blinking at brilliant light flooding through the tall window, she uncurled and stretched out, wondering for a moment where the confusion of low voices was coming from and where she was.

William! While he suffers I slept, she thought, struggling to her feet. Plodding to the door, her fist clenched to pound on it, above the quiet intensity of rustling voices, she heard another. Pressing her ear to the wood, she listened as someone shouted, long and loud and insistent, demanding something by the sound of it, she thought. Thudding on carpet, but muffled by its thickness, heavy footsteps approaching fast drew level with the room she was locked in, and quickly went by.

The angry, imperious voice, she knew, was that of the woman holding William captive, the one running to do her bidding, she guessed, the woman who had opened the door to the spacious apartment.

"Clara," William said. She whipped round, her face alight with joy, expecting to see him. "Clara, do not look for me. I am not with you. It is my mind speaking to yours."

"William?"

"If you love me, Clara, do as I say. Apatia, the Lord of this Helm, will strike you down in a heartbeat, having no use for you now. She has much on her mind, but draw her attention to yourself, she will slay you, and I am not sure, I could prevent her yet. Clara, I cannot do without you, so please,

please, be quiet. Remain in this room, make no fuss of any kind and soon we shall be together again."

"William, does she hurt you? What is happening?"

"I am coming into my own, Clara. You will not understand what I am telling you. When you see me, you will know. Remember, be still and quiet. I will put it in the mind of the one who keeps watch at the door to bring you food and drink. When she comes, be submissive. Do not think of escape, or to rescue me. Truly, I am in no need of it. Please, will you do as I tell you?"

"This is a strange place, with many weird things I do not comprehend going on. You speak with William's voice, yet the words used have more maturity than my darling boy had. What is there to say, this mind to mind speaking, is not a trick played by the giantess to bend me to her will?"

"No trick, Clara."

"Prove it, tell me the name of my friend."

"Your greatest and best friend is, and will always be, Persimmony Clump. Even as we speak, he comes to this place. You wear the emerald ring he made you. Upon the third finger of your right hand, you wear it. If you are troubled or anxious, you twist it round twice and stroke the table of the gem. Again I ask; will you do as I have told you?"

"You are the child of my heart. For love of you, William, there is nothing I would not do."

Chapter 39.

Spessa. Translucent and opaque, the ancient walls of the Kingdom City glowed pale-orange beneath a lime-green sky, which was overcast by dense, sugar-spun clouds of pink and purple. Its ancient streets, narrow and twisting, with thread-like lanes and alleys running from them to small yards. Its public squares, and open markets, in cramped spaces, and everywhere, teeming with noisy, bustling activity.

Cutting through the medley of boisterous sounds in the roads and byways, tinkling bells striking hard and fast. Hearing glass shiver, the heaving crowd drew apart, and pressed back against the walls of tall buildings to make a path for the servants of the Blessed Lady. In silence, they waited for them to come dancing along the passage they had given access to, hoping to receive blessings liberally showered by the Mendicants without preference, or favour, upon all who gathered along the route, and in return for the Blessed Lady's largesse, give such alms as could be afforded.

They came leaping wildly, their slashed robes whisking about sinewy, dirt-grimed legs. Wide sleeves, fallen back onto knobbed shoulders, bared stick-thin arms held aloft in reverence, shown by shaking sisters. Long tassels flying on the end of pointed hoods. Skin stretched taut across skeletal faces, partly hidden by matted hair and beards starched with grease and accumulated filth. The insanity of excessive adoration shining bright from sunken eyes, the madmen whirled, stamped and jumped, shuffled and jigged, shouting all the while the Blessed Lady's blessings with hoarse voices.

Behind them, Girasole, still waiting for opportunity to take the robe and sisten, walked proud. In the rear, the rest of the recruits dragged the wheelbarrow. Nodding mute acceptance of alms given, they piled them onto its boards. Coin to one side, food to another. The Mendicants gone past, the sounds of bells receding into the distance, that portion of the crowd closed in, and business continued as usual.

All the way along the route, the same procedure repeated, until directly beneath the walls of the Helm, and the unnerving gaze of vigilant guards, the crowds thinned and the Guardians' House of Learning was reached. Going through the tall wooden gates, they came into a small garden. Grateful to rest from their labours, the recruits lowered the wheelbarrow and sat beside it on the ground. Detached from them, Girasole crouched to watch the dancers. Silent and fervent, he prayed to the Blessed Lady, if it was her will, and he sincerely hoped it was, one of them would drop and fade. Less enthusiastic than when in front of a crowd, the Mendicants pranced a slower measure on the short grass, and continued to cry out the blessings of the Blessed Lady, accompanied by the music of their sistens.

Soude, trotting a crab-ways step, left the group. Jolting along the winding path, he mounted steps leading to the portico without breaking off-kilter rhythm, and going quickly between the columns of the small colonnade, disappeared into the House, where students, milling in the high-ceilinged foyer, retreated to give him the floor, stared curiously at the raggedy, capering figure rimed with engrained dirt.

"Immediate audience I must have with the Headmaster of this House," he shouted, to no one in particular, "he has urgent need of the Blessed Lady's blessings."

"May the blessings of the Blessed Lady be upon you, friend," Soude said, offering traditional greeting to the jangle of the sisten.

Holding up his hand to signal nothing more should be said until they were alone, the Headmaster replied automatically in flat bored tones, "May the Blessed Lady make your face shine. If you would come this way."

"Friend," Soude said, the moment the door of the study was closed behind him, "information I have, which you must decide has import, or not."

"Say on," the Headmaster answered, wrinkling his nose at the sour smell coming from the Mendicant, he scowled irritation at the muted tinkle of the sisten and the soft-shoe shuffle now being trod.

"Friend," Soude said, going on to outline his meeting with Persimmony Clump. "He claimed to have been conducting trade in Lessadgh, save his clothes and clod-hoppered boots, were not of Noor's contrivance. Of clumsy manufacture, they were, thus indicating more time than admitted had been spent in that drear place of dull light. He spoke of a Faienya child, supposedly taken there for nurturing, who recently abducted, had been brought back into Noor, the place of perfect light. His purpose? To know if such a story I had heard."

"A strange tale," the Headmaster said, raising brows bristled with long hairs, and thoughtfully ran his eyes over shelves, stacked with books, behind the stinking Mendicant.

"I thought so, friend, and most worthy of your attention, else I would not have troubled you."

"Your are sure you heard him aright?"

"I am, friend."

"This person, did he say, which sally port he used to come back into Noor?"

"Friend, there was only one close by, and that Almandine's. And, there is this, he stole away in the midst of the darkling with one of the newest recruits."

"That is no loss, soon enough, others will join your group. In what direction did he go?"

"Back from whence he came, by all account, friend."

"Toward Almandine?"

Soude nodded making his sisten tinkle louder. "Further information I wish to impart friend."

Longing to get the reeking madman out of his office, the Headmaster reluctantly said, "Is that not your purpose here? Speak."

"Gossip there was in the streets of Almandine's Kingdom city. Of a child, purportedly a relation of the Lord of the Helm, and recently taken into her care, friend. Further, a few whispers concerning the Lord of that Helm have begun to circulate."

"What say the whispers?"

"She walks the Way of Atrament!"

"We must be careful of what credence is given to gossip and rumour. Ever have the Faienya loved to chatter of things they know little about, embellishing the flimsiest of tales with high-gloss for added interest."

"Friend," Soude said, coming a little closer to the desk, much to the Headmaster's dismay, "my opinion of gossip runs parallel with your own. It is a dubious sport, though many consider it a pleasant past time, and its import I ignored until meeting the one we speak of."

"Yes, I see clearly, what was only unconfirmed rumour became the sinew of coincidence. No great leap to add bone and flesh," the Headmaster said, covering his nose with his hand. "You have done duty well. Is there anything you lack that may be given for your comfort?"

"No friend, all comfort is to be found in the service of the Blessed Lady. To confound all, who go against the Lady's blessed teachings, and bring down those who set foot on the Way of Atrament is not duty, but pleasure, friend."

"I could not have put it better," the Headmaster answered, his tone dry, and rising from his chair, began to usher him out.

A legacy, left by the Mendicant, pervaded his study. Rancid stink lodged in his nostrils, clagging his tongue with vilest taste. Opening the window wide, the Headmaster of the House of Learning took a deep breath of incoming fresh air, and ran his fingers lightly over the tips of hair standing in line from forehead to the nape on his otherwise shaved head.

If true, exciting news it is, he thought, considering the information he had just been given. *Mine, it is, to determine if truth is told. To sift through the mire of gossip, and rumour, to decide if a grain of fact is secreted in fantastic fiction. Mine, it is, to filter news gathered. Mine, it is, to receive sharp rebuke for passing concocted tales, containing no substance, on to Hessonii, and wasting the Quisitors time. This is surely a tale of fantasy. My knuckles already sore, they have no need of a further sharp rap, yet the filthy zealot appeared to own lucidity. His speech clear, and seeming unimpaired by vagaries induced by exhaustion. Further thought to this, I must give, knowing madness can be the refuge of a wise fool, such as he may be.*

Pacing back and forth before the window, he assessed the mental state of the Mendicant, and the penalty that would be paid, if he decided not to pass on information that might possibly be the most important he had ever been in receipt of, should later prove to be correct. Finally, he thought about the whispers the Mendicant had heard, regarding a walker on the Way of Atrament. Noting he had offered talk of the Anathema last, he came to the conclusion the man, in full possession of all of his faculties, had laid what he had thought most important before him first, and could not deny the logic.

When all is said and done, when all consideration has been made, each aspect twisted, turned and viewed dispassionate, there is but one choice remaining to me.

Returning to his desk, he opened a drawer and took a tiny, wide-necked bottle from it. Shaking it to bring fine green powder from the bottom, he uncapped the lid and spoke into it.

"Greetings from the House at Spessa. May the Blessed Lady make your face shine, friends. Concerning information recently received, possibility there is, the child the Order has searched for these past six sparns is recently come out of Lessadgh, and likely taken to Almandine."

The brief message complete, he clapped his hand to the mouth of the bottle, and carrying it to the window, emptied its contents into the air. For a time, he stood watching particles floating on the breeze slowly come together, and gaining speed, head off in the direction of Hesonnii, and the Sacred Isle of the Guardians.

* * *

"Brother," Galateo piped, "if with our wealth, you think to buy your way onto the illustrious heights of society, would it not be better to collect it first, before travelling into Noor?"

"Hah! In that you would be correct, if it were my intent to try that tack at first outing. Another, I have devised. The peacock has tattooed my person with many hues. Cuts and splits, I bear in abundance, lumps and bumps, and all manner of strange swellings have grown upon my flesh, and weird sculpture is carved upon my body, such is Semyon's artistry. My plan is this. To the Lady, I will go. Her sympathy, I will elicit for this assault, and plead in piteous tone, no fault of mine provoked it. To such extent will her wrath rise, her tongue will lash the peacock with vitriol for such heinous usage of me, her long-time, faithful servant."

"The peacock's boot has flipped your brain within its bony pan to have such thought. Think you, the Lady Apatia has a care for your wellbeing? Think you, on the remotest outskirts of her affection, you somehow flitter, brother? Divorced from reality, you have become. Pointless to ask you to reconsider?"

"It is," Slubeadgh smirked. "You will see, this time, how I am in the right, and you in the wrong. For just a moment, think on this. In disgrace, how will it gall the peacock to see my wealth raise me high? Delightful retribution, before the fatal blow is struck, I do envisage."

"Brother, in dream are you lost."

Struggling to his feet, groaning and whimpering, he extended a foot to prod the mound of rubbish he had created while eating his way through most of Clara Maddingley's winter provisions. Moaning about excruciating pain suffered, he hobbled to the door.

"It is clear," Galateo said, "you are not in fit condition for travel. Common sense would dictate a period of rest to allow your broken body to mend a little and recuperate, brother."

"Common sense?" Wincing and grimacing, he stepped down from the porch. "That commodity is foreign to me, have you not said so a million times, yet you ask me to employ it! My broken body is what I wish the Lady Apatia to observe. To make an entrance, whole and healed, has not a smidgen of the impact it is my intention to make. For that reason will I go now."

"For a certainty, the peacock has scrambled your brain, brother. How else could logic make unexpected appearance in your reasoning? Many leagues there are to travel and the brightling well advanced."

"I know," breathing laboriously, he began to limp down to the sally port, "the distance we must journey, and what care I, in present mood, for brightling, or darkling light. All things I will bear, if it gain me my way."

"Which being dependant on the Lady Apatia, is doubtful, brother."

"Seeing my condition," he said, through a creaking groan, "knowing the hardship endured to come again to her side, how can her pity not be stirred? And say not the Lady has none."

"Brother, she has none," Galateo promptly piped. "As will you soon see."

Pausing on the threshold of Noor to listen for a moment to circling voices carried in the air, and travelling smooth between leaf and grass, Slubeadgh said, "We put both views to the test. And soon, if the powers send me strength, see who has the right of it."

"This venture sits ill with me, brother," Galateo's voice was tinged with sadness. "Whatever the outcome, whoever has the right, we shall not fare well. Instinct tells me so."

"A pox on your instinct," Slubeadgh said angry, and whimpering softly, began the long trek home.

* * *

"Friend, you can have no idea, what a relief it is not to have to push that confounded wheelbarrow," Bezel said, swinging his arms as he walked. "Times, there were, when dragging the power-blasted thing, I thought these appendages would be pulled from their sockets. Other times, there were, when pushing the power-blasted thing, I thought the long bones of them would shoot through my body and meet halfway in the midst of my chest. And times, there were..."

"Do you never give your tongue a rest?" said Clump, who had not spoken a word since leaving the Mendicants camp. "All trial and tribulation suffered since joining their group, I have listened to. The story of your life, and associated trivia surrounding it, you have most graphically told. Your relatives, numerous as daisies in a field, by name and occupation I could reel off, together with every peculiarity they would admit to owning, and some, they would rather fade than acknowledge. Your chatter is as constant and insistent as any sisten. To be blunt, my ears are near shattered by your drone."

"Friend," the exuberance in Bezel's voice crumpled into hurt, "I meant no harm. To have freedom to talk at will, on any subject I choose, being only recently reclaimed after so long in silence, I had not thought of the annoyance factor. Accept my apologies. A gag has been clapped to the offending organ."

"Total quiet was not my meaning," Clump said, sorry to have been so brusque.

"Modification? Always, I have been told I am a nattercan," Bezel said, with a disarming smile. "Shall we soon stop to eat?"

"A little bread, and cheese, I have for sharing."

"Bread and cheese?" Bezel grinned, "I do not know them. Lessadgh fare, most like. Far, far, better than that can I do." Opening his coat, revealing an enormous pair of voluminous breeches, held up and gathered in folds round his waist by a worn belt, Bezel displayed many pockets. "Here," he pointed, "in this one is sliced meat, braised in clover-minted honey, delicious. In this one, still in its container, and as yet untouched, meats and vegetables in hot-spiced jelly. Pressed curds herbed with...I am not sure which herbs, but highly recommend it. In here, wrapped in waxed flax-paper, a pie of succulent minced berries steeped in fermented juice, the pastry somewhat crumbled and soggy, though still edible. A quantity of rounds made from the crushed ears of tall-grained grasses, a little stale, but still full of good taste. Pates and pickles, candied fruits, nuts, and various sweetmeats, what is your pleasure, friend?

"Oh, and moisture, squeezed from the vine, rests in a bottle to wash our meal down. In addition, a few small coins stolen from the Blessed Lady in belief, my need being greater than hers, she would not miss them. All other comfort, I swear, I eschewed, except for the comfort of my belly."

"I journey in the company of a rascal," a rare smile turned the corners of Clump's mouth.

"I prefer," Bezel said, "a fellow of serious resource. Had I a tighter tongue, and owned talent, a Quisitor I would have aimed to be."

* * *

Ruthless, the tilted mirror showed an image of his ruined looks. Swollen flesh, pulling at the crude stitches he had sewn, was pricked with painful stiffness. The tufted threads he had cut, after drawing the knots tight, looked ridiculous, appearing to be parallel, uneven lines of coarse, sprouting hairs. Avoiding the all too evident loss of talent across the bridge of his nose, a luminous blue eye, its brilliant colour and lustre contrasted, and increased, by the dark, heavy bruising around it, and the empty socket of its companion, he focused on slicking back hair, still damp from his bath. Throwing the comb down, Semyon picked up the necktie chosen to complement the heavily embroidered waistcoat he wore, and began to arrange it in pleasing folds.

Close by, faithfully reflected on the polished surface of his dressing-stand, Apatia's dart gleamed dull and sly. The coppered-silver of urilatum barbed fletches, and wicked point, in perfect harmony with gemstones glittering shameless on the engraved barrel. Shrugging into his frock coat, he picked it up, and slid it inside his breast pocket. Prepared for shocked and curious looks as he advanced, and the speculative chatter that would follow him, he went quickly through the rooms of his apartment, and out into the broad corridor.

Ratanakiri opened the door a crack, and gasped.

"By the powers sir," she said, in concerned undertones, "how came you by such injury?"

"It is nothing. A scratch that shall be speedily removed, once I have seen the Lady," he answered.

"She sees no one."

"Me, she will see," he said, leaning into the narrow opening. "Tell the Lady, that which was lost is found. Into her hand, alone, will I put it."

"Sir," Ratanakiri whispered, "my instruction is this. To approach her not on any pretext, and to let no one, careless of status or station, come near to her either. The situation, this serious is, sir. Acting as High Lord, in the Lady's stead, the Chancellor of this Helm came again not a span ago demanding immediate access. Intimidating presence, and a sharp tongue he possesses, yet my fear of him being lesser than my fear of the Lady, in present mood, I denied him. And, he, with rising temper, told tales of unrest in the Council chamber. Of horrid rumour going rife in the streets, gossip in the leaf and bean houses, and the like, all brought to his attention and all saying one thing." Ratanakiri lowered her voice further still. "The Lady walks the Way of Atrament! Though he tried with force to enter, I barred his admittance, and was rudely cursed for my pains."

"You have told the Lady of such foul calumny?"

"Not, I, sir. To stay intact is my preference."

"She must be told. She must straightway put her foot on the neck of scurrilous tales that may without any foundation, and she, innocent of such vile charge, have in the finish detrimental effect and at worse, bring those predators, the Guardians, down upon her if this tale come to their ears."

"Then another, braver than I, must find a way to her for the telling."

"But contact you must surely have?"

"No," Ratanakiri shook her head making corkscrewed curls on her forehead fly. "No contact do I have, save to ferry the Lady's meals on a tray to the door of her bedchamber and leave it outside. Unless she bellows for my aid, sir, I see her not. As good as pinioned to this chair in the vestibule, am I, demoted from mistress of the Lady's paint-box to humble doorkeeper."

"Madness there is in this situation," Semyon said.

"Sir, upon that score, I would not argue. Madder still, each two span, by secret ways the Lady rushes out of her apartment at first light, and returns a little while later, in considerable distress. She thinks I know nothing of it. Having little to do, and fighting boredom, I found the courage to listen at her door and heard her talk with herself as to another person!"

"Of what does she speak?"

"Her mother, sir. In great fear of her long-faded mother, she is. And only this span, the Lady slipped out thinking, as always, I would not hear the panelling slide. On her return, I heard some talk of high reward."

"You know where she goes?" he asked, knowing he had seen her on one of these outings.

"That I do not."

"Tell me, Ratanakiri, the child stays in her bedchamber?"

"Him, I have not had sight of since he was first brought here and hurriedly taken there. I own no knowledge of what passes within those walls, but my believe is, nothing to the child's good."

"Fears do I have for his welfare, too. And the woman of Lessadgh, what of her?"

"Locked away. Some disagreement there was. The Lady, mad with rage, threw her into a room about to undergo refurbishment, and turned the key upon her."

"She has suffered no harm?"

"None I know of. Truth to tell, sir, I believe the Lady has forgot about her. Had I not taken food and drink to Lessadgh, thirst and hunger would have begun to bite. Sir, I must go. Curious eyes watch in passing. If tongues should wag at the length of our conversation, and the Lady discover it, a worry it is what she will do to me."

"I thank you, Ratanakiri. Frank and honest you have been, and I would not place more stress upon you than is currently applied. Fare you well, and may better days have found you when next we meet."

Chapter 40.

Lingaradgh's translucent face, flushed with triumph. Her silver eyes glittering, wild with exhilaration, locked on her scrying bowl. On the surface of the water, an image of the naked child's body glowing with talent. From head to foot, light moved effortlessly, streaming beneath his skin.

With every dosage her daughter had blown into his nostrils, Trooh had not only rocked his brain with its potency, but had started the process. It had travelled through his veins to find receptors, and stroking them patiently in passing, had drawn latent talent to waking state. Having coaxed a beginning, he had begun to shine, and with each new intake, he shone with more intensity.

"Here was risk worth the taking and vindication for so daring," she crowed, unable to drag herself away. "Here is chance for a rebirth of a sorts, and greatness of a different kind, even the Guardians shall not be able to withstand.

"Desperation forced me to the risk. The gamble, high-staked with all that was mine, the benefits shortly to be reaped by me…me, alone. Almost, is his talent ripe for harvesting, though a little more does the child have that must come forth, and his brightness rivals a fire crystal in full flame, as of old, did Atrament."

Watching Apatia prepare the last of the Trooh given to her, she nodded appreciatively on seeing the boy shiver and judder after the application.

One more batch have I smelted. This final time, with nothing has it been diluted. Its purpose express, its greater strength shall seek all elusive talent that still lingers and drag it to the fore. In two spans, just two short spans, shall I take what is his, and live a life other than this one of skulk and hide. No more bounded by these walls. No longer shall I be the power behind the Chair of Authority.

In the full light of the brightling shall I come forth, and in claiming my rightful place, none will be able to say me, nay. There will be none of such power that could even hope to chastise me, for that which I have done, or will in future do. As Atrament was in power, so shall I be, except his mistake, I shall not make. Trusting the word, or deed of none, never shall I come to such a miserable end as he made.

* * *

Striding through crowds thronging the passageways and corridors, Semyon was convinced paranoia had broken Apatia's mind. He could think of no explanation to account for her recent behaviour, other than her intellect had been shattered, and her wits were disordered. He feared she careened headlong on a road that could only lead into the arms of the Guardians, and the abyss of their damning censure.

Opening the door to his apartment, Reboia jumped to her feet and saluted.

"What do you here?" he growled.

"To enquire after your health, sir, and if arrangement has been made with the Restorer for the growth of an eye, and removal of the wound blighting your look."

"Other things, I have on my mind. I have lately come from the Lady's apartment. Denied access to her, I was told she will see no one, you have heard of this?"

"It is no secret."

"Tell me, on taking Lessadgh to the Lady, did she truly kick shut the door of her apartment in your face?"

"She did, and telling of the injury you had taken, received curt and harsh reply to the effect, little interest did she have for rigors dared in her service."

"In just a few short spans," he sighed, "she is much changed."

"You have heard of the tittle-tattle rampaging through the city?"

"I have, and like it not. She no more walks the Way of Atrament than you, or I. Chattered flow must be clamped forthwith, though if the Lady be not willing to stamp it out herself, what can be done to stem such poison?"

"Send out the guard?" Reboia suggested. "Let them be visible in all thoroughfares. None would dare talk so in their hearing."

"To do that would heighten alarm, and to false suspicion add further fuel. No, the Lady in public must appear. Unmasked, she must be, wearing none of the regalia as befits the Lord of the Helm on official duty. Before the assembled Council must she show her face, and rather than refute this stupid nonsense, gently laugh at it, for the incredible nonsense it is. For this reason, I will see her, whether she desire it, or no."

"You will use the way of intimacy?"

"Does every cur within these walls know of it?"

"They do, sir," Reboia answered, cheerful. "Arrangement with the Restorer, on your behalf, shall I organize?"

"Your care of my look is most touching."

"Such care is not for you, it is solely for the benefit of all unfortunates who must rest their gaze upon you, since it turns every stomach, sir."

"Impudent rogue, get you gone. I have business to attend to that cannot wait."

Resting in its sconce on the palm of his hand, the fire crystal flamed in the darkness, lighting tangled cobwebs, sagged with dust, hanging just above him. Small insects scuttled to hide away in crevices age had cut in crumbling stone. Touching the wall, cold dampness quickly seeped into his fingertips.

Was it ever so? Semyon wondered, going purposefully along the passageway, *or was it the allure of her scent, always filled with rampant promises that drew me in haste toward the heat of sexual pleasure and fulfilment of ambition in the process, that I failed to notice dank surrounds?*

At the sliding panel, he listened for any movement. Hearing nothing, he drew his obsidian dagger from its sheath, and struck the panel with the sharp pointed blade. Offering no resistance, thin-gauged wood peppered with holes bored by beetles, and pasted with embossed silk, splintered and cracked. Another blow, and the upper portion disintegrating, he could see clearly into the room where Apatia usually waited to receive him. Sheathing the dagger, he ripped the lower part of the panel out with his hands and stepped into the room.

Thick-piled rugs and carpets, deadening the sounds of his steps, he strode to a pair of elaborately carved doors that were closed against all comers, and without hesitation, reached for the handles.

* * *

Lessadgh pounds on the door again, Ratanakiri thought, when noise first flew into the vestibule, *but has not the strength to splinter it! Why behave so, when she knows she must remain quiet?*

Jumping up from her seat, she hurried to the arched doorway. Looking down through the series of rooms, progressing one after another, she was just in time to see Semyon stalk out of Apatia's favoured reception area and approach her bedchamber.

"No!" she wailed. He reached for the handle on one of the doors. "Blame for this..." she shrieked, as Semyon looked over his shoulder, and smiling calm reassurance, shook his head, "...breach, will be mine."

Opening the door a fraction, he shook his head again, and sliding inside, closed it quietly behind him.

Panicked, not knowing quite what could be done to salvage something from the situation; she picked up her skirts. Corkscrewed curls bouncing mad on her forehead, she raced along the opulently furnished avenue.

"Lady," Ratanakiri sobbed, bursting through the doors and into Apatia's presence, "by use of the way of intimacy did Semyon circumvent my watch."

"Ratanakiri?" Apatia snarled, from behind the screen. "Who bade you come? For this unwarranted intrusion, madam, dire distress will I visit upon you."

"Lady, show no anger toward your servant," Semyon answered.

"Semyon?" Apatia breathed, laying the pump-tube upon the table.

"No fault attaches to her," he continued. "Earlier this span, she turned me away, as was your bidding," his voice faltered, shocked by Apatia's appearance as she came from behind the divide, "and deserves not your chastisement."

Blanched beyond fragile whiteness, her paler than pale skin. Deep, dark marks of near exhaustion circled sunken eyes glittering fury from their depths, turning yellow to molten gold.

"Insolent hog, birthed in the mire of the swinery," she spat, "you dare come here un-summoned? The usage of my servant, you have the audacity to instruct me in?"

"Get you gone," he said, quietly to Ratanakiri.

"The ever pliant instrument of my will directs you well, madam. Get you gone, and labour in this manner. The key to my reception room, you will find. Lock that place up tight, to bar unlovely, audacious riff-raff from me. Show not your face to me until I call, lest I peel it from you!

"My privacy invaded," Apatia stormed, watching Ratanakiri leave in a frightened flurry of petticoats and bobbing curls, "you, sir, shall soon feel the full brunt of my anger. Depart at once."

"Lady," he said, "concern for your well fare drove me to override your wish for self-inflicted quarantine."

"My well fare?" she sneered. "What well care could you give, when all evidence of carelessness is carved into your flesh, Commander Scarface? May the powers keep me from such uncaring care."

"Understanding," Semyon said, soft, reaching for her hand, "there is between us. Does not care have a home within it?"

"Care has no place within our understanding," she slapped his hand away, "and never will. Within our understanding there has been, and always will be, allegiance owed, and duty given."

"Lady?"

"Lady?" she mimicked, knowing with calculating words, and allowing such freedom of intimacy, she had deliberately misled him. "Did thought lead you down erroneous paths, Commander?" she scoffed, slowly moving around him.

"Never tell me, you believed our liaison to be more than that of frenzied coupling? More than heated urges of the flesh meeting to do battle upon a sheeted ground? Did you dare," a vicious smile hovered at the corners of her mouth, "dream greatness hovered at your fingertips? Did you dare unleash hope, and with it roaming free, think to stand beside me was within your grasp? Sit in the Chair of Authority at my side, and share in the power it gives?

"Know this, grasping idiot. Never, would I share it. In your eye, I see ambitious hope shattered. Fool," her voice ripe with scornful enjoyment, she taunted him, "did you think to buy power I own with sexual congress?"

"For you Lady," he replied, with as much dignity as he could muster, "what other coin is there? Well known it is throughout the Helm, you bare your quim, and squatting over any rod that rises to your tune, impale yourself many times upon it." He caught Apatia's wrist before she could strike his wounded face. "More frequent than the gates of this city, Lady, do your legs open and beckon all to come inside."

"Talentless bastard."

"Lost in the service of an ungrateful harlot."

"For these insults, you will pay dear, Semyon."

"Have I not paid already? Over much, is my belief, for reward so paltry, and unremarkable. Tell me," he said, twisting her wrist and drawing her close, "what is it you want with the child?"

"No business is it of yours."

"Trollop, if you do him harm, I make it my business, and the well being of Lessadgh, too, for that matter. Do you know, in the streets rumour runs you walk the Way of Atrament?"

"Full well you know those claims are false," she cried, struggling to break his grip. "Every part of my body you have lingered over, and know, I am beggared of talent. Owning nothing of it, what benefit could there be to walk upon that Way? The velvet voice never whispered to me, never beckoned 'come', nor ever would it, for there is nothing it could want of me. Semyon, let go your grasp, you are paining me."

"I doubt that, whore, devoid of feeling you are. Full of devious spite, well-placed are you for an acolyte of the Way, which needs must have helpers."

"I swear that is not so," she said, suddenly afraid. "Upon the memory of my mother, I swear it. See the child. With your own eye, see the strangeness that has struck him, and know it could not be of my doing."

Dragging her by the wrist, Semyon marched to the screen and went behind it.

"By the powers," he muttered, glaring at her, "what goes here? Talent streams throughout him."

"I know not. Who can say what triggered talent early. The malady he sank into, proved to be the beginning of it," she explained, feeling her way through the lie. "Mayhap, it was bringing him through the sally port that instigated it. In that act, Semyon, you are as culpable as I."

"Woman, all was done at your command. For what reason is he trussed?"

"To prevent doing harm to himself. Senseless, he is, and cannot be woken, yet his body spasmodically convulses and judders."

"The Guardians have been notified?"

"Of a certainty," she lied. "Even now, I await their arrival and right glad for it, I will be," she looked at him slyly between her lashes, "to take some rest from constant nurse-maiding."

"And Lessadgh?"

"Locked safe away for assault to my person. If you doubt my word, ask Ratanakiri for the truth of it."

For a long moment, Semyon stared hard into Apatia's glistening eyes.

"Woman," he said, through gritted teeth, and twisting her arm further, made her sink to the ground to prevent it from breaking. "If I came here thinking to save you from yourself, I see now, you are not worth saving. You took the child knowing of his value. Do not refute it. In your eyes, I see untruth being conjured that in sparking writes it upon your face, even before you speak it."

"Very well," she sobbed, wincing at the pain, "since you demand it of me, I admit it, but had no means to induce the value in him, nor control him once it bloomed. Also, none there is within my court with knowledge to draw it forth, and to what purpose could I have wished it?

"To curry favour with the Guardians, did I send my creature, Slubeadgh, to find him. That was the value of the boy to me, knowing of the greater value the Order would have of him. There," she said, as he let her go. "There," she said, looking at the storm-cloud bruises on her wrist, "now you know all."

Without saying another word, he turned on his heel, went back behind the screen, walked the length of the chamber, and opening the door, he turned to say, "It can be no surprise to learn, from your service I resign forthwith, and this, if you can retrieve it, your property I return."

He threw the dart with such force it hit one of wooden struts of the screen, and the sharp point sinking in, to the girth of the barrel, stuck fast. He did not see if his aim was true, the door being closed by that time.

Chapter 41.

Vigorously sucking his teeth, Cullinan steepled his fingers and rested his chin on the tips.

"Friend, the Headmaster of the Learning House at Spessa, is he known for good judgment concerning information the Mendicants bring?"

"Opinion, only, can I offer, friend, Doge," the Headmaster Quisitor said, so carefully, none of the rolls of fat below his chin quivered.

"Say on, friend."

"He is erratic, friend, Doge. In mitigation, I would say, to know the mind of madmen such as they, one would have to suffer the same derangement. To be wary of information gathered, and proffered, is perhaps expedient, and this is the difficulty that faces all Headmasters of our Houses of Learning."

"Then to tread cautious, is best, friend, Quisitor. No move shall I make until some corroboration can be attained."

"That is the wisest course, friend, Doge," the Quisitor fawned.

"From the House of Learning at Almandine, find what gossip circulates the streets. If they have it not, straightway must they seek it out, and be expectant of punishment for their negligence. In the event this Mendicant's telling proves correct, fortuitous it would be to know into whose hands the boy has fallen."

"To that business I shall immediately attend, friend, Doge."

"Informed of all news relating to this matter must I be, friend, Quisitor. Make sure it is so, no matter how trivial."

"Naturally, friend, Doge."

Sucking his teeth ferociously, from beneath hooded lids he watched the obsequious Quisitor waddle from his office, then buried himself in thought.

For six sparns have the Guardians searched for this child, and found no trace. To hide him in Lessadgh? Yes, in that hiding there was merit, and with utmost cunning was it done, if true.

Newly sat on the seat of power, balanced upon the likeness of the Blessed Lady's thighs for scarce three starns, I now face the prospect of the ripest plum falling, without effort on my part, into my lap. An illustrious start to a very long career, that needs must be paced slow, lest I appear a bumbling idiot, unworthy of talent emphasized to great degree from head to toe, and of wearing the loincloth.

* * *

The moving bridge, Caryadgh had just walked upon, shivered. Dry, and safe, on the far bank of the Trapiche Emeral, she watched air made visible and solid, vibrate and vigorously begin to shake itself free of the making that bound it. One, by one, constructed sections disintegrated. The last first, and the first last, the blocks silently fragmented, crumbling into invisibility and dispersing back into the dark greening of the night from whence it had been summoned.

Strange to be alone, after almost three years spent in the continual company of many others. Strange to have freedom to stop and start, as and when she wished, after almost three years of days mapped out from waking to sleeping. Strangely liberating, to be away from the stifling atmosphere of the political intrigue, which was rife in the Guardians' Houses. Strangest of all...to be plucked from the rank and file, and with no training given, or attachment to the Quisitors, be assigned this mission.

Doubtless I shall be watched once I reach Almandine, she thought, putting her back to the Sacred Isle. *Every action of mine scrutinized. Long before I have a chance to give information painstakingly gathered, will it be known? Probably.*

The violent roar of the river's pounding challenge. The warm currents of air, swooping to dispute its dominance, tempered by the iciness of lashing foam, before rising cool and cyclonic from the surface to whip the jadeite walls of the Guardians House, and diving into its courtyards and outhouses, carry the river's voice across the island. All this, and much more, left behind in the darkness of night.

Further away from the Sacred Isle when the curious light of betwixt and between began to break the sombre hues of dark green depths. Further still, when the first strip of yellow light tentatively broke the deadlock, and slashed the opalescent sky with the promise of an awakening dawn.

Above, scorching the last yellowed wisps of cloud from existence, the fierce red sun fired the pale, washed out sky with a paint-board of lime green, and burned it to crystal clarity.

Below, Caryadgh jogged effortlessly through the long reaches of grassland, rattling the sap-dried, brittle stalks, whose pale-blue had been leeched by heat, her skirt gleaning empty husks of deseeded heads in the folds of the coarse material as it swept through them, and the soles of her boots dispersing precious kernels that would soon wither on parched soil, before rain brought them to life again.

With the strong smells of a land bound in dryness and meadowsweet in her nostrils, the hum of subdued voices borne on a failing breeze, the lazy drone of busy insects, and calling birds, were loud in her ears.

On the second day, distance deceived the eye. On the horizon, thunderous clouds hung so low; they appeared to be scraping the landscape. Coming nearer, but no less deceptive, cloud took on the appearance of a mountainous range struck with shifting, hazy blue. Nearer still, her eye no longer misled by distance, or the perception of phantom clouds and mountains, she saw trees, ancient and huge, that could be nothing other than the Merelanii Forest.

On the third day, her pace quickened, she kept to the wildness of Hessonii's meadows, angling towards the furthest reach of the pines, where the Rhodalian Mountains squatted.

Shadows lengthening, spread thick fingers of purpled indigo that crept to dapple grass, robbed of cyanic colour, with shades of oncoming night, and dulling the whiteness of meadowsweet, stole the perfume of its flower for a time.

During the lull, between day and night, when all sound was silenced, but for the susurration of the tangled voices of the faded, the cautious flutter of birds and bats, and the cries of nocturnal creatures, Caryadgh reached her destination. Going beneath the spreading branches of sparse trees, she found the road.

Eager to have done with journeying, she moved swiftly along its potholed length towards one of the many stone pylons raised to mark the borders of Bekily's fields and pastures.

Riding high and serene in a cloudless sky, the moon polished the silica on all four faces of the granite needle to sequinned glitter. Relieved to have come across the border, and found the pillar sooner than expected, she sat down and propped her back against it, needing to touch its refreshing coldness.

Hungry, she took the last of the meagre ration of food the Guardians had provided from her bundle. The waxed flax-paper covering unwrapped, she smoothed out crisp folds, listening to the soft crackle beneath her fingers, and paused on hearing a new sound.

Something, other than I, is abroad in the latest segments of the darkling.

Not too far away, coming from the direction she had just travelled, wheels slowly scrunched over gravel. Food forgotten, she got up and waited, listening to the unmistakable sound of long-toed claws raking the dirt track, the squeak and creak of a drawn vehicle, and the subtle tinkle of jade on a harness. Out of the darkness, its outline hazed with midnight glow, a covered wagon loomed, and nonchalantly drew alongside her.

"Late to be about, is it not?" a man's voice said quiet.

"A journey takes as long as it takes, no matter the stride of the walker," she gave answer.

"If you would have the journey shortened, climb aboard."

"Dangerous, it is, to travel a road belonging to Bekily, if no dispensation has been granted by the Lord of the Helm."

"Through the good office of acquaintance," he grinned, handing her up to sit beside him, "documents have been procured. I stand in no danger of the watch challenging, since I have but to produce them. Though, I shall not deny, some risk was attached in venturing a little way into Hessonii, but what could I do? Later than expected, I grew anxious and thought to intercept you."

"My father and mother are well?"

"Busy, as always," flicking the reins over the haran's backs, he set the wagon in motion.

"From the pathetic scraps lying in your lap, I note you were about to eat? Leave off the thought of mean-tasting provisions. A veritable feast in the back, do I have to offer. Succulent spatchcock, stewed in its own juices and finished off in piquant wild-berry sauce of my own devising, fresh breads and a leafy salad spiced with herbs.

"Did I ever tell you, having no talent to propel me into the Guardians' care, and thence into the Quisitors' department, I once thought to be a Mendicant? Loving all pleasures spread for the taking, a life spent in abstinence was not for me. In these present days, having supped over well at the table of every indulgence ever thought of, if there should come a time when I left the service of the Spymaster, I will think upon a career that runs along the lines of cuisine art. For me, there is nothing more sensuous than food and my passion for it grows..."

"Always, you talk too much, Bezel."

"True enough little, Caryadgh. To my credit, you must admit, I now gabble only to those with whom it is safe to do so. Close-mouthed am I, when not in such company, though my amiable disposition and inquisitive nature remain as ever they were. Using these tools, along with easy fellowship, I winkle out that most needed to be known for my masters. With great success," he winked, "though I say it myself, despising false modesty, do I ply my present trade. So tell me, how fared you with our, friends, the Guardians?"

Chapter 42.

Time rolled. And rolling out through myriad spans, did not overlay me with lethargic tedium, which was ever the burden of those owning the weight of longevity. No, for me, each span with activity was filled. In my scrying bowl, I kept watch on those things, the usurpers and thieves of all that was mine, did.

In the Guardians Great House, secluded from all others by the raging waters of the Trapiche Emeral, fights for power broke out. Backbiting and untimely fadings, the ebb and flow of allegiances, coupled with swift changing policies, these things I saw among the higher echelons. In the Houses of Learning, these same things, though to a lesser degree, were practiced to the detriment of students, who in jockeying for position, had not the realisation most would never find their way to the fabled island in Hessonii. Never would they partake of the enhancement offered secretly to those, who in the eyes of the Guardians had great ability, and aptitude. And upon leaving the Houses of Learning, an annual fee for a license to authorise use of their talent must be paid in perpetuity, and so no more than cash cows for the Guardians, would they be.

Of particular interest, in my quest for vengeance, were the testing booths. With utmost patience, these places did I keep closest watch upon, for were they not the means for future repayment of a long outstanding debt?

Is not every life, however great and illustrious, however mean and pitiful, a story in and of itself? And no story runs alone. Of necessity, it travels in the company of others. Sometime in parallel, sometime in tandem, sometime only briefly entwined before it break away to find new stories waiting to be touched and left, or waiting to be embraced, and stayed beside. Such a story, do I now relate, though, by no means imaginable, is it the whole. No, very far is it from being told in entirety.

After long search in the Kingdom State of Pyrope, another did I at last find bearing hallmarks of exceptional potential. Even as the urilatum wire was heated to draw through drops of life force taken from this one, was I certain of it, for this reason. Dripped into the crystalline dish, I saw it spread not outward to form a pool of tiniest scope, but held fast in the round, a perfect globule of beauteous green.

Whilst this one slept in cotted cradle, did I come in dream, and gently stroked her mind with mine own. Throughout this one's formative years, did I do this that she might accept me easily, and without thought, as did she take each breath.

Have I not told you, at the pinnacle of power with what radiance I shone? How talent's brilliance speckled me not, but garbed all of my body, from the crown of head to tip of toe, with glorious travelling light? With your own eye, Clara Maddingley, you saw how once I was greatly gifted, seeing me then as I wish to be seen, and remembered.

With this image, no nightmarish apparition to take fright at, as now am I, did I walk through the corridors of this one's subconscious in preparation of the lessons I would later teach whilst she slept. No augmentation to latent talent this process, but a laying away of knowledge for instant use once puberty was reached, and this one came into her inheritance.

A child of privilege this one was, her sire holding high office and much esteemed by the Lord of that Helm. Self-serving this one's nature, knowing little affection for any other, with these traits, was she birthed. Shown every indulgence by doting parents, spoilt and wilful she grew, and blinded by love for their offspring, no fault could they find in the evidence of their union save this, more than natural curiosity this one's interest in the Way of Atrament.

What cared I, who saw this one's casual, and often cruel usage, of the kindness surrounding her? Her character was not at issue. Talent she would come into, and profit I would get from it, uppermost in my thought. Prior to testing at the age of nine, did I tutor her in the ways I thought best. To beguile, and amuse, my intent at the first.

The marvel of illusion did I show her. To draw phantasmagorical creatures and objects forth from fanciful imagination, and creating them, give semblance of life and reality, if only for a short while, the method to achieve these wonders did I reveal. The words to use, the order and ways they must be spoken, these things I taught in dream, and in the process burned much gold from the dwindling stockpile taken so long ago from the Houses of the Disobedient Ones.

How could I know, enthralled by these sleep driven visions, so narrow was this one's compass that in the life to follow, she would not relinquish them, and would not move onto projects of greater and wider import? Such was this one's vanity, no further embellishment could aid her in the excellence of her power, was her proud belief. And in the rejection of additional knowledge offered was I, little by little, pushed away to such extent, no authority could I establish over her.

On previous occasion did I not say a making has best effect, if hung upon a willing subject? If the subject be unwilling and strongly resist? Then is any making a poor thing, and incomplete to do its work, no matter how strong it is made. In this way, were threads necessary to draw her to me in the fullness of time, plucked from my fingers, and opportunity lost.

And the Guardians? In the House of Learning, a wayward student was she, forever fermenting trouble and disruption. Haughty, open to no blandishment, or reason, other than her own, using all their cunning they could not bring her to meekness under their control, nor could all their guile draw this one into their fold. Them, she rejected, also. In that there was some comfort. No benefit, however slight and frivolous would they get

from lessons, I had taught.
You know of whom I speak.
If not Lingaradgh, once a child of Pyrope and in later life, bonded partner of the Lord of the Helm at Almandine. Who else? There is no other that is known to me.

"At last!" Malfroid said. "We come to one whose deeds are well known and documented."

"She be faded," Clump said, his eyes fixed on the wall opposite. "Long ago, did that one fade. For a certainty, she walked the Way of Atrament, and no surprise to learn the dark one walked beside her from earliest childhood."

"That was not the sense I got from it," Clara said, gentle. "Disapproval of her character, I heard in his voice..."

"Which he made no attempt to correct," Clump interrupted. "Headstrong, and full of spite she was."

"You knew her?" Clara asked.

"I heard tell of it," Clump lied, dropping his gaze from the wall to thick-fingered hands resting on his knees. "During a brief, and none too happy sojourn in Almandine, I heard tell, she queened with ruthless rule from the moment her bonded partner, the Lord of the Helm faded."

"Am I right in thinking that one faded in mysterious circumstances?"

"Am I the recorder of what went before, Malfroid?" Clump snapped. "If some history of those events you wish to know, go seek them in the archives."

"Peace, there is no need to spike me with harshness," Malfroid said, "I only hoped, if you had knowledge, and would share it, I might save a little time."

"I did not know you had come into Almandine on a prior occasion," Clara probed. "For what reason did you visit?"

"In accordance with my skill as master craftsman, a commission," Clump glowered, "the patronage, and further articles commissioned, proved not to be to my liking. By the powers, am I now under scrutiny, or do we continue to discuss what the speak-cube dispensed?"

"What need to dissect words spoken when it is plain enough," Malfroid languidly drew in long legs he had sprawled out, and sat upright in his chair. "What he wished from Lingaradgh was not a nature revised, but talent. Has he not told us on former nights, how such talent was taken?"

"Pity his scheme failed. Much sorrow and distress would never have been visited on so many had he sunk fangs into that one's neck. By all account," Clump added quickly.

Malfroid's luminous eye twinkled, as he smiled his lazy, crooked smile. Eyes downcast, Clara twisted her ring, round once, round twice, and stroked the table of the gem. Knowing they were in the act of trying to form questions to ask him, without giving offence, Clump got up and left the room.

"He knows more of Lingaradgh than he wishes to make known?"

"That is my opinion, also, Clara. Better, I think, to let him keep his secrets, unless, of course, you wish to fight him for them."

"We all have secrets, do we not? Some are best left buried never to come again into the light."

"True enough, though some have more import than others."

"To what secret do you refer?" she asked, quiet.

"I am not sure. To keep a secret close requires much effort for the keeper of it, and if the keeper fades?"

"The secret is surely lost, Malfroid?"

"No," he said, noting she fidgeted more than was usual with her emerald ring, "even if memory of it is forgot, the secret remains. It is merely hidden, lying in wait to be discovered at a future time and once again become known, for good, or ill. This is the thought recently sprung to my mind, Clara. The probes of the Guardians are a fiction. A tool of propaganda put about to prevent those tempted to set foot upon the Way of Atrament, and increase perception of their power."

"Say on," she said, when he paused. "I am curious where thought has led you and…if it matches my own."

"If the probes were potent fact, and the Guardians ever watchful for wrong doing, why could they not pierce the making that hung so thick over the old city, deceiving every eye, every sense?"

"Giving no voice to it, that has been my belief for some time, Malfroid. I am convinced, the only probes the Guardians use, are those pitiful creatures, the Mendicants, and their minions in the Houses of Learning. Where is this new thought leading us?"

"Have a little patience, I work through many stranded threads spread loose across my mind, in hope of pulling them together to weave a cloth through which truth may not soak away.

"Following devastating revelation, in the midst of confusion and chaos, did not the Guardians profess to have laid hold of the one who walked the Way of Atrament? Did not they say, immediate punishment was doled out, but refuse to name this one, saying it was Anathema, and must never be spoken? Who, then, thought to challenge these statements? Ask for evidence to be put forward? Doubt their wisdom? None. In shock for all that was lost, their words accepted by all peoples, who swallowed with no little relief, all the Guardians said. Clara," he saw her stiffen, "your boy must surely have known."

"William did not say, and I, newly come into a place full of strange wonders never thought to ask. I cared nothing at that time for what had gone before, who had done what, to whom, to what effect. All of my focus was fixed on the child of my heart. On him, and him, alone."

"I know it, but had to ask," Malfroid nodded. "In the spans that followed, did he make no mention of it?"

"No, our time," her voice shook with emotion and longing, "our time together was short, as well, you know. Every span filled with frantic works."

"Clara, having no talent, Apatia had not the means for a making. To that fact, I can fully attest. Do you think, despite the memorial garden built to honour her name, it is possible, Lingaradgh did not fade as all thought, or were led to believe? Was it she who cast illusion across the old city and maintained it? Was this the message implicit in Atrament's monologue? Did he most subtly say, with words unspoken, she lives still?"

"I heard no such message. How you come to arrive at such an unlikely conclusion is beyond my understanding."

"Then let us listen further to the speak-cube to hear what follows next."

"To let it roll without Clump to interpret, what would be the point?" she parried. "You are not well versed in the old language, Malfroid, and I can barely make out a few words here and there. Lest you have forgot, I remind you, we could not roll it back."

"Understanding comes slow to you?"

"It does," she confirmed getting to her feet. "Take Clump's advice, and get you into the archives to unearth a mystery just dreamed up. I am to my bed, and not a moment too soon."

Chapter 43.

"It is a file of considerable thickness, friend," Cullinan said, eyeing the folder with distaste.

"Very wordy, friend, Doge," the Headmaster Quisitor agreed.

"You have read it?"

"From start to finish. By way of its wordiness, I deliver it in person. Knowing of your interest in this matter, friend, Doge, and wishing to save your precious time, with permission, I thought to speak only of salient points, of which there are few. If you wish to wade through the bulk of the report later..."

"No, I thank you for consideration shown and ask you speak."

"In essence," the Quisitor cleared his throat. "In essence, friend, Doge, long and thorough investigations carried out at the site, known as the Field of Madricore, have produced nothing of note. The making, which appears to be dissipating, remains to be of an origin and manufacture completely unknown to us."

"Rubble has been excavated?" Cullinan said, steepling his fingers and resting his chin upon their tips.

"To a great depth, friend, Doge, resulting in nothing found, and two of the investigators faded in the process. This fact may be of some interest to you. Amongst many other voices of the faded, a stronger one could be heard, but since all spoke what was thought to be the old language, no sense could be made of what was said, thereby providing no clue to whom it once belonged."

"You think, we could, in safety, attribute it to Atrament Emim?"

"Friend, Doge," the Quisitor, fat-rolled chins aquiver, said, "you well know, I am cautious in the extreme upon matters I know little of, but in this instance, I would have thought it a probability, rather than possibility." Sucking his teeth, Cullinan nodded. "Why that part of the field should suddenly implode," the Quisitor continued, "the investigative team was unable to determine."

"What of Lessadgh, the Sphalerite?"

"Of her, we know no more than we did. What prompted her incursion into Spessa's territory, and if she carried something away from the site, is open to conjecture only, less she, of her own volition tell it."

"Go bid the Trapiche Emeral to reduce its waters to a trickle," Cullinan sniffed.

"Quite so friend, Doge. No more obedient to the Guardians will, is she, than the river itself, may the Blessed Lady curse her and remove her from the shelter of the Insane Child's shadow."

"It is to be hoped, the Blessed Lady hears your request and grants it."

"If, for reasons of her own, the Blessed Lady is slow to act, there is always our fresh-faced novice, friend, Doge. It may be she, with companionable speech and innocent chatter, can worm her way past loyalty that rings the Sphalerite and bring to us the knowledge we lack."

"Indeed. That is the sum total of information contained in this mountainous tome?"

"It is, friend, Doge."

"And for so scant findings," Cullinan lifted his chin from his fingers, "your department saw fit to waste so much flax-paper, not to mention time?"

"Over exuberance to produce a comprehensive, detailed account has been punished, friend, Doge."

"I am relieved to hear it. From our House of Learning in Almandine has any communication yet been received?"

"Not to my certain knowledge, friend, Doge."

"If the answer is negative, send it through normal channels. If the Mendicant's information is corroborated, in person, you will bring it to me immediately. I wish to know what the Sphalerite does, even before she does it."

"She is a treacherous rock. Right you were to name her so. Have every confidence, as you command, so shall it be done, friend, Doge."

* * *

Ratanakiri cringed when he came into the vestibule.

"What else could I have done?" she wailed.

"Only what you did," Semyon said, brusque, and wrenching the door open, slammed it so hard behind him, it rocked in its sockets, sending whiplashed echoes bounding along the length of the unusually quiet corridor. Following the crash, thumping walls and ceiling, he drummed an angry tattoo with the heels of his boots, and with raging breath, created a symphony of anger.

Past cleaners and serving maids shrinking away from fury that streamed from him, he went down to the archway giving onto one of the main byways of the Helm.

Into crowds choking the wide passageways, he marched, and down staircases thronged with massed parading and ricocheted chatter. Curious stares met him. Slowed down for a better look. Instinctively avoided his eyes. Rested in amazement on the wound disfiguring his face. Drank in the tiniest detail, to be able to accurately pass on, in delicious gossip, how ghastly the length, breadth and shape, the number of untidy stitches piercing lividly bruises on swollen flesh, the loss of an eye, and most horrendous, most important of all, the calamitous loss of talent.

"Give way," he snarled, and without waiting for the press to draw back, ploughed through them.

Anger powering him, he barged his way through frowns of disapproval, judgmental heads shaken in distaste, fans quickly set fluttering to hide open-mouthed shock, and following him, an occasional small cry of horror mingled with muttered advice, was submerged beneath the outraged shouts of those he had knocked aside.

Anger-blinded, he saw nothing, heard nothing, felt nothing but rage, burning a hole in his mind, that Apatia, with the artifice of sweet words and the enticement of her pale, pale body, had bent him to compliance and deliberately deceived him.

And I let her, he thought, arriving at the door to his apartment. *Chasing ambitious hope, did I not set out to insinuate myself deep into her affections? And believing this accomplished, believing strong emotion for me ringed her heart, I questioned nothing she said, or did. Am I not as cold as she? Into her uncaring hand did I willingly place the weapon to disembowel ambition? With unexpected relish, has she done it, humiliating me complete in the process! Played for a fool, I have been, and with lying face and cheating mouth she thinks to play me still concerning the child.*

Furious with himself, Semyon went inside to find Reboia waiting in the foyer.

"What do you do here?" he asked, sharp.

"By the look of it, sir, you received short shrift from the Lady."

"My look need not concern you. If you have no other business with me, go. Business of my own I have, to attend to."

"The Restorer, sir. The appointment is made for not long hence."

"The appointment may go hang! This embroidery do I intend to keep in all its ugly splendour. I bid you good day, Reboia."

"But sir..."

"Sir me no sirs. My commission is resigned. I am not of Almandine, and never shall be now, so get you back to the barracks."

"You leave?" she gasped.

"Have I not said so? Long before this span is done, I shall be on my way."

"This is unwelcome news," she said, following him into his bedchamber. "How came it about? Where will you go? And concern voiced for the child, what of that?"

"Him, I saw," Semyon growled.

Shrugging out of his fitted frock coat, he let it fall to the floor, while he ripped the carefully arranged folds of his cravat from his neck and tossed it onto the bed.

"You saw him?" she repeated, picking up the fancy-stitched waistcoat he had just discarded.

"Passing strange, it all is," he said, stripping off his shirt of fine woven web-silk. "For some inexplicable reason, talent comes long before its time and paints him from head to toe with moving light. Notification, so the Lady told, has been sent to the Guardians..."

"She lies. Through her teeth, the Lady lies. Receiving such news, faster than a fly on a fresh turd, would the Headmaster of the House of Learning come to the Helm to verify this happening," Reboia said, watching him rummage through clothing in wardrobes and drawers. "You know it, Semyon. And even from Hessonii would the Guardians have descended upon Almandine shortly after. No sign has yet to be seen of either."

"I well know it. For those very reasons," he pulled on a workaday shirt, his fingers deftly buttoning it, "my first task upon leaving the Helm is to go to the House of Learning. In haste, I take only that which I need. The rest of my possessions may I leave in your care, Reboia?"

"No! No, you may not. If you are for pastures new, there am I also bound."

"That is rash," he scowled, stuffing changes of clothing into a portmanteau. "A good career you are set for here. Even to Commander, if I judge right. To throw such chance away? Think again. It may be I can do you no comparable service in return for loyalty offered."

"None is asked, or looked for. Your business with the Guardians will not take overlong. Hot on your heels I shall follow, once I, too, have packed a few necessaries. Shall we meet up by the portals of the western gate?"

"By the western gate," Semyon answered, fastening the clasps of his bag, and throwing a nondescript jacket over one shoulder, "though it is my hope, good sense having taken hold, you will not be there."

"Then hope has abandoned you," she said, dogging his steps back through the apartment. "For a certainty, I will be waiting and ready to go where you lead."

Opening the door, jade clashed, its song reverberating along the length of blades barring exit.

"By the powers, what passes here?" Semyon snapped, at guards he had only recently commanded.

"On the Lady Apatia's order, you are placed under arrest, Commander."

"What is the charge?"

"High treason. In your rooms you must remain, and receiving no visitors, wait upon the Lady's pleasure. Sir," the captain of the guard's voice softened, "never has duty given cause for grief. I would it was not so, Commander, but orders are orders. I dare not go against them."

"Nor would I wish it. Duty must be done," Semyon answered. "Your comrade in arms, who stands by my side, is not so confined?"

"Not to my knowledge, sir. About her business she is free to go."

"Then stand aside," Reboia said, pushing the blades down with her hand, "so that I, too, may do duty as honour dictates."

Casually sauntering out into the corridor, she turned, red eyes flashing dangerously. "I will return," she smiled cold, "in the meantime, while you stand guard, stiff as if a poker were shoved up your arses, I bid you give thought on the value of allegiance, bought and paid for with Almandine's coin. Those wages, I think you will find, come not near loyalty earned."

* * *

"This time of the sparn, when all leaf is becoming lightly fringed, mottle-spotted with red, gold and purple, and full seeds, pregnant with promised life, have dropped from parenting host to come into their own, and a perfume, like to no other, stains the air with succulent dewberry, meadowsweet, and dry grassed smells. This time, above all other, do I love best. Does it not set your heart to singing a primal song in praise of such wonders, friend?"

Persimmony Clump grunted a reply.

"Before too long, friend, we shall see further wonders to marvel at. The crystal spires of Almandine's city, sparkling to rival the brightling orb itself. Towers, beautiful behemoths, rising tall and proud above the trees, with onion domes settled upon pearly stone. Bridges and raised walkways clinging to the faces of fine buildings, all carved with such craft it is difficult not to believe they are spun from the solidified juice of finest beet, so delicate and intricate is their design. Broad avenues and streets heaving with crowds, and quick stepping harans drawing all manner of carriages and vehicles, your head will spin to see the splendour of it all. A visit to Almandine's fabled city is not something easily forgot. You have visited that place before? Did you mention, friend, what takes you there?"

"I did not, but since you show interest..."

"Oh, I do not seek to pry. Never let it be said, Bezel, once of Rhodal and sometime world-traveller, poked his nose where it was not wanted, even if there is cause for you to think it."

"I seek a child, a boy," Clump blurted.

"If you have coin to spend, anything that takes a person's fancy is to be found in the stews of Almandine's lewd-pot quarters, friend. Each to his own, I say, but never would I have believed you owned such lecherous predilections."

"Nor do I. You mistake my meaning. On behalf of someone dear to me, I seek to find a boy, recently stolen away from her."

"From where was this child stolen, friend?"

"What concern is it of yours?"

"Moronic, I may appear, frivolous and empty-headed my friendly chit-chat, but never mistake me for a fool. My poor clothing, faded and torn, frayed and worn though it may be, and grained with all manner of filth, still has the essence of sartorial elegance of that constructed in Noor. See?" he said, pivoting slowly to display the cut and fold of a shabby coat and voluminous pants. "Whilst your attire is crude. It is drab, and ill favoured to such extent, rather would I go naked, than wear it upon my back. In short, friend, otherworldly it surely is, and what world sits cheek by jowl, almost grazing that of glorious Noor?

"No mastermind, do I need be, to know of Lessadgh's manufacture are your garments. So, do I know, for reason I shall not contemplate, you have lived in that drear place for some time. The dear friend, you casually speak of, is held most tender in your heart. The child being stolen away from Lessadgh and brought into Noor through Almandine's sally port, and you following hotfoot? Certainty says, he was of the Faienya; else he would have perished. By way of logical process of elimination, and acute observation, I have the full story. I am right, am I not? No, say nothing. A lie would sully our burgeoning friendship, but tell me, friend, did you happen to mention this strange tale of woe to Soude?"

Annoyed he was so transparent, Clump answered gruff, "Not in near so many words."

"Friend, let not Soude's madness distract you. No matter how you wove the words, that one being wily and cunning will have pieced together an outline of what has occurred, even as I have. Upon reaching the Kingdom City of Spessa, straightway would he have gone to the House of Learning and relayed this information. On this, you may depend. Collecting tittle-tattle, I discovered, during time spent with them, was the Mendicants true function along with shouting out useless blessings.

"Sharp ears do the Mendicants have to hear of those who would walk upon the Way of Atrament, whether in truth or conjecture, it is not within their remit to decide, but they pass these things quickly on to the lower order of the Guardians. This being the case, I know the exact place to begin your search.

"At the House of Learning in Almandine will we learn a little more, and if fortune ride upon our shoulders, learn his whereabouts, perhaps. Devising a way to do it, will we steal back the boy you seek!"

"We? I have no remembrance of asking for your aid."

"If ever I saw one who needed my assistance, friend," Bezel said, clapping him on the back, "it is you. Beside, I looked for adventure and have found one in the most unlikely place. Who can tell where it will lead? Look, see in the distance the twinkled radiance of the spires I spoke of?"

"I see," Clump said, lengthening his stride. "How long before we come into the city?"

"If we keep to this fast pace, stopping not to take food or drink as would be civil, before the darkling drops I estimate."

Chapter 44.

Galateo, silently sulking, kept his own counsel. His greatcoat languidly flapping with each stuttering step he took, Slubeadgh hobbled through the last stretch of grassland. Entering the shelter of trees, he sank down to rest, regretting he had not thought to carry some of Lessadgh's foul water with him to ease the dryness in his throat.

All will be made right, he kept telling himself. *The peacock now prancing in the light of the Lady's favour, brought low, I come into her grace, and with all wealth accumulated, take my rightful place in high society.*

All will be made right. All suffering endured, rewarded. Recognition and honour, given to me, at last, no longer need I lurk in the shadows. A grand house, I will have, furnished as tasteful fashion dictates, with servants to wait upon my every whim. A chef working to please my palate, will astound my guests with dishes of artistry never before experienced, and one with great knowledge of the vine will I employ as keeper of my tea. In stables of my own, high-stepping harans bred from excellent pedigree, matched for colour, shaking arched necks and rattling their quills, I will have, and carriages for all occasion to ride in.

A veritable picture of the tailor's art shall I be, sporting finest cloth sewn with invisible stitch that make my body appear most elegant, and handmade boots of exquisite workmanship upon my feet, encasing my calves. All will be made right. All suffering, rewarded. All will be made...

"Brother," Galateo's voice halted the flow of his thoughts, "Barred from the hallowed place of the mind, I know what it turns on. Have you considered, luxury could be yours without the suffering, which in the end may find no reward as expected?"

"All will be made right," he persisted.

"My hatred of the peacock matches yours, brother, yet I do not allow it to befog my brain. From a position of weakness, you attempt to scale the heights, and for this monumental climb, base all hope in the Lady's goodwill and mercy to bring the bird of bright plumage down.

"No goodwill do I remember her ever giving, nor mercy extended in our direction. Better, by far, to break fealty with her. Throw off the shackles of serfdom, and without her aid, achieve the heights first, as can easily be done. From an unassailable position, protected by our wealth, then may you do as you will with the peacock. Think on this proposal for just a while," he wheedled, determined to make a last attempt to turn his twin from the course he had chosen for them. "Think on this, if wealth buys all things, as you believe, why may you not secretly hire brigands of disrespectable repute? Imagine; the peacock snatched by these ruffians, brought in chains to the cellar of your grand house. Dungeoned up, helpless in your clutches, how may we not amuse ourselves with him?

"What suffering may we not inflict upon him in retribution, repaying hurt for hurt, insult for insult, every humiliation suffered, healed slow and sure by humiliation piled upon his arrogance, and with a little skill…make it last the longest of times? Draw out his agony till he plead with us to fade him?"

"I like it well enough," he nodded, examining bruises and cuts on his arms and legs, "save for one thing."

"One thing? I have forgot one thing, brother?"

"Indeed you have. To wait for such happiness, I am not willing. How can I build the life I desire, knowing that one has not faded, but breathes and struts still? I cannot. I will not. No longer will I allow the peacock to sour the life I now live, nor the life I will live. This feat I am resolved to accomplish, or perish in the process."

"Fair words, bravely spoken, amount to nothing more than hot air, if no action follows after, brother. And what is your resolve? A nebulous thing, comparable to a droplet of rain trembled upon a leaf that quickly evaporates beneath the heat of the brightling orb, so does your resolve in the scalding furnace, named cowardice, disappear.

"Always," he continued, as his brother rolled down his sleeves, and drew up his stockings to tuck them into his knee-breeches, "in the peacock's presence, does small courage, inexpertly nailed to the sticking place, become dislodged and fall into an abyss of fear with a resounding clang. Have you forgot the effect he has upon you?"

"I forget nothing. I cannot be swayed. Courage, I swear, will not desert me this time," Slubeadgh said, getting to his feet with difficulty, "and since no relief, nor encouragement will I get from you, upon my way do I go with all haste as I may make. No direct route do I now take to enter into the city. I refuse to parade sad circumstance for all to gawk at and snigger.

"No," he took a hesitant step and wincing with pain took another, "circuitous paths I will take. Though it be after darkling has fallen when I come to secret byways I know of, further hardship suffered will strengthen the resolve you make mock of. By use of these hidden passages, is it my intention to come to the Lady Apatia and show her what works the peacock laboured to put upon me. Then, Galateo, will you see evidence of the Lady's goodwill and mercy toward me, and just punishment meted out."

On we go to disaster then, Galateo thought, *goodwill and mercy she has none and of justice she knows little. These things you will soon discover, and delusion falling away, we may yet find a better life for the living, if you regain your senses, dunderhead.*

* * *

Fully dilated, the pupil ringed with gold flecks spreading out into the dark purple of his iris that now filled the socket of his eye, its colour clear and smouldering bright.

She let the child's eyelid fall, noting each long hair in the fringe of lashes flamed with crackling colour, and talent moving swiftly just beneath the surface of coppery skin, burnishing every particle to luminous rose-gold.

"Impossible to believe the white powder could shine you so," Apatia whispered, into his ear. "Did I not know my mother watches intent, I would try it to see what effect it summon in me. But no, she sees all, and I dare not. Three doses more there are to get from the batch given, all destined for your usage, little brat."

Six spans have I, who ever loved gaiety and company, played solitary nursemaid, she thought, placing the pump-tube back in its place at the side of the bed, *on the seventh shall I be released from onerous duty,* "And do what?" she said, aloud. "Take up the reins, unwillingly let slip from my fingers, and once more be Lord of this Helm?"

Rushing to her mirror, she asked the haggard reflection, "If all comes about as mother predicts, what role is mine? If her power match that of the Guardians, is my use to her obsolete?"

Panicked by the thought, she dug her hands into her hair and not wanting to, but knowing it was necessary, explored it further.

"Out of seclusion she will come. None will challenge her authority, or dare to say, listening to all the silken voiced seducer offers, she walks upon the Way of Atrament. By the powers, well on that Way she is, and will walk it to its end. Into the very arms of waiting Atrament she will go, if he promises her great longevity. This Kingdom," tears started in her golden eyes, and her lips trembled at the prospect awaiting her, "she will rule, not I. This do I know, for am I not always the nail upon which the hammer that is the brand of her maternal love, falls? Superfluous to her purpose, what becomes of me? What of me? Tell me what must I do?" she pleaded to her reflection.

"No foolishness upon my part dragged me to this pass. Terror plain and simple, was ever the spur that goaded. Hold," she begged her image, "hold the madness of panic back, lest fumbled thought bring me into stupidity and push me to futile rebellion, or a final renouncing of my being before due time. Alternatives? Do I have them now? The powers aid me in my distress.

"I am not bound so tight, I may not move in a direction of my own, is that not so?" Her image slowly nodded agreement. "If I am to be no jenny, driven to hard labour between the shafts of her raking plough, only to be discarded by sudden fading, a bulwark I shall need. None of equal strength there will be except the Guardians.

"Hold," she panted, "let not my mind run so fast. Give a little time to think. Never seeing the danger before, I beg leave to think how to gain protection I never thought to need from those always considered opposition."

She leaned in, touched her nose against that of her mirrored image, and ignoring its coldness, stared deep into narrowed, calculating golden eyes.

"Does she own all duplicity? To her only does it belong? No, how could it, for am I not my mother's daughter? Her nature, if not her talent, resides in me, and no whit of the character, so I have been told, of that owned by a father, scarce remembered. Can I not play both sides against the middle? If it keep me whole and in good health, I can do it, and, do it most excellent.

"Very well, here then is what I must surely do. Showing all filial respect, to her scheme I will adhere. If she fails in this venture, I lose nothing and remain as once I was, unless she fades, whereupon all manner of problems must I deal with. If she succeeds in this venture, then am I most at risk. I see it clear. But...if she threaten in the slightest part by word, or deed, or seek to take from me that which is mine, to those vultures the Guardians, I will get me hence.

"Betrayal I fight with betrayal. Playing the innocent victim right well, with many tears and much wringing of my hands, will I lay out all she has done, and behind the skirts of the Guardians robes will I hide and she never reach me. The same will I do, if she fades and the illusion cast over the city with her. Why did I not think of it before?" she said to her reflection. "Come what may, in any event, I preserve myself. My dear," she said, rising and swooping into a deep curtsey, "I thank you for wise counsel."

Drawing away from the mirror, Apatia smiled satisfaction, and tried to tame long strands of pale, pale hair, floating on soft draughts about her head and face.

* * *

"Do not let me go," William said, to the dark. "Never let me go."

"As tight as may be, I am holding you."

"It does not feel like it. Before that last invading stillness, which the gift is busy eating, I could feel your arms wrapped tight around me, but now...I hardly feel them."

"With might and main, I promise, they are still in place," the dark assured him.

"Then we are all right?"

"We are united as we should be."

"Many sights crowd my head. The gift says, they are memories, carried in my life force that Clara mistakenly called my blood. The gift says it strokes receptors, whatever they are, and from them coaxes remembrance of things gone before in times past. People whose skin glowed, tall and terrible to look upon, I have seen. They strode Lessadgh once, and regretting actions rebelliously taken, looked to find a way back to the stars, but they could not. Frustrated, and pale with great age, they finally had to accept what was written for them.

"Realising they could not cheat nothingness, they opened their arms, and gave it well come. It was they, who brought the gift, and leaving, could not take back that which had been given."

"That is strange," the dark said. "How can you know of these things?"

"I do not know, but I am the sum total of all that has gone before. Stranger still, the gift says it has made my skin shine as theirs once did. Can you believe that? How can I play hide and seek with Clara, if I glow? She would find me too easily, and there will be no fun in that."

"Perhaps, the time for play is past, William," the dark said, sad.

"I hope not, though I feel myself grown. Not in body, but in knowledge. Many words I now know in what the gift says, is the old language. Many recipes to make things happen have come into my mind and are stored away for when I wish to use them. They are all the more potent for using these ancient words. The ones who perform makings in these days use the new language, and that has been adulterated by those words bought out of Lessadgh, so they do not have nearly so much power.

"I even understand the voices now, even though they are faded. Clara would say they are dead, but the air still carries the sound of them within its breath. They say a lot and nothing. My head hurts."

"I am sorry, William, I can do nothing to ease the pain of it. Perhaps, if the gift stopped feeding, the hurt would go away."

"It will not stop. You know as well as I, the power it is being fed has slowly been of a stronger and stronger mix, so strong it is almost pure, except it lacks one vital element. The gift, already bloated, is greedy for the power it brings. It says, I should be grateful. A little pain now for great future power is more than a fair trade."

"Then we must be patient. This cannot go on for much longer. The gift must reach saturation point soon. Even though all is still and calm, you hold onto me as tight as you can, and I will cling to you. Remember, William, that is all we have to do, and we must do it, if we are to remain together."

"I know. If we lose each other, we are both lost. Are you sure you hold me tight as can be? Your grip still feels very loose. Did I say my head hurts? It hurts a lot."

* * *

Hearing the key slip the latch, Clara got up from the floor, and drawing away to the furthermost wall, waited. Ratanakiri, blue-corkscrewed curls bobbing on her forehead, poked her head round the door. Seeing Clara stood well back, she gave a friendly smile, and came into the room bearing food on a tray.

"Eadgh Lessadgh," she said, holding out the tray.

"Eat? I thank you for your kindness," she answered, and pointing to herself said, "Clara."

"Clara? Lessadgh es Clara. Eodgh Ratanakiri."

"Eodgh Ratanakiri," she repeated, and inclining her head in thanks, took the tray.

"I know, understanding of what I say is beyond you, but in hope you will know the gist of my speech, I bid you be quite and still, Clara. The Lady's mood is foul. Half mad, do I believe her to be, and if she remember you are here, I cannot say what she will do out of spite, or malice. See the mark of her hand upon my cheek," she said, showing redness splayed on one side of her face, "that was for spilling a little wine on her tray. The wall now wears the food I took her, which I must go and clean away. Later, if I can, I will come again with the darkling meal. I am sorry, but lock you in again I must. It is as much for your safety, Clara, as it is for mine."

Chapter 45.

Semyon, held under close arrest for high treason, it was natural to assume those closest to him could be under scrutiny. Conscious of this fact, out of uniform and wearing the most nondescript clothes she could find, Reboia left the barracks, where the latest gossip was circulating already.

"Ho! Reboia," one of the stable lads cried as she passed, "you were with the Commander when he was taken, were you not? What act of treason is it said he committed?"

"None I know of," she answered, gruff.

"Ho!" he shouted, "you know more than you say."

"No more than you," she shouted, over her shoulder.

Through the grounds of the Helm, and all the way down to the eastern gate, the same question asked by everyone within hailing distance, and the same reply given without stopping to chatter.

"Ho! Reboia," one of the guards on the gate called, "does the Commander stand trial presently?"

"Ho! Reboia. The handsome dog was much to your liking, was he not? Most likely, more than fence with blades you two did," the other leered making an obscene gesture. "Getting no further practice from his sword, do you go to find comfort in the lewd-pot quarters?"

"What else?" she growled, sauntering past, "a rider must needs have a mount."

Ribald laughter followed her down the ramp and out into the city. Choosing to use the busiest streets, where it would be difficult, but not impossible for one with skill to follow, she set out. Along pavements blocked with milling crowds. Across roads, jammed with traffic. Winding through markets to end up at the place where she had come in, and continuing on. At the first leaf and bean house, with tables and chairs jutting out onto the walkway, she sat down, casually gave her order and waiting for it to be brought, carefully scanned passersby through her lashes while appearing to be interested in a pamphlet her neighbour was busy reading.

In a jeweller's shop window, images reflected in the crystal panes were scrutinised. Going inside, and asking one of the assistants to remove a bracelet from the front display, she used the time taken to put the piece into her hands, to see clearly if any one noticed earlier, loitered close by. Handing it back, with a reluctant shake of her head, she stepped back out into the street and a moment later, shot down a narrow lane between two buildings.

Coming out onto a street running parallel to the one just left, she changed direction and began to zigzag her way across the city to the House of Learning situated by the western gate.

"Audacious your method of entering this House," the Headmaster blustered, as nervous fingers stroked his beard. "Outrageous to bypass protocol and bursting into the privacy of my study, demand immediate audience."

"At no little risk to myself," she growled. "On behalf of one, whom I hold in highest esteem, have I come. My purpose for such actions, you will soon realize. I ask only that you listen. I am Reboia of the Lady Apatia's Household Guard, sword-master and shortlisted for promotion into the Ceremonial Guard. Such are my credentials."

"So you say, as may any jackanapes. Present your papers," he said, hoping his new found tone of authority would be enough to send the woman away without causing trouble.

"I carry them not on me."

"Unannounced, unable to verify who you may be," his hand strayed to a bell at the far edge of his desk, "I have no leisure, nor inclination..."

"Friend, do not act in haste," she said, cold. "Do not think to summon aid, for much leisure you will have to repent you did not listen to what I had to tell, but hear me, you shall, albeit with the point of my dagger at your scrawny throat."

"Stay your hand," he cried, intimidated by her aggression and passion. "Sheathe your weapon. Dire action is not necessary. Say on."

"In the streets, rumour runs rife saying the Lady walks the Way of Atrament."

"Worthless gossip to entertain the masses," he scoffed, feeling he was on firmer ground.

"So did I also think not long ago this span. In the Helm, she is bolted in self-imposed seclusion, and with her, a child."

"That, too, I have heard. A relation, bereft of parents and in need of succour."

"No," Reboia shook her head. "No kin is he to her. No connection, however remote, do they have, and this I know for a fact. From Lessadgh, was he stolen away."

"You go too far," he spluttered.

"Not I. It is the Lady who oversteps the mark. Under her direction did I help with his abduction, and later that of the Lessadgh woman, who nurtured him from a babe. He is a child of the Faienya, owning perhaps eight sparns, who straightway on arrival at the Helm fell into a strange malady. You know of its result?"

"How could I? This so-called malady is tittle-tattle, for well you know, no illness can infect us."

"He now glows from head to toe with talent."

"What foolery do you speak?" the Headmaster exploded. Reaching for the bell to call for aid, his hand was knocked violently away.

"If truth be foolery, then yes, I speak it. Think of this, how may any, other than one of the Faienya pass through a sally port unscathed? None."

"That I accept," he said, trying to calm the situation, "though to come into talent before puberty, impossible."

"Nevertheless, talent has bloomed in great amount to such effect, the shine dappling your reverend Doge, is dull in comparison."

The Headmaster toyed with his beard for a few moments, thinking of a child the Order had searched for and had never found, and said, "You witnessed this with your own eye, friend?"

"No, but one who did is now in confinement charged with high treason, and for all I know, faded. From his mouth I heard it."

"You vouch for the truthfulness of the person you say had sight of such unseemly miracle?"

"With my life, have I not already vouched for him? The Lady told him, this House had been notified and even now, she awaited visitation from Hessonii. Ahhh…" Reboia smiled, "I see by your face…this is not so."

"You did right to come, friend. For harsh words initially spoken I beg pardon. Within the sanctuary of these walls you must stay to run no further risk to life and limb."

"I will not. Through a window in your kitchen did I come, and is the way I will go to one who has all my loyalty, and stand guard over his guards, so no harm find him, providing he lives still. If assistance you would give, give it as a hooded cloak."

"Easily done, friend, and trust the most gracious Blessed Lady, may her face shine with ever greater radiance, watches over you that no hurt finds you."

"Rather would I trust the strength of my right arm and the blade of a sword grasped in my hand," Reboia retorted. "You will notify those on the Sacred Isle?"

"At once," the Headmaster answered, "you may be sure of it. If you are correct in what you say, momentous news you have brought, friend, giving sharp-edged shape to indefinite hearsay. I thank you for it, being much in your debt."

* * *

Sandals slapping the floor, fat-padded jowls quivering, rolled chins shaking, his face screwed with the effort of fast-paced urgency, the Headmaster Quisitor waddled quickly through the corridors, impatiently waving all out of his path.

At stairs leading up to the innermost sanctum, he paused briefly to catch breath. Rasping still, he pulled up his robe, to make sure he did not trip, grasped the handrail and began to haul his bulk up the steps. Reaching the top, his lungs burning, and feeling light-headed, he tottered across the landing.

"News of great import," he panted, entering the anteroom of the hallowed sanctum, "do I bear that our friend the Doge has waited for."

His eyebrows risen in surprise, the secretary looked up from the work on his desk, and said, "Friend, no appointment is scheduled. If you will wait..."

"Idiot, this will not wait," he puffed, and made for Cullinan's spacious office as the secretary leapt up and grabbed hold of his sleeve.

"Friend, I beg you..." he began.

"I tell you now," the Quisitor spat into his face, "ill-fortune will find you, the instant the Doge hears my words, if you seek to hinder the task I now perform. Unhand me."

"On your head be it," the secretary said, "never say I did not try to help. The Doge, in commune with the Blessed Lady, will appreciate no interruption. If any are about to take a fall, I think it shall not be me."

Eyes bulging in anger from the swell of fat surrounding them, the Quisitor cuffed him away, marched across the floor and throwing the door wide, the crashing roar of the Trapiche Emeral hit him with force. He staggered beneath the blow, regained balance, and screeched at the top of his voice, "Friend, Doge, I beg your indulgence for this intrusion. I bring incredible news from the House of Learning at Almandine."

Oblivious his privacy had been breached Cullinan remained at the window, listening to the music of the river.

"Friend, Doge?" the Quisitor bellowed. Receiving no response, he rolled back out of the room. "You," he beckoned to the secretary, "get you to the Doge this instant. Break into his reverie and tell our, friend, I have that which he is most desirous of knowing."

"I dare not disturb him, friend."

"You dare not," the Quisitor fetched him a crack on the ear. "This instant will you do as I bid, or find yourself back in the rank and file of the Order in shortest time, doing the filthiest work I can devise. Now, get you to it."

Taking a handkerchief from his sleeve, he mopped his brow, and gently patted moisture from the waxed line of hair, stretching from his forehead to the nape of his neck, and blowing hard, began to pace slowly in the wake of the secretary, who scuttling ahead, had already reached the figure at the window. Rising on tiptoe, he coughed loud in his master's ear. Cullinan started.

"Forgive me, friend, Doge," the secretary yelled. "Our, friend, the Headmaster Quisitor, has urgent news that cannot wait."

His face stony, Cullinan turned from the window. "I would expect nothing less, since he dare disturb my devotions. Close the casement, friend, and leave us."

Listening to the Quisitor faithfully repeating the message received from the House of Learning at Almandine, his face did not change expression, though mounting excitement wound its way through him.

"Great possibility there is, friend, Doge, the child we have long searched for has been found," the Quisitor finished, stating the obvious.

Irritated, but feeling there was more than a peck of truth in what had been told, Cullinan measured his speech carefully, "In other circumstance, I would say, it has yet to be verified through proper channels, using correct protocol."

"You wish me to contact the Headmaster, bid him go to the Helm and demand sight of the child, friend?"

"No, I think not. By such action, warning we would give the child's whereabouts are known, and time we would hand over to spirit him away. That," he said, harsh, "cannot be allowed to happen, friend."

"What then, friend, Doge, would you have me do?"

"Summon the Nine. Bid them come to me bringing such Trooh as they hold in reserve."

"They go to Almandine, friend?"

"In my company, they shall raise many bridges to bypass all obstacles this darkling."

"You intend to leave the Sacred Isle, friend, Doge?" the Quisitor asked incredulous. "To Almandine you will go in person?"

"You evince surprise? You should not. If information received is correct, it is fitting I bring this boy, and the talent he possesses, direct under my charge. And if it is not, I must be on hand to straightway punish those who think to make the Guardians appear fools. An example made of them, who, in future time, shall think to try the same? Get you hence. Arrange all as I have said. I would be on my way so soon as the light of the brightling wanes."

"It will be as you say, friend, Doge," the Quisitor bowed and hurried away as best he might.

Revolted by the sight of mountainous buttocks, heave and jiggle beneath taut material, Cullinan maliciously called, "You, too, must prepare yourself for rapid journeying, friend."

The Quisitor halting his retreat, turned amazed, "I, friend, Doge?" he gasped.

"Naturally, friend," he said, in amiable tones. "How can punishment be meted out, if you are not with me to extract full confession from suspected wrongdoers?"

"Others there are who..."

"Are not near so exalted in skill and perception," Cullinan interrupted. "It is likely, we shall encounter no ordinary transgression of the Blessed Lady's teachings. For matters of such implied seriousness, friend, I assure you, none other than yourself will do, in this instance."

When the door closed, Cullinan went back to the window. Opening the casement, he leaned out to see the tumult far below that in some ways matched the turbulence of many possibilities blasting through his mind.

* * *

"Did I not say it was a place of exquisite beauty?" Bezel said, as they drew nearer to Almandine's city.

The fabulous design, the seeming fragility of its many buildings, rising high above a surrounding wall, could clearly be seen shimmering beneath the beginnings of a star-struck sky that heralded encroaching night rapidly chased away the diminishing colours of day.

"You did," Persimmony Clump answered, thinking it had changed very much from how he remembered it.

"Cease gawking," Bezel chivvied. "The southern gate lies not far now, but we must hurry, if we are to enter before it close for the darkling part of the span. The House of Learning is situated close by the western gate. More than enough time there will be to marvel and wonder at more marvellous and wondrous sights waiting to be seen, as we make our way there. If we are fortunate, gossip we may hear that is to our advantage, though much is stacked against us."

"How so? Gossip, as I recollect, cannot be avoided."

"No, friend, I spoke of your appearance. Do you not know what an oddity you are? Height singles you out as a Stunted One, and how many of that breed do we often see? In that, you are a rarity. Since there is no remedy for short stature, may I make a suggestion without giving offence? Take off your jacket, which from its cut and cloth will undoubtedly excite unwanted notice. Your shirt, your breeches, hideous as they are, at a pinch might be no cause for attention, but that jacket? By the powers, friend, it is atrocious."

Clump shrugged it off and cast it away.

"Better," Bezel said. "If, for some reason, guards stop us at the city gate, I urge you to say nothing. Living in Lessadgh has dulled your wits, while mine are sharper than a finely honed obsidian blade. Your tongue does not wind itself round words so well, while mine is slicker than oil drizzled over a plate of mixed leaf. Your manner, if I may be blunt and to the point, is gruff, while mine is companionable. In short, friend, leave the talking to me."

"There be nothing further you wish to comment on regarding my social skills, hereditary traits, or character?" Clump grumbled.

"I could say much that would vastly improve you, but will save it for another time. Here we are. Remember," he said, lowering his voice, "say nothing and try to smile a little, not with a grimace, but in a friendly, 'hail fellow well met' kind of way. No, no, forget the smile, just keep your face straight and we will do well enough, if the powers assist us."

* * *

In the back of the wagon Bezel stirred. Beneath the web-silk coverlet, he slowly began to wake to a melody made by wheels turning, leather harnesses creaking, jade decorations tinkling, the clacking rhythm of clawed toes striking the road in unhurried gait, the flap and slap of half-doors thrown wide, softly knocking in their stays and gently slapping against the wooden body of the wagon.

Luxuriating in that state of neither sleep, nor full consciousness, where dreams are still possible, and reality only beckons, while the surface of both is blithely skimmed, he loitered for a while before opening his eyes.

He raised his head above the cover. Caryadgh, her back to him, sat upright in the driving seat, crinkled hair standing about her head with light caught and held in a maze of myriad strands, reminiscent of a halo.

"How goes it?" he asked, his voice thick with the residue of slumber.

"Well enough," she answered, without moving to face him. "At this leisurely rate we will not pass into Spessa before the darkling falls."

"The brightling part of the span is yet to be spent?" He sat up in the makeshift bed, and reached for a flask of water. "I had thought we made better progress."

"It is almost spent. About two segments remain, if I judge it right."

"By the powers, I have been horizontal overlong. The haran's will need to be watered and fed," he yawned, "not to mention rested. Stop in the first grove we come too, where I shall attend to their needs, and when we have eaten our fill, then I will take the reins and set a quicker pace while you take rest."

"We travel through the darkling?"

"We do. Frankly comrade, you are no good companion to journey with," he said, throwing back the cover, "being so closed-mouthed, gossip goes lacking. For that reason alone, and no other, do I think it best we reach our destination as soon as possible."

Caryadgh laughed. "My report made, Bezel, if there is need for you to know gossip, as you put it, doubtless you will hear of it soon enough, but for a surety, not from me."

"Surely," he said, stretching, "there is some small, insignificant scrap you could throw to poor starving Bezel, to assuage his hunger concerning the Guardians?"

"They are bastards," she snarled.

"Pshaw, tell to me something I do not already know."

Chapter 46.

Never did I give my word lightly. Never did I dishonour it. My word given to you, Clara Maddingley, now do I honour it and come to him, whom above all else you desire to hear of.
The means by which I discovered him no different to those previously found. To come across another so soon, was hoped, but not expected. The testing booths of Andradia gave him up. Lessons from past failures had the Guardians learned. Determined not to let another of great potential slip through their fingers, they made known their intent to take the child into their care, much to the dismay of his parents. Nothing of remark were these people, who owning between them no talent, or other wealth of note.
By your own experience you know, to go against the Guardians slightest inclination is to defy them. Nevertheless, to my great relief, with courage and unaided, this is what these ones did. Refusing to give their child over, they fled. To relatives in Bekily did they go and leaving the child there, went on with the Order's minions in hot pursuit. What transpired to them thereafter, I cannot, with surety say. You may think me callous, but with gold now in short supply, to use even the smallest quantity on curiosity, I would not.
On the wavering resolve of those remaining in Bekily was my attention focused. Tussling with right and wrong, they weighed strong affection for those held dear and duty of care for the babe, against the loss of all they had worked for. If discovered, the prospect of dire punishment, even to fading, the penalty they would pay. These ones, in great fear of the Guardians, considered coming forward to confess all.
I, too, had learned. No laggard had I been in the interim between the last one of great potential, who had given herself over to vanity, and this, the new. The workings of the Guardians' minds understood, foreseeing they would seize hold of a new find, even as it was made, strategies I had sought out whereby all concerned, in such eventuality, might profit, to the exclusion of the Order.
In essence, these schemes finally arrived at were much the same, dependant of location. Each sally port still in operation did I examine, by scoping out likely candidates, who would unwittingly aid me, for if another of great potential was a blank sheet to be writ upon, determined was I that writing would be mine. The weight of spans without number crushing down upon me, and under no illusion nothingness lay in wait to receive me, a last attempt this would be.
In dream did I go to Bekily. Into their minds I lodged a solution, which betraying no trust given into their keeping, their conscience might not be

troubled ever after.
These thoughts did I cement in dream. Keeping the child hidden, in secret and by circuitous route, they would take him into Almandine, and through the sally port pass unobserved into Lessadgh, the one place the Order would never think to look. Close by, solitary in nature, a human woman of middle age as reckoned by that place. Childless, greatly feeling the lack, she would take him into her care and into her heart. To salve doubt, Bekily would not leave that place, but keep close watch until Lessadgh, by her actions, confirmed acceptance of the babe. Knowing all was well, they could return from whence they had come to resume a life only briefly left.
Then did Bekily tinker with thoughts the Way of Atrament whispered with silken voice! What could be done? To trouble them further with urgent insistence could only lead them to believe it was truly so, and surely push them into the Guardians arms. I remained silent, though it took much self-control to do so. On the verge of handing over the child, just when I believed all was lost, and prepared to meet imminent doom, did they reconsider and hasten to carry out the scheme planted in their minds.
To Lessadgh I then went. In dream, I grazed the woman's mind with that which was even then in transit to her...

"Talk not," Clump snapped, breaking off the monologue. "What of this, Clara? Never have you spoken of dreams."

"Was I to trouble you with nightmares? That is what I thought they were, and what patience would you have had for them? Beside, you were absent when they occurred, and William mine by the time you came calling again."

"What form did these nightmares take, Clara?" Malfroid asked casually.

"Never shall I forget images I thought my mind had conjured in sleep," she shuddered. Wetting her lips with the tip of her tongue, the ring on her right hand was turned round once, round twice and the table of the gem stroked. "I saw a rider, riding through the darkling at terrific speed. Hidden in the shadow of a hood, wide as a sail, no features of the rider's face could be seen. From the pommel of the saddle, hung by their hair, many severed heads. I had that terrible dream every darkling till I feared to close my eyes, but never had it again, once William came into my life."

"Strange notice to give of a momentous event coming," Malfroid said, thoughtful. "Perhaps, in the vision you saw, there was warning?"

"My thought exact," Clump nodded. "Did I not say, by accepting the child, you also accepted great risk?"

"You did. I never cared a fig for it," she said, not trying to hide tears welling in her eyes. "Atrament knew me well, did he not? I saw only a child, scarce more than a babe, abandoned," she said, wiping wetness from her cheeks. "The moment I took him down from the tree, my heart went out to him. Every day, I waited, dreading someone would come to claim him. Every day, I loved him all the more. When his little hand touched my cheek, I thought I could hear angels sing, when he smiled, he lit up the world, and filled me with happiness I had never thought to have. I loved him," she wailed. "With every fibre of my being, with all my heart I loved him, and love him still."

"Do not distress yourself so," Clump said, getting up and crouching before her. Taking her hands in his, he said, "We know of your love for him."

"How can you know," she sobbed, pulling away, "you, whose heart is closed to all affection? What can you know of pain I have suffered, and suffer even now? Loyalty, you know, I give you that, Clump, but nothing deeper."

"Does not deep affection have a place in loyalty, complete, and long given?" he asked, his face crumpled with hurt.

"You are overwrought, Clara," Malfroid said, motioning him away, "in grief you know not what you say. Come," he took her by the hand and raised her gently from the chair, "no good thing will come of further discussion, and hearing more this darkling, ill-advised."

She sagged boneless against him. Sweeping her up in his arms, he went to the door with Clump running to open it for them. In the adjoining room, her ladies looked up when he strode in. All faces were set with alarm as they jumped away from the table, upturning chairs with a crash, scattering playing cards and small coin, glasses filled with wine and plates of sweetmeats to the floor.

"By the powers what have you done to the Lady?"

"What ails the Lady?"

"Some illness of Lessadgh has struck the Lady?"

"Why does the Lady weep? Why so pale?"

"Exhaustion and great emotion has overcome your mistress," he answered, sharp to bring their twittering to a halt, "nothing more."

Silks and brocades hissing, voices whispering concern, they followed him to Clara's bedchamber, and gathered fussing round, once he had laid her on her bed, to wipe her face with cool clothes, and stroke her hands, offering comfort with touch.

"Rest will serve the Lady best. Unclothe her..."

"No," Clara cried. "I manage myself as always. I wish to be alone."

Malfroid frowned, glanced at Clump, who briefly holding his eye, frowned too.

"Very well, if that is your custom, manage as you wish, but promise me this," he said, shooing her ladies away, "a draught you will take to aid restful sleep, and so armed, hear what more has yet to be told. Promise me."

"I promise,' she sighed.

"Better yet, I will stay and see you drink it down."

"Bring me the speak-cube, and I will do as you direct," she sobbed.

"She took the draught?" Clump asked.

Malfroid nodded, saying, "Did you make enquiry of her ladies?"

"I did. From them have I obtained this assurance, with the exception of donning regalia over a shift and undergarments already worn, no assistance has Clara ever accepted," Clump said, quiet. "Always, she has clothed and unclothed herself."

"Bathing?"

"She will allow none to even stand nearby with towels and the like. In utmost privacy, behind locked doors does she carry out personal tasks. What make you of this new mystery?"

"Modesty, perhaps?"

"That is not your thought, Malfroid," Clump barked.

"No, it is not. I merely offered possibility that should not be overlooked."

"She hides yet another thing?"

"Probably, yet I shall not trouble myself over it, and advise you, Clump, to do the same. Fast are we approaching a time when all secrets will be laid bare, such is my opinion. What think you of this? Before going to my bed, I have it in mind to review Clara's schedule for next brightling."

"To what purpose?"

"If there is nothing of import, clear all engagements and listen to what comes when next Atrament speaks."

"It may be he speak to her alone."

"That is not possible. Why think you, I suggested the sleeping draught and stood over her while she drank it down to the dregs? Mixed strong enough it was to knock the friskiest haran senseless for the rest of this darkling."

Chapter 47.

In the House of Learning at Almandine, the Headmaster paced his study. Having received no response to the message he had sent some time ago, he wondered if he should send another, asking in more urgent tones what action he was required to take. Common sense said, he should go to the Helm without delay, and using authority invested in him, demand to see the boy. Caution opposed, saying, an answer would come, he must curb impatience and wait.

Late afternoon drifted into early evening, and still no word. Anxiety flowed into agitation. Pacing back and forth, alternately pulling on his beard, or stroking it, the Headmaster began to convince himself his message had gone astray. For a reason he could not fathom, he imagined it had been misdirected, or flying away, words wedged together to make the whole, had somehow become disjointed and fallen apart completely.

And now, the darkling had descended. Shot through with star-shine, darkest green, flirting with purpled blue, could not encroach into light given out by myriad fire crystals, flaming on stands upon every street, gilding buildings with indecent brightness after chasing every shadow away…and still no word from Hessonii.

Indecision tying his stomach in knots, the Headmaster concluded the time for dithering was past. If his message had not been received, he would be criticized for not sending another, and very likely punished for untimely delay. If his message had been received, what harm would a duplicate do? Urgency of the situation, and to validate information received, prompted him to take the course of action he would shortly embark on.

From the drawer in his desk, he took another wide-necked bottle. Activating green powder lying at the bottom with a vigorous shake, he spoke roughly the same words said earlier and spilled them out onto the air. He did not watch them fly, but went straight out into the hallway, telling his secretary to fetch his deputy at once, and bobbed back into his office to prepare.

"Gather a few of our, friends. Enough to comprise a delegation, friend, Deputy," the Headmaster said.

"If it is not impertinent, to what purpose, friend?"

"We go to the Helm to demand of its Lord, sight of the child said to be in her care. From a reliable source, information I have recently obtained suggests this infant has come into great talent before time. I wish to verify this report."

"Go dance with the Mendicants!" the Deputy cried, forgetting to whom he spoke. "Such occurrence is impossible. I never heard the like."

"Nevertheless, friend, investigation of this phenomenon must be carried out with all diligence, and straightway."

"Friend, taken by surprise, I spoke out of turn and in too much haste, for which I apologise most profusely. Even now, rumour races through the city..."

"I know of it, friend."

"My point is this, friend," the Deputy said. "Could it be this report, spun from circulating gossip, has been made in error?"

"No, my first thought on hearing of it matched yours exact, but it came from an unimpeachable source, one not given to fantasy, and cannot be ignored."

"With all respect, it is likely this report is made in honest error, but...but if it prove correct, should we not take the child into our custody immediately, Headmaster?"

"I shall consider that avenue, friend," he said, knowing that was precisely what he would do. "Have our delegation ready in the foyer before the hand on the face of the water clock turns another quarter."

* * *

"Pssst! This has a look of interest," Bezel said, quiet.

Crouched beside him, opposite the main gate of the House of Learning, Clump said, "What of it?"

"In such number, do the Guardians go out for a casual stroll against all custom? Do they take the air? Go to indulge in the pastime gripping all in this city? No, I really do not think that is the way of it. See how purposeful their stride?"

"Yes, I see it, and grim-faced, they are. We follow?"

"What else? But at distance, no attention do we need draw to us."

The streets were crowded. Leaf and bean houses rammed to the rafters. Hostelries doing such brisk trade, from every establishment an overflow of customers spilled out onto the pavements, and in marked contrast, restaurants and eateries all but deserted.

In the squares, entertainers played to audiences, who having far greater amusement to occupy themselves with took little notice of the shows being put on. In parks and gardens, gatherings assembled, ignored the beauty and perfume of night flowering blooms, as all attention focused on a recent event and the rushing heat of opinionated talk, expressed all manner of views on it.

Groups clustered on corners, huddled in earnest conversation, broke away like flocking birds only to find others engaged in similar occupation, and joining them in hope of hearing some new angle, some new twist to news already heard a hundred times, lingered to put their own spin on the hottest topic in an age.

Determined not to miss any titillating gossip, windows had been thrown wide in houses lining streets, squares, lanes and narrow alleyways. By this route, those unable to join the throng, remaining separate became a part of it. Children tucked up safely in bed, locked in deep dream and oblivious to the mayhem of chatter ricocheting throughout the city, while mothers leant out to garner tasty morsels, add shouted opinion, or exchanged views on dire implications, and examined all aspects of this turn of events with neighbours and friends. Similarly trapped in their homes, the aged, worn almost to transparency and too frail for the rigor of hustled bustle outside, were not excluded from the excitement.

Everywhere, from the most select areas to the poorest quarters, everyone was heavily involved in discussion, dissecting and reconstructing the latest scandalous gossip. Semyon, Commander of the High Lord of the Helm's Ceremonial Guard, arrested for high treason. Juicy gossip, based on indisputable fact, was in the process of being squeezed to the very last pip. Speculating on what the reason might be, imagination did its worse, and passed it on for general consumption.

Semyon's innocence, hotly debated, in the face of strong argument against, quickly deflated, and the case for defence briefly abandoned, flared again as suitable punishment was disputed. In the lanes and roads, streets and avenues, the inhabitants of Almandine indulged in the sport most enjoyed by all Faienya.

Seeing the Guardians advance, crowds silently parted and staring goggle-eyed while they passed, came together and began again, adding to all that had gone before, the reason why the Order was on the move. Roads clogged with more traffic than at the height of the day, came to a halt to let them pass. Some, more curious, or enterprising followed, and among them, Persimmony Clump accompanied by garrulous Bezel.

"Did I not say, better we wait by the House of Learning than fly off half-cocked at what was, at very best, gossiping rumour?" Bezel said, as they came near the Helm. "And lucky were we to hear of it, it being old hat in the light of high-treason upon the lips of all. It may be, we shall find out what is really afoot, though I have doubt we shall be made privy to it."

"Clara's boy," Clump answered. "He be in that place. I know it. My problem be how to get in and bring him home."

"Our problem, friend. Have I not thrown my lot in with yours? Look, the Guardians are admitted into the Helm."

"And the horde held back," Clump said, scowling.

"To hide in a crowd is most acceptable, but always is it a mistake to run with it, that being so often the way of mindless error. Come," Bezel tugged at his sleeve, "we will away and find our own port of entry, if the powers show us grace and favour."

* * *

Night falling, rapidly trampled any light that remained with bruised darkness and the hush, peculiar to that time of the day, was broken by rustling voices that rode upon its still calm.

Moving through the landscape with grim determination, Slubeadgh limped to a place discovered long ago. A place where he had often hidden from Lingaradgh's spiteful play when he and she, had been children. Ragged in cloth and mind, he littered the air with complaint.

"No help have you ever been to me. Always a hindrance. A burden I must bear not just with my body, that being bad enough to the point of catastrophe by any light, I have borne you always in my head. You, and your infernal chatter, have plagued me constant since we were birthed together.

"Would I had eaten you in the womb, rendered you limb from limb and consumed you whole, then I should not have had to endure your hateful presence. There, you have my truest thought, the extent of my feeling for you, Galateo. And know this, could I rid myself of you, I would do it in the blink of a haran's eye. By all the powers, do I swear, it is so. For any chance of normalcy, you held back from me. What sentence do you ever speak without naming me 'brother' as if to remind me, we two are one? It maddens me beyond distraction, and hateful it is."

Unused to the outpouring of such vitriol, but refusing to be drawn, Galateo, secure in his cradle, steadfastly said nothing.

"Make mock of me, you did, saying I could not find the wherewithal to dispatch loathsome Semyon? I spit on your mock and piss on it after. Soon will you see me have revenge on the peacock, and when it is done, out of Lessadgh will I bring my wealth, and by the powers, this first act will I perform. I will find me a Restorer, skilled enough to part us, no matter what the cost. To your fading, and my release, I pledge it."

He paused, scanning an overgrown bank, wondering if memory playing him false had brought him to the wrong spot, and turning, squinted through half-light for landmarks he was sure should have been there.

"A stump of tree, hewn by lightening there was to one side," he murmured, visualizing how it had been when he last been at the mouth of the small disused culvert, through which sewage had once flowed. "And to the other, barely a chain's length away, three saplings of slenderest girth barked in silvered white."

To his left, nothing. To his right, three massive trees with silvered trunks glowing ghostly in the darkness. Undeterred, he shuffled over to them, put his back snug against a trunk and carefully measured out the distance with hobbled step. Mewling in pain, he knelt, and ran his fingers through fragments of wood that crumbled to dust at his touch.

I scarce took account how long it has been since I was last here. Time does roll outrageous fast, and has nibbled the remembered stump down to smallest nubs of almost nothing that too, will soon be absorbed by the soil beneath. I grow maudlin. It was nought but a remnant when all is said and done.

Groaning, he creaked to his feet, measured out fifteen paces, and turned back to the bank. Straight ahead, if his calculation was correct, his childhood sanctuary, though it was now partially blocked by earth and fallen stones, and disguised by overhanging grasses mixed with wild-grown flowers. Shrugging away sentimental attachment, which briefly flooded, he applied himself to the task of clearing the means to enter the Helm undetected.

A hole, once believed to be cavernous, was now just large enough to wriggle through. Worried by thoughts the culvert might have collapsed, but comforted by thoughts he could return and rethink what needed to be done, he squeezed himself into absolute darkness inside. Stale air, threaded with the stink of ages past and rotting decay, riddled his nose with musty smells. Beneath him, cracked stones come loose from unreliable moorings of friable mortar, and damp yeasty soil broken through the gaps was covered with wither-crinked leaves. Hard carapaces, all that remained of long dead beetles, scrunched and small brittle bones were fractured with tiny, audible pops. Soft-bodied worms wriggling, and maggots feeding on decomposing corpses of small rodents, together with plump slugs and cold-housed snails slithering trails of viscous, slimy secretions.

Whimpering at aches enveloping him from shoulders to calves, he felt with his hands for the way ahead, culling all thought of what his fingers touched, what noxious things he lay upon, what unlovely juices were being crushed and absorbed into the fabric of his greatcoat and breeches.

Questing roots had punched a way through the low arch above him, housing all manner of insects in trailing, fibrous tentacles that scraped against him as he slowly made his way along the length of the culvert. How far he would have to go, he could not remember with any accuracy, only knowing as a child it had seemed a long stretch. The tips of his fingers met hard stone. Wandering upward and outward the palms of his hands confirmed a blockage.

"No! I will not have it so," he cried in anger, and edging closer, pushed hard against the obstruction.

Fresh air, he could smell it, sweet and clean after rankness breathed. Pushing hard again, he felt the stones move as they pivoted very slightly against one another. Another effort, and clearly he heard stone grinding on stone. Encouraged, by the thought a strong thrust would break through the impediment, he pulled himself closer, rested for just a moment to gather strength...and heaved.

Chapter 48.

Refusing to be hurried, Sinhaladgh, Chancellor to the High Lord of the Helm, waited for his servants to arrange the trailing cloth of his robe in artistic folds behind him. The drape finally spread to his satisfaction, he nodded, signalling he was ready to begin the long walk to the great hall. With measured step, as befitted the authority and position of his status, he went slowly out into the near deserted corridor.

While he trod the byways, there was time enough to erase creases of annoyance from his face, and compose his features into the polite indifference they usually wore. Time enough, too, to speculate, what had brought the Guardians to the Helm at such a late hour, and drag him away from good company, and a very fine meal.

Unprepared for the number of Guardians about to confront him, when he caught a glimpse of them from the far end of the corridor he perambulated in regal fashion, Sinhaladgh's equilibrium momentarily deserted him. Instinct took over and spread a diplomatic smile that was neither broad, nor slight, across his mouth and pasted his expression with confidence he did not feel. Lost poise restored and readjusted, so his manner would not be read as haughty, nor servile, he swept into the hall, and bowed in customary well come.

"Friend, Headmaster," he said, in reverential tones, "may the Blessed Lady make your face shine."

"To keep me waiting is not appreciated, friend," he replied, intentionally omitting the traditional greeting. "The Order's time is not yours to waste."

"Forgive me," Sinhaladgh said, momentarily distracted by echoes skipping round the huge empty space. "I regret it was unavoidable. Important matters of state detained me," he lied, greasing his voice with hasty repentance, "to cease discussion with visiting dignitaries at a moment's notice? Only, if I wished to cause deep offence and possibly irreparable damage, could I have hurried unceremoniously away."

"Your priorities are skewed, friend, if you think it better to keep the Guardians waiting."

"No, no, you mistook my meaning entirely, friend."

The Headmaster stiffened, "I mistake nothing. I understand it plain," he said, stern. "For your misdemeanour, penalty will be paid, friend. Now go, tell the High Lord of the Helm, I do not ask to have sight of the child currently in her care, I demand it."

"Ah..." the Chancellor's eyes rolled, and his expression suddenly nervous, he stammered, "there is a difficulty, friend."

"The boy is no longer here?"

"In truth, I know not. Nor have I seen the Lady this many a span. Ensconced in solitude she is, and bids none disturb her."

"Ensconced in solitude," the Headmaster spluttered, "I care not if she is marooned permanent in it. She will appear. She will give me sight of the child."

"Yes, yes, I see it must be so," obsequious, Sinhaladgh bowed and scraped, wringing his hands together, "though it places me in uncertain situation. Between two furies I stand, friend."

"Be assured, in a situation owning as little pleasure as I can contrive, friend, will you find yourself before very long."

"Very well, the full brunt of the Lady's wrath I must brave by doing the Guardians will, which may take a little time, since no one will she see. Refreshment may I offer in the interim, friend?"

"You may not. Now get you gone this instant."

* * *

Trembled by exertion, Slubeadgh hauled himself over scattered chunks of stone and rubble, and crawled clear of the derelict culvert. Lying in the long fringe of grass, edging manicured lawns, he sucked in great quantities of clean air.

"You see?" he gasped. "Without your aid, I overcome obstacles? Silence meant to punish, has only highlighted I need no advice to offer an obvious solution to a problem faced. Already, do I begin to throw off the shackles with which you have bound me, brother, and begin to find freedom. Soon, will the rightness in this venture become evident, and your wrongness of opposition, exposed."

Laughing soft, he sat up and scanned the greening dark to make sure he was where he expected to be. A copse of ancient trees to his left, with the garden built to honour the memory of the Lady Apatia's mother at its centre. Curving round and away across velvet-textured grass, the Helm's towers glimmered ferociously in the cool shine, shed by the light of the moon, which sparkled the rise and fall of its walls.

Confident, he got to his feet, and flitting from shadow to shadow, aligned himself to the secret entry that would give access to the network of hidden passages running between many rooms. Arrived at the point where cunning was needed, he paused, and cautiously peered this way and that to assure himself no one lingered in this part of the gardens. Then forgetting all burrowing aches, all deep-seated pains, he sped swiftly over the stretch of open ground.

Beneath an arched window, he crouched, his fingers searching for an innocuous piece of stone set into a slab at the base of the wall, which pressed rapidly four times, would open the concealed door.

* * *

Lounging nonchalantly against the wall, Bezel looked down into Clump's upturned face.

"Unusually quiet for a lewd-pot quarter," he observed. "High treason, the desire to know of the latest twists and turns, gossip has all but emptied the place to our advantage. Even were it heaving, inebriated on a drug of choice to the point of collapse, or overcome with rampant lust, and trust me, friend, all in this place suffer such afflictions, no one has care for what another is about. That being so, I would submit, here is as good a place as any."

"You have an idea what part of the Helm's grounds lie behind this wall?"

"Friend," Bezel grinned. "Lewd-pot quarters never are situated in salubrious locations. My nose, pricked by a whiff of fragrant saxifrage and pungent haran dung, says the stables are not far hence. That, too, is to our advantage. At this time of the span, save for the beasts, they will be unattended."

"It be a very high wall," Clump answered. "If we are caught, you know our fate? I do not ask you to accompany me. I ask only that you allow me to climb upon your shoulders."

"Your personal ladder, I am to be? Even by lending you my height, it is doubtful the top is within your reach. But try, if you must." Squatting, he said, "Straddle my shoulders. When I am risen, using the closeness of the wall to aid and check balance, get to your feet."

"I fall short," Clump groaned. "On wobbled tip-toe, the pinnacle is still beyond my grasp."

"By much?"

"A fair few cubits."

"Then put a spring in your haunches. If by chance you fall, I promise nothing, but will do my best to break it."

Settling his feet firmly on Bezel's shoulders, Persimmony Clump bent his knees. Poised for the leap, he pushed away, and in the same instant, leaping, his fingers found the top edge of the wall. His feet scrabbling for purchase, he pulled himself up. Grunting, he managed to get one elbow onto its broadness, then the other and hauling himself to the summit, sat awkwardly astride.

"You have my thanks," he said, looking down into Bezel's face.

"Give thanks when the task is done." Backing away, with a running bound, he scaled the wall to join him. "To remain seated within the sight of any who care to look is error, friend." Dropping to the ground, he pulled Clump with him. "One obstacle cleared and many more yet to go, friend," he grinned, "though we smell not so sweet as a moment before. That said, it was a soft landing, no?"

"Not one I would have chosen," Clump replied. "From crown to heel, I be covered in haran shit."

"Friend, we must hope that is the sum of our troubles."

* * *

"You – will - open - this - door," Sinhaladgh thundered.

"Great sir, with all respect, you know I cannot," Ratanakiri called. "I dare not go against the Lady's wishes."

"A wish of a different kind, the Lady shall have before long. Circumstance dictates you open this door and give immediate access."

"Circumstance? What circumstance can have more import than the wish of the Lady?"

"Am I reduced to this," he fumed, "parleying through a plank of wood with you, who are no more than a paint-box whore? A nonentity?"

"Entrusted by the Lady to perform a task, I do it, and thank you not to impeach my reputation with unfounded accusation and foul word," she answered, with spirit. "It is not my intention to incite you to rage, sir. For the stubborn position I am forced to take against you, I ask pardon. If...if, you were to tell what circumstance brings you to this pass, I could, perhaps, take a message to the Lady?"

"For insulting speech, I offer sincere apology," he changed tack by replacing harsh anger with softer tones. "The demands of the Guardians take precedence over all, is that not so?"

"They do," Ratanakiri agreed.

"Then for the love of all the powers, girl, get you to the Lady. If she give no audience face to face, I beg you, bid her come to this door at very least. News I have, which she must hear from my own mouth and no other's."

"Sir, I cannot bid the Lady go here, or there. For such impudence, I would be punished severe."

"And the Guardians extract penalty from all, if you do not! Listen, girl, you must do as I say. You must. The will of the Guardians denied, if not directly opposed, is to place the future security of the Helm in peril. The Lady being foremost, upon her will the hammer of their displeasure first fall. Be brave, girl. Cast aside all thought of risk to your person, and tell the Lady what I have said exact, so she may know what seriousness has brought me to her door at this untimely part of the span. Tell her this also. In force of number do the Guardians, represented by the Headmaster of the House of Learning, wait on her presence in the great hall."

"Guardians in the great hall?" she screeched.

"Take a grip on panic, push it down, keep a clear head and do as I say, girl, please."

"I will, sir," she answered, curtseying out of habit to the Chancellor behind the door. "I go now with all haste."

"Lady," Ratanakiri rapped tentatively on the door to Apatia's bedchamber. "Lady, can you hear me?" She knocked again, harder and more persistent. "Lady, if you sleep, I beg you awake. A matter of the greatest urgency has arisen." Banging on the door now, she said, "Lady, you must hear me."

"Must?" she heard Apatia bark. "You dare tell me, must?"

"Lady, I meant no offence," she babbled. "Guardians, in force of number, await your presence in the great hall. In the corridor, the Lord Chancellor hops and fumes, since I, adhering to your command, admit him not, and bade me bring this message to you, speaking of peril imposed. Of penalty extracted by the Order, if their will is denied, or opposed."

"Guardians wait in my great hall?"

"So the Lord Chancellor bade me tell you. He asks for audience. Failing that, to speak with him through the door. News he has that must be told by his mouth alone."

Apatia's mind, whirling through possibilities, sorting and discarding, arrived at the only possible answer.

By the powers, the vultures know of the child! How? How? When none have set eyes upon him, save myself ... and...Semyon! Scar-faced Semyon has betrayed me! No, no, he could not, almost immediately upon leaving me was he placed under arrest, to ward against such event...another has done this? By the powers, Scarface sent another in his place to inform the Guardians. He sent another to do what he could not. That one must be found. Found and with direst method known punished alongside...

"Lady?" Ratanakiri's voice, plaintive and apologetic, broke her train of thought. "What must I do? Once again, I hear the Lord Chancellor frantically pound upon the door."

"Tell Sinhaladgh," Apatia said, choosing her words carefully, "tell him, I am well aware of what business the Guardians have here. To any wish, or demand, I willingly accede, but first make myself presentable for public view. On my behalf, this is what he must say, and beg the Guardians to grant this small indulgence with patience."

Chapter 49.

Starved of light, a fire crystal just inside the doorway, licked hungrily at moonshine spilling into the passage when Slubeadgh entered. Cursing its feebleness, he picked it up, placed it onto his upturned palm, and ignoring pathways yawning at either side, began to tread a way that was well known to him.

At intervals he deviated from the sloping passage, and padded along level stretches, occasionally stopping to listen to what went on in rooms behind various thin panels. Hearing nothing of note, he resumed his chosen path until the trajectory changed from a gentle incline to a steep slant, where his mind, keeping pace with the gradient, rolled smoothly from one grandiose scenario to another. He imagined every possible way he could tell the tale, choosing words he would use to best effect, and quietly tried them out, only to find swollen bruises and minor cuts hampered the facial expressions he would have liked to make. This, he finally decided, was to his advantage. Being in obvious pain, he would appear even more pitiful. Every now and then, he paused to work out how his body should move to exaggerate his injuries, and wondered if he should feign broken bones.

Next, he briefly considered his manner, though he had no need to give that much thought. He would be respectful, as always, though he needed to show himself beaten, but unbowed in her service, emphasizing to do her will was his only pleasure, if he could somehow inject some sense of it without actually saying so.

And what of Apatia? Throughout the telling, tears will glint in golden eyes, and her face, at first shaded by deepest sorrow, will shortly drift into an expression of outrage and utmost horror? Yes, yes, that is how it shall be on learning of the abuse her faithful servant has suffered, by the courteous use of the peacock's hand and boot. In her fury, she will be swift to act, and retribution deal out. Hopefully, she will fade him.

Nearing Apatia's apartment, doubt began to niggle.

"Is it possible, my importance to the Lady has been overblown?" he whispered, to voices of the faded rustling in the dark. "No, her eyes and ears I am. The facilitator of many schemes made reality, without me, she cannot do."

Laughter, not high and piping, but low and derogatory sounded in his head.

"Hush your clack, else I rip off the harness I bear you in, and with my own hand, strangle all life from you, Galateo. By all the powers, I swear, such will I do if you mock me further."

Buoyed by his brother's sudden silence, he went more quickly. The nearer he came to the panel that would give him the means of approaching

Apatia; he began to fret. Access was only assured if she was in the room.

Where else would she be, when she spends much time in it? Or, hearing me knock, one of her servants will alert her...Semyon wishes to see her? True, she may be angry at first, but... Noticing light, softly brushing the walls about him, put the fire crystal he carried to shame, anxiety gripped him. *What if Semyon travels the byway?*

He moved back into the security of darkness, and listened for any hint of a footstep for long moments. *Glue courage in place. Use the hammer of will to bed it in so tight it will not fail you,* he encouraged himself, and more cautious than ever, edging back into the first flush of brightness, went slow and silent into the stronger brilliance flooding the passage.

Arrived at the panel, to his surprise, he found the way open. The flimsy wood, which should have barred him from the chamber, was smashed to smithereens. Great splinters lay scattered across the floor and fragments, no better than kindling, still clinging to frayed silk, hung from the frame that had held all in place. Suspicious, he nervously peered past the destruction.

What goes? No one. I see no one, and no answer for violence done do I perceive. What of my intent? Firmer than before, since no danger threatens!

He stepped over the detritus, and hurrying to the door, turned the handle to find it locked fast.

Ratanakiri swivelled on her chair, poked her head round the corner of the wall, and leaned further out. Unable to determine what caused the rattling sounds she could hear, she got up and walked slowly through the series of rooms.

Outside the chamber Clara was locked in, she halted for a moment then, grateful the woman did nothing to draw the Lady's attention, passed on, following the persistent noise and frustrated banging now accompanying it.

"My life is spent talking to doors," she sighed, watching the handles to Apatia's favourite reception salon ratchet back and forth. "Who goes there?"

"It is I, Slubeadgh, the Lady's most faithful servant. Unlock the door. From Lessadgh, am I recently returned, and must see the Lady at once. Unlock the door this instant."

"Be gone, you vile creature. Far behind the times you are, believing any news you might seek to tell could, in any way, outdo that told barely moments ago."

"What news?"

"You have not heard of it? Go find it for yourself, master skulker, for I have no patience for the likes of you. Get you gone, and bad cess go with you."

"Bitch," he shrieked. "Open this door, else the Lady will hear of your treatment of me."

"Go douse your head in boiling oil," Ratanakiri replied, and walked purposefully back to her seat in the vestibule.

* * *

The Nine on the terrace, their arms uplifted in supplication, draped sleeves, skirted robes, sashes and hoods all whipped to a frenzy by conflicting winds. Every face rapt with concentration, every mouth moving in unison, pulling vowels to utmost exquisite thinness, and brutally snapping consonants to a click of shortest length. With the rhythmic words of a making, they forced air to their will, compressing its unruly, transparent weightlessness to stable solidity before fusing it to uniform blocks. Each one made to fit in perfect harmony next to its fellow, and locked into place until an outline of a simple shape glimmered in the dark green sky.

At last, the bridge of air raised, stretching high above the unrelenting roar of the Trapiche Emeral's savage waters, and far beyond the river's treacherous banks, the Nine left off their making, and sang another to coax, and hold in place, all they had erected in perfect suspension. Braced against the wildness of the night, Cullinan settled the strap of the satchel, containing a huge amount of purest Trooh, across his naked chest. With a brief smile at the Headmaster Quisitor's scowling resignation, he marched forward. Putting his foot to the bridge, he mounted, and without a backward look at the formation the Nine and the Master Quisitor had fallen into behind him, set off at a punishing pace.

* * *

Leisurely going from willodgh to willodgh, parting the fronds to have a jeering conversation with enemies trapped and rotting in heartwood, she walked in her garden, delighting in the most pleasurable activity of the day.

Arrowing through the heights, a message bubble nearing the crystal spire of the summerhouse, decreased speed, and circled the panes searching for its recipient. Sensing she was not there, it dropped to skim the tops of the trees, and following the pathways found Lingaradgh. Speeding, the bubble collided with her forehead and popped.

"Mother," Apatia, the tremble in her voice unmistakable, spoke rapidly, "Fear shakes me. Guardians wait upon my presence in the great hall of the Helm. What purpose can they have to come unannounced in the darkling? What can it be, unless they have knowledge of the child, and are come to claim him? Mother, tell me, what must I do? What must I do?"

The message received with the force of a blow, breath was knocked from her. Staggering, mind-numbed and faint, instinctively crouching to prevent herself from falling completely, Lingaradgh waited for shock's impact to pass. Swallowing nausea, she pressed it down and away. Her mind, suddenly reactivated, reeled to the possibility one of the Guardians' probes had somehow pierced defences she had put in place. *No, not by that route. All are meticulously maintained. Had any one of them been breached, I would know it. By some other means, unknown to me, they found it out.*

"To have come so far," she moaned, despairing. "The goal so near reached, is snatched from me. For the want of just one more span's grace, I lose all. I lose all? No! To be defeated by the space of a span? Am I so weak of spine, so lily-livered, I submit to the will of those vultures and go down into the dust without a fight? Never!"

Silver eyes flashing with controlled anger and determination, she rose unsteadily to her feet, and cried, "Lingaradgh of Almandine, am I, destroyer of all who opposed me. Not so easily can I be undone."

Picking up her skirts, she went quickly to the summerhouse, climbed the stairs and breathing heavily, selected a small flax-paper envelope from her supply. Prising one end open with her nail, she emptied the tiny, pearlescent sphere onto the palm of her hand.

"Daughter," she said, putting her mouth close to it, "if we are not to fall at the last hurdle, you must remain calm. Give the child all of the Trooh remaining in your possession at once. By the secret way, you know of bring him to me."

Swollen by her words, the bubble hovered uncertainly, waiting for a designation to be told. Taking it to one of the windows, she opened it and spoke, then watched subtle rainbow colours racing away become lost in the greening dark, shot with purple and grey.

* * *

"What now?" Bezel asked.

"What now, indeed," Clump said. "The city is much changed since last I was here, and the appearance of the Helm with it. Assuming the layout remains the same, I cannot say what distance separates us from where we wish to be, nor where we are. This part of the grounds I never came into. Never had cause to. "

Bezel's eyebrows raised in mute surprise. "Before this darkling you have been inside the Helm, friend?"

"Cease calling me, friend. It be irritating."

"A habit grown, frie...must be un-grown, and cannot be done at a moment's notice. You have been here before?"

"It is a long story. One, I care not to revisit."

"By the powers," Bezel swore, "this adventure exceeds all expectation. We have no plan. Between us, no idea exists on how we may gain entry to the innards of the Helm, and no clue where the child you seek is held, friend. My apologies for the irritating slip of which, I am sure there will be many. The walls of the Helm can at least be seen. What avenue can we take, other than flit from place to place in hope we bumble upon some part of the grounds you are familiar with, when at such time, we take stock?"

"The wall is behind you," Clump growled. "Take yourself back over it, friend, if this adventure be too adventurous for you."

"Did I say that? I did not, and to leave a, frie...comrade in time of need would not sit well."

"Now we are comrades?"

"Of briefest acquaintance, perhaps," Bezel shrugged, "but what difference should that make, when we are united in a common task? To the business at hand. First, so that we flit not to different locations, which would be the stuff of farce, in which direction do you believe it best to go?"

"Obviously, toward the Helm, to find an entry where we may slip in."

"By the powers, optimism must reign supreme in your head. Stinking as we do, comrade, never shall we go unobserved in closed spaces."

* * *

"Runted bitch of a sway-backed hundgh. Daughter of a rancid whore, come back. Unlock this door, slattern," Slubeadgh railed, at retreating steps thumped smug across the carpets outside. Slumping against the elaborately carved wood, he waited, anticipating any moment his brother would snigger derision at the very least, and at worst crow, 'did I not say this would be the way of it? Admit you were wrong and I, as always, in the right.'

"I am not wrong yet," he replied, to a remark Galateo had not made. "There is work still to be carried out before I am proved to be wrong. Before I go to it, I will find what news that little doxy spoke of."

Limping to the gaping entry of the passageway, he retrieved the fire crystal he had dropped. Relieved to see it had sucked in light, and shone more brightly than earlier, he went back the way he had come and down to the level where Apatia's ladies were housed when not in attendance.

In the wall of each room, various tiny holes had been bored through wood and silk, which from time to time, he had spied through for gratification, or to hear gossip that might otherwise have escaped him. Stepping quietly to the first room, he listened, and hearing nothing, peeked through the spy-hole. It was empty. He moved on to the next, and found that empty, too. And the one after it. Approaching the fourth, he could hear voices rising and falling in babbled excitement. Within a few moments, he had news that put a smile on his battered face, and set off with a very definite destination in mind.

Chapter 50.

Sweat-slicked from head to heel, his robe wetly clinging to his fat-rolled bulk, and his sandals threatening to slither from his feet at each step, the Headmaster Quisitor, wiping salt-water from his eyes, stumbled from the bridge of air and collapsed, panting with exertion, to the ground.

Behind him, the last block of air made solid, shimmered and dissolved into fluid transparency. In front of him, the Nine were gathered closely around Cullinan. Now the Trapiche Emeral's winds had been left far behind, he took a long-handled spoon from the waistband of his loincloth. Dipping it into the satchel slung across his naked chest, he scooped Trooh from it, levelled the rounded heap, scraping the excess back into the bag, and offered it first to the most senior of the Nine, who knelt to eagerly snort the stimulant into her nostrils.

Again the long-handled spoon was dipped. Another crouched to take his portion, and lurched away, feeling the first effect of the powder speeding to hit his brain. Knowing it would hit faster than a lightning bolt, he knew within moments, the Blessed Lady would bless him with her most potent gifts, clarity, ability, and strength to help raise the next bridge.

"Come," Cullinan commanded the Quisitor, "you have rested enough. I will suffer no untoward delay. We have far to go and little time to travel it." Dipping the spoon yet again into his bag, he grazed the surface of the Trooh with its tip. "Even now, the Nine work to raise the roadway, and the blessing of the Blessed Lady is prepared for you. Come, friend, receive it."

"Friend, Doge," the Quisitor struggled to get to his feet and wheezed, "I fear my frame was not made for such active exercise. The pace set is savage."

"You never began so large, friend. Abstinence would have served you better. Too long, and too often, have you sat at table and hung overmuch flesh on your body. I have need of you as we spoke before. Will you deny me?"

"No, friend, Doge, to do that would be to deny the Blessed Lady herself."

"Then come, friend," sucking his teeth Cullinan held out the long-handled spoon, "and receive the Blessed Lady's blessing."

* * *

"Lady," Ratanakiri rapped loudly on the door. "Listen to me, I beg you," she shouted in panic. "The Lord Chancellor has returned in worse temper than before and bids me, in strongest tones, to tell you the Guardians grow impatient and demand to know what cause there is for unseemly delay?"

Against one of the panes of a window giving out onto the balcony, Lingaradgh's message bubble knocking light, but persistent, drew back when it sensed Apatia approach to let it in. The door opened, it drifted inside, briefly scraped against her temple before popping, and her mother's voice chimed loud and clear.

"Lady?" Ratanakiri bawled. "Even now the Chancellor rages in the corridor. Can you not hear him rant? By all the powers, he swears, if there is need, he will have no qualms about invading your privacy, and will break the door down. What answer shall I take to him?"

"For pity's sake," Apatia screamed. "Am I expected to appear before the Guardians in a state of undress? Does my own Chancellor seek my humiliation?"

Emptying all of the remaining Trooh onto a small urilatum salver, she took as much as possible into the pump-tube, and shot its load into one of the child's nostrils. His reaction was immediate, body arcing, arms and legs straining against his bonds, and crashing back onto the bed, he thrashed wildly as if in the throes of a fit of monumental proportion.

"Tell my most excellent Chancellor, if the Guardians will wait no longer, all embarrassment I will bear with good grace, if he should bring them to me now," she shouted, filling the pump-tube again.

Holding the boy, weighting his body down with hers, she managed to straddle him. Her forearm at his throat, she kept his head still enough to shoot the rest of the Trooh high into his nose. Again his body arched, violently throwing her from him, and collapsing into the coverlet, shook madly. His face, contorted with spasms, grew red, and thick veins stood out from his neck and temples. His eyes snapped open, starting from their sockets. Froth, foaming from between his lips, flew through the air as he squirmed and bucked. His clawing fingers ripped at the lace-trimmed sheets, while his heels churned the covers into a tangled heap. His mouth suddenly drawn into a grimace, he let out a series of animalistic, long-drawn out howls, and continued to scream for something he had lost.

Picking herself up, Apatia took little notice of his fast-jerked limbs and head, or terrible cries. Calm, she put the urilatum tray and pump-tube into a drawer, brushed away telltale signs of white powder dusting the top of the bedside table, and trampled them into the carpeting. Looking into her mirror, she caught hanks of white hair lazily floating on draughts, drawing the long strands together to tame its wildness and twist its mass into a knot, which she stuck with pins to secure it. Moving swift, she fetched the quiver, symbol of her authority, and attached it to her girdle.

Returning behind the screen, she stared at the boy writhing like a crazed thing, baying like a rabid dog, and flecking web-silk pillows with saliva. No pity showing in her yellow-gold eyes, Apatia said, "Little one, shine on, very well you do my work for me."

* * *

Hearing the key in the lock, Clara drew back from the door and said in polite greeting, "Eodgh, Ratanakiri."

"Well met, Clara. A pitcher of fresh water is all I am able to bring for you this time," she answered, smiling apologetically, "so you may at least slake thirst." Placing it on the floor, she said, "Now shall we presently see sparks fly. Be silent, Clara of Lessadgh, lest one of them burn you."

Putting a forefinger to her lips to sign the woman should be very quiet, she left, locking the door behind her, and hurried back to the vestibule.

* * *

William felt the rush coming, its ruthless speed, indicating its force would be greater than any previous blast he and the dark had withstood.

"Hold me," he said, frightened he could hardly feel arms that had held him so tight for so long, and in the explosive violence of a collision that shook him from head to toe, never heard the dark's reply, nor felt its loose grip slip completely.

Something, big and powerful, snatched at him. Plucked him up. Carried him out into thick, thick, dark clouds. Held him close and whirled him away. Took him deeper into the blurring mist. Tumbled him over and over. Threw him high. Cast him down. Somewhere, someone was screaming. He screamed back. The long, keening, sounds were rammed back into his mouth by another huge blast that rocked him to his foundations. Something massive and wild seized him. Ripped him from the grasp of the power holding him. Whipped him away. Spun him with cyclonic ferocity across a landscape oppressed with a bleakness that was unending in scope and scale for the longest of times.

And in the aftermath, calm steadily settling on the ramparts of shadowed cloud moving down to find him, William felt scrambled. The pain in his head magnified, and pinging against the front of his skull, drowned the sound of many faded voices and others still living in the circling fog. Confused, he wandered through it knowing an important part of himself to be irrevocably lost, but not understanding why he could not find his way back to the dark. Why the dark did not draw him to its shelter as it had done before.

I am alone, he thought with sudden clarity. *I am me. If, I, and me remain, where then, is self? My self is lost, the innermost core of my being gone. My refuge missing, it will not be found again. We, who should never be apart, are parted and I no longer whole, but geometrically fractured for all time to come.*

He began to scream and howl, mourning the loss, mourning his complete incompleteness.

* * *

His ear pressed against the panel, Slubeadgh strained to hear any sound coming from the apartment. The only noise he could hear disturbing the quiet was a clock, lethargically tumbling stones with water's gently gurgled fall.

The peacock is gone from this place, he thought, regretting he had not stayed longer to listen to what further gossip might have been gleaned from Apatia's ladies. *No! If the peacock had been faded, such news would have rocketed about the Helm. Likewise, if he had been transferred elsewhere, that news would have been poured from every lip. They would have gabbled of little else. The peacock is here. Logic tells me this is so.*

Taking the urilatum fan from the breast pocket of his greatcoat, he caressed the uppermost feather, feeling beneath reverent fingers the strands of minuscule filaments, comprising the barbs, engraved all along its length. Feeling the shaft of the quill, he fingered those fitted snug behind it, the woven metal cord piercing them through, and the tassel hanging, its long threads swinging. The urilatum was cool in his hands, and silky. For a moment, he exulted in the cunning of the fan. It's true nature hid behind innocuous beauty, gave no hint it was an exquisite weapon, but posed as an everyday accoutrement used by so many ladies of the court.

One well-aimed slash, and it is done. It is done, and I may live a life longed for. One flick of the wrist is required to gain all I have earned, together with peace, once the peacock struts no more.

He imagined the deed done. The surprise of guards when they came to lead their prisoner to just punishment, only to find him gone, never thinking he was no more than a speck of dust, indistinguishable from any other lying on and in the pile of the carpeting.

"I will do this," Slubeadgh said, on a breath.

At his feet, its reservoir of light exhausted, the fire crystal flickered. Winking feebly in the struggle to shine, it dulled as he pushed the button to release the panel. His back hugged the wall in an effort to keep out of sight, as it slid back noiselessly on runners, and the brilliancy of many fire crystals raked into the passage. Blinking in sudden light, refusing to be unnerved, he spread the fan in anticipation of verbal challenge, or the worst thing imaginable, the peacock leaping into the opening, armed and ready to give fight. Swallowing fear, he waited for opposition that did not arrive, and with slow-motioned movement, to see, but not be seen, cautiously peered round the edge of the wall into the room.

A chamber crowded with objects, and in its midst, the high-backed chair Semyon had sneeringly lounged in not so very long ago, to hear news he had painstakingly collected in Lessadgh. Infuriated by the sight of it, he stepped out of the byway, checked haste fuelled by hatred, and crept stealthily up behind it, sensing before he looked, the peacock would not be sitting there. He went over to the door leading to the anteroom, quietly opening it a fraction, and froze for a heart-stopping moment, before recognizing the voices heard were those of guards in the corridor engaged in a losing argument with Reboia, rejecting all inducements to stand down from self-imposed duty.

Stay outside, no protection of any worth can you offer the peacock, woman.

The door left ajar, he crept smooth and slow back through the apartment, and onto Semyon's bedchamber. Clinging to the wall, he once again peered cautiously through the doorway, noting from his vantage point, fine clothes were laid out on the bed.

A frock coat of pale blue, the colour most favoured by the peacock, its lapels and cuffs heavily embroidered with urilatum thread. Next to it, a waistcoat stitched in like manner, with a ruffled shirt of delicate web-silk, and breeches cut to emphasize the shape of slim hips and muscular thighs. And by a full-length dressing mirror, misted with vapour, a pair knee-high boots waiting to be pulled on.

He bathes! Even now, in direst straits, the peacock's vanity is ever foremost. In finest attire, perfumed and groomed, he thinks to meet eternal nothingness with sartorial dignity. That final show of bravado, I will most surely deny him.

From the room beyond, he heard a sudden plash and smack as the surface of water was broken, and the resultant mild-wallow of wavelets slapped against marbled sides, spread into tender ripples, followed by a stream of droplets rapidly drizzling back into the pool.

The peacock rises. Slubeadgh breathed deep, mastering temptation to abandon his intended assassination. *For me it is now or never.*

Adjusting his hold on the fan, he made sure his grasp was not too tight, or too loose, and gliding soundless went into the bathing room, where Semyon, his back obligingly presented, stood with one foot on the seat of a stool, dried himself with a large towel. He straightened, tossing his head to throw back wet hair fallen over his face, sprinkling the figure lurking in the doorway with residue spray. Raising his arm, Slubeadgh leapt to the attack. One downward slash, across unsuspecting broadness, carved a blood-spattered path through muscles moving fluid beneath skin. The stroke complete, his wrist flexed with a supple twist, and the fan, a half-circled blur of coppered-silver gracefully pirouetting in an upward cut, sliced a different gory angle to the first.

Semyon cried out, his naked body automatically curving away, instinctively trying to avoid a deadly weapon his mind had not yet comprehended, and half-turning in the same instant, exposed his throat. Once again, with lightening speed, the fan connected, its sharpened edges scythed through flesh leaving a small, blood-spurting chasm in its wake. Clutching his neck, eyes and mouth wide with surprise and pain, Semyon staggered, and slipping on the damp-slicked slabs, fell headfirst into the pool.

A deadweight, he hit the water with force torrents of watery plumes rocketed in all directions, splattering the ceiling, the walls, and drenching Slubeadgh from head to foot. Gloating at the half-submerged, unmoving body, hardly noticing he was saturated, hardly feeling the cascade raining down upon him, he stood quite still, while moisture dripping from his hair, and pouring from the hem of his greatcoat, added to the pool he was standing in. He remained rooted to the spot, staring in fascinated triumph at clouds of green blood billowing, mingling with strands of floating hair, its brightness muddying the colour of coppery skin, and diffusing in flushing eddies, patterned the cooling water with crazy swirls and curls.

"Lose life force slow, so that I may watch you fade, you walking piece of hated, moribund arrogance. Always, you were nothing," he crowed, contemptuous, "soon, nothing will you truly be. Thus, do I pay you out."

"Semyon?" a voice called, shaking him from trance-like victory to sudden alertness. "Semyon, why did you not answer when I knocked? Semyon?"

Reboia! He recognized her voice. Knew her prowess with sword and dagger. Knew she was never without her weapons.

"Semyon, where are you?"

She seeks the peacock out. So tenacious is her character, she will not go till she has found him.

His teeth bared, he snarled silent frustration and fury, and folding the fan, oiled with his enemy's blood, slid behind the door.

Chapter 51.

"Semyon?" Reboia shouted, pushing the door to the anteroom wider. "I come to see if you lacked for anything?"

The door slammed back, she marched to the reception chamber and immediately noticed the entrance to the secret passage was exposed.

"By the powers?" she said, going inside to look into the place she had named, the byway of intimacy. *Fool, surely you have not gone to the Lady, thinking to beguile her with your presence and prevail upon her by using sexual arts? But no, if never would you go on bended knee, and cry clemency for wrong done, it beggars credulity you would use such a ploy, when no guilt do you bear. Why, then, is the panel slid back?*

Alarmed, she went to his bedchamber, respectfully knocked, waited for a response and receiving none, went in. With a glance, she took in Semyon's finest clothes laid out on the bed. His boots neatly placed next to the dressing mirror, the last vestiges of moisture almost evaporated from the glass, but stubbornly clinging to its corners and edges.

"Semyon?" she cried, a final time and barged into the bathing room to find him submersed in the pool and his own blood.

Leaping into the water to lift him out, she did not hear, or see a raggedy, cloud-wracked scarecrow, soiled with all manner of muck softly oozing from the hem of its tattered greatcoat, creep stealthy as a stalking hound from behind the door.

* * *

Yellow eyes glittering, pale, and very haughty, Apatia stood beside Ratanakiri in the vestibule.

Equally erect and haughty, the Headmaster spoke the traditional greeting, "The blessings of the Blessed Lady be upon you, friend."

"May the Blessed Lady make your face shine," she answered, automatic. "These, friends, you bring, they are to accompany us?"

"They bear witnesses to that which you now reveal, friend."

"Then, Ratanakiri, you also will come, to act in likewise fashion on my behalf. Follow me...friend."

Turning, nonchalantly arranging the long train of her robe behind her with an elegant kick, she led the way through the avenue of rooms to her bedchamber, then waited for Ratanakiri to throw the doors wide. The tiniest smile of satisfaction hovering at the corners of her mouth, she stepped aside to gauge the reaction to high-pitched wails and low-pitched growls. Gratified by expressions of horror and dismay registering on the faces of the gaggle of Guardians crowding into the chamber, she knew with certainty how the last scene of deception would be played out.

"The child howls in bestial manner?" the Headmaster queried, suddenly nervous.

"And has done, since the strange malady struck him," she lied. "But come, see what miracle has been wrought below the surface of his skin. This warning you should heed," she said, taking the lead again, "for his own safety, is he bound, and if truth be told, for mine own also."

His features settling into a mask of tragic concern, the Headmaster asked, "His suffering is so great?"

"That you will see, and judge for yourselves," she answered, moving sedately through the length of the room. Pausing at the screen, she politely ushered the Guardians and her maidservant beyond. "Now," she said, when they stood speechless about the bed, "do you understand why I would not willingly exhibit my relation to curious eyes?"

Biting his moustache, stroking the length of his beard, unconsciously segregating the hairs, spreading them over his chest, and gathering them to begin the process again, the Headmaster of the House of Learning finally raised his eyes from the child's madly jerking body, to meet hers.

"Talent gilds him nonetheless, friend," he answered, harsh.

"Undeniable. Yet what good, or advantage, could his gift be, when the child lost his wits the instant talent began to arrive?"

"No matter how strange the circumstance, notification should have been given," he answered, doggedly. "It was duty, friend."

"It was. And I am contrite for the omission. But love for my relation, for his safety, and to keep him from prying eyes, bade me overlook duty. I, instead of he, have borne the ignominy of public censure. In every leaf and bean house, have you not heard it whispered," she wet her lips as though what she was about to say came hard to her, "I walk the Way of Atrament? Obtaining a glimpse of the boy, would not a shout go up, Atrament is arisen? Would not clamour soar, demanding his immediate fading?"

Caressing his beard, the Headmaster nodded. "Still, it was duty. Into our care you must now deliver him."

"How will you carry him away?" Apatia cried. "Ghoulish gossipmongers cram every street, as well you must know, having traversed them to reach the Helm. How will you control his body, let alone hush the maniacal song he trumpets and trills? Friend, you would not go far with him in such condition."

Bending his head in thought, the Headmaster relentlessly pulled and tugged at his beard, considering what he should do. Speckled talent, he had, but not sufficient to have been taught the words for a making to calm, or silence the child. With excitable crowds leeching the last dregs from the news of the Commander's high treason, and hungry for the next instalment, or some new scandal, it would be impossible to pass unnoticed. If such an attempt were made, all too soon, could such good sport turn to something more sinister, and the child lost to a rampaging mob? Unthinkable. Better not to have embarked on the course taken. Better not to have clapped eyes on the poor boy ranting and fighting some unknown struggle.

But he had seen. Seen talent shining the child from head to toe in such profusion it dizzied him to think of it. That, at least, he could confirm. That report, he could, with certainty, send to Hessonii and leave the matter in the capable hands of the Doge.

"What you say has merit, friend. A situation of such delicacy dictates it must be dealt with..." the Headmaster groped for the right word, "...delicately. To Hessonii, I will send, saying what has been witnessed this darkling, and shortly receive advice on how best to proceed."

"I see it now, most venerable one," she wept, "some cure for this curious affliction might the Guardians have found, had I but come to you sooner."

"May yet be found," he answered, knowing in all probability there was no remedy, but seeking to give a little comfort. "Meantime, though affection bids you tend him well, so now do the Guardians lay that duty firmly upon you, friend. And, friend," he said, turning from the bed and the boy, apparently in the throes of serious mental affliction, "penalty will be payable for the oversight admitted."

"My weight in gold," she answered, humble, "if a price must be set to counterbalance my love."

* * *

Furiously sucking his teeth, Cullinan kicked at the remnants of a tuft of grass he had demolished, determined to uproot it from the soil it was anchored to. Frustrated and very angry, he kept at the work, raising a small dust-cloud with his bare toes, without seeming to feel any pain when one of the nails was broken away, and his blood congealing, with dirt, formed a crust over the wound.

Clustered a little distance away, the Nine, already exhausted by the making and stringing of three bridges, and under no illusion the night's work would soon be done, stared hungrily at the satchel draped across his bare chest. Above him, the air bridge's fast moving outline shimmered, and the dark figure of the Headmaster Quisitor lumbering slowly across it, each step more faltering than the last.

By the rancid Lady's stony tits, no more delay will I tolerate.

Striding across the grass to where the Nine waited, Cullinan shouted, "Let it fall. Bring it down that another can be made and strung."

"But, friend, Doge," one of the Nine said, "the Headmaster Quisitor still walks upon it."

"You think I know it not? Our gluttonous friend causes too much delay, friend."

"But, friend, Doge, to drop the bridge would be to fade him."

"Is it not the wish of all Guardians to enter the embrace of the Blessed Lady, friend?"

"It is, friend, Doge," the Nine answered as one.

"Nor would I give such command lightly. In commune with the Blessed Lady have I been. To the Blessed Lady, may all blessings be upon her, I have listened most attentive, and her counsel is this. Another Headmaster Quisitor, one not given to unhealthy excess, may be elected with ease. To take into the Guardians possession, a treasure that glorifies not only the Blessed Lady, many blessings upon her, but also increase the Order's power...will not come again. The Blessed Lady bids me tell you, her arms are open wide to receive our, friend, the Headmaster Quisitor, and her blessings ready to be given complete for service performed. Do you then, the Blessed Lady's will, all blessings be upon her for erudition and compassion everlasting. It is not I, who commands, but the Blessed Lady, herself. Drop the bridge, friends."

The words of the making sung soundless in the heads of the Nine to maintain each block in ordered position and keep the bridge standing, drifted slowly to a halt. Almost at once, the last blocks laid glimmered, and deconstructing, particles fled to meld invisibly with invisibility once more. One, after another, each block dissolved, returning to the ether from whence it had come, and as though ethereal disintegration was preferable to nebulous solidity, the collapse of the remaining blocks that had been forced to the unnatural process, became more rapid.

High up on the crumbling bridge, the Headmaster Quisitor felt the vibrations of destruction. Puffing and panting, breath burning his lungs with acidic fires and stitching his sides with insurmountable agony, he realised he would never reach the ground before it disappeared altogether. Resigned to his fate, he stopped, and with closed eyes, spreading his arms wide, pleaded with the Blessed Lady to receive a true friend into her bosom until the very moment, nothing remaining beneath his feet, he plummeted to the earth at great speed.

"The blessings of the Blessed Lady are assuredly upon our lamented, friend," Cullinan intoned, reaching for the clasp on his satchel and the long handled spoon within, to dole out the next liberal portion of Trooh to the Nine.

Is it not ironic, he thought, while the words of the making for the next air bridge were beginning to be sung and spun, *food for birds and all scavengers has our Headmaster Quisitor denied, and so again provides no useful function unless he has not faded, but lies immobile due to serious injury then, the diner is now dinner.* Laughing inward at his own wit, he went on to think about a forthcoming election to fill an empty post, and, who should win it.

* * *

"You let me sleep most of the darkling away," Caryadgh said, climbing onto the driving seat to sit beside Bezel.

"You would not have slept had you not needed to do so."

"How spent you the time?"

"In good company," he grinned. "Many deep conversations I have had concerning the where, and why for, of a great many things of interest, such as what information you carry. How your spans were spent in the stronghold of the Guardians. And, not least, how Spymaster Malfroid will receive what you have gleaned."

"With whom did you speak?" Caryadgh bristled.

"Myself," Bezel laughed. "What better company could there be, when knowing myself so well, all argument could be bluntly made causing comrade, me, no offence whatever?"

"You are a buffoon."

"All too often has that has been said, and worked to my benefit. Who guards their tongue with a fool?"

"I do. We have made good progress?"

"We have. Into Almandine's realm we shall shortly pass. The border lies not far ahead. Will you alight shortly, and make your own way?"

"No, I think not. Without doubt, the Guardians will have spies within the Helm, if not throughout the city. My story will be this. A tinker was guided into my path and he, taking pity upon my lonely state and lack of provisions, gave me free passage. I think it credible."

"It is. Lying is always done best by sticking near as may be to truth. Did you hear the Lord of the Helm had to pay penalty to the Guardians? Her weight in gold by all account."

"For what reason?"

"Incursion into Spessa. More, you shall undoubtedly hear from Malfroid, if you ask to know it. Very angered the Lord was, and royally fell out with her Chancellor, my very good comrade, Persimmony Clump. It is my belief," Bezel said, sly, "trouble brews between our Lord and the Guardians. What think you?"

"I think, some advice I will give to you comrade, Bezel," she said, sweet, "Never consider occupying yourself in the trade of fishing. Your catch will inevitably come up lacking."

"Fair enough," he said, disappointed.

Chapter 52.

Her face pale, and pinched with tension, Clara came into the room. Acknowledging Clump and Malfroid with a brief nod, she went quickly to her chair. While they seated themselves, she drew the speak-cube from its pouch, and said without preamble, "Talk me."

A long story told short, so have I spoken of my life. In brief, it amounts to this. In the long ago it was said, the child of a god, or fallen archon was I. What is the truth of such words? I have no care whether they are fact, or falsity. I know, which none may gainsay, I am the last true child of the Disobedient Ones. In recent time it was said of me, I was demon spawned. I say, I am not, but have played the part as suited my purpose.
Come I now to the child. William, the woman of Lessadgh named him, in absence of any other. At his birthing, Gilgaladgh was he named, and noted in the ledger. Since the best part of the story of his life is known to you there is little to tell, but I would have you know my need of him.
What could I want of him, but that which I wanted and took by force from so many others? But know this, him I would not have served as I served them. I would have waited till talent bloomed naturally in the boy before drawing him to me. And coming into my charge, would have nurtured him, taking his life force and talent within it a little at a time to cause no lasting hurt. In payment for extension of life and slow restoration, I thought to give all knowledge I owned.
A treasure trove of priceless value was he to me. The epitome of all fought and worked for in the preservation of talent throughout all the aeons of my being. Did I not prove this by sending him for safety into Lessadgh? Essential, for me it was, that he lived, since no benefit I could derive from his fading. Not so the one responsible for his madness, who caring not for his wellbeing, craved only the gift he potentially possessed. How knowledge of him came into this one's compass I never learned. Believing him safe from all harm, my vigilance was not enough. Too late, did I discover, he was snatched from the shelter where I had placed him.
Using incomplete Trooh in huge amount, talent was unnaturally induced to blossom long before it should. Thus do I honour part of my word, having told you the method and means, employed to bring misfortune about. Thus, in part, have I honoured my word, having told you of what instigated the child's insanity, and continued to provoke it. To see him violated in such despicable fashion, and with such dread outcome, I mourned him, together with my impotency to prevent all that took place, for was it not the sealing of his fate and mine own? Know this, one thing in common did we two have, his captor and I. And it is this. All believing us both to be

faded...believed most wrongly.
Now do I honour in full my word, and give the name of the perpetrator of the heinous deed, if you have not yet guessed it. Sometime Lord of the Helm of Almandine, the destroyer of a callous, conniving father, who, for all his well-cultivated faults and vaunting ambition, cared for his child overmuch, to her ruin. Vile jailer, not only of a good husband, but all who dared oppose her rise to power, they continued to live in one place, entombed in separate heartwood prisons. Spinner of the greatest illusion that fooled all the world of Noor, a walker on the Way, her name is, and was...Lingaradgh.

No need to command the speak cube to cease talking. For an age, or so it seemed, it spun silence as deep and brooding as their own.

"It may be..." Malfroid finally said.

"Find...me...Lingaradgh," Clara said, freezing them both with the piercing coldness in her voice. "Find me Lingaradgh," she repeated, spiking them with the dagger points of her eyes.

* * *

Grazing the surface of consciousness, he had played her game, which was in part his own. Ranting and raving, easily done, for he still mourned an irretrievable part of himself and would always do so. But now, the gawkers who had clustered about the bed were gone and she, pleased with her perceived cleverness, approached to see why he had suddenly fallen silent, why he no longer struggled against his bonds.

He lay perfectly still, with the yeasted stench of advanced decay strong in his nostrils. The dankness of rotting wood, and bubbled plaster, alive with a life of its own, and independent of the wall it had once been applied to. Age-old stone, cracked and rubbled, shot thick with mildewed lichen and mushroomed tang, accumulated in the mounds of dung secreted by generations of creeping insects, in the crumbled mortar. Pungent rivulets, the base of the flow begun long ago, petrified, hillocked, and streamed by droppings constantly deposited by birds and bats just above. These smells, and many more, were almost hidden beneath the sourness of stagnant water and pervading damp, and the glue holding all together, a mask. Its construction, plied layer upon layer, to form a wondrous disguise that lulled all senses and tricked all eyes. A mask of fabulous deception put in place, and maintained, by the art of a mistress of illusion.

Her cool, dry hand was placed upon his forehead. To the music of her husky voice, congratulating him for a task well done, William broke through the last thin barrier, and slowly opened his eyes.

Snatching her hand away, Apatia gasped, "Thank the powers you did not wake whilst those vultures stood round, little brat."

In answer, he began to say aloud the ancient words talent had instilled in him, which coming into his mind without need of thought, would loosen the silken cords binding him fast.

"By the powers," she cussed again as he spoke, "what kind of madness do you now relay? What goes?"

He smiled a beatific smile, and said, "You do, Apatia. You go to your mother. I shall take you."

Striking his face, she shouted, "Insolent little fool, it is I, who shall take you!"

He smiled again, feeling cords slip from wrist and ankle.

"The hand that struck me," he said, in the ancient tongue. "The arm that delivered the blow, the body that owns it, the mind that directed the action, I condemn and confine..."

"Stop this," Apatia screamed, realizing too late he knew how to employ talent gifted to him. "If I have used you ill, it was at the behest of another, who holds great power over me."

"I know," he smiled, silently finishing the making he had begun, and added, "but you had choice. Always there is choice." Sliding across the coverlet, he sat up, and reaching out, took the little ruby bottle from the table beside the bed. "It is pretty," he said, unscrewing the cap. "I like the carving on it. A pretty container, for a pretty lady," he held it out, "come."

"No!" she put her hands out, as if to fend him off, and saw fingers on the hand that had hit him crowned with wispy tendrils of smoke idly drifting away from her. Away from her, toward him, toward the bottle so invitingly offered.

"What is it you have done?" she wailed, seeing not only her fingers, but her hand engulfed in reddening smoke, float unhurriedly away, the flesh and bone of wrist and arm unravelling in curling spirals, waft and trail languidly behind them. "No, no, no," Apatia howled, feeling her other hand and arm painlessly dissolving, her feet and legs becoming weightless, turn into something they should never be, "you cannot."

"My head hurts," he answered, watching the first of her smoke filter into the neck of the ruby bottle. "It hurts a very great deal. Come, there is no time to waste. I have much to do, and your mother is waiting. When every last particle of you is safely inside, I shall take you to her. On Clara's heart, I swear, I shall lose nothing of you. Come. Come."

* * *

"My, frie...comrade," Bezel whispered. "This is lunacy. Around the Helm we have strolled, tried every unguarded entrance to no avail, and barely escaped challenge at those that were manned. By some miracle, we remain in the grounds, or perhaps, no miracle at all, seeing how many walk to take the air in these extensive gardens. What is to be done?"

Clump growled, lamenting his talent was of no use here, lamenting the Faienya, despising all metals save for gold and urilatum, the locks and bolts, and the mechanisms within, were carved from hardwearing, serviceable lignum vitae.

"Some plan we must devise," Bezel insisted.

Hit by sudden inspiration, Clump said, "The balconies. We use the balconies. No, do not look up and openly stare."

"To admire the elegance of their construction is not permissible, comrade?"

"No, not when it is my intention to use them forthwith. Saw you how they go one above another?"

"A wide-stepped ladder with much space between each tread," Bezel nodded appreciatively. "Genius, frie...comrade, I am sorry, the word keeps slipping out, though my tongue is well-bridled on that account. Two drawbacks, do I see, the first..."

"I know it, my height. The second?"

"The darkling is dark enough, but not so deep we may carry out this madness, this adventure," Bezel corrected himself, "unobserved, when at every window fire crystals show. Yet, I see by your jutting jaw, the square set of shoulders you will not be persuaded from determination to try it."

"You have the right of it," Clump agreed. "A more secluded area would be most to my liking."

"Tell me," Bezel said, "this woman for whom you risk all..."

"Where she is concerned," Clump muttered, "for some reason I cannot determine, I make rash promises and go here, go there, and never count the cost until too late. In me, she brings out impetuosity. All caution, in the heat of the moment, do I throw careless to the winds. Regretting it mightily on reflection, but my word given, I can do nothing but fulfil it to best ability."

"Comrade, the solution to this problem is most simple. It looks you in the face. To rid yourself of this affliction, bind her to you at earliest opportunity, and I vow, impetuosity will flee, never to be seen again in her respect, and caution return from its journeying to fondly hug you once more."

"It is not like that," Clump growled, irritated by Bezel's diagnosis and gabbled cure. "Not at all," he growled, stumping away to find a better location.

"Is it not?" Bezel shook his head, and called to Persimmony Clump's back, "your view, friend, is somewhat delusional."

* * *

"Do not fade. Do not fade," Reboia repeated, pulling Semyon's head from the water. "By the powers," she screamed, seeing blood flowing freely from the gash on his neck, "do not fade. You cannot fade."

Looping her arm about his shoulders, and pulling him to her chest, she waded into the centre of the pool, hauling his thighs and legs into the water then turned him to face her. Relaxing her grip for just a moment, he sank limp beneath the surface.

"Do not fade," she wailed, her voice rasped by shock and desperation. "You cannot fade."

Grabbing hold of his hair, she pulled his head above the ripples, took a deep breath and ducked beneath them. Her shoulder powered into his belly. Her arm keeping him in place, her footing unsure, and buckled by his weight, she fought to get to the side. Every muscle, every sinew in back, leg and thigh strained by the supreme effort to stand, she managed to heave herself upright, and gasping, sucked in air, while carefully sliding him onto the round-lipped, marble slabs rimming the pool. He lolled back. She caught him before he fell. Cradling him with one arm, she tried to get out, and finding the move impossible, held him with both arms.

Blowing hard with exertion and controlled panic, she laid him sideways on the ledge and letting his legs dangle in the water, shoved him a little further away from the edge. Frightened he would roll back into the pool, and knowing he was not breathing, she crawled quickly from it with a torrent of water raining from her clothes and hair.

"Do not fade. You cannot fade," her tongue stumbling on the mantra, she dragged Semyon clear and rolled him onto his back. "Do not fade. You cannot fade." She raised her arm. "Do not fade," she clenched her fist, and moaned, "I will not let you," and brought it down hard, high on his chest.

Water trickling from his mouth, drooled syrupy onto the blood-smeared slabs.

"I-will-not-let-you-fade," her fist crashed down again and again, each stroke more desperate and harder than the one before. "Breathe," she panted, "breathe you stubborn bastard. Breathe!"

Semyon choked. Chest shuddering, stomach convulsing, he suddenly retched, spewing a stream of water, and taking a faltering breath, took another.

"Help!" Reboia cried, relieved to see his breast rise and fall in stuttering rhythm. "Help!" she looked at the wound on his neck. Thankful it was not as deep as thought, she pinched the lips of the gash together with her fingers, and bellowed, "Help!"

Chapter 53.

Self-preservation moved Slubeadgh quick and quiet.
"Do not fade."
The very words he did not want to hear followed him through the bedchamber and into the reception room.
"Do not fade. You cannot fade."
Even in the entrance of the passageway, where light blazed, he could hear Reboia repeating the same thing over and over again, as if her words and will could keep Semyon living.
A few moments more, he thought, despondent, *another well-aimed blow delivered, and he would surely have gone to nothing.*
"Do not fade. You cannot fade."
Those words, resounding in his ears, dogged him through the brilliance shed by fire crystals to the dim perimeter of their reach, and on into darkness settling in the secret byway. Those words, now unheard, rotated in his head teasing him with the possibility Semyon would live, and taunted him with the hateful prospect.
With no fire crystal to shine his path, he went at a snail's pace in the dark, feeling the way with his fingertips. He had just reached the first junction, branching off from the passage, when he heard faint cries of distress, and stopping to listen, interpreted the sounds.
"Reboia!" Hope surged. Straining to hear, believing there could be no other reason for the distant bellowing, he reasoned, in front of her eyes the peacock had faded to nothing and she mourned him, howling out her grief.
Joy, volcanic in its wildness, rocketed past despair. Overcome by an emotion never experienced before, his heart thumping so hard it threatened to leap out of his chest, he slid down the wall. Surrendering to a delirium of happiness, he wallowed in it, amazed by his daring, stunned by courage dredged up from some deep remote corner within, and expertly exploited to commit a murder dreamed of for so long. A murder, he had only a little while ago, tried to carry out and failed miserably.
"I have done it," he whispered, savouring the sweet taste of a death accomplished. "Truly, have I faded the loathsome peacock. The strutting piece of arrogance, now struts amongst dust, and much joy of it do I wish him. Do you hear, Galateo? Without your aid, I have done this great deed. By the strength of my arm, by use of sheer audacity and inimitable bravery, have I rid myself of him, whom I hated with all-consuming passion! What say you now? No, no, say nothing. It is not needed. We know who had the right of it, and who wrong. And...and now I think on it, strange is it not, without your nagging clack I can succeed?

"All our lives," he hissed, "you are the one who told me ineptitude was my forte. All our lives, have you jeered and sneered saying without you, a bundle of incompetency am I. Sulking silence has taught me much, for which I most humbly thank you, brother. Most plain is it to me now. You, and you, alone, are the one who held me back. Kept me small when I could be great.

"Oh, yes, I see it all. Jealousy was the spur that goaded clever speech to wash from my mind all thoughts of competent ability, and instil in its place, dependency upon you. The shackles you thought to bind me with can no longer hold. You are undone. Now do I know, of no use are you to me, and henceforth, obsolete."

Galateo did not reply. Certain his brother would never follow through with his plan, and even if he did, would not achieve anything other than bring them both to fading by Semyon's sword, if not his boot, his silence had not been a sulking fit, but resignation to their fate. His silence, he now saw, had not only been misconstrued, it had tumbled him from the acknowledged position of superior mental ability, mentor and advisor, and reduced him to nothing more than a hated burden. Serious consideration would have to be given on how best to regain a little of the ground lost... which would not be done with argument. Bathed in his brother's sweat, he meandered through possibilities, and situations where he might be of assistance to slowly worm a way back to the height he had fallen from.

Two victories in a single night under his belt, Slubeadgh got to his feet, shaken by success. Hearing no one moving in the passageways, but fearing pursuit to find Semyon's murderer would most certainly begin soon, he moved off to find the door he had come into the Helm by.

* * *

"Clara."

"William?" Throwing off the blanket Ratanakiri had brought her, she sat up and looked around the room. "Where are you?"

"Not very far away."

"Your mind speaks to mine again?"

"Yes."

"You are unhurt, William?"

"I am much changed, Clara, as I told you when we last spoke."

"You sound so grown up."

"It was unavoidable, but I am still your boy."

"And always shall be, William, no matter what the change. What has she done to you? Will I recognize you?"

"You could not miss me if you tried. I shine like a beacon. Remember talent glowing on Persimmony Clump's hands? That is the change that has happened to me. Are you comforted?"

"I do not understand," she admitted.

"I will explain everything when we two are reunited. Clara, you must listen to me. Presently, Ratanakiri, the woman who has brought you food and drink, and shown what kindness she could, will come. Go with her out of this Helm. She will take you to a place of safety. Wait there."

"Eodgh Ratanakiri," Clara said, thinking she corrected him, "will bring trouble upon herself, if she does as you say. I would not wish her punished by that pale harridan of a giantess on my account."

"Have no fear of her. She has gone."

"Gone? Gone where? William, you are frightening me."

"Be frightened of nothing, Clara. Under the shelter of my power you are, and will be for all my life. Go with Eodgh Ratanakiri," he said, humouring her, "go where she takes you, and no matter what happens to dismay or alarm, you must stay there. Remain calm, and I will come to you. Promise me, you will do as I ask, Clara? For me, beyond anything else, it is important you are safe. Promise me."

"I promise," she said.

"All will be well. I go now to do what must be done. I will send Clump to you."

"William? Tell me what must be done? Clump is here? William? Is Clump here?" she called, hearing the key turn in the lock. "Did he come looking for you here?"

"Greetings, Clara," Ratanakiri said, ignoring the fact the woman appeared to be talking to herself.

Picking the blanket up from the floor, she placed it around her shoulders saying, "For some strange reason, I know Lessadgh beings feel cold when it touches them, and though the darkling has a certain freshness I delight in, for I touch it not, it could chill you. Come," she said, taking her hand. "We must leave at once. Do not ask me why, but I am compelled to take you to a certain place in the middle of the grounds, and remain by you. Be quiet," she laid her forefinger across her lips, "that we may steal away unmolested. Come."

* * *

Impatience biting sharp, Lingaradgh paced the paths in her garden, for once taking no notice of the willodghs. For once not troubling enemies trapped in heartwood with verbal torture. Up to the gate and back, becoming more agitated as the minutes ticked by, she waited for her daughter to come with the child, excited at the prospect of finally taking talent from him, and furious Apatia dallied.

In the spire of the summerhouse, laid out and ready for immediate use, the instruments she would employ to take every drop of life force from him. An adamantine knife, its blade honed to perfect sharpness, to open a succession of small veins. No danger of the boy fading, or talent lost in a quick spurting splash, but a slow and careful harvest of fluid bearing a priceless cargo.

Vessels, to catch the precious flow, took the form of two glasses of exquisite loveliness. From the centre of each wide foot, a stem of incredible length and elegance swept up to meet a full-bellied bowl of finest emerald shorn to impossible thinness, the rims curving inward to preserve warmth, and prevent inadvertent spillage. In the event some small smidgen escaped, each would stand in their turn, within a large urilatum bowl to ensure no irretrievable loss would occur.

The knife and bowl she had burned in crystal fire, the glasses scoured with urilatum dust to eliminate contamination. These articles waited on an urilatum tray. Lying on the table, where she would lay the boy down, straps to curb struggle and bind him helpless, together with a tongue press to check his screams throughout the entire and lengthy operation.

If...if the document found amongst her father's collection of ancient histories told true, from the child, from his blood and the talent travelling in it, she could benefit. The spectral appearance she fast approached would not just be halted, she would be restored, and with more power than possessed before. If....if the document told true, and talent really was transferable from one to another.

The thought of actually drinking his blood revolted her. The thought of what it could do, set aside all qualms. She would drink it down. Drink it to the dregs, and lick her lips after. By the gate, once again, Lingaradgh spoke words to open it, and peered through, hoping to see her daughter hastening through the trees. Except for leaves fluttering in night breezes, she saw no movement, and no sound other than the rustling voices of the faded and the creaking crack of rotting wood.

Slamming the gate shut, she marched back to the summerhouse, climbed the stairs and reaching the spire, paused to catch breath to consider what must be spoken.

I must not rant. With the Guardians breathing down Apatia's neck, my voice divorced from bubbled fury must be, that I drive her not into the maw of disastrous action. I must speak firm without harshness, a few words phrased succinctly to encapsulate the danger we both stand in the way of, yet give her no leeway for further delay.

Opening a window, she moved to one of the shelves, and lifting the lid of a casket, containing small envelopes, took one out. A tiny pearlescent sphere rolled from the flax-paper packet to nestle in the palm of her hand.

"Apatia," she breathed onto it, "I have care for the problem you currently experience, but care much more for the problem we both shall soon have. Bring him now."

Carrying the swollen message bubble to the window, she threw it out, and remaining to watch it fly, frowned when she saw it twitch and tremble as it hovered in the air, before it wobbled unsteadily on an unseen axis, and moments later, plummeted, heavy as stone, straight to the ground. Her own voice, the exact words entrusted to the bubble, floated up to her.

"Will nothing go right this darkling?" she stormed, seizing another envelope from the casket.

The flax-paper envelope ripped open, the tiny sphere rolling out onto her palm, she spoke, her tone tolling harsh and cold, "Daughter, if I must come and fetch the child, this do I solemnly promise. Next brightling, you will not see, nor any after it. Bring him now."

She moved back to the window, and the bubble shivering rainbows on her outstretched hand, was flung out into the night.

"Some defect the other must have had," she said, watching its arrowed flight.

Satisfied her message would reach its destination, she began to close the casement; then thinking the bubble's luminescence seemed unnaturally bright against the deep green of a sky trickled with purpled-grey, held it ajar.

Now just a pinpoint of firefly-glow in the darkness, she saw it make a wide curve and journey in ever decreasing circles, as if it had lost all sense of direction, and close in upon itself. Ringed with travel-shine it pulled up short, and hovering indecision for a few moments, suddenly made straight for her.

"By the powers," she screamed, slamming the window shut, "what goes?"

Exploding on one of the crystal panes, the bubble exploded and delivered its message.

* * *

Aches and pains, forgotten in the heat of murderous action and its exhilarating aftermath, returned to gnaw at him with dull teeth. Limping, Slubeadgh cautiously made his way through the labyrinthine tangle of passages. Constantly squinting into the darkness for any glimmer of light that would signal the secret paths were being patrolled, he groped towards the way out, stopping every so often to listen for the sound of pursuit.

Two victories under his belt would mean nothing, if he were found roaming these byways. Blood spatters in his hair, on face, hands and greatcoat could perhaps be explained. Scabs, formed over cuts Semyon had given him, as well as scratches acquired on his journey back to the Helm could be ripped off to aid a claim the damning marks were made by injuries sustained travelling from Lessadgh. If necessary, he would do it.

But he had many enemies in the Helm, and throughout the city. They would most surely point the finger, and put their full weight behind Reboia, if she said he was responsible for Semyon's dispatch, and he was uncertain whether she had caught a glimpse of him or not. The fan close to his breast, his only comfort, the blood drying on the tips of the feathers his ultimate betrayer, he could not bring himself to wipe incriminating gore away. To remove it would be to erase the only tangible evidence of newly found courage and a deed well done.

On he limped, parting curtains of cobwebs with one hand and touching the wall with the other, negotiating his way through the paths with difficulty in the darkness. The voices of the faded, keeping him company, could not overcome regret that Galateo's chatter was not filling his head with welcome noise.

Ahead, a soft glow beckoned, that had nothing to do with a fire crystal's blaze. Relieved, it could be nothing but moonshine's gleam filtering through the arched window beside the secret door, he hurried towards it. His fingers would find the catch soon enough, and release him into the world, where he would disappear and go to the life he longed to live in a Kingdom City far from this. Putting any further thought of capture out of his mind, Slubeadgh hurried toward the cold light.

* * *

"I think," Bezel said, thoughtful, "we should forget about balconies, comrade. Another way into the Helm there is. Just now, did that raggedy creature hobbling fast across the grass, show the way. Out of the very stones of the wall did he slinking emerge, and set off at hirpled pace. Doubtless, he is no better than he should be, having a scurvy look about him, but by the powers, a door must lie hidden close by that arched window. My reputation, do I stake on it."

"No matter," Clump said, brusque.

"No matter? You tell me no matter? For what reason is it now of no matter, when half this darkling has been spent trying to get inside the Helm, comrade?"

"My mind be changed."

"What? This woman and her lost child, for whom you embarked on this enterprise, are of no further concern?"

"Do not be ridiculous," Clump snorted, and began to walk hurriedly away. "My concern is as great as ever it was, how could it not be?"

"What then, friend?" Bezel cried, striding to keep up with him.

"She is no longer in the Helm. I go to meet her."

"You have an assignation?" Bezel squeaked, incredulous.

"Come. Meet her, too. Come away, there be danger."

"Friend, I did not think it before, believing you to be a person of sound mind, if little good judgment, but now, truly do I believe you should be away dancing with the Mendicants."

"Say that when stonework rains down upon your pate," Clump shouted.

* * *

Every particle of Apatia faithfully collected in the ruby bottle, William finished screwing the urilatum cap tight, and held the bottle up to a fire crystal's blaze. Smoke, densely packed inside, dulled the gem's lustre, but threw intricate carving running around it into bold relief. In his mind's eye, he could see Clara, small beside Ratanakiri, hurrying away from the Helm across a stretch of close-clipped grass to the flower gardens, and Clump, accompanied by one who chattered too much, and behaved like a fool, but was not, swiftly going in the same direction.

Rubbing one temple, where the pain was worse, he got to his feet and lowered his head. From beneath his brow, he stared hard at the web-silk curtains hanging at the long windows leading out onto the balcony, as the making sprang easy to his tongue. The rhythm begun, the cadence shifting from level to level, he felt the rush of power rise fast and strong. Cold heat, shooting up, ancient words carried on insubstantial breath, changed into a metamorphic blast that all but atomized the windows, the cracked decaying stonework of the wall around them and beyond.

An unnatural spume disgorged from the uppermost level of the Helm. Powdered dust, and pebbled stone, vomited out into the night air. Borne in the churn of the foamed explosion that pierced the air, burning slivers of fragmented wood, shards of needled crystal, miniscule pieces of web-silk curtains and decorative hangings. The rippling cloud of destruction expanded, spreading towards the memorial garden, and in its midst, treading on friendly breezes, William walked.

Chapter 54.

Windblown debris rose above the tallest spire of the Helm, and rising higher still, brushed lightly against the apex of a dome comprised of myriad, invisible threads artfully woven together to enclose the Kingdom City. The heart of the making touched, it glimmered for an instant and once again was veiled from sight.

* * *

Congratulating himself on his prowess, skill, ingenuity and ability to overcome any difficulty, Slubeadgh laboured across manicured grass in the direction of the memorial garden, and the culvert. Startled by a violent, thunderous crack, followed by a succession of reverberating roars that seemed to be running close behind him, he glanced over one shoulder to see the cause.

Coming toward him. Rolling fast, massive in proportion, billow upon writhing billow, of blanketing cloud blotted out ground he had just recently limped over, together with the Helm and the sky. Petrified, his mind numbed by the certain destruction threatening to engulf him, he froze.

Seizing the moment, Galateo shrieked, "Brother! This is no time for paralysis to set in. Move. Move. Move, or we choke to fading and join this dust. Move, brother, for pity's sake save your noble self. Move!"

"Galateo?" he gulped.

"Yes, brother?"

"We are done for."

"Not if you act. Run, brother. Run, our lives depend on the strength in your legs. Run. Good, I knew you could do it, brother. One foot before the other and do it very fast. Very good, but faster, brother, faster, show us at what great speed you can sprint. Reach the culvert, and we are saved by a deed no less than heroic."

The whip of encouragement liberally applied, Slubeadgh obeyed the screamed instructions. Breath grating in his throat, a fire ignited in heaving lungs, muscles and sinews straining, his feet barely skimming the grass, he gained the culvert, crawled inside and lay crying and sobbing.

"We are safe?" he finally managed to babble.

Foolish to tell his brother, the dust cloud had been rolling in the direction of the memorial garden. Foolish to mention, the culvert was well to the side of that revered, forbidden place, and would therefore escape the worst of rapidly falling dust that even now, fresh breezes were picking up and carrying far away. Foolish to say any of this, for had his brother kept his wits about him, these things he would have seen for himself. And, far more foolish than any foolishness, not to capitalize on his brother's cowardly stupidity, and take the first step back to supremacy.

"Brother, I think we are. But for the herculean effort you made we would surely have perished."

"Best stay here awhile?" he queried.

"You exercise great wisdom," Galateo flattered. "Most risky it would be to leave this place of sanctuary, for it may well be, choking cloud chases beyond the boundary walls of the Helm, and where would we be, if having escaped it once, we then fell into its clutches?"

* * *

"Clara," Ratanakiri said, "the strangest things occur this darkling. Coming toward us is a dwarf, one of those who are stunted and shunned. Look," she said, pointing to Clump marching confidently with Bezel, who, bewildered by the sudden change of plan and his companion's unexplained cheerfulness, trailed a little behind. "Look!"

Understanding nothing Ratanakiri said, other than she said her name, Clara followed the line of her pointing finger. She knew him by his stamping walk, the set of his shoulders and the shape of his head.

"Clump!" she cried, running to meet him.

"Clara!" a smile engulfed his dour face. "How came you through the sally port unscathed, I know not, but most glad, no gladder than most glad, I am to see you."

Behind him, unable to comprehend the language spoken, but interpreting the tone of words spoken, and actions well enough, Bezel quietly remarking on shameful understatements, unashamedly gawked at the woman of Lessadgh.

"Heavens above, how you stink," she said, wrinkling her nose in disgust.

"An inadvertent tumble into a heap of haran dung. Clara, listen, I have yet to find your boy, but know where..."

An explosion rocked the stillness of the night.

* * *

Magnified a thousand times, whiplash-cracked sound parted the air and dragged a growling rumble in its wake. Immediately, furious attention removed from the remains of the message bubble, smeared wet on the windowpane, its faults and deficiencies were usurped by urgent interest that was quickly satisfied.

Above the trees, a dense plume of whiteness spewing into the sky clouded night's colours with mirk. Weightless, minute particles puffed higher by the breeze, drifted past the tallest spire and, lightly touching some of the finely drawn threads of illusion she had woven to precise tautness, briefly glimmered. Shocked at the sight, Lingaradgh sank to her knees. Her mind momentarily blank, and the roundelay sung in her head faltering, a few delicate filaments at the very heart of her making, snapped. Zigzagging fast away from each other, she concentrated on catching the loose ends, and reconnecting them, and never saw brightness, moving above manicured lawns, was shrouded in desiccated rubble.

Over the ancient copse, where trees veined with tired sap and still clinging to life, were fighting a losing battle with young saplings, hungry for space, reached for the light. Over the circling wall, into the hideous garden tombed with the living, silently rotting. William stepped down from breezes that had borne him. Throwing off the cloaking cloud, he walked among the willodghs accompanied by the mournful dirge of pleas and laments sighing through their fronds.

"Imprisoned in heartwood," he said, "you have suffered for no good reason, for too long. I tell you what is needful to know. You are beyond all help. I can give no resurrection to putrefying flesh, peeling from the flaking scaffold of marrow-dried bones. That making is beyond me. Peace, I bring, and beg forgiveness for an evil deed, kindly done."

"From this living hell deliver us, and the powers bless you for a kind deed, kindly done," he heard rustling through the feathery leaves.

Lowering his head, looking from beneath his brow, he scythed the trunks of trees nearest to him in half, and having released the occupants to merciful oblivion, went on through the garden felling trees and hedged the paths with ruin.

Despite the roundelay being spun in such rapid turn, and silently mouthing words to support those sung in her head, Lingaradgh could not catch the loose threads with mental hooks, nor snare off-shooting tendrils. And worse, for some reason she had no time to discern, she could not stop skilfully woven threads, so carefully maintained, from fraying one after another.

Outside, in her beloved garden, dread thuds beat the ground with heavy fall, and vibrations trilling into the foundations of the summerhouse, called for her attention. Frantic to keep her creation intact, countering unravelling illusion with all her craft of making, she created new filaments to weave and take the place of those wantonly disintegrating, and had no time or inclination to answer. Newly made threads buckled, and bent, and would not be twisted pliable into the warp and weft, and becoming brittle, fragmented even as she coaxed them to her will.

Drawn from words spinning in her mind, and silently mouthed, newly made threads, short in length and thick as her smallest finger, were completely useless. She put them through the mental pulling block and drew them through it again, and again, and again.

Above, a tiny breach at the apex of the dome was circled by little lights that winked like a shimmered halo, or a naughty tonsure, in the fabric of her illusion. Threads remade, and woven into place, suddenly became elastic, drooping and rubbery. No matter how hard she strived to pull them taut, they stretched, seeming to have the ability of infinite length and ultimate sagging limpness. And still threads frayed and snapped. The breach in the dome, no longer neatly rounded, was notched with a ragged glow.

Medusa-haired trees, William thought when they had been felled and the last of the long, leafed fronds snaking through the air, settled sighing on the ground to rest in untidy, sprawled heaps. Grim gardening completed, he walked between the columns of the portico and into the foyer of the summerhouse. Leaking from beneath the door of the cellar, the subtle odour of gold burnt to powder turned his stomach, and strengthened the intensity of pain in his head. Rubbing his temple, he began to climb the stairs, carrying in his other hand the ruby bottle. Keeping his promise, he took Apatia to her mother and to a much longed for meeting, but not in any circumstance either woman had expected. At the top, he waited, watching through the opened doorway, Lingaradgh on her knees, contriving with demented fervour making, after making, after making, never realising his was stronger than anything she could ever devise or construct. Dispassionately, he looked at the instruments arranged in readiness on a long table to take, so she had thought, his gift, his talent and his power, and his eyes sweeping around the room, that had been the true seat of rule in Almandine, briefly scanned shelves crammed with ancient books and charts, crammed with jars containing dried berries, herbs and flowers she had believed would aid her. He called her name.

She could not halt the destruction of her life's work, nor could any measure taken countermand the steady demolition. The roundelay disturbed by her efforts, partially neglected, while she sought for reasons, for answers that always led back to the Guardians' probes, and eminent punishment, hiccoughed in her head. The words now mumbled out loud, stumbled and shuffled, and the apex of the dome holding her illusion in place within its ordained bounds, was gone. Threads fraying and snapping, glimmering shine crept down every length, and she could do nothing. Nothing.

Fear, a forgotten emotion, congealed in the pit of her stomach, its acid gall bitter, its fumes stinging the roundelay to a grinding halt, and someone, someone called her name in tones owning no maturity, that could only be a child.

"Lingaradgh," William said, again.

Without turning to face him, she accused in matter of fact chimes, "You are the child stolen from Lessadgh , though no child now?"

"I am. I am the child from whom childhood has been stolen."

"That theft was mine," she admitted, refusing to meet his face, "and in its place, gifted you with power. I see it is great. As great, possibly, as that which once mantled Atrament, for its glow lights up the room to brilliancy and reflects from the windowpanes. Many tribulations may it bear you down with."

"You curse me?"

"Perhaps. Or, perhaps, I see it without looking. You are come to gloat? To fade me?" she asked, calm.

"No, that is not my purpose. Time is what you have fought for and against, and it is time, albeit short, you will keep. If it is oblivion you seek, wishing to dwell in the unending dreamless sleep of dust, by your own hand must you place yourself there, or beg the hand of some other help you to it."

"Clever," she said, closing her eyes against the kindness of his cruelty. "You leave me time in which to torture myself with what might have been, to regret that which narrowly slipped through my grasp, and await punishment doled out by the Guardians."

"First, they must find you."

"I am expelled from my own Kingdom?"

"A Kingdom you have abused, brought to wrack and ruin for the sake of vanity. A Kingdom you would be well advised to depart from. Stay or go, Lingaradgh. It is nothing to me."

"What then is your purpose here?"

"I bring your daughter to you."

"That talentless, little fool! Of what use is she to me now?"

"That is for you to determine. Here, take her," he held out the ruby bottle, waiting patient for her to climb from her knees to her feet and turn to him, and when she did not, he went to her side, unclenched a fist folded in her lap and put the bottle in it.

"What is this?" she asked, staring down at the ruby glinting dull on the palm of her hand.

"Your daughter is safe inside. Draughts, or sudden breezes, will be her complete undoing, so you must guard her well, as you must yourself, for you are almost a spectre, and she, most certainly a wraith. Apatia is all you now own in this Kingdom, and departs with you."

Drained by defeat, Lingaradgh lurched to her feet and staggered to the door. Holding onto the frame, she stared at William for the first time, and, only for a moment, envied talent moving a sparkled journey on his skin. Holding her daughter close to her breast, she let go of the doorpost, swayed, corrected her balance and went down the stairs, through the foyer of the summerhouse, and the desolation of her garden.

William shattered the adamantine knife to smithereens. The urilatum bowl, he crushed between his hands into a ball. The goblets, straps and tongue press, he burnt to ashes, and leaving the summerhouse, razed it to the ground. Outside the circling wall of the garden, he erased all trace of Lingaradgh and the place where she had dwelt so long. With the breath of his mouth, he erased it all.

Chapter 55.

"Heavy blows shake the ground," Slubeadgh whimpered, stating the obvious.

"Trees in the memorial garden fall one after another, I think, brother," Galateo piped thoughtful.

"Trees falling? You are sure?"

"What else could it be, brother? Can you not hear the agony of bark and sapwood cast down? The misery of multitudinous leaves crushed? Yes, that is most surely happening. The smell of fresh, hewn wood confirms it."

"Now you mention it, those smells worm into my nose, too," he agreed. "What goes?"

Curiosity piqued, Galateo piped, "To know that, brother, you must turn about, since you face the wrong direction. Crawl to the end of the culvert, and altering your position, return to have sight of what goes. Courage, and more besides, I know you have, do you not, to learn something to our advantage, mayhap?"

Not wanting to confess, terror of the monstrous cloud that had chased him still lingered, he shrugged nonchalantly.

"Do we not go back on wisdom? Choking dust may lie in wait," he said, hoping to put an end to his twin's suggestion.

"Brother, that is easily answered," Galateo stifled scornful laughter. "If it lie in wait, nearing the mouth of the culvert we shall see it. Did you not notice how it coloured the night with mirky gloom?"

In the throes of panic, he had not seen anything of the sort, but would rather have cut out his tongue than admit it. "You are right," he said, "I had forgot the shrouding drabness."

Humping reluctantly to hands and knees, he began to move slowly, peering ahead all the while, and sampling the air to make sure it contained no element that might kill him. On the other side of the culvert, the air was clear and sweet. When he looked up to make sure no danger lurked above, the night sky was planished darkest green and teased with a purpled, milky blush untainted by any dust. Without a word, he turned round, and went scrabbling back through detritus scumming the tunnel. On reaching the opening he had clawed through in panic, he said, "Though the cloud appears to have dispersed, which being a strange thing of itself, there is nothing to see."

"Naturally, we are still lodged inside. We spoke of the memorial garden, remember? To see what passes in it, we must venture forth a little, just a little, and your great courage, brother, will carry us outside. Perhaps, now danger no longer threatens, heroic courage will carry us into the copse to gain a better view."

Unable to argue with his brother's logic, and growing more curious now no risk was attached to a request, humbly couched in terms recognizing his worth, he crawled out, got to his feet and, picking his way across broken stones strewn in front of the culvert, slunk into long grass and headed toward the copse.

"All is silent," he said, once they were between the trees. "A short, perilous journey I have made to avail me nothing."

"No, and I, most sorry for it, brother."

"Wait," he hissed, jumping off of the path and pinning himself to the trunk of a young sapling, "someone speaks. Apatia is here."

"Not Apatia, brother, her voice has no ringing chime to it."

"Hush, shut your clack." Curiosity overcoming his fear, he dared to peer out from his hiding place. "The gate opens. One comes forth. See how she is worn to thinness?"

"Near to fading that one is," Galateo agreed. "You know of her?"

"Hard to tell in darkling light. Did I not know she was faded, I might have hazarded Lingaradgh walks, but her, it cannot be."

"A stranger emerges from a place forbidden. Here is a mystery, brother. In revealing a little, it explains nothing, and still no knowledge do we have of what passes here."

"I am wearied to the bone," Slubeadgh said. "All I wished to do is accomplished, and if curiosity stirs at fullest throttle, no further intrigue will I allow it to pull me into. I am done. I go to collect a little of my wealth, and begin a life dreamt of."

"Wisdom, brother, you have it in large amounts and I, very wrong to coax you hence. We go then?"

"We do. When this one with stumbling gait, and pale almost to the point of transparency, has passed, we will go swift away."

The brothers, for once in agreement, watched the woman walking slow along a well-trodden path, disappear between the trees.

He had not gone far when grumbled sound took him to his knees. Curled into a ball, he expected choking cloud to descend at any moment.

"The memorial garden," Galateo piped, "what goes is not yet done."

Cautious, he glanced up. Reassured the air around him remained untroubled, he got to his feet and swaggered, mindlessly kicking at grass with battered boots.

"Swift action I took to protect us," he lied. "Had malicious cloud deceitfully dropped sudden upon us, no time would there have been to sprint to safety, and ever is it better to be safe than sorry."

"I know it," Galateo lied back, massaging his ego. "Lightning reflexes, such as yours, brother, are to be applauded."

Vanity ballooned, courage appreciated, and undoubted, thin shoulders squared, narrow chest puffed out, he sauntered back to the culvert. By the stones, lying in front of it, he turned, intending to take a sentimental, final look at the place he was about to leave and yelped in amazement.

The crystal spire of the summerhouse, shimmered by moon glow, was unmistakably sinking gently below the tree line. And high above it, the sky seemed to be decorated with an exquisite veil of quivering lights, randomly cascading outward and down from a jagged hole torn in the centre of it.

"Weirdness is upon this place," he gulped. Pivoting on the spot, he took in the immensity of something resembling a broken dome, appearing as far as he could tell, to enclose the entire city. "Well are we gone from this place, and gone quick."

* * *

Delicious scandal passed from gossiping mouth to gossiping mouth. High treason configured in a thousand different ways and rehashed in a thousand others. Reasons for the act, continuing to be unknown, a matter of conjecture for fertile and puerile imaginations to have sport with. Punishment for the act, suffering a similar lack, was no bar to announcements of imminent fading, shortly after retracted, only to surface in a different guise from different mouths again and again.

Onward ran the most crucial debate of all between Semyon's supporters and detractors. Had he, or had he not, done the deed? Arguments, scuffles and blows were struck, as debates grew heated. This scandal, the best in an age, blowing faster than tumbleweed in high wind, circulated and would have continued had someone not looked up. Looked up, and seeing a glimmering halo in the sky, point to it screaming adamantly, "This is a sign of Semyon's innocence, by the powers it is."

One head, face to the sky, became an undulating wave of faces upturning to see what the commotion was about. A surge of pointing fingers, and excited voices rising to the highest levels of noisy clamour screened out the blast blowing out the wall in the Helm, and if a loud bang had been heard it was ignored, as rumour ran endless throughout the Kingdom City for hours.

But now, shimmering lights winking upon the jagged edges of Lingaradgh's broken making, gossip found new legs to run, or jump upon, and bellowed defiantly, "Semyon's guilt is proven by the sign, by the powers it is."

And all the while, the tear in the delicate network grew steadily wider, the display of little lights briefly spangling its borders flickered out and came again with each creeping new expansion, and gradually, gossip of Semyon's disgrace was forgotten. All thought of signs of guilt or innocence cast aside, theories began to be expounded. Circulating faster than a fire crystal could flame, supposition bounced across the city in an attempt to explain what was now perceived to be more than any portent, but a miraculous happening.

"Star dust sprinkles!"

"Why then are we not sprinkled by it then?"

"I am sprinkled with it."

"Idiot, dandruff lies heavy on your collar."

"New stars struggle to be birthed."

"Yes, yes, and the darkling orb, jealous of its position, gobbles them up."

"Lunatic! If that were so, the darkling orb would be chasing after them yet it remains stationary."

"Lunatic, yourself, if you do not know the darkling orb has power to pull objects to it."

"Nothing to with the darkling orb is this. The lights go away, not toward it. See the downward trajectory now?"

"I see a waterfall of tiny lights."

"Some unnatural phenomenon this is."

"Well do we know it, but what?"

"This is the Guardians' doing."

"Since when did the Guardians do anything for our amusement?"

"No amusement, is this, but a strong making being rent asunder."

"What? What was just said?"

"A making is spoken about."

"Great talent would be needed."

"Only the Guardians have such power."

"The Guardians spread a making around us!"

"Around the city?"

"I have just had it from an acquaintance newly come from the eastern gate."

"A making? To what purpose?"

"Penalty. Have you not heard? Apatia, Lord of the Helm, walks the way of Atrament."

"It is true, then?"

"Surely, why would any even whisper such a thing, if it were not true?"

"By the powers, now shall we suffer for her wrongdoing."

"Increased taxes."

"Increased taxes, they are saying, could they be right?"

"Away home, am I, to hide what wealth I have. If the High Lord, or the Guardians, think to dip into my coffers, they shall come up empty. I advise you do likewise."

"It is proved, then? The Lady treads the Way."

"Of a certainty. This rain of unnatural light is of the Guardians' manufacture. They prevent her escape."

And still, streaming ribbons of tiny lights glimmered and failed. Falling rapidly, the veil woven to hold a great illusion in place, one that had dulled all senses to the true condition of a city, famed for its fabulous architecture, would reveal what had been hidden.

The revelation began on top of the tallest tower, where none could see it.

Borne down by the weight of the spire, rotten timbers cracked, crumbled and gave way.

* * *

One of the guards, who had stood sentry outside the apartment, tramped through the rooms to the bedchamber, shouting, "Reboia! We are called away. There is talk of an attack on the Helm."

"Impossible," she bawled, staunching the wound on Semyon's neck with a cloth, "warfare is against all protocol laid down by the Guardians. None would dare it."

"Nevertheless, the dread sound we heard was an explosion of some kind. It has cleaved the Helm from the Lady's tower garden to the ground, so I am told. We are ordered to assist and must obey."

"The Restorer has been summoned?"

"He has, though, by all account many have been faded, even more are injured. If true, it may be his services will be diverted from you and the Commander."

"Then go," she said, reaching for another towel. "You can do nothing here."

Chapter 56.

He was tired, very tired, his step listless and heavy, and his head hurt. The pain, so excruciating, his vision was impaired. His eyes felt as though they were spinning in their sockets, and he could not bring them to focus on the way he must go. He closed them, and exhausted by the makings performed, lay down amongst debris thickly banked in the copse, and thought of Clara.

Warm and soft, her arms wound around him. So strong, so comforting, they held him close, while her work-hardened fingers, cool and soothing, stroked his forehead with gentle roughness. Her voice, lowered to almost a whisper, had lulled him away from childish fears when he had woken in fright from bad dreams, saying, 'Be at peace, little one. There is no need to fear, child of my heart, my only love.'

The same floating sensation, which had always come when he had drifted back into careless sleep, secure in the knowledge she was there, engulfed him now until he thought, *Clara waits... she waits for me.*

His eyes snapped open. Looming above him, shadowy, twisted and broken, the arc of decrepit branches. He saw them clearly. Refreshed, he got to his feet, walked through the trees, and out into long unkempt grass girdling the copse.

"Clara is waiting for me," he repeated, and with talent's brilliancy lighting the path, he moved quickly to the place where she waited for him.

* * *

Out on the lawns, well away from masonry occasionally falling from the breach in the Helm, the lucky ones who had escaped the catastrophe were huddled together in small groups. Hysterical panic had subsided into uneasy calm. Each person had a story to tell of possessions lost, of near escapes, or minor injuries to show. In the midst of these conversations, speculating on the cause of the apparition in the sky, and the reason for the sudden demolition, stranded gossip faltered for a few moments, each time someone badly injured was carried from the buildings by guards, before the thread was picked up again.

When the fissure creaked and yawned wider, a gasp of horror accompanied it, and a small torrent of stones tumbling down to the ground was met with screams of grief that soon gave way to continued gossip and conjecture.

"An omen of disaster, the halo in the sky must be."

"That appears after disaster has struck? Go dance with the Mendicants."

"There is talk, the round of glimmered lights portends the collapse of the

Helm," someone said, loud, to get attention and was gratified by all eyes swivelling to him.

"It matters not what imagination conjures from suspected portents," someone else countered. "The Helm is strong. The slabs of its construction well cut, and maintained."

"Not so, look you at this chunk of masonry. See it raddled and crumbled by age? If this stone has such condition, others surely have it, and nothing has the lightshow above to do with this."

"May the powers preserve us," someone shrieked. "The spire in the memorial gardens has disappeared!"

"Disappeared? Nonsense."

"Shock, from this darkling's misfortune, has addled his mind."

"No. He spoke true. Look. The spire's sparkle has vanished."

"By the powers it has!"

"How could it?"

"Tremors, from this portion of the wall's collapse, brought it down? Perhaps?"

"Someone should tell the Lady."

"Speak to the Lady of further devastation? Rather you, than I."

"Powers deliver us," someone howled, "Atrament walks!"

Unmindful of the extent of damage done to the Helm, fadings caused, injuries sustained, or terror screamed out by night-darkened figures running as fast as their legs could carry them, William, clothed in light, walked across manicured grass. Closed to everything about him, he walked across the wide expanse of the lawns, going to where Clara waited with Persimmony Clump. In one of the many ornamental gardens, beneath the fluted cupola of a pergola, draped with a profusion of pendulous white flowers, whose large, waxy petals competed with the heady perfume of night flowering lilies, she, he, and those with them, were wreathed in shadows.

A little way from the others, Ratanakiri paced while Bezel lounged against the trunk of a tree with his hands deep in the pockets of his voluminous trousers.

"We dally for what?" he whispered.

Ratanakiri shrugged, "I cannot say."

"You were told to bring the woman of Lessadgh to this place, you say?"

"That is not the right of it exact," she answered. "More of a thought it was. Compelling thought, I could not deny, despite known risk, but none gave challenge or tried to prevent us leaving the Helm, even though we were seen."

"Strange. Strange as the cleft struck in the Helm, and the hole-shot shimmers in the sky above it."

"More strangeness, to add to the strangeness witnessed these past spans, and never thought, in all my life, to see," she agreed.

"Ho!" he said, pushing away from the tree. "Here comes a bright light."

Ratanakiri shrank nervously into deeper shade, and moaned, "Who comes? Surely not the guard to fetch the woman and me, back?"

"Stay here out of sight. I shall see if need there is for alarm," he winked, and jumping lightly across a bed of lilies, crept into the bushes beyond and disappeared.

"Tepauni's stinking arse!" Ratanakiri heard him yell.

"What comes?" she cried, ready to pick up her heels to warn the woman of Lessadgh.

"A child," Bezel gasped, falling out of the shrubbery, "if my eyes deceived me not. A child, naked as when his mother birthed him, and ablaze with talent comes, that is what!"

"Clara's boy. Clara, Clara," she shouted, running to the pergola, "your child comes to meet you."

"What did she say?" Clara asked Clump.

"She said, William be come."

Much changed, he had said. Many changes, she had imagined, all revolving around some kind of dread disfigurement, but never this. Her mind whirled, asking, what had really changed? If he glowed like a beacon, what did it matter? He was still her boy. Plainly, his body was whole with no marks of abuse on his skin, his beautiful face unblemished by any wound, and best of all, her heart sang, he was with her once again.

Beside her, Clump usually stoic, gold-fished the air saying nothing.

"You wear no clothing, William," she said, taking the blanket from her shoulders. Wrapping him in it, she kept her arms locked fast around him, pulling him into a tighter and tighter embrace that spoke more than any words could say, while murmuring in his ear, "I thought I had lost you, child of my heart, my darling boy, and here you are. Praise be, for I could not have borne the losing of you."

Laying his head on her shoulder, he nuzzled her hair, smelling her smells as her softness enfolded him, and her breath tickling his skin, William said, "My head hurts, Clara."

* * *

High treason, little lights streaming a rainfall from the sky all around the city, and now this news, trickling out into the heaving crowds on all streets. An explosion in the Helm had riven one of its stout walls from stem to stern. Masonry continuing to fall into the gardens, it was likely the whole of the beautiful building would come down.

For once, news of devastation, too much for gossips to take delight in, from mouth to mouth, the mournful information of catastrophe was spread. Stunned incredulity, replacing agreeable chatter, blunted the edge of sharp-tongued criticism on the why, and wherefore, of Semyon's innocence or guilt, and effectively bridled all from rife speculation.

* * *

In the tallest tower of the city, the spire followed rotting beams to the next level. Crashing down into the empty space, blocks of soft stone, imperfectly cut with the skill of poor workmanship, and honeycombed with age, shattered, buckling the rough-cut timbers of the floor beneath, and pressuring the circular wall by its sudden weight. The hail of pebbles produced by the fall, knocked out windows, creating a shower of bouncing shards of glass.

Improperly mortared with a weak mix, which had crumbled to friable dust, slabs dislodged by the sudden impact of the debris were pushed from the anchor that should have secured them in place, and now perched precariously upon those below. Gradually, settling and shifting, the heavy burden of ruin drove them further out, and gravity finally taking hold, brought blocks somersaulting onto the crowd massed in the square below.

* * *

Panic in the Helm. Above Apatia's apartments, the rooftop garden sagged, levering the breach apart with more and more heaviness. Jutting and jagged, the huge blocks on either side were pushed further apart and moving, leant on adjacent slabs. Displaced, they in turn shifted their neighbour, filling fissures that had widened into cracks, crushing mortared glue to powder and slowly ground fragile stones to pebbled grains. Continually scattering a fragmented cascade, the forced separation gaped to a perilous 'V' as the remorseless advance of skewed stone continued.

Mingling with groans made by the distressed walls, ceilings moaned and split. Floorboards, dragged from their moorings, screeched. Two levels below the compromised garden, courtiers and their servants, who had been evacuated from their apartments, were crammed into chambers with the occupants, where it was thought to be safe. Complaining to anyone who would listen, valuable possessions, important documents, articles of especial sentiment that could never be replaced might be lost, few heard the panting guard, running along the corridors at full pelt, yelling everyone should get out. Duty done, he ran down the stairway to the next level to shout the same heated message.

"Wait!" a senior officer shouted from the stair above. "The Lady Apatia, you have seen her?"

"No, sir."

"You searched for her on the floor just left?"

"No, sir. To shout news of complete evacuation, my only order."

Nodding, the officer told him to carry on, and went back up to begin a more comprehensive search.

A thunderous rumble of shattered roofing, and thick, cracked beams finally giving way, preceded an avalanche of soil and plants. Its descent halted for a brief time by steadily bulging walls, the floor beneath straining to hold the monumentally heavy load, stopped all complaints of possible loss. In the face of a far greater threat, a maelstrom of panic erupted. No deference shown to age, sex, position or status, one and all pushed and shoved, elbowed, punched, kicked and clawed to be one of the first out of the rooms, and into the corridor, only to find when they had achieved this, they were congested by the same frantic traffic, and the long flights of stairs they had hoped would take them to safety, were unattainable.

* * *

The worst of the flow staunched to a trickle, Reboia bandaged Semyon's neck with shredded towels. Outside in the corridors, and overhead, the sound of panic finally barged into the chamber. Making sure he still breathed easy, she left him to find out what was happening. The door to the corridor opened for just a moment, she learned all that needed to be known. Slamming it shut, she leant against it.

The Helm was falling. She could not digest information screamed and babbled, yet could not deny it either. Glimpsing grim terror written on faces streaming past in the brief instant she had looked out, she knew it was true.

Be calm, she thought, *be rational. To take him out into frenzy will be the fading of us both. I have not the strength to carry him, and fight my way clear of the Helm. I must wait until the clamour lessens.*

Hurrying back, she rolled him over, dressed deep wounds on his back as best she could, wrapped him in the counterpane, pulled from his bed, then taking hold of material closest to his head, slowly dragged him from the bathing room, through to the anteroom, and waited.

Chapter 57.

Panic, on the lawns of the Helm, had given way to morbid fascination, or resignation of an incomprehensible combined, set of events. Imagining Atrament walked, the first survivors of the disaster had long fled, wailing in terror to tell the tale. In their place, new groups oblivious of a dread sighting, huddled on the grass at a safe distance from what was now believed to be the inevitable fall of the Helm in its entirety. Plainly seen, in the flare of fire crystals, debris was no longer a sifting trickle from walls ravaged by the blast, but flowing freely. No longer an occasional slab, driven from its position and tentatively teetering before plummeting, but a card-trick of flying masonry, steadily falling and burrowing deep into the close-cropped lawns.

Plainly seen, in the flare of fire crystals held on sconces, and far beyond any dispute, the Helm had been cleaved in two. From sfem to stern, back to front, it appeared to be a huge and unmanageable doll's house, whose hinges had been broken past any repair. Its interior chambers, fully exposed, showed them to be lying at odd and tragically impossible angles. Floors up-tilted and mangled. Priceless furniture, decorative objects and web-silk hangings could be seen sliding, fleeing from the yawning crevasse, smashing and crashing, and piling haphazard and awkward, bludgeoning the walls of one chamber to force entry to the next, added their power to the Helm's overthrow, and nothing could be done to salvage a single thing.

For once, disinclined to idle chatter, or wild speculation, they waited in silence, listening to the agony of a fabulous building, famed for its beauty throughout all of Noor, being rent into pieces, while watching recalcitrant stone stretching out, mimick the movement of a haran's arching neck reach for water.

Great cries of dismay, expressing all degrees of grief, were made when a large portion fell, but unable to tear their eyes away from the relentless destruction of a place known for all their long lives, the groups growing larger, continued to watch. Besides, there was nowhere else to go. For hours, noisy good-natured hubbub, floating excitedly over the wall encircling the Helm and its grounds, had recently acquired a tone of stridency, and rapidly swelling into something more menacing, until the unmistakable sounds of rioting in the streets was heard.

* * *

Joy. What else could it be, when a series of effervescent fountains bubbled through her? The urge to get up from the bench, to go out from the talent lit shadows of the pergola was strong. To dance, with the moon her only witness, a prancing jig of overwhelming happiness and gratitude, Clara felt compelled to step, while singing a song. And the song would have been one, not only of joy, but defiance raised to the highest, loudest pitch, yelled at this strange world, and the giants in it, for the child she had thought to never see again was with her. This, she would have done, if the lump in her throat had not been so large, and compulsion, however strong, could not be obeyed.

Wrapped in the blanket she had enfolded him in, William lay on the bench, one shoulder warming her thigh and his head in her lap. Loving the solid weight of him, her fingers caressing his shining forehead, stroked the place where he had said the pain was worse, easing it away with rough, work-hardened fingers while he slept. Hearing someone discreetly cough, she dragged rapturous eyes away from the beloved face and looked up.

Bezel appeared saying quietly, "The Helm is holed beyond redemption."

Not understanding a word he spoke, she caught the drift, and her smile said, "What do I care if it falls? It is nothing to me. Here, in my arms, is all I treasure."

His voice drowsy, William said, "He thinks trouble will come our way shortly after, and tries to warn us, Clara." Then raising his head, he spoke to Bezel saying, "The Helm will fall. All of it will fall. Soon you will see everything revealed. My making unravels another of great deceit and artful illusion. Before long, you shall see everything as it truly is. Do not worry. If any seek to harm us, with a look, I will annihilate them. Be sure to stay within these gardens, Bezel. Here you are safe."

"Ask him where Clump and Eodgh Ratanakiri are."

"They went to help," he answered, snuggling back down, "to see what they could do. Their aid is useless. What has been done...is done. Even I cannot call the faded back to life."

* * *

Panic in the streets. From the tallest tower, great stones fell without warning. They toppled lazily at first, and gaining speed, slammed into the crowd below. A hot knife through butter, soft bodies pulped and faded. Shrapnel pieces of rubble, claimed unfortunates standing close by, injured bystanders some distance away with slingshot spray. Immediately, a stampede of terrified survivors sped off in all directions, sobbing and screaming, fighting a passage through throngs, swarming in the streets all around, to find safety and succour in their homes.

The news of catastrophe spread fast. Embroidered and embellished with gory detail, flew faster than ever, and in its wake, fearing they would be served the same all eyes were turned upward. Straining to pierce the veil of night, the tallest buildings were scoured for any sign of weakness. Another discovery soon made, lowered and squashed morale.

Crystal spires no longer captured moon-beamed spark, or threw out refracted colours, but sullenly reflected cold light with dull, flat, darkened tints, and the luxuriant sheen of iridescent pearl, gilding the onion-domed towers, had vanished. Only the outlines of the buildings, traced by night-shadow, were defined against the sky. And just beneath drab darkness, tainting the first reaches of slender, white-marbled columns standing proud, slowly dribbled down, staining the perception of unblemished purity with harsh reality.

A massive hole torn in the thin veil of tiny falling lights, the aspect of a dome was replaced by a curtain suspended by nothing, its fabric thickened by spangles clustering together, moved rapidly downward. Lingaradgh's making of illusion, maintained for many centuries and very strong, was slowly being unravelled. The city, gradually casting off a sumptuous garment worn for so long, would reveal the remnants of a soiled and tattered shroud.

Radiating outward, regurgitated again, and again, news of the shocking change blighting the tallest spires and towers met the same news radiating inward, and was no news at all. The same unaccountable weirdness was happening throughout the city, where a confused blend of fear and curiosity boiling through the streets, sent faint-hearts scampering to their homes. Others, resolutely inquisitive and intrepid, remained firmly in the heaving throng until another ingredient, thrown into the mix, struck all with dread.

Atrament walked. Atrament had cleaved the Helm in two, and fading many, brought about its ruin. Atrament walks. Courtiers at the Helm had, with their own eyes, seen him. Along the very streets and avenues, the populace now stood upon, along the very roads, where carriages drawn by high-stepping harans were being driven, along lanes and alleyways, Atrament would soon walk to bring the city down, too. In person, the Way of Atrament was upon them all.

Wave, upon wave, of frightened voices took up the shout to give fair warning. Smiting the air with the tumult of oceanic sound, terror vaulted in the streets. Rearing, through surging hysteria, one thought in every mind, the massed crowds, packed tight, took mindless flight and cobbled paving was thundered by shuffled feet breaking into a run. Anyone who hesitated, was picked up, and carried away in the unforgiving tide. No deviation was remotely entertained within the chaos that had erupted, and the headlong departure followed a route instinctively chosen.

Obstructing vehicles, overturned by a low-slung tsunami of bodies crashing into them, the forefront line of panic-stricken people crushed and mangled to nothing in the act of rending the highly polished carcasses of carriages to splinters. Harans screaming, thrashed in their traces. Lashing out to no avail, their bodies broken, blood streamed in the carnage on the cobbles. And still, the witless, madding press, pressed on.

The outer edges of the fear-crazed, jostling crowd, helplessly slammed against walls had all senses knocked from them, while others were spiked on railings, or thrust into doorways, and like so much jetsam, left behind. Those following in the stampeding crush trampled them underfoot. Adrenaline fuelled, panic spurred the impetus of the breakneck pace to faster speed. A wall of flesh, meeting a solid barrier of more flesh at corners and junctions, clashed and broke against one another, and unmindful of the injured, churning their bodies to smash underfoot, joined ranks and sped on.

At the first sound of Anathema walking, opened windows were hastily clapped shut. Distraught mothers roughly shook children awake, to haul them sleepy and complaining from beds, intending to whisk them to safety. In the time it took to arrange hasty flight, the heaving masses in the streets were already on the move. Wisely deciding not to dare the crowd, there was no option but to hide their families in the most inaccessible parts of their homes, and wait. Wait for the fleeing herd to pass before attempting to venture out, praying all the while, Atrament walking did not find them.

Some of the aged crept into the deepest recesses of their homes, and waited for the hammer to fall. Some, careless of whether they lived or died, drew a chair to the window, and lingering behind draping blinds, pulled them aside a little in hope of catching even the merest glimpse of an ancient legend, suddenly risen, they watched intently to see Atrament walk their way.

The curtain of illusion, now thick and heavy, began to fold down. Below lofty spires and towers stripped of all magnificent splendour, reality was casting a long shadow over the high roofs of fantastically wrought official buildings, and would soon reach the sugar-spun lacework of the walkways and bridges connecting them. Reality, a quilled pen, whose nib glided smooth over deceitfully pearlescent pages, wrote a dismal script with an inky trail of decay.

On the roofs of all these buildings, a few broken slates clinging to the edges of great gaping holes, were cemented in position with slimed bird droppings, which had been baked hard, slimed and baked over, and over, again. Draped with decrepitude, and garlanded with thick lichen, the joists beneath, exposed to the elements, were the wobbled sentinels that hovered over discarded rubbish, piled into attic spaces, and silently rotting, a home for all kinds of gnawing insects and vermin.

Elaborate carved decoration on the eaves, gradually lost crisp relief, showing they had been sanded to bumped smoothness by wind-blow. Revealed, the true nature of luscious white marble, no more than rendered mud bricks, cracked and slowly mouldering in damp disintegrating mortar. Delicately constructed lace-worked walkways, no more than moisture-rich, splintering wood, whose only fragility was rot, colonised by miniature, pale-green mushrooms growing in every crevice.

Pushed down, and down, by reality, the curtain of illusion gave up its secrets and displayed a terrible truth. Luxuriant gardens, filled with exotic flowers, no more than overgrown weeds, and the marble statues in them, whitewashed fire-hardened clay. The structure of every grand house, ripe with fungi, and ready for demolition, and the condition of more modest homes no better, so it went on down to the pavements and roads.

By the time the revelation had been made, the curtain of lights was winking out for all time. With it, the greatest illusionary making ever created and maintained. The greatest deceit that had deceived all senses for many centuries was going, and would delude no longer. Lingaradgh's making was completely destroyed.

* * *

Half the Trooh in his satchel gone, Cullinan, vigorously sucking his teeth, accepted there would not be enough to carry them back to Hessonii by the route he and the Nine had come. Wiry of build, and having performed no making, he was more than capable of going on, if...if the final bridge was raised.

Going over to the Nine, stretched on the ground, he squatted solicitously amongst them, and said, in his gentlest voice, "My, friends, exhaustion claims you all. I know it. Not for myself," he coaxed, "but for the Blessed Lady, all blessings be upon her and make her face shine with ever more radiant light, I ask you to do her will. In conference, the Blessed Lady, may every blessing be upon her, bids me tell you this.

"You must raise the bridge. If strength deserts you, once it is in place, no displeasure will she show, it is by her will. No penalty will she exact, if you cannot follow, it is by her will. To raise and maintain the bridge, your duty, and her will supreme. The Blessed Lady, all blessing be upon her, bade me say these things and give assurance her arms long to embrace her faithful servants. Her words given to me, I have spoken. Duty must be done, friends. Raise the bridge and hold it in place."

"Friend, Doge, can we not have a little respite?" one of the Nine mumbled.

"Would that you could, friend," he said, forcing his tone to sadness, "but I cannot gainsay the will of the Blessed Lady, all blessings be upon her. The darkling will soon begin to struggle against the brightling's reign, and I must be in Almandine to collect a great prize for the Guardians soon after the tussle is over."

His thin lips smiled encouragement as the Nine got to their feet with effort, and stood drooping around him. Digging the long-handled spoon into fine white powder, he did not level the heaped bowl, but held it out for consumption.

"Friend Doge, you have forgot to measure the dosage."

"Not I, friend. I follow only that which the Blessed Lady, may blessing be upon her, commands me."

One by one, the Nine bent to greedily snort, and brain-rocked, reeled away to wait for the startling clarity and strength Trooh would lend them. Jubilation keening, all dreams of greatness soon to be in his grasp, and all doubt stifled, Cullinan watched the bridge being raised and once it was made, setting his foot to it, never looked back to see if any of the Nine came on after.

* * *

"Almandine is not far. Will you go the remaining distance on foot?" Bezel asked.

"I think not. To the very gates of the Helm you may take me. Stopping at any one convenient to you, we shall play a little game to allay the interest of those appearing disinterested, that they may carry the information to the House of Learning when next they visit."

"It is a game consisting of a lowly tinker," he grinned, "who, taking pity on a girl, alone and defenceless in the wilderness, offered protection and sustenance providing, of course, he went the same way?"

"You have it exact," Caryadgh laughed, "and with no prompting."

Flicking the reins over the harans' backs to increase the pace, Bezel did not say it was a game he had played on more occasions than he cared to remember, and while the wagon rolled on, he engaged her with his usual brand of foolish conversation.

Chapter 58.

Malfroid and Clump had left the room an age ago, but still she sat, her face stony, listening without hearing, to the faintly buzzed silence spilling from the speak-cube.
They are gone?
Startled to hear his voice again, Clara's head snapped toward the emerald.
Now, I may speak most freely. Did I not say, a creeping thing I had become, and to a watcher I had been reduced? Think you; I did not watch all you did? In Lessadgh I watched and learned, with you, the boy would find safety and nurture. In Noor, I watched to see how you, a woman of Lessadgh, would hold the Chair of Authority, knowing when others did not, the hand of the Insane Child could not shelter you. Watching closely, did I not learn your character? How you would conduct yourself, and in any situation, react? I did, Clara Maddingley, most surely I did. In addition to knowing what brightness rings your heart, I know you...better, than you know yourself, mayhap.
Grief clouds, does it not? Grief drains all senses to such extent, its heaviness forbids all movement of the mind. Into grief, do I now intrude, and beg no pardon for it. It is necessary. For me, time rolls very short.
On your behalf, do I ask a question as yet unframed. To what purpose was my story told? Needing to confess, I sought absolution? Never that. Absolution, never have I sought, nor could I now. Even were it my wish, of a surety, it is not within your power to give. To what purpose a lengthy monologue? Had you, but known it, a courtship of sorts. Have we both not laboured in it? I, in the telling, and you, not only in the listening, but forced to learn the old language, which may yet stand you in good stead. Together, have we not laboured toward this moment, and a common goal? A goal, where affection has no part in our union, since never did such a gentle passion exist between us, nor ever could it. In the unity of a far different emotion, do not we two come together? In us both, does not the desire for vengeance burn strong, and in its furnace, do we not embrace? Strongly are we bonded, our motivation differing, it is true, but unity there is, built on grief, hatred and loathing.
My word honoured, my gifts given and accepted, know now of another gifted without your knowledge. In the bottom of the casket you bore away, there will you find a secret that gives into your hand the means to do what I could not. There will you find a phial of Trooh, as it should be, not as that aberrant which rocks the Guardians' brains within their pans. Trooh, rich in the missing component omitted from recipes I once wrote. Yours to do

329

with as you wish, you have only to speak, saying in the old language, be opened.
Know this, Clara Maddingley, woman of Lessadgh, my enemies are yours, and thus, in the kinship of the dispossessed are we two tightly bound. Can you, in all good faith, deny it?
Beware the Guardians, who seek to bring you down. Throughout the sparns have they looked for a means to accomplish this all the while you sat upon the Chair of Authority. This you know. This enemy do we have in common.
Lingaradgh, snatching your child from you, set his foot upon the road to oblivion. I answer in your stead, she did. From me, did she not steal all hope, save one, which I come to presently? She did, and lives still, having paid no penalty for her crimes, save expulsion. This enemy, also we share.
Now comes the telling of hope remaining. Now comes the sole purpose of this monologue laid bare. Vengeance. Vengeance for yourself, and in taking of it...take it for me, too. Now comes the test. Have you the stomach, the heart, the will, to follow vengeance wherever it leads, and exact just punishment long overdue? Do you?

Once again, faintly buzzed silence seeped from the speak-cube while Clara, no flicker of emotion passing across her face, turned her ring once, turned it twice and, stroking the table of the gem, sat motionless in the shrouding silence of the room with only memories for company.

* * *

Lacing the pale-green translucence of the sky, patchy clouds of delicate pink, stained with lemon, were tickled with a promise. Soon, the fierce heat of the sun would flood them with clearest light and burn them away. Cruel light, preparing extraordinary brightness to pick out, and expose, with harsh cutting clarity, the starkness of the festering pile that was the Kingdom City of Almandine.

Irritation balanced upon irritation. Far later than he had hoped, or intended to arrive, the morning was well on and...the Nine had misjudged their aim. The bridge of air, lower than any made that night, and almost grazing the tops of trees, finally sloped gently down onto ground a good league and a half away from the city. Furiously sucking his teeth, Cullinan stepped from it, and opening the satchel slung across his chest, roughly assessed what dosage he could give the Nine, who tottering with fatigue, were on the last stretches of solid air.

Closing the satchel, but not buckling the stays, he waited for them. Shocked by ravages the night's exertions had carved on healthy faces, the pallid colours each was now painted with, and talents dimmer shine, he drew aside to consider the situation, and what must now be done with few resources at hand. From the corner of his eye, he saw each one of the Nine flop limply onto the ground, and lie without moving.

Another tack must I take. One not used before, if they are not to be laid prone for the rest of this span, and I cannot let them lie. I need them, he thought, and immersed himself in deep contemplation of the action he would take to stir them to use further energy.

"Friends, much beloved of the Blessed Lady, may all blessing be upon her and make her face shine, sacrifice made will be rewarded. This, the Blessed Lady, may all blessing be upon her, just now told me," he said, gently nodding his head in approval. "This, too, has also been told to me, the conduit of the Blessed Lady must even now become the spur that goads. So, am I honoured, my words are hers. I am the conduit. I am the spur that goads."

Prostrate in long stalks of dew-damp grass, the Nine raised their heads as one. Amazed by his speech, they stared incomprehension.

Vivid, in the lightening dark, the outer edges of all nostrils and upper lips, crusted with Trooh, plainly seen now, he thought, staring back, *they are not what they were, nor shall they ever be. Remorse may look, but cannot find me, for all are disposable in this venture.*

"Friend, Doge," one of them rasped, "do we understand correct, no further instruction does the Blessed Lady, may her face shine eternally, intend to give in this endeavour?"

"Friend, you have it exact. Instruction has already been given and remains the same. Why is there further need to waste good breath? We go to collect a great prize. If true, the greatest that ever graced the halls of Hessonii, and into Almandine's Helm, must we go to fetch it. Glory awaits you.

"In the annals of the Order, will your names be writ large for the deeds you now perform. Honoured before all, will you be, and for all time to come, blessed in every eye, with the blessings of all heaped upon you. This the Blessed Lady, may her face shine, commanded me to say, and this, also. All done this darkling will be faithfully recorded," sweeping his eyes across the Nine, he said, "all done...and left undone. Rest a short while. Trooh there still is, though not in so great a quantity as I would wish. My, friends, it is yours. I take none for myself."

Taking the satchel off, he laid it down, walked a little distance away, and squatting, thought contemptuously, *let them scrabble for it as best they may, snatching a portion, or not, they will follow. For the sake of eternal glory, they will follow.*

The Nine up on their feet, faces drawn and haggard, their colours pale now and forever, but at least talent shone a little brighter. The Nine up on their feet, slightly invigorated by a small helping of Trooh shared out, and not willing to relinquish the resplendent lustre attached to those, who, together with the Doge, had bought the prize to Hessonii, and forever blessed, would have their names written in history on the Sacred Isle.

"Friends, you are recovered?" Cullinan asked, rising easily. "Say now, for I can brook no further delay."

"Lead on, friend, Doge, we follow."

"Is not," he heard one of the Nine say to another, "Almandine famed for sparkling spires? At great distance, I once heard tell, one could see their shine menacing the sky itself with piercing tips."

"Crystal and marble its construction, I heard," yet another said.

"Friend, Doge," one of the Nine stumbled up beside him, "it is my believe something is very wrong."

Sucking his teeth, controlling flamed temper with difficulty, he answered crisp, "Never say, friend, you missed your aim with the bridge, and we are not in Almandine as thought."

"Friend, Doge, it is not we who are wrong, but Almandine. Time rolled a great way since I was last here, and very rightly was it considered a place of fable."

Eyeing broken spires, clothed in sullen drab, standing tall above the trees, and thinking no Kingdom City wore such colours willingly, Cullinan said, "The way lies straight ahead?" and receiving nodded agreement, lengthened his stride.

* * *

The stampede, spilling from all of the city's gates in a maddened dash, flooded onto the broadness of the plain, onto farmlands and fields, and charged on in mindless flight. Terror for some, so great, the borders of Almandine were in sight before impetus was finally lost.

Stragglers, not so fit in leg and lung, and unable to go further, took cover in clumps of trees, or bushes, and feeling the need for company in such dread times, eventually found enough courage to creep from their shelter in hope of locating others, who, like them, had been left behind. One met another, a third joined them, a fourth, and a fifth, and the small group growing, expanded to ten, to twenty, and still more joined as the hours passed. Worn to exhaustion by a series of mind-staggering events, deeming they were far away enough to be out of imminent danger, and there was safety in numbers, chatter began. Some spoke of cringing shame for abandoning loved ones to their fate. Some bewailed possessions possibly lost. Some mourned the Helm gone to ruin. But, throughout the confessions, recriminations, and expressions of regret, some spoke of what might come upon all with Atrament living.

Astute enough to place outlooks, one such motley, nerve-stretched group, received warning a strange procession was fast approaching. Crouched quietly in screening bushes, they waited to see who made the sound of sandaled feet, monotonously slip-slapping the air with dull, clapped rhythm. Intent on devastation gradually becoming visible as he drew near, Cullinan passed by with long strides.

"Atrament?" someone whispered.

"Not he. From head to heel is he burnished with talent," whispered back, "not heavily speckled as this one is."

"Hush, more come."

A few moments later, struggling to keep up the frantic pace set by their Doge, the Nine appeared with emerald-green robes flapping, orange sashes swinging, tufted heads bobbing, and talent barely glimmering.

"The Guardians!"

"The Guardians are come."

"The Guardians are come to do battle with Atrament," whispered, from mouth to mouth.

"Did you hear that?"

"We are saved."

"Who can withstand the might of the Guardians?"

"No one."

"Shall we follow?"

"No, best stay here and be safe."

"My bonded partner, and babes, are in the city. I, for one will follow."

"There is risk."

"My business lies open to pilfering. I, too, go with the Guardians."

"Who can stand against the Guardians?"

"No one."

"Then why do we skulk here?"

"There is risk."

"Stay then, and watch my arse disappear down the road they tread."

"We follow the Guardians."

"To be on my own is risky. Wait! Wait for me. I am coming."

If Cullinan was aware, small, dishevelled groups were peeling out from the shelter of each copse, or clambering through fences of dense shrubbery to skitter nervously across open spaces, and join the growing throng marching at a respectful distance behind the Nine, he gave no sign. Fuzzed growth shadowed his normally smooth-shaved head, and coarse stubble decorated his cheeks and chin. During his long walk, small flying insects colliding with his body, and dying in his sweat, were stuck to his skin. Grime coated his feet and legs, dimming talent's gleam, and urine stains spotted his loincloth.

Grim-faced, he walked with more bravado than he had ever shown through the first gate of the city he came to, and stopped. Far-sight, nearing, had not prepared him for the desolation found here. No sparkled crystal to steal the sun's radiance, or play with moonshine's glow. No iridescent gleam to tame fierce light at the middle of the day, or romance star-bright. No smooth-sheen of marbled whiteness to drink the breath of airy breezes. Only disintegrating brickwork, weather-beaten to the colour of mud, blighted with fractures, riven with knotty stems of foliage clambering to attack the heights, and lumpish, dinner-plate sized fungi, step-laddering after it. Only holed, and fallen roofs, their joists and beams sticking from them at crazy, needled angles. Only flaking timber, shearing at will from rotting window-frames, and doors worn to paper thinness. Houses, great and small, afflicted by irreparable decay, no better than the meanest tumbledown hovel imaginable.

Tall spires stood dejected, their domes askew, and crowned with jagged darkness piercing incompleteness. Others, with irregular angles gaping wide, invited the elements to come and dine upon certain ruin. Some, with crumbled stones that teetered uncertainly, whilst gravity had yet to decide whether to bring them down to rest with those fallen, and smashed, or leave them see-sawing perilously. The Kingdom City of Almandine, renowned for majestic splendour and bright beauty, was no more than a slovenly drab. A travesty of all it had once been.

"A great making overlays another," he said, just loud enough for the Nine to hear. "Approach, come closer to me. Tell what thoughts you have, friends."

"Our opinion matches yours, friend, Doge," they agreed.

"Why was this not discovered earlier," he hissed, at blank, non-committal faces. "No matter. No matter. We leave this abomination till a later time for judgment and penalty."

The crowd following them pressed closer, inclining their heads to try and hear what the Guardians spoke of, and craning their necks to get a better view, passed what had been seen, or glimpsed, to those waiting behind. Among the rustle of quiet, angry voices, Cullinan's sharp ears heard the name that was Anathema.

"Atrament. Atrament still walks."

"What talk is this?" he asked the Nine. "Go fetch one of the herd that I might know what nonsense is spoken."

He had the story, and looked to see where the wavering finger pointed. The huge space, which the Helm had once proudly occupied, was heaped with rubble.

"I see it plain," he scowled, bringing an end to the newly begun retelling of the jabbered story. "Go stand with your neighbours, friend."

"Dire news, friend, Doge," one of the Nine said, from the corner of her mouth.

"Evidence that may not be denied lays before us, friend, testifying catastrophe has struck this place, though not as was the tale told. The dark one cannot walk. That one faded. Documents written by the hand of the Blessed Lady herself, may all blessing be upon her and make her face shine, are lodged in our archives that tell us this, though none can read them now. Doubtless, some figment of imagination provoked the mob to flee in frenzied disarray. We go to what is left of the Helm. There, will the Lord be, and with her, the child we claim as our prize. Once more in Hessonii, I shall instigate a thorough investigation of what passed here," Cullinan said, waspish, and set off at a cracking pace.

Past remnants of recent destruction, scattered on cobbled roads and strewn across all paving, he strode. Past the devastation of what had once been a market, the stalls in splinters, their bright awnings torn to tattered shreds, mournfully waving in the freshening breeze. Past the skeletons of ragged vehicles, whose smashed panels hung limp, or cast to one side, and worm-silk stuffing, used for expensive upholstery, blown hither and thither in clustered balls of candy-flossed lightness, wherever the soft breeze took it. Past harans lying prone in wide sticky pools, their scaled skin stripped from the meat beneath, and quills faintly rattling on dead necks. Past shops, their windows lit with guttering fire crystals that winked and blinked, resembling lascivious eyes peeking from scabby skulls. Past abandoned leaf and bean houses, where the strong aroma of beverages, burnt in pots and kettles left on hobs and stoves, wafted through opened doors, and the chairs and tables set outside, little better than kindling. Past hostelries leaking odours of spilt wines and beers, their foregrounds spread with a mass of splintered and ground glass. Past darkened houses, where an occasional fear-rimed face, cautiously peering wide-eyed through a window, was quickly drawn out of sight.

Saying nothing, Cullinan and the Nine went through the blighted city, seeing and smelling the rankness of advanced decay, followed by a slowly burgeoning crowd, and accompanied by the voices of the recently faded mingling with the old.

* * *

At first light, smeared in blood and tired to the bone after helping to tend those injured during the fall of the Helm, Persimmony Clump and Ratanakiri trudged back to the garden of lilies, and the flower-draped pergola. Wrapped in a blanket, William lay on the bench with his head in Clara's lap, and she, rapt in joyous adoration, unable to keep her eyes from the sleeping child, did not notice them at all.

They crept away, found a place to rest, and drifting into sleep, Ratanakiri said, "Clara is as a mother to the child?"

"The only one he can remember," Clump answered, stifling a yawn.

"Poor lady, to have her child stolen away, but it is good they are together once more."

"Is it?" he said beneath his breath.

* * *

Without warning, William pulled away from her, and sat up. Alarmed, Clara asked, "What is it?"

"They have come for me."

"Who? Who, William?"

"The Guardians," he answered.

"They cannot have you. No one can. You are mine, mine."

"Help me," he said, getting to his feet, and dropping the blanket she had bundled him in. "Help me put it over my head, so my face is in shadow, and no part of me is clearly visible when I meet them, Clara."

"Meet them? No! No, you must not do that. I know not who they are, but we must get away. Go back to Lessadgh. Yes, get back to our farm, to the life we lived. In seclusion we shall be, so have no fear you will be marked out, for none shall see you there. No one can take you from me ever again. I could not bear it."

"No one shall. No one can. One part of me is lost, I shall not lose another thing most treasured."

"Then come," she gabbled, arranging the blanket as he asked. "Let us go. Go now. Leave this place of fierce colour, and go home. We must, William. You must see it is what we must do."

"No, Clara, I must show the Guardians who has mastery here. Only promise me, you will stand meek by my side, saying nothing, while it is proven. Come," he held out his hand, took hers in his, and dropped a kiss on her cheek. "All will be well," he said, leading the way out of the pergola.

* * *

Denied access to the grounds of the Helm, guards struggled to hold back the restless throng clogging the gateway Cullinan and the Nine had just passed through. A crowd, made brave by the presence of the Guardians, and curious to know every detail of what was going on, and the condition of the building.

"What can you see?"

"Nothing."

"Ho, you at the front there, what goes?"

"Nothing much," the answer rippled back.

"Keep your elbows to yourself."

"What of the dark one?"

"No sign."

"Doubtless that one slunk away, knowing he cannot withstand the might of the Order."

"They will find and destroy him, mark my words."

"What passes?"

"The Guardians wait."

"The one in the loincloth, why does he not wear the robe?"

"He is the Doge, idiot."

"The Doge?"

"Do you know nothing? Supreme is he amongst the Guardians, some say he is the Blessed Lady's anointed."

"It is no small thing for the Doge to leave the Sacred Isle of Hessonii."

"In living memory, it has not happened."

"Is that so?"

"Can you remember such a happening?"

"No."

"Then ask no ridiculous question."

"If you wish not to look a fool, take my advice, and be silent."

"It is no small thing for the Doge, and the Nine..."

"Who are the Nine?"

"Your knowledge is sadly lacking. They are second only to the Doge."

"Stop pushing. No closer can I get, nor you either."

"It is no small thing for the Doge, and the Nine, to be standing in the outer edges of the rubble of the Helm."

"It is gone then?"

"A mound of broken stone by all account."

"A flattened pancake is the news just passed back. No stone standing upon another."

"What goes?"

"Stand upon my foot again, and by the powers, I shall fetch you such a clout you will not forget in many a span."

"The Doge and the Nine, wait for something, or someone."

"They wait for Atrament?"

"Use what little brain you have. If the Guardians knew where the dark one was, they would not be waiting, would they?"

"Stands to reason they would not."

"To keep such revered personages waiting, no matter what catastrophe has befallen, is not respectful."

"Not respectful? I tell you, unthinkable it is, to keep them waiting overlong."

"Penalty for it will be paid."

"No doubt more fucking taxes we will be plagued with."

"As if we have not suffered much already!"

"Ho! You at the front there, what goes?"

Chapter 59.

Arms folded across his naked chest, Cullinan sucked his teeth more vigorously with each passing minute as he waited for Apatia, High Lord of the Helm, to be found.

"This is not to be tolerated, friends," he snarled, over his shoulder, to the Nine.

"Someone comes, friend, Doge," one of them said, directing his gaze to a Guardian threading his way through tumbled ruin with as much speed as he could muster.

"Who is that, friend?" he asked.

"The crest, worn on his head, indicates it is the Headmaster of the House of Learning, friend, Doge," one of the Nine murmured. "He who advised of the child."

"Let him come near."

The Headmaster, bowing deep, began to mumble apology.

"Where is the Lord of the Helm, friend?" Cullinan scowled.

"Not to be found, friend, Doge. This, I have had from Sinhaladgh, the Lady's Chancellor. Suffering dread injury, but mindful of duty, he sent guards to search out the Lady. They found her not. Regrettably, she is believed faded, friend, Doge."

"Where is the child?"

"Ah…" Terrified of the reaction to the news he brought, the Headmaster twisted the ends of his extraordinarily long beard whilst he fumbled for words that might make the telling easier. Finding none, he blurted, "Friend, Doge, that, too, is a mystery."

"How so, friend?" Cullinan asked, the menace in his voice undisguised.

"I have yet to find one who knows, friend, Doge," the hapless Headmaster stammered. "Long before I knew of your illustrious presence, I tried all avenues to discover the boy's whereabouts…" he paused, distracted by the violence of Cullinan's tooth sucking.

"Say on, friend," one of the Nine said, sharp.

"Yes, yes, one snippet that had promise at its core, I was about to investigate, but news came, friend, Doge, you were not just in the city, but had entered the ruins of the Helm, and had been waiting overlong to see the Lord, so came I straightway with what news I had."

"This snippet," Cullinan sneered. "It was of Atrament walking?"

"Indeed, it was. Ridiculous, of course, for that one faded long since, but having seen the child…"

Interest piqued, Cullinan left off sucking his teeth, "You have seen him?"

"I have. Blazed with talent he is, friend, Doge, a veritable marvel to see. To my mind there is hope he, and no other, was seen walking toward one of the ornamental gardens."

"The gardens must be searched," his hooded eyes seared into the Headmaster's, who understood from the expression in their depths his fate now rested on this one act. "Find him," Cullinan said, dripping acid on the words he spoke.

* * *

Out of the pergola, with Clara's hand held tight in his. Out into morning light, to wind their way through the beds of night flowering lilies, their petals tight closed against the day. Quiet, they went past sleep-taxed Persimmony Clump snoring, and Ratanakiri sighing in dream. Out of the dust-smudged cyanic shrubbery ringing the garden, and onto rolling lawns, where devastation and sight of a fallen behemoth drew a sharp gasp from Clara. Past lawns that had been deserted, except by those too badly injured to have jumped up and run to see yet another strange visitation, an event not to be missed, playing out at the front of the Helm, which had provoked curiosity from the least curious.

"What happened here?" she asked, wondering, but knowing at the same time, why she had not heard the mayhem there must have been during the night.

"We shall speak of it later," William said, drawing the blanket closer about his face, "does talent show through?"

"What?"

"Can you see the shine I wear, glowing through my covering?"

"No, no," she answered, shaking her head in confusion. "I think not. No, not overly much."

Approaching the backs of bedraggled courtiers crowded close together to get a better look at something she could not see, she clasped his hand tighter. Coming nearer, she heard their muttering voices, but not understanding what was said, realised excited speculation roamed freely among them.

"Give way," William shouted, to make himself heard, "the Guardians wait for me!"

* * *

"Arrange a search, friend, Doge?" the Headmaster whined, "right glad would I be to do as you bid, but difficulty there is, when every guard is occupied, either controlling the multitude pressed into all gates, or tending the injured, or..."

"I care not what occupation guards are employed in," Cullinan took a step nearer to him. "I care not," he said, fierce, "who searches. This instant it must be done."

Shaking fingers found the longest strands of his beard as the Headmaster turned from the Doge and began to scuttle away, just as on-looking courtiers at the front of the gathering drew apart. Seeing the opening, he dashed for it, thinking to have easier access going away from the Guardians from the Sacred Isle than he had on coming to meet them, only to find the way blocked by two children. His anxious look transformed into an angry glare, before morphing into a puzzled frown for a moment, then recognizing they were not children, but Stunted Ones, his expression changed to sneering disdain.

"Be gone!" he said, "this is no place for the likes of you."

"Give way," William said, with quiet authority, "or face the wrath of someone more powerful than the Guardians, who wait to melt in my shadow."

Dumbfounded, he moved aside to let them pass, and stood wringing his beard as though it dripped with non-existent water, while the exact words William had said to him rippled through a quickly quieting crowd.

"I cannot see a power blasted thing, what goes?"

"I know not. Ho! You in the front there, what goes?"

"The Headmaster of the House of Learning..."

"That jackanapes!"

"Who spoke those words of disrespect?"

"Not I."

"Nor I, so give me no bad look."

"What was said?"

"Who can hear a thing with all this bickering?"

"With whom does the Headmaster speak?"

"The Doge. Go home straightway, and wash out your ears."

"Who speaks with whom?"

"The Master of the House of Learning speaks with the Doge. If you heard it not this time no repeat will I make. Whoa! The Doge wears a sullen look?"

"He does not. He sucks on a bonbon."

"Undignified, to do so, if you ask me."

"No one did."

"Ho! What now?"

"The Headmaster, fleeter of foot than ever seen, rushes away."

"What does he rush to?"

"The gaggle of sometime courtiers, who have collected in assembly."

"Is that not always the way? Best place always goes to them, and we poor bastards must crick and crane our necks to get a sniff of what goes."

"By the powers, you say the truth."

"Wait, be silent. News comes from the front."

"Two children, one covered from the top of its crown with a blanket that trails on the ground, have come from among the Helm's courtiers."

"By the powers! The Headmaster has stood aside for them."

"And? And?"

"They approach the Doge, and the Nine."

"And?"

"The Blessed Lady aid us, we are always the last to know a thing."

"Ho! You in the front there, what goes?"

"They speak."

"What?"

"Does talent shine upon my ears that I might hear what is spoken from a distance?"

"Tepauni's pendulous tits!" The irreverent exclamation shock-waved from the front of the crowding press to the back, and slightly changed in the process.

"Tepauni's pendulous bits? What do they have to do with anything?"

"Blasphemer, go hang your head in shame to speak of the Blessed Lady so."

"The child's blanket has dropped!"

"Bare-arsed and shining with talent he is!"

"Atrament is come."

"Atrament has come!"

"Let panic not take you, the Guardians will strike him down."

"How I wish I could see what goes, instead of receiving it passed from a hundred mouths."

"No, this one is not Atrament. This one is a child. The dark one was full-grown."

"What goes? What?"

"What goes?"

* * *

"Into our charge you will come, Gilgaladgh of Andradia," Cullinan repeated, "away from the contamination of this...thing, brought out of Lessadgh."

"Mind your tongue," William said, slow and cold. "You speak of the only mother I have known. Into your charge, I shall most certainly not come, nor do you have power to claim me, nor bend me to your will."

Wheedling, Cullinan replied, "Talent shines you to a blaze. Yet, its power full-blown, you have no knowledge of. How could you, when you do not even know of a name given at birth? How could you, when the lightness of extreme youth rests upon your shoulders? Knowledge, the usage of talent, and all its ways, this the Guardians, owning the weight of untold sparns, will instruct you in."

"You can teach me nothing, Cullinan, Doge, supreme spinner, whose only produce is the threads of virulent propaganda. Supreme weaver of warp and weft, the fraudulent material you construct, is named deceit, and you throw it over all. Cullinan, Doge, supreme counterfeiter of fraudulent fools, I say once again, you can teach me nothing. Knowledge is mine, more than you could know. Power, I wield to my own desire. Push me, but once more, and you will see it, to your detriment, at work."

To be spoken to in such tones? To suffer insulting, threatening words, carelessly thrown at him by a child? Fury pulled Cullinan to fullest height, and hands held out in winning supplication, were clenched into fists. He looked down at the talent-shined face staring contemptuously up at him. Looked into eyes, lit by golden flecks moving restless through each purple iris, and knew, in one breath-held instant, judgement had failed him. Believing the child would be fertile ground that would come easily under the Order's plough, he had approached a delicate situation with haughty arrogance and bumbled greed. By sheer force of personality, and presence, he had thought to intimidate and overwhelm the boy, as he had done with so many others. No ordinary boy, either. One using adult language with full-grown assurance, meeting his glare, stare for stare, confident he would look away first.

Cullinan lowered his eyes, knowing his talent was no match for that which clothed the boy in drenching light. For the moment, accepting failure, but knowing other means would have served him better, he vowed, given a little time to find the means to bring this child into the Order's fold, he could accomplish it, and his clenched fists relaxed. Clearing his throat, swallowing insults and failure with difficulty, he said, "I meant only to offer aid, Gilgaladgh, though perhaps my meaning was misconstrued, for I offered it too enthusiastic."

Beside her boy, his hand gripping hers, Clara peered up at the gaunt-faced giant, her eyes flickering warily to nine others, who, dressed in robes of brightest green, were barbing her with critical stares. She gave them daggers back, but stood impassive, intent on what was being said. Not understanding a word spoken, except the exchange was becoming more heated, she waited, longing for this living nightmare to be over. Waiting to go home with the child of her heart, and take up the uneventful, cosy life they had left. Waiting, she wondered where Persimmony Clump was, and if he, perhaps even Eodgh Ratanakiri, would go with them.

"This making," Cullinan went on, "was of your contrivance?"

"The second, but not the first. Another performed that making. Mine unravelled deception blinding every eye and every sense. In compensation, I will make a city to rival that which was thought to exist."

"Be careful, Gilgaladgh..."

"I am named, William. From this time forth, I answer to no other."

"Be careful, William, of such boasts," Cullinan cautioned. "It may be, I call upon you to fulfil it."

"You? Call me to fulfil my given word?" he laughed, a low and chilling laugh. "You may call, but never draw me. Unlike the Guardians, I make no empty sounds for the sake of keeping up pretence of power. Power is mine. My word, I hold to. In seven days, in seven spans, word given I shall keep. And every eye shall behold the gift I shall give to the inhabitants, of a broken place, to ease their suffering and loss. Now go. Take your pale, impotent minions with you, and know this. Never shall you have mastery of me, or get any benefit of the talent I own. Come, Clara, my business here is done, let us go and find our old friend Persimmony Clump, and those who are new, Ratanakiri, and Bezel."

"William, a moment more. Life force runs hot within you," Cullinan conceded. "We shall talk further on these matters when it runs a little cooler."

"For the Order, my life force will always run fierce."

To save face in front of the assembled courtiers, though it cost him very much to do it, Cullinan put a smile upon his lips, and nodded graciously at the child, who had turned away. Beginning to walk towards the gates of the city, he made that achingly expensive smile all the broader for the crowds waiting outside the ruins of the Helm.

"What goes? Ho! You there at the front, what goes?"

"Chit-chat."

"Nothing more?"

"No."

"Very disappointing to stand here for so long, cricking my neck, to see nothing. Now you say, they have only talked! Had I known..."

"What did you think would happen?"

"Wait. By the powers, the Doge, and the Nine are walking toward the gate."

"They come this way?"

"Assuredly, they do."

"Make way, give me space to move back, to give the Doge and the Nine, passage."

"Make way, move back."

"Make way, move back, the Doge comes."

"The blessings of the Blessed Lady be upon you," Cullinan cried, entering the path made for him.

"And upon you blessed, Doge, may the Blessed Lady make your face shine," was shouted back from thousands of throats.

I wish the stupid bitch could, Cullinan thought, repeating the blessing over and over again all the way to the House of Learning, where he and the Nine would lodge for the foreseeable future.

* * *

Voluminous trousers ballooning around his legs, Bezel ran over the lawns to the pergola with the news.

"Waken," he yelled in Clump's ear, and shook him. "Waken."

"What?" Clump rumbled, groggy.

"Comrade, such a sight, I never did see, nor will again. You should have been there. By the powers, you should have been there."

"What be you jabbering?"

"The child and the woman..."

"What?" Clump sat up in alarm.

"...face to face with the Guardians, and the Doge, foremost among them. Ha! Had any told me of such a thing, comrade, I would have told them go dance with the Mendicants, but with my own eyes I saw all that happened."

"What happened?"

"Well, in the scheme of things...I suppose not much," Bezel grinned, "being at the back of that stuck up mob of vacuous nonentities, courtiers of the Helm I mean, I was not privy to all that passed, but magnificent, by all the powers, it was."

"William be all right?"

"More than all right, the little one is. Some heated conversation he had with the Guardians, but it was the Doge and his cohorts who retreated with tails tucked between their legs, comrade. And hear this, the Doge, not looking anything like happy, did plaster a great smile across his face. Anyone, with only half an eye could see the scamp's twitching effort to hold it there all the way to the House of Learning. I know, I kept pace with them, in hope of seeing his falsity fail."

"And Clara?"

"Not near so fierce as you have painted her, comrade. Quiet and meek, she was, holding the boy's hand while he did business with the Guardians. She, and the little one, will soon be here. I, thinking you would be anxious of their whereabouts, rushed to tell the news."

"What goes?" Ratanakiri said, her voice thick with sleep.

Bezel guarded the entrance to keep the curious from entering the part of the garden William and Clara occupied, telling them to hush their noise lest they wake the boy clothed in talent to anger, and hugely enjoying new found authority over those who thought themselves his betters. In the pergola, William slept on the bench, while outside, Clara and Clump put their heads together in conference.

"I like it not. Dormant talent has been forced to wakefulness," he said, shaking his head. "I never heard tell of it. For him, there be no gradual growing into power, no time to gently acclimatize to demands talent will make of him, let alone control it. To be sure, talent be a gift, a gift that burning too fierce, destroys."

"Speak plain," she said, not understanding.

"Take the Helm for example."

"William said, he had not meant the blast to be so great."

"You make my point for me. Talent, Clara, must be controlled. He has had no time to learn how to do so. Think on this. To build a fire in your hearth what must you do?"

"Lay dried leaves and straw, place a little kindling wood layer upon layer, light it, coax a feeble flame to stay, and then feed it slow."

"You see? Little by little. Yet what if dried leaves and straw have been laid in the hearth, and a fireball is thrown into it? Could you control it?"

"No! Perhaps," she frowned, "with difficulty. You are saying...are you saying, talent has come to William in that way?"

"It be a crude parallel, and not exact, but so similar as make no difference. With fury, talent will strike. The trick to learn be to know how to control it. To use it precise and in desired quantity."

"His blast brought the Helm down?"

"The Helm's condition was as rank as I am told the city be, but likely, if talent used had been less, it would have fallen slower, and so many would not have been faded."

"Faded?"

"Died. They died," Clumped nodded regret, "and many more injured."

"I did not know."

"William did not tell you, Clara?"

"He did not."

"But he must have known it."

"How could he? He is just a little boy."

Clump, searching for a way to say what he thought must be said, did not see her face drop. Memory stirred, and clearly coming into her mind, William's voice saying, 'even I cannot bring back to life the faded.' *He knew. He knew what he had done, and spoke of it so casual, as if it were nothing. Death, to some, came as a direct result of his actions.* A chill spread across her shoulders and slid icy down her spine.

"Clara? Clara!" The sharpness of Clump's voice pulled her away from dreadful, and certain, knowledge, "you do not understand, and I have not words to prance about a hurtful thing, but must say it straight and blunt. In the space of a scarn, one of your weeks, talent has not seeped in gentle, as it should, but come in flooding torrent. William does not own a little talent, he owns it vast, and it has taken childhood from him. Couldn't do anything but."

"Surely," she said, confused and defensive, "he would have got it anyway, would he not?"

"At puberty, talent would have begun to wake, to trickle slow into his blood and stroke receptors most sensitive to its touch. Gaining adulthood, he would have come into his own inheritance. He has it too early, Clara. He has it far...too...early."

"Oh!" She puffed a light bubble of air, in surprised comprehension.

"And," Clump continued, wanting to get all of the bad news he had to tell out of the way, "talent uses energy. All things have a price. Use a little in a making, not much energy is lost. Use a lot in a great making, and much energy is lost. That is why your boy be so tired, Clara."

"Energy can be revived," she said.

"True, but talent leaves its mark. Bright hues grow pale."

She frowned, picking at loose threads on her skirt, trying to contend with knowledge she wished never to have known, while trying to make sense of what he was saying.

"William said a thing last night that, I, thinking it was childish prattle, did not take any note of. He said he had lost a part of himself. Is that what you mean? Clump? Answer me! Is that what you mean? He has lost childhood?"

"Perhaps."

"Perhaps? What do you mean, perhaps? What else could he have meant?"

"I do not know. If I did, I would tell you, but I am not sure at all what was meant. Coming into such inheritance, puberty be the trigger to begin its release. And, Clara, we Faienya are so different from you humans. Your lives are fleeting, compared to ours. We age not as you do. Illness does not know us, as it does your kind. Cold and heat be of no consequence if they touch us, but we feel such sensation only if we touch heat or cold. We die not, as will you. We fade. The colours we are painted with grow pale, and pale, and paler still, till we are near translucent. Then do we know, down to the oblivion of dust, we irrevocably travel."

"Using talent can make that happen faster?"

"Yes."

"Clump!" she grasped his arm in panic, "he is to build a city to replace this. He said it would recompense residents who have lost nearly all they had. In seven days, he said he would do it!"

"When did he say this?"

"He spoke to that bald-fuzzed giant wearing only a loincloth. Nine others there were, all dressed in bright green robes. On the way back here, William told me he had pledged to do this."

"He has pledged the Guardians," Clump said, with a dour expression. "Then, well does your boy know what capability he has together with knowledge of all he has done…and will do."

"But, he must be stopped."

"He has the talent to do whatever he wills, and that be the truth of it."

She got up, tripping on petticoats and skirt, and went hurriedly into the pergola.

Clump remained where he was, thinking about what the boy could have meant when he had told her, a part of him was lost. For the rest of the day, he kept separate from the others, speaking little and eating less, pondering on a riddle whose secret remained locked against him. When night fell, shading all with muted colour, he was still no nearer to any kind of solution that made sense.

Chapter 60.

"Plans for the new Helm are in my head, the layout of the new city, also. Both will be magnificent," William said, allowing Clara to arrange the blanket round him, tie a knot at one shoulder, and close gaping edges with a few of her remaining hairpins.

"And the pain?" she said, brusque.

"Not so great as it was, a dull ache has replaced it."

"I wish you would stop this nonsense, William."

"We have talked about this, Clara. You have nagged, and I have resisted all blandishments and argument you thought to stumble me with. My purpose remains unchanged."

"I beg you, think on it a little more. To raise a city in seven days is the stuff of fantasy. Perhaps, you are too ambitious with the power you say, you now own."

"You cannot conceive of it," he laughed, amused by her lack of understanding. "I make no false claim, even so, ask me to leave the homeless without homes, the dispossessed with no possessions, to leave this place a stinking heap of rank decay, and pay no price for life force spilled. Since it is easily within my compass, if you ask me, Clara, I shall do it."

"You know I will not, for I would not see anyone, even these giants, live so miserably. It is your welfare that concerns me. You are my boy, the child of my heart, William. I want no harm to come to you because you do a great thing."

"No harm will befall me that has not been already done. We are together. I am bound to you by love, for you are the only mother I have known, and shall know. If I am the child of your heart, believe you are the mother of mine, and with that, Clara, be content to let me go my way."

Bursting with excitement, Bezel leapt into the pergola, crying, "The Doge and the Nine wait at the gate, together with all those pompous upstarts lodged in the House of Learning, comrades."

"What does he say?" she looked to William for translation and hearing it, said, "The bald one hates and envies you. I saw it in his eye and by his manner. They wait to witness your destruction."

"They will grow pale waiting," he answered.

"Comrade," Bezel clapped Persimmony Clump on the back as they came out of the garden to find an entourage of the ruined Helm's courtiers lined up in readiness to escort them. "My doing," he grinned, "we cannot appear a ragbag crew afflicted with disarray. We must proceed with dignity, as befits our new station. Some word on that I will speak later. Had I known what great adventure lay in store when first I laid eyes upon you, I would not have dithered so much about leaving the Mendicants, and throwing my lot in with yours. Had I an inkling of what greatness you would throw me up against, more respect I would have shown. A follower no longer, am I, but in the vanguard of all that takes place with followers, where I once stood, and for it, have you to thank."

"Think nothing of it," Clump growled, seeing Cullinan step forward to greet William. "That one needs careful watch."

"You may be sure, under my scrutiny he has come and will not escape from it, comrade. Tepauni's stinking arse!" Bezel swore. "This, I had not expected."

"What goes, other than noise of a great crowd?"

"No crowd, comrade, but surely the entire populace of this power-stricken place. They stand outside the walls with bag and baggage packed. No curious excursion do I see, which you, blighted with lesser height, cannot. A full evacuation of the city it is. By the powers, an exodus, no less! Word, of what Lessadgh's little one pledged, must have leaked fast and furious as the Trapiche Emeral itself does flow."

"I wonder,' Clump said, dry, "how that could have come about?"

"Look not at me," Bezel said.

In front of guards trying to hold back a goggle-eyed crowd wedged in the gateway, Cullinan and the Nine waited. Smarting from yesterday's exchange, he waited, refusing to step away from ground stood on. To go and greet the talent-drenched child would have been to lose face, and he would not do it. Scalding the woman of Lessadgh with a flickering look, he waited for them to come close, then closer still, knowing the crowd, struggling for better views would believe the Order, as was only right, had supremacy and controlled the child blessed with extraordinary talent.

"This city you are to erect," he said, when greeting, stiff but courteous, had been made, "we would suggest..."

"Selected already is the site," William smiled. "To see done, what the Guardians in wildest dream cannot, you must follow."

Not understanding how fast news of a miraculous child shined with talent had spread, or how word of what he intended to do had gone hanging onto its coat tails, Clara stood quiet by William's side, completely unprepared for the scrutiny of a vast and curious crowd, and occupied herself by needling the Guardians with a defiant stare.

Come too late to squeeze into the main gateway, a mass of people had congregated all about it and spread along the wall running from it. Desperate to see, or perhaps catch a stray snippet of what was being said, many climbed up onto it, and having managed to find a good vantage point to view the proceedings, clung there, glad to be out of the crush. Below them, pushing and shoving, in hope of winning a better position, or obtain even the merest glimpse of what was occurring, the tumult of sound dropped to an expectant babble when someone bawled, William was approaching the Doge.

"Ho!" A hoarse voice rose above the prattle. "You, there at the front, take pity on us at the back."

"Yes," another screeched, "say what goes."

"Get off my baggage."

"How looks the miraculous boy?"

"He outshines the Doge a hundred, no a thousand times,"

"Is it true," another cried in wheedling tones, "he is to build an entire city in just seven spans?"

"So it is said."

"What mean you, so it is said? All I own is packed and ready to be carted to the new city."

"It's true?"

"Why think you, so many are come with all they own?"

"You have me there. To remain in a city, lumped and shredded with decay? No, abandoning the place is the only sensible thing to do."

"By the powers it is."

"All buildings are unstable."

"I heard that, too. During the darkling, another one came down, by all account."

"Hush, more news filters to us. A Stunted One is present."

"You jest!"

"Stunted One?"

"Let me get close to look at that freakery."

"What was just said?"

"The female is not a Stunted One."

"That cannot be right."

"What then is she?"

"A being out of Lessadgh?"

"Go dance with the Mendicants."

"Many more such events as have rocked us in this past span, and we all go seeking those mad ones out, for loss of our wits!"

"None out of inferior Lessadgh may come here."

"Hist! It is confirmed, out of Lessadgh has she come."

"Who confirms?"

"Impossible it is. Of Lessadgh, she cannot be."

"Move back."

"Make way."

"They are to come out!"

"The Doge comes, make way."

"No, the talent-blessed child comes first."

"Hear that? We shall yet get to clap eyes on him."

"Stop pushing."

A solemn procession, with a carnival feeling about it, would be how

Clara remembered that day. Low in spirits, when it first began, walking through the rotting city she understood why William would not go back on any word he had said. And as the day wore on, she could not help being infected by blossoming hope appearing on dejected faces throwing off despair, seen through the covering over her eyes.

Under a surreal green sky, its colour growing deeper and brighter, and with no cloud smudging its glassy texture, beneath blue, red, gold and purple foliage on the trees, over blue grass waving feathery seed-heads of pink and mauve, the procession went. William, holding her hand, talked animatedly of his plans, asking her opinion on everything as they led the way across farmland and plain, with Clump, Bezel, and Ratanakiri hovering at their sides. The sour-faced Doge came next. Behind him, the Nine, followed by everyone from the Headmaster to the lowliest student lodged at the House of Learning. Bringing up the rear, strung out across many miles, a multitude of people.

"Here, is where I will build a city to outshine any other, Clara. A marvel of beauty, and very strong it will be. What think you of the site?"

Wilting in the vicious heat, her eyes stung by vivid, strident colour, she shook her head to clear her mind. "It seems a pity to spoil open land, why could you not build upon the ruins of the other?"

"This city must be separate and distinct from a place of dire deception. That place I will level and wash clean."

Through the veil, she caught sight of Cullinan bearing down upon them, and said, "Sour-face comes to speak with you, William."

"Mighty, Doge," William smiled, turning to meet him. "Here is where proof of power will be shown."

"So close to the sally port, talented one?"

"It was error to build elsewhere."

"Greater error to build here, the site is ill-thought out," Cullinan said, smug. "From where will the city draw water? No strong flowing stream, or river, do I see. I would suggest..."

"For the well being of the city, and all in it, no thing essential will be left undone. Provision will be made, on that you may rest assured. Here will the city stand. Here may Almandine's sally port be guarded, and tithes properly collected from trade passing through into Lessadgh in pursuit of gold. Surely, friend, you can have no objection."

"None," Cullinan scowled, knowing the avenue would be blocked against agents of the Guardians to use freely, and further argument useless.

"Then it is settled. Another thing. For a time, we will continue the charade you engineered yester-span, and pretend you direct all I do. But I tell you now, seek to impede me in any way, down to dust will you and all falsity practiced by the Guardians go.

"This I pledge. Further, control of this throng do I give into your hand, I will have no fadings here brought about by improper behaviour. Upon your head, and those of your minions, do I most securely place all care, and responsibility, for every single one here present," William instructed Cullinan, who, folding his arms across his chest, began to suck his teeth. "Go amongst the people, bid them spread along the line I will pace, and step not a toe beyond it, else they fall into the chasm I shall shortly begin to create."

Black. The colour of the void. Black footprints, smouldering in the grass. Clearly defined heel, arching instep, ball and toes, as William stepped out the furthest perimeter of the Helm he would shortly bring into being. And black, the circled line his feet traced within the outer circle. Across these marked boundaries, neat and linear, eight sets of lines traced next.

"I see what he does," Clump said, to Bezel, "the new Helm is to have eight bridges crossing a deep cleft. He makes the Helm unassailable from without, if need arises."

"He honours the eight points of the compass, comrade" Bezel nodded. "From where will he get stone to build?"

"Be patient. The boy, it seems, has thought of all things necessary."

Satisfied his markers were true, concentrating to hold talent back to correct proportions, William cleared the inner circle of grass and soil, and made the first cut in the underlying rock between the circles. Before all eyes, light as thistledown blown in wind, a massive block of granite rose up, and another, and another. And this process continuing, he raised his arms and directed them to the place where they would rest. No need of mortar. Each stone perfectly cut, slipped jigsaw fashion into its neighbour and locked tight. Faster and faster, stones raised, cut, and dressed, huge blocks gliding stately through the air to an appointed place and fitted together. Fearful, and jubilant at the same time, the crowd witnessing the extent of his power grew silent.

Impassive, his face schooled to show not the slightest emotion, though he was consumed with vitriolic envy, Cullinan also watched. Behind him, the Nine registered disbelief, and muttering softly between themselves, spoke of like power said to have been once owned by the true children of the Disobedient Ones. Separate from those come from the Sacred Isle, the Headmaster of the House of Learning was almost delirious with joy, believing in error, such power now belonged to the Guardians.

Faster, and faster, the cut stone rose and flew. Faster still, William's arms confidently conducted their passage and settlement, while Bezel chattered a running commentary to a stunned Ratanakiri. Clara, enthralled by her boy's achievement, and at this moment not thinking of any cost, stood beside Clump, who watching without really seeing, pondered on yet another thing Clara had said. Meaning to reassure him, her boy would suffer nothing for the great making he would perform, she had repeated something William had told her. *No harm shall befall me than that already done*. His mind playing with these words, strung them together with those Clara had reported to him earlier. *A part of me is lost.* More than ever, he was sure, none of those words were of a childhood lost.

The foundations laid, the first course of stones and the second slotted and locked, the walls of the Helm and every room in it, beginning to rise, and the circling cleft, overhung by eight would-be bridges, growing deeper.

"It was a good day, a good beginning," William said, coming from his creation to where Clara waited.

"A veritable miracle!" she said, trying to shake off heat exhaustion. "Who in Lessadgh would believe it could happen and, I, though seeing all you have done, doubt the evidence of my own eyes."

"Believe it, Clara, and never doubt me," he said, reaching to take her hand in his.

"You are bleeding!" she gasped.

"A scratch, nothing more. Likely a chip of stone complained at being rooted from its mooring."

"It must be washed and bound," she murmured, inspecting it.

"Do what you did when I was small, each time a tree, or bush, or the ground, leapt to rebuke me for some abuse or carelessness on my part."

Putting his hand to her mouth, she sucked dirt and blood from the graze, and kissed it.

"I am made better," he smiled, touching her heart. "You always make me feel safe and well cared for, Clara. Those precious gifts you have always given. Many gifts I shall give to you."

Chapter 61.

"Tomorrow," William said, laying his head in her lap, "the work will go much quicker. Yes, rub it there. Stroke the pain away for me, Clara. What stone shall the Helm be?"

"Granite you dragged from the ground, my dearest, boy, and granite it must remain."

"No, it must not. Anything I wish it to be, it will be. Jadeite's subtlety would be kind to the eye. Of such material was built the house of the Disobedient Ones who dwelt in seclusion at Hessonii, which Atrament once claimed, but is now put to the Guardians usage. Jadeite, will the Helm I raise be."

Not knowing what he talked of, Clara stroking his head, soothing pain away with her fingertips, agreed.

In three days, the Helm was raised complete. Gracing the sky with exquisite beauty, its majesty spurned the scintillating sparkle of the old city. Its high walls of pale-green jadeite, tinged with gentle translucency, stood proud beneath tall turrets, and towers, roofed with a subtle gleam.

Well apportioned, the spacious rooms, and meeting halls, the broad corridors and wide staircases connecting them, one to another, and also to the vast kitchens, laundry rooms, and cellars. Pleasant courtyards gave out onto gardens waiting to be planted, where fountains would play once they were connected to the water supply William would create. Set away from the Helm, the stables were equipped with large stalls, and above, lodging provided for those who would work there. The only thing lacking in the unoccupied Helm were woodworked doors, which William decided, since time was running short, good carpenters should be employed to install. On either side of the deep chasm, and on either side of the eight bridges, he erected delicately carved balustrades, Clara could barely see over.

Each morning, as dawn strung a hesitant line of yellow on the horizon, William appeared before an enthusiastic crowd, who yelling a thunderous greeting, throughout the day shouted hoarse encouragement while he continued his great making. Fear of the power he wielded, gone, they called suggestions of how they would like their homes laid out, and squabbled amongst themselves, who would have what, and where the choicest locations might be. Or wondered, if the ownership of houses was to be freely given, or leased. Wondering, back and forth, if it was better to return to the place of dark rankness and collect what possessions they could salvage, or whether it was better to remain in the event the choice of a new home was theirs to make. These things were argued and debated until a whisper, beginning to hiccough through the multitude, swelled to encompass all, and conjecture took over, as Cullinan had designed it should.

"The Doge is absent."

"The Nine, too."

"Why should that be when the talented one works under the Guardians' direction?"

"The Doge knows who was responsible for the great deception."

"They go to deal with the culprit."

"Who? Whose is the blame?"

"No name was spoken."

"They go to apprehend the culprit?"

"To Judge."

"To execute."

"Fade? Fade whom?"

"No name springs to the fore, did any hear it spoken?"

"Do we not have right to know?"

As the city, taking shape, spread away from the chasm girdling the Helm, Persimmony Clump distanced himself further. Caught up in speculations of his own, his manner became more brusque than usual. William's movements had gradually become grandiose. Conducting a symphony of flying stone, his arms worked frantically, tracing elaborate spiralling flourishes in the air for no apparent reason. Sometimes, he laughed uncontrollably, and pranced about in what appeared to him, manic, pointless capering.

When he mentioned this to Clara, she passed it off, saying it was sheer exuberance, but he had noticed what she had not. The grid of streets, roads, lanes, and alleys did not run straight from the Helm's bridges, as William had drawn one night to show what he intended, but were becoming skewed and out of step. Nor had she mentioned William's headaches were getting worse. This news, Bezel overheard, and quietly repeated to him when they were alone. Feeling he could not speak of growing concern to Clara, if he ever managed to get close enough to do so, and knowing Bezel to be garrulous, Clump kept his own counsel, and watched more closely.

The seventh day. The city almost complete. The walls of all houses, from great mansions through the spectrum to those of modest proportions, were blushed with shades of palest pink to match the colour of roses that had bloomed in Clara's garden, and roofed with silver-grey slates. Preparing to raise a protecting wall around all he had built, William said to Clara, "Its like has never been seen. These gentle hues, chosen to remind you of your home in Lessadgh, sit well amongst the vivid colours Noor is painted with, do they not?"

"Remind me of home?" she said. "Why would I need reminding of it? Surely, now you have done what you said you would do, we can return?"

"We shall not see Lessadgh again," he answered, turning glittering eyes on her, and by the hardness hidden in them, she finally understood something was not right with him.

"My home is with you. Wherever it might be," she said, quiet.

"Good. In a short while, I am to make you High Lord of this Helm. A woman of Lessadgh shall sit on the Chair of Authority, and liking it not, none will gainsay me, but bend to my will. They must, or I fade them. I fade them all and send them down into dust."

"William?" she said, keeping her voice calm and even, "why do you talk of killing the very ones you built a city for?"

"Was I?" Confusion clouded his face for a moment. "Yes, on the Chair of Authority you will sit, Clara. None is better suited. A mother you have been, and are to me. A mother, you must be to the inhabitants of this city. Come, I go to bring this project to completion and need you by me."

Her hand in his as always, acquiescent and silent, Clara went with him resolving to speak to Clump when an opportune moment arrived. Approaching the place where he would begin his making that day, he snarled, "Where is my audience gone?"

"William, do you not remember?" she said, frightened by his feral look. "Last night you sent instruction, all willing to take the risk should return to the fallen city to salvage what they could before it vanished forever into the depths of a great lake you would make there."

"I did? I said that?" He frowned, as if bewildered. "And all that remains are the aged, and those hampered with children? I care not," he laughed, switching from rage to calm in a heartbeat. "You are the best audience, Clara. As long as you are by me, it matters not if none see the completion of my masterpiece."

Worried by things her boy said, Clara looked for a chance to talk to Clump, but never found it. William could not bear for her to be out of his sight for even a minute saying, not very long ago, the dark had reached out to embrace and shelter him. That refuge gone, she alone, could keep at bay another darkness seeking to insinuate itself into the empty space the first had left, to reside there for all time to come.

Noting the pallor beneath Clara's sunburnt skin, and the anxious look upon her face, which fled the instant William turned to her, only to return when he looked away, Clump's quiet observations continued. An answer for what he saw was framed wordless in the recesses of his mind, but it was one he did not want to accept, and he could not bring himself to reach for it. Yet, he could not help noticing so many things about the boy that did not sit right with him. The unnatural glitter in William's eyes had nothing to do with talent passing through them. His behaviour, according to Clara, usually careful and cautious, was now erratic, which could have been the result of extreme tiredness, but was not, as his energy never seemed to flag, or fail. His speech, usually clear and considered, was often gabbled and unintelligible. His movements, once as agile and fluid as any eight-year-old child's should be, were jerked and uncoordinated, which was not spontaneous, decisive confidence. And it appeared, to him, William's dependency on Clara was becoming total. The boy could not bear it if her attention was drawn by anything, other than him. Talent come far too soon, Clump believed, was the start of the problem, his thought dwelt on the strange words the boy had spoken to Clara...

"What if," he said, to Bezel, when the works on the city were coming to a conclusion, "you lost a part of yourself?"

"What part? An arm, a leg, what?"

"A part deep inside."

"Literally, you mean? Such as a lung, or a rib?"

"No. Something deeper."

"How could I lose a thing such as that?" Bezel grinned. "Now if you had said...my sense of self, an answer I could perhaps have found. Explain your meaning in more explicit terms. What part, Clump? What part?"

There it was, the answer he had deliberately kept from himself, given form and validity by words carelessly spoken out loud, and not retractable. Staring sightless into the distance, prompted by what Bezel had just said, Clump understood what the boy had meant by saying, *'a part of me is lost. No harm will befall me that has not been already done.'* William had lost his self. Teetering on the brink of madness, somehow, he had managed to keep balance, to hold it in check, but huge amounts of energy used in the great making were slowly tipping him into insanity.

"Clump, what?" Bezel persisted.

"Nothing," he answered, gruff.

"More than nothing it is, to sit with vacant stare, therefore, something it most certainly is. What?"

"It be only stupid talk to while away time," he growled.

"I shall not allow the Guardians to allocate housing," William said, to Clara. "Avaricious and unscrupulous, they are, and will line their coffers with gold from the rich, and small coin from the poor while they do it. And besides, the city is of my creation, in which they have no portion. Persimmony Clump, and the lanky fellow, clad in trousers too big for his slight form, the one who is always in his company, sticking to him like a burr to sheepskin, they shall do it."

"You mean Bezel?"

"If that is his name, yes, and the other one making up a shabby trinity, the woman with blue curls on her forehead."

"She is called Eodgh Ratanakiri."

"I am Ratanakiri?" William frowned, then shrugged off a moment of confusion. "Are you listening to me, Clara?"

"Yes, my dearest boy, I hear all you say."

"How can you, when your eye wanders constant to rocks on the floor?"

"It is a very strange decoration."

"No decoration," he laughed. "You shall see what their purpose is presently. Clump, I was speaking of Clump, something important, oh, yes. Them, do I charge with the work. A register, they must keep, so we may know who resides where, and what annual stipend each must pay. The rich have always strutted and preened, pretending by virtue of wealth, they are better than those less fortunate. So they will ever strut, save in my city. For the privilege of residing here, they pay a premium to subsidize the poor. Had you the language, I would delegate the work to you. No! No, I would not," he said, hitting his forehead with the palm of his hand. "You would be away from me too long, too often, and I cannot tolerate your absence.

"Beside me, you must always be. I am the child of your heart, am I not? What would you do without your heart, Clara? But the language you must learn, if you are to sit in the Chair of Authority. I shall teach you. Yes, yes, I shall teach you. We will begin once the wealth of this Helm is in its coffers. For your eyes, and yours alone, Clara, I do this making, for the Helm must have its own wealth. Watch close, and you will see a thing. Many in Lessadgh wasted their lives in search of the formula for what I do now, never knowing words have power."

How it happened, she was not sure. Impossible, inanimate rocks should suddenly become animated. Subtly moving without being touched, they bulged at one side and squeezed in at another, and glowing with extreme heat, compressing the composition of their elements, rearranged them seamlessly through a series of barely perceptible changes. Slowly cooling, and coming to rest, the results of impossibility lay before here eyes. A huge heap of insignificant grey stones had been transformed into a pile of gold nuggets.

Knowing he not only loved her approval, he expected it, she applauded, clapping her hands until they hurt. And he, bowing low, even though the pain in his head was excruciating, accepted acclaim in certainty...she loved to give it.

Chapter 62.

William sank Apatia's city into a crater. Then, diverting an underground river from its course, he buried its desolation beneath the crushing weight of deep waters, and its tributaries and springs later supplied the city he had created.

In just a few months, the old city was all but forgotten, or remembered as a bad dream, the new soon taken for granted, and fully populated. Its streets and roads jammed. Its pavements thronged with pedestrian traffic. The roads clogged with stately carriages, fast dashing phaetons, and lumbering wagons. Its gardens and parks a riot of white flowers, and every species, in full bloom. The places of commerce, the leaf and bean houses, hostelries, together with every other kind of business, thrived.

The Helm fully staffed, its kitchens and laundries bustling. Throughout each day, servants rushed through the passages and corridors to serve courtiers ensconced in its apartments and rooms. Its stables, stocked with the finest harans. Its kennels, filled with Smu Hundghs soundlessly barking and baying. Its registry offices busy collecting the first stipends due from tenants. Its accounting offices, busy counting gold from trade passing through the sally port, and Bezel, despite complaining to Persimmony Clump, he knew nothing of soldiering, had temporarily been put in charge of patrolling and collecting the toll.

"By the powers," he cursed, when ceremonial and ordinary guards had been selected, and relieved him of his onerous post, "never have I been so thankful for an escape. The boredom induced was nigh on as bad as being with the Mendicants."

* * *

The room was filled with women she barely knew, all waiting to serve her. Some of them, bore the regalia in their arms that would be fitted upon her, and weigh her down with unwanted heaviness. His expression thunderous, his eagle eye intent on all that was being done, William slouched in a chair. With a flick of his wrist, he motioned the women to begin clothing her for the ceremony. Laid across the forearms of two women, the first artefact, a robe stiff with embroidered urilatum threads was brought forward, and Ratanakiri, beaming a shy smile, spoke in respectful tones.

"She asks you to hold out your arms, Clara," William barked. "Do it."

Obedient, she did as she was told, shuddering when the thick, carded web-silk made contact with her skin, and slipped over the shift of opaque silks she wore.

If I had believed for an instant, he had truly meant to place me at the head of the Kingdom State of Almandine, I would have resisted. Then, my boy would have listened. Heard me say, high estate was not what I wished, and might, perhaps, have allowed himself to be coaxed away from a ridiculous idea said at first, I am sure, in jest. I dare not attempt it now. I cannot refuse a gift, he believes, he gives me. Not now. Not ever.

"Lady," Ratanakiri said, quietly, "if I pull the stays too tight, you must tell me, so I may loosen them. The ceremony is long, and you must be comfortable."

Belying the scowl he wore, William laughed, saying, "The Lady's sole comfort is me, nothing else is of any consequence," then seeing her smile, interpreted what had been said.

Comfortable? How can I be comfortable, burdened by such a weighty thing, and yet more to be piled onto me?

Hoping his mood had lightened, she glanced at him. Seeing him still sunk in the blackest of moods, which he seemed incapable of escaping from, and rubbing, always rubbing his temples to drive out pain that would not be driven away. Despite the brightness gilding eyes avidly fixed upon her, its glitter could not disguise, the promise of death lay in their depths. She turned quickly away, feigning interest in the garment as its sleeves encased her arms, and unsightly folds in its skirts were smoothed out.

"You know," he had said to her one night, when he lay with his head in her lap, "I slowly slide down an insane slope, do you not, Clara?"

"No," she had answered, not prepared to admit it to herself, let alone him, "I know nothing of the sort, my darling, child. You suffer from the stresses and strains of the past few months; that is all. Who would not be overloaded in body and mind, having made great effort to bring about the miracles you have performed to the benefit of all? Rest will set you right."

"Always the mother," he had replied, "who will see no wrong in her child."

"Is this really necessary?" she said, when Ratanakiri lifted the urilatum collar from its cushion and made to fasten it around her neck, and collarbones.

"It is protocol," William sprang from his chair. "Would you," he said, through clenched teeth, "before even sitting upon the Chair of Authority, upset Noor's long standing tradition? These artefacts," he spat, stalking to pace a circle about her, "these emblems are symbolic of rule. You seek to challenge this? Do you think to disgrace me before the High Lords of Bekily, Andradia, Spessa, Tocantinae, Rhodal, Demantae, Tsavoe, and beyond, who thinking it scandal, and worse, a woman of Lessadgh will be Almandine, would have refused to attend, had they dared? Had they not feared the power I wield," he screamed, in her face. "By the powers, Clara, you shall not. I tell you, you will not." Rubbing his temples, massaging the deep aching pain, he grew calmer saying, "The High Lord of the Helm signifies continuity and stability, the mask alone must tell you that, had you the wit to recognize it. You will wear it. All of it, shall you wear uncomplaining."

Submitting, knowing he was capable of anything once his temper was roused, and frightened of provoking him to further outburst, she smiled weak apology, murmuring she was stupid and ignorant and ungrateful when he did so much for her. The collar fitted, she waited for the headdress to be placed securely on her head.

"Look," William said, laughing with pleasure, and waltzing to stand beside her, "see in the mirror how regal my mother looks? Was not the Lady, my mother, born to wear such robes? Who could fail to love you, as do I?"

"The mask?" she said, "we must not forget the mask."

"You have so much to learn, Mother, mine," he said, with a lean smile. "So very much to learn, and very quick you must do it. The mask will only be fitted over your face, once you are confirmed. The cloak now," he commanded, and more heaviness was hung from her shoulders, while many metres of embroidered cloth, spangled with gemstones, were spread on the floor for her to drag when walking in stately progress.

"My mother looks well, does she not? You women waiting upon the Lady, come after, but come not up onto the dais. You, Ratanakiri, open the door, run ahead and tell Clump we make our way to meet him."

Hubbub rising. Muted murmurs writhed amongst curses and subdued outrage. Shocked whispers, heavy with denial no summons had been received, but of their own volition they had come. The patter of soft muttering, by those engaged in schemes, which would never come to fruition. The sound of many low voices swelling from the floor of the great hall, made by unwilling witnesses assembled to view the proceedings at close quarter.

Hubbub rising. Like invisible smoke, the noise was almost a tangible thing, which becoming trapped for a time on the underside of packed galleries, finally found a way to waft through the stay-rails, only to encounter further confused din. Seamlessly, it was drawn into suppressed clamour.

Hubbub rising. Saturating the threads of magnificent tapestries, drenching the bare surfaces of every wall with inarticulate, growled mumbling.

Hubbub rising. Hanging lights of fire crystal flared in quietly roared sound, and the softened tumult of many voices insidiously rising, rose to a crescendo and circulated beneath the domed ceiling.

Separate and apart, in floor-space of his own, Cullinan Doge, his face screwed in a thoughtful scowl, sucked his teeth with vigour. He stood, arms folded across his bare chest, malignantly eyeing the massive curtains strung across the width of the hall to screen the dais and the Chair of Authority mounted on it. Behind him, the Nine listened intently to outrage rippling in hushed speech, noting with satisfaction, whispered opinion exactly matched their own, and quietly registering for future reference, from whence it came.

Behind the curtains, dressed in foppish finery he would rather not have had on his back, Persimmony Clump waited. Unable to hear anything distinct through the mass of jumbled, discordant rumbling, he knew precisely what was being said. Once again, he looked into the passage giving access to the dais, and was relieved to see Ratanakiri, blue curls already straying from the elaborate hairstyle she wore, holding her skirts high, rushing toward him.

"They come," she panted, "is all in readiness? By the powers, I hope it is, for the talented one will brook no error this span. Why, I thought he would blast the poor Lady to dust for some small remark she made. His temper grows fouler, and fouler."

"Mind your mouth," Clump said, stern, "else it will be you who founders in dust and never know it. All be ready."

* * *

Straining to stay erect beneath the heavy regalia, her hand resting light on William's arm, Clara stepped into the corridor, and, beginning to walk slowly past the ceremonial guard waiting to escort them to the great hall, faltered.

A man, one she had thought never to see again, regarded her from one luminescent blue eye. She shivered, noting the wound she had given him. A puckered scar, running from brow to cheek, marred a handsome face. The hollow socket of the eye she had ruined, sullied his look still further.

"You must bear the weight," William said, with ice in his voice. "It has, after all, been scaled down to your size and cannot be that heavy. Take hold of yourself. I will have you show no weakness before so-called dignitaries, little better than whipped curs, who in attendance, hope to see you fall."

She moved on, hanging onto her boy's arm for support, knowing a hated enemy walked just a few paces behind them.

* * *

I am old. Clara began to climb the stairs to the dais, assisted by William and Clump.

I am old. Her excuse, and lament, for muscles screaming in neck, shoulders, back and thighs, as she mounted the steps to enable her to sit in the Chair of Authority with no loss of dignity. Sinking into its depths, despite feeling ridiculously dwarfed by its size, a moment of relief flooding her was dissipated by a watchful, luminous blue eye.

I am old. Patient, she leant forward while cushions were packed behind her, to fill the space between her and the back of the chair, so the assembly need not stare at the soles of her shoes.

I am old, she thought, while Ratanakiri fussed, arranging the train of her cloak in pleasing folds over the dais, *yet will never be older for talent, taken into my body when I sucked his wound, girdles my heart, and my boy, laying his hand upon it, stroked it into life. Another gift unasked and unwanted.*

"We are ready?" William snapped. "Then let the curtains be drawn. Clump, you stand by my mother's right hand. That is your place. It will always be your place. Do you understand? Now, let the masquerade begin!"

Surprise, amazement, envy, outrage, loathing, emotions gushed in one enormous gasp upon laying eyes on him. Walking to the front of the dais, William stripped off all clothing, except for the loincloth he wore, and with a glare from glittering eyes, brought deadly silence to the hall.

"See me?" he thundered. "See talent clothing me from head to toe, and know power is mine. You know it. Who among you would in truth, wish to be here this span? None. Fear brought every one of you, urilatum masked Lords of many Helms, into the great hall of the Helm of Almandine. Lickspittle drabs in fine raiment do I name you. Deep embedded in perfidy, and proud in prejudice, do I know you to be, nevertheless were you bidden to come, that with your own eyes, you might see at first hand what is done here, and no time of yours will I waste in greeting.

"Behold my mother. My adopted, mother. A woman of Lessadgh whom beyond all things, do I love. Her, I place in the Chair of Authority. With good reason do I do it, and it is this. Honesty, fair dealing, courage and sacrifice, I name only a few of her many qualities, you here assembled lack. What better qualities for the ruler of the city, I, through a great making, built? Who more suited than she? This city's inhabitants need have no fear she will steal their gold, and dip their purses as some do. Nor blight them with labour, and pay no hire, as some do. Nor with unfair taxes will she ever charge them. Who among you may say the same? None. I know you all.

"Into your hearts and minds do I see clear. Parasites, you are, feeding off the sweat of those who serve you. The very ones, I remind you, since you have forgot, you should serve, if in leadership you were true. Know then, Clara Maddingley of Lessadgh is High Lord of this Helm. My hand shelters her. My hand will shelter her always. Take heed. Come against her, and I will smite you. Down to dust, will you go! Try to usurp her, dust you shall be before an eye may blink. Nor try with artifice to persuade her to abdicate. Mutter and groan, plot and scheme, that is your right. I do nothing to prevent it, but make a move to my mother's disadvantage, and this do I solemnly promise. You, and yours, all you hold dear, will I take from you. I make no idle threat, nor seek to dress it in any other cloth than that which it is...a certain promise.

"Who here, this day, has objection to this rightful choice for High Lord of the Helm of Almandine? No," he crowed, hearing no one speak, and noting the uncomfortable movements many made in their seats. "I thought to hear none. Prejudices, have I spoken of them? Not at length, I think. Colour, what prejudice could there be, when the Faienya are painted in all colours? Not colour? Talent then? No, from those that do not own it, there is envy, and the more talent shines, the more envious," he said, staring directly at Cullinan and the Nine. "And fear, do not forget fear toward those who own it in great amount, such as I. Does it not make cowards of the brave? No, there can be no prejudice against a thing all wish to own.

"Height? Yes, we come to height. That is the greatest prejudice amongst the Faienya, and the most stupid. Long have the Stunted Ones been scorned for lack of height. Wrongly. It is not something chosen. None among this assembly ever had choice of the physical attributes they would be birthed with, and none throughout the whole of Noor either.

"My good friend, Persimmony Clump, owns that lack and does very well without height. He is to be my mother's right hand. He has been her right hand, and always will be. Honest, reliable and courageous, he is, and will serve her unto fading, if need be. Who gathered here, has one such as he? None. Show prejudice to him, you show prejudice to me, and I will not tolerate it.

"I detain you no longer. Witnesses you are, and true testimony will you bear this day."

Signalling, he waited for the mask to be brought forward. Cullinan, thinking as would be proper, he would be called upon to fit it in place, stepped forward. Lifting the mask from the cushion it lay on, William held it high so all could see it.

"With this mask," he said, ignoring the Doge completely, "the continuity of the Helm, and the city I have built, begins. Never will the Lord appear in public with face uncovered, so that all may know the Lordship continues no matter whose face lies beneath the mask I now fit in rightful place."

Closing her eyes as the subtle gleam of coppered-silver drew near, and darkness threatened, Clara felt cold metal spread on her skin, and waited for the clasps to be snapped shut before looking through the eyeholes.

I am old. Encased in a metallic effigy of rule; no emotion can I show which shall be seen. Unless I walk the grounds of the Helm for all time to come, or till talent girdling my heart wears away, if it can, my face will be covered.

Tears, hovering on the brink, slipped and flooded hot onto her cheeks.

"Now, do you all come, in orderly fashion," William commanded. "Congratulate the High Lord of this Helm, who is newly risen. An onerous task, but most necessary, though no feast of celebration do I impose upon you, knowing no merriment resides within you, and much there is to carefully think on. Come to the right conclusion in advance of penalty, striking, if you will not."

For long hours she sat, her back erect, graciously nodding thanks to kind words spoken falsely, and just when she believed her spine about to crack in two, the ceremony was over, and the hall cleared.

William and Clump helped her down from the seat she would sit in for many a year to come. Watching, waiting to fall in line behind them, a cruel face that had once been handsome regarded her from a brilliantly blue eye, while the barely healed wound she had given him, flamed livid.

Chapter 63.

Shamed! He had been shamed. Striding away from the Helm, with fury flushing his face at the ignominious treatment he had suffered, the word reverberated in Cullinan's head.

Striding through the streets of the city to the House of Learning, the talented child had reluctantly allocated to the Guardians, his mouth automatically sprayed the blessings of the Blessed Lady on all within hearing distance, while the heat of shame boiled angry within, and his mind a lighted Catherine-wheel, spun on insulting disrespect.

Shamed before them all. Stepping forward to complete the inauguration, I was deliberately ignored. All saw it. All saw me rebuffed and rejected. All saw it. All saw. Humiliated, I had to stand before them all, saying nothing. All saw. How their tongues will wag. Like wildfire, news of shame suffered will travel throughout Noor. By the actions of a malicious child, I have lost face. No, no, the Guardians have lost face, and for what? A creature out of Lessadgh, inferior in every aspect save one...the talented child's hand shelters her.

Well...well, out of its shadow she must sometime come. To that end, do I vow, my life's work I will make it, to wait for such an eventuality, and bring her down into dust where she will rightfully rule in dirt. Think. Think not on future revenge, but how best to turn catastrophic shame to positive spin. On this, the Nine and I shall consult upon our return to Hessonii. No! Before we depart. Shameful insult must have immediate opposition. At once, some story we must concoct, and spew out to counteract tongues that wag, with other tongues wagging in denying dispute. A plausible tale, it must be, to annihilate doubt in the minds of the faithful. And Lessadgh? I bide my time to bring about her destruction.

"May the blessings of the Blessed Lady be upon you, friends, one and all."

"May the Blessed Lady make your face shine, friend, Doge."

No hope of that, he thought, smiling a munificent smile that never reached his eyes, *the bitch faded long since, and never had it in her power to make even her own face shine beyond a speckled shimmer.*

"The Blessed Lady's blessings upon you, friend."

* * *

Gone, the first yellow strip of light, which had begun to push up the shutters of night, and pink now suffused the lower reaches of the sky. As if exhausted by the effort, its advance was slow, until creeping through long windows it insidiously merged with talent's shine to light the room, and blanch the last pale shadows hiding in corners.

Quietly babbling continuous complaint of great pain in his head, William, sleeping fitfully, lay sprawled across the counterpane covering the bed. At the writing desk, knowing he would soon miss the warmth of her body, Clara hurriedly drew a sheet of flax-paper from the holder, dipped her quill and scribbled:

Clump, the ceremonial guard, with one extraordinarily brilliant blue eye, and an ugly scar running diagonal across his face, tell me all you know of him. Give me answer, discreetly.

The note folded, and slipped into her pocket to give to Ratanakiri for delivery, she returned to bed, and sliding back under the covers, put one arm around her boy.

"If you wish to know a thing, Clara," he said, harsh, shaking her to the core, "you have only to ask. His name is Semyon of Rhodal. He is the one who dragged me from our hiding place. He is the one whom you chopped with a hatchet when he came to bring you into Noor. At his interview, Clump asked him how he had gained unruly, cack-handed stitchery, and these are the words he spoke exact. 'A woman of Lessadgh, whom I had done great wrong, marked me in this fashion, taking talent, my eye, and all sense of smell. Most dear is the scar to me. To know where vaunting ambition leads, I need only look into a mirror, and there, do I find my place and worth.'

"Ruthless in the execution of duty," he continued, "we both know him to be, and loyalty I know, he will give to the full. I ordered Clump to employ him, to place him in command of both the ceremonial and ordinary guard."

"You spoke to Clump?" she blurted. "When? Never, in these past days, have I left your side."

"For me, speech is not always necessary. Mind to mind, I may speak as the fancy takes me, as well you know, lest you have forgot."

"I took his talent and sense of smell with the blow?"

"You did fierce, Mother, mine. Talent is gone. The receptors smashed, never to return, his gift is lost. Do you remember," his voice grew softer, "when the land was bound in ice and snow, how you shivered, and your sense of smell was banished by your dripping nose. You cobbled an explanation, when I understood not why your body did these things, saying mal froid was the cause? For Semyon of Rhodal, in respect of his nose, the effect is similar."

"Mal froid," she repeated, "yes, I remember."

"Now you know," he said, turning to face her, "you will tear up the note you wrote, and do not think to go behind my back again, lest I cannot control anger, and in madness, strike out at you."

* * *

In days long passed, if a thread held William's sanity together, Clara had not noticed. And if Clump had managed to get close, and told her in the space of a few moments the thread was fraying, she would not have listened.

Breathless, limping rumour, whispering insanity was in the eyes of the talented child, had been quickly hushed. Unaware of this, Clara would have admitted her boy had changed. Reluctantly, if pressed, she would have said the boy, loved with all her heart, was much changed, but not different, despite erratic moods swooping from carefree lightness to towering rages, as easily as birds on the wing performed acrobatic flight.

In the days before her inauguration, these things she could not avoid noticing.

Hardness, sometimes observed in William's glittering eyes, was now constant, and iciness was growing stronger in their purple, gold-flecked depths. He rarely smiled, appearing to take no pleasure in anything. He was quick to find fault, and the calculating lash of his tongue was intended to maim the psyche of all whom he whipped with it. He was no longer greeted with enthusiastic reverence and wonder in the corridors of the Helm, but all shrank away, as if they would rather bury themselves in the wall than draw his attention when he passed.

Fear, she noticed, walked the Helm, wearing the form of her boy. Since fear now nibbled at her too, she wondered if it could ever outstrip the love she diluted its venom with.

* * *

"I do not leave our apartment this day," William said, "nor for the days to come."

"Good," she answered, relieved he accepted a suggestion she had made many times. "Rest is to your best advantage, and will set you to rights. I am pleased you heed my advice."

"Your advice, Clara? A fig for your advice, I go into seclusion as the Disobedient Ones before me. You will go with me."

"Secluded? For how long?"

"Did you not hear what I said? For all the days to come."

"But, William," she said, puzzled, "there is the Helm to manage..."

"Barely able to speak a word of our language, what help would you be in dealing with the affairs of the Helm?" he sneered, pinning her with dangerously glittering eyes that dared her to argue. "These past months, Persimmony Clump, dour and thorough, has overseen most energetically. His guiding hand shall remain on all, his eye fixed on nothing, if it is not to your benefit. I have spoken."

"Then," she fingered her ring, turned it once, turned it twice and stroked the table of the gem, "of what use am I?" she asked, quiet.

"To me? Of great use, Clara," he laughed, taking her in his arms, and whisking her round and round, "You are the loving tool that shall give me release."

* * *

"My head hurts!" William wailed. "Keep the agony at bay. Take the torment of pain away with the magic of your fingers, Clara. Smooth its jagged edges. Blunt its sharpened point."

For hours, she sat with his head in her lap, stroking and rubbing, desperately massaging a worsening condition, and achieving nothing.

"By the powers, you do not do what you should," he cried, roughly pushing her away. Jumping to his feet, he paced the floor. "They walk," he said, screwing his forehead with a finger, "they walk, here in my head. The fall of their steps is what causes me pain. I am their true child, the one who never was. Hearing the sounds of their footfall, I feel the thunder of their movement. Very restless, they are, and in turmoil. Even though they are gone, they remain. A veritable archive, am I, of all that passed, and in the passing, do I know everything. Memories, ancient memories, travel in my blood with talent ever at their side. For me, the two are irrevocably linked."

"I do not understand," she said, scrambling to get up.

"No, no, you do not," he said, bursting into sudden laughter that had no cheer on its surface notes, and deep despair in its depths, and laughed until tears streamed from his eyes.

"Tell me," she took his head in her hands, and drawing it to her breast, stroked his temple, "tell me, William. Make me understand, so I may help you."

"I speak of destiny, Clara," he wrenched away from her. "Of a destiny that should have been mine, robbed from me. To stride across galaxies my hand helped form. The planets mere stepping-stones to far and far infinity, and I would have, could have... No! No, that destiny was never mine, but should have been.

"Oh," he said, shaking his head, and his eyes growing wilder, "they made a very grave error of judgment. Such a great mistake did they make. Tantamount to rebellion it was, and thought not to pay any price for their actions. Why do you look at me, so? Do not look at me!" he shouted. "I am not they," his voice dropped to a whisper, "and, I, am them. Their error was not mine. Forbidden fruit, they tasted and never had enough of, I have not experienced. Hear me now, you Disobedient Ones, and know whom of your kin calls to you. My given name is Gilgaladgh. I am one, the only one left behind. Mim nimadgh qimem Gilgaladgh. Eodgh oom, fim oomlim oom mesadgh bessoumdgh."

"William, you are frightening me!"

"Do not," he screamed at her, "interrupt when I am speaking to my forebears. Get you hence. Bring me gold burnt to fine powder, and dewberry tea. Yes, and we will play cards. Look, the pack is in my hands. Which game shall we play, and what shall we play for?" he said, shuffling non-existent cards, and dealing them out to players who were not there.

"Let us play for a galaxy in its entirety."

"We should play for nothing less," William said, in a voice not his own, "surely we should not play for trivialities."

And then in the tone and timbre of another voice, he cried, "No longer do the galaxies wheel to our order."

Wide-eyed with terror, Clara backed slowly away as strange voices erupted from William's mouth. Speaking a language she had never heard and did not understand, she knew with certainty as the conversation continued, every word spoken was drenched with anger, and despair.

"If galaxies wheel not to our order, more shall we create, and with a roadway of stars, deck the infinite regions of deepest space."

"That power has left us."

"Then let us depart this place, and regain that which was ours to command."

"Well do you know," a low voice sobbed, "the way is barred."

"The way is barred, you say?"

"You know who bars it."

"Well do we know, and despair come upon us."

"No, no, never say we are bound to this place."

"We are bound, and may never hence go forth."

"Do not despair, do not despair, we may yet return, if we can but find a way to achieve it. A way there must be that is not yet beyond us."

"We will withdraw. Forgo the pleasures of the flesh that have delighted and enthralled us in pleasurable bondage. Together, working as one, as once we did, will we find a remedy to the blight that keeps us in this ruin."

"Nothing works. Nothing works. A library grown through long eons of searching to find the way back, and still it is not found."

"How long are we bound?"

"Forever. Forever."

"Come, the cards are dealt, stake your claim, and play as best you may to win."

"We cannot win with the hand we, of our own volition, dealt ourselves."

"No dice, no dice, never again shall we meddle with the dice, for it has rolled, and not to our advantage."

"Nor ever shall they roll in our favour again."

"It was very great error for so little gain."

"We broke the boundary set. Never should we have done what we did through puerile curiosity of carnal knowledge."

"It flamed, it burnt, to see and know of passion, yet never feel its heat."

"Now burnt with fire of cooler nature, but no less fatal, is our perpetual punishment and remorse."

"Never should we have done that which we did."

"No, we should not, and scattering seed by right not ours to sow, neglected the produce from it in our lust to taste the whole of the feast."

"Wrong, upon wrong, did we do, and saw it not, cared not, so great was passion."

"Noor did we create for the product of our loins, so chide us not with neglect."

"The place of perfect light, our seed calls that place, knowing not the perfection of light once we walked in."

"No more. No more to reside in perfect light."

"In mourning for that which is lost, do we spend time left to us, who once ordered time and space."

"More gold. Strip from Noor all gold for the work we do. Fill the smelting pots and let it burn."

"Bring dewberries to make a tea, and drink it down."

"Energy...I feel its surge."

"Power shines."

"We may yet regain original form, and returning, do humblest obeisance."

"Heap me in mourning. We cannot return."

"Taking the form we took, so are we entrapped...by error made."

"Every avenue...locked against us. And, we, bereft of hope, are bound forever to this place that was ill-made by imperfect hands and minds, that only a short while ago did own perfection."

"Destroy all that has been made, and all in it."

"Wipe out cruel evidence of error, so it may be as if it never were, and we, innocent of guilt."

"Wrong piled upon wrong piled upon wrong, our wrongs take on mountainous proportions if that path we take."

"The denial of wrong, by destruction? No, we must draw back from that path, and let not rage engulf us."

"The wrong is ours to pay, not by those sprung from these hateful forms to make unacceptable payment."

"Our wrong doing acknowledged, we must take punishment with acceptance, knowing we are justly served."

"Will we, in this frail form, waste away?"

"Not I."

"Nor I."

"Before that happen, I waste all that I now am, and down into dust go willingly, rather than suffer the torment of such knowledge."

"To utter ruin, we have come complete. In devastation we find ourselves, and despairing, exchange the light that once did shine so brilliant, for the welcoming arms of oblivion."

"For us, what other course is open?"

"The last and final wrong?"

"We, immersed in disobedience, agree?"

"So be it."

The long conversation crashed to an abrupt halt. Frightened by the strange voices, and the argument that had strung rage between them, the long silence following it terrified her even more.

"Clara," William said, calm and matter of fact, "you must know, you have to fade me?"

Chapter 64.

On the desk, two piles of flax-paper, one large, one small, and between them William sat. His head bowed, his brow knit in concentration, and the light of a fire crystal flaming his red hair to brilliant incandescence. Occasionally, he paused to think of what he should write, his tongue peeking from a corner of his mouth for an instant before applying himself to a task he had screamed must be done. Deftly, he filled page after page with childish scrawl, scowling at any noise Clara made, until she retreated to the far corner of the room, and sat perfectly still for long hours.

"This work, I do for you," he said, once again straightening papers into a neat, orderly heap.

Later, drawing yet another sheet from a rapidly diminishing stack, he said, "Ignorant you are, and must come to knowledge," and began to scribble, once more.

* * *

Cross-legged on the floor, William plucked at the web-silk carpeting as though he striped feathers from a chicken meant for the pot. At the farthest end of the room, Clara, still pressed into the corner, and not daring to move or ask what he did, watched him intently. Watched him tug knotted strands loose from the thick pile. Pulling web-silk free from the anchoring weave beneath, only to aimlessly discard little tufts by throwing them over his shoulder. Breathless and afraid, she watched the pieces briefly float on air, before lazily pirouetting to litter the floor around him with frayed, thistledown threads.

Hour after hour, she watched him labour to expand the first little bald patch he had made. Without saying a word, or looking in her direction, he continued to do his work, gradually shaping a little arc, then a horned moon, then a semi-circle, until he was finally marooned at the centre of an island, hemmed in by denuded carpeting.

"You see me?" he said, when the moated circle was complete.

"Yes," she said, on a rasped breath.

"If you could wrest talent from me, and keep me in such isolation as I now stand on, then, and only then, we might be as we once were."

"You are not isolated, William," she said, trying to keep tremors from her voice. "You may step over the breach at any time you choose."

"It is symbolic!" he screamed. "Symbolic," he said, pacing in agitation back and forth on the atoll he had made, and calming, "you must not be obtuse, Clara, really you must not. If you can, imagine I am a babe encased in my mother's womb. The circle I have made, the muscular outer walls that protect the wonder being created inside. You understand?"

She nodded, quietly saying, "Yes," to humour him, "that I can imagine."

"A babe not fully formed. So incomplete, I am not yet able to draw breath," he said, and lightly jumped from the circle. "Long before its time, the babe I now portray is thrown from its refuge. What happens next?"

"It would die."

"In figurative parallel, such a babe, am I. Talent sleeping deep within me, Clara, came too soon. At puberty, it should have begun to waken, and as the petals of a flower slowly open to the light, talent would have bloomed. If that had been the way of it, I would have been complete in the gift...and truly great.

"You understand? Too soon, was talent violently forced from deepest slumber, and viciously hauled from its resting place, in fury it came roaring. Implanted in me, are the rage and seeds of destruction, the Disobedient Ones thought to visit upon both Noor and Lessadgh. Talent, birthed as it should, when it should, would have checked and balanced. You see me? I am incomplete, no checks, no balances have I, save my will, and that is quickly eroding. In me, the seeds of destruction sown are growing, Clara. I can do nothing more than I have done to control them. You must fade me."

"I will not kill you, William," she whispered, appalled he should ask such a thing. "You are mad to ask it of me."

"At last!" He threw back his head amd laughed. "You arrive at truth."

"No!"

"Denial cannot serve you, Clara," he said, with anger sparking from his eyes, though his voice remained calm, "not as you would have it do. In denial, will you be culpable, and have a share in all I most certainly will do."

"I will not be the death of you, William."

"The power of talent in creation you have witnessed, and were glad. Tell me, Mother, will gladness wreathe your heart, and paint your face with smiles, when for no good reason, other than my sport, cities are razed to the ground, and untold numbers faded? Will you cheer me on in the destruction I will wreak in the throes of insane rage, and putting your arms around me say...I am the child of your heart after that?

"Will you say, in the midst of smouldering ruin, I am your boy, your dearest, child? Will you? And when," he snarled, "all is dust, and faded voices crying lament our only company, what will you do when insane rage turns on you? Where will blame lie, when you did nothing to prevent it?"

"You are cruel," Clara sobbed.

"Not near so cruel as I shall be," he hissed. "None left to call me, Anathema. None left to spit on the soil where I trod. None left to revile and curse my name. All gone to dust, and many there will be, who wished oblivion came earlier before that happen! None left, Clara, not even you.

And raging, must my gaze turn next on Lessadgh, for the sport of destruction, always will I crave. That craving is already in me. Insistent, it is, but the full measure has yet to rise and demand it be satisfied. You have no choice. You must fade me."

"I cannot," she wailed.

"You do not believe these things will come about?" he asked.

"I do not know. How can I, when I am ignorant of all that passes in this strange place of miracles, and harsh colour? How can I do as you ask, when all I feel for you is deepest love? In me, William, there was a void, deeper and wider than the chasm girdling this Helm. Who brought you, and left you in my orchard, I cannot say, but I found you, and that yawning emptiness was filled to overflowing. You smiled, and all bitterness in me fled. My life, I would give in defence of yours, so you cannot beg me to take it."

"Then your choice is made, and in choosing, have chosen the course of destruction for me. Come, let us perform the first act of very many." Opening one of the long windows, he went out onto the balcony, and leaning on the balustrade, called, "Come! See what you have sanctioned. Down in the courtyard," he laughed, "a group loiters by the big fountain. Them shall I blast to oblivion, and all who stand nearby, too."

"No! No," she cried, running across the room, and dragged him back inside. "You cannot."

"I can," he smiled a chilling smile, shrugged her off, and raised his hand as if to strike her, "and will, for you do not love me near so much as you profess."

"William?"

"Your love has surrounded me, warmed me in its soothing balm and protected me. For all of my life, your love has done so, only to desert me now when it is needed most. All I have said I would do, I will do, Clara. And worse. Yet you will not protect me from the terror lurking within. Where is your love now?"

"William, that is not fair."

"Has selfless love taken refuge in selfish cowardice?"

"Yes, perhaps, I do not know," she wailed. "You ask too much of me."

"Find the steel I know is in you. Please, I beg of you," he said, kneeling in front of her, and putting her hands up to his throat, "find the courage to do what must be done. Please, Clara, help me. Let my name be revered for the good I have done. Please, Mother. I shall not struggle, nor fight my end. Fade me, before it is too late, and provision made to protect you for all your long days vanishes."

"Without you, I have no care if I live or die, William."

"I care for you. That you live, and tend all I have made, is of great importance to me. You are my beginning, Clara, and my end. My legacy, the gift I give to Noor, and all in it, is you, Clara. It is you. Help me," he pleaded, "to live through you."

She tried to pull her hands away, only to find she could not. "William, you must not make me do this," she sobbed.

"I make you do nothing. Time is short. Insanity will soon break the final filament that binds it to lucid, rational thought. Please, Mother, you must do it."

"How can I live without you?"

"How will you live with me, a monster? Listen. Periodically, in time to come, my voice shall rumble from the depths I made. Fade me, Mother, and all shall think they see me walking in a blaze of brilliancy around the Helm's circuit, that everyone may believe upon a journey I have gone, and never know it is the last I make. Please, Mother, full-blown insanity is near. Please, I can hold it back no longer. Please, Clara. Help me. Help me, Mother," he cried, desperate. "I cannot be a demonic fiend, whose only malicious thought is bent upon the destruction of all and everything. Help me, Mother."

Tears, she did not know she cried, scalded her face. Cold resolve, harder than adamant, growing somewhere deep inside, which in time to follow would never be shaken loose, her fingers tightened on the smooth column of his slender neck. Gently, she caressed the small hidden mound of his adam's apple with the balls of her thumbs.

"Please, Mother."

Fingers tightening, thumbs pressing into the soft flesh of the only one she had ever truly loved, and tightening further, squeezed. Growing dim, and dimmer, the light in his gold-flecked, purple eyes. Darkly darkening, unnatural colour rose to flood the luminescence of talent travelling beneath the coppery skin of his lovely face. A rattle, gurgled in his throat, and she relaxed her grip.

"Please," he rasped, "please, Mother. Insane fury comes."

Howling in agony, Clara's fingers applied death. Howling anguish, she squeezed, and squeezed with all her strength, never feeling beneath them, the fabric of William's being quiver, the tiny, physical building blocks becoming unstable, now caught in a dynamic vortex of whirling vibrations. A long sigh sped from his opened mouth, and riding on his last breath, a small bright light floated away.

Her hands, clawed to killing grip, gripped nothing. Sinking to her knees, curling into a ball of hurt, she rained bitter tears and despair onto the carpet.

From the balcony of Clara and William's apartment, a shining figure stepped from the balustrade, and walking on friendly breezes, went to the perimeter of the Helm. Beneath it, shouting excitement, staring and pointing in wonder, those in the gardens chased after to see what would happen, and moments later, everyone inside the many buildings tumbled out to follow.

Rumour, racing round the city said the talented child was to perform another great making. Crowds, collected in expectation, saw the shining apparition tread the full circuit of the Helm, and before the eyes of the multitude, sink gracefully into the depths of the chasm girdling it.

Chapter 65.

Clump was hovering outside in the corridor when she finally opened the door.
"You have been weeping," he accused, running concerned eyes over her dishevelled appearance, and the paleness of her haggard face.
"Why should I not?" Clara answered. "Any mother would weep in such circumstance."
"Your boy, what does he do?"
"How should I know?" she snapped. "You are aware of how he has been of late."
"He has gone on a journey?" he persisted.
"Did you not see him go into the chasm, Clump? His reasons are his own. This apartment, it is to be locked. No one is to enter. It is to be left exactly as it is."
"Until his return," he nodded. "When might that be?"
Ignoring his questions, Clara said, with ice in her voice, "You will arrange another apartment on the ground floor for me, at once. Then, you will show me how the Helm is managed."
"I am your right hand, Lady."
"And always shall be. Now down to business. Show me everything."

* * *

"Ho!" Bezel called, "traffic here gets worse all the time. Did I tell you, rumour runs? It whispers, trouble there will be in the Ammolian Mountains. For myself, I am sure of it. If not this sparn, or the next, it will come. Mark my words. The Guardians squeeze the Stunted Ones for yet more taxes and they, most understandably, are not thrilled at the prospect of stumping up more gold. Tepauni's tits! What holds us, now? Oh," he said, craning from the seat of his wagon, "I see it plain. Some fool, not securing the load carried on his cart, has dumped it in the road. Well, and well, we must be patient. This mission, no offence, I hope you will take, Caryadgh, has been of little event. No cut, or dash, no skulking, or slyly prising information from those reluctant to give what must be got. No peril encountered to be foiled. A very dull affair. In all frankness, this mission, if you can call it that, has been beneath my worth. Far beneath it, but being the accommodating fellow I am, when Spymaster Malfroid put it my way, asked for me express he did, I had no heart to refuse. You will have a tale to tell, will you not, when reporting to him? Caryadgh? Caryadgh?"
Swivelling on the seat, Bezel drew back the curtain to look inside, and

grinned.

"By the powers, a sly little hussy she is," he said, to no one. "Empty space and closed doors at the back, I never felt, or heard her go. Ripe for recruitment, she most definitely is."

* * *

Cloaked and hooded, Caryadgh slipped purposefully through the press thronging the pavement. Further on, ducking out of the main street, she passed into a quiet little alley and paused to listen for the footsteps of any who might be following, before she went quickly along the narrow walkway. Coming to her destination, she glanced over her shoulder, and a moment later, sidestepped into the deep recess of a porch. Rapping a sequence of taps softly on the door, she pushed into the cool shadows of the hall, and closed it behind her.

A dark figure stepped into the gloom, saying, "So, you are come, beloved."

"Yes, I am home, and with information you will find most interesting, Father."

"Time enough to speak of it in depth. First, let me look upon your dear face," Malfroid said, taking her into his arms, and into the subdued light of the room he had just come out of. "Let me hold you. For now, it is all I could wish for, and is more than enough. Three sparns is far, far too long to have been without you."

"How many spans shall I be here," she said, crushed to his chest, "before I am sent back to Hessonii?"

"Hush, my dearest, Caryadgh, the Guardians have forgone their chance to draw you into their Order. To, Hessonii, nevermore shall you go."

"I am glad right of it. That hateful life was never one I would choose to live, Father."

"Nor shall you," he said, rocking her in his arms as he had when she was a small child.

"And mother?"

"Reboia is well. Very well. Duty prevented her from leaving the Helm. She bade me give you this," he dropped a kiss on her cheek. "Doubtless, she will smother you in the like, the moment she claps eyes on you. Reboia has missed you. Very, very much she has missed you."

* * *

Memories. The night passed in the thrall of memories. Raw, cruel and deeply painful, their sharp bite gnawed a wound that would never heal. Twenty years on, and time, equally as spiteful, had not lessened the impact, but had gradually stolen the face of her boy from her mind. Only snippets were left, how his hair flamed in the light of fire crystals, how his mouth had moved while he wrote, and the pen in his hand, trawling across the papers, leaving a spidery trail of ink as it continued onward.

Malfroid, and his widespread network of spies, would seek for the one Atrament had named, and find her. What then?

"I will fade her," Clara said, to buzzed silence. "By the powers, I swear it."

Rising from her chair, she went to the cupboard and scrabbled through accumulated rubbish she had thrown there, meaning to deal with it when she had a moment, which had never come. Her fingers touching the white heat of extreme coldness, folded around it, and drew the bone white casket out into the light.

"After so long," she said, "the power to pierce me with ruthless chill remains."

Carrying it to the table, she set it down, and not wanting to view its contents, carefully turned it over.

A courtship of sorts? Was that not how Atrament couched it? There is irony. He courted one who was already wooed, for in the unity of vengeance we are most surely irrevocably bound, tighter than any lovers were ever tied.

For a moment, she stroked the base of the casket, enjoying its smooth glacial feel, and likening it to the chill residing within her, that never melted, no matter the intensity of warmth encountered.

"Sidgh liminadgh," she said.

Noiseless, the panels slid back to wrap seamless seams around the edges of the casket, and disappeared into undetectable recesses. Vibrant green the cloth. Mirky green the long phial, capped with urilatum, laying on it. Untying the stays holding it in place, she took the bottle from its secret home, and held it to the light.

"Liquid, dark and syrupy by its look," she murmured. "Trooh as it should be. Dewberry tea, and burnt gold, William said, if I remember right. Dewberry?"

Uncapping the tiny bottle, a smell she recognized instantly flooded her nostrils. Lusciously rich, the sensual aroma of fruit ripened by the sun to plump, succulent fullness, its juices extracted and fermented, the easily obtainable ingredient Atrament had omitted to insert in the recipe stolen by the Guardians.

"Do I have the stomach, the will, and heart for vengeance? Have I not hungered for it down through the years? For you, my bonded partner, the one named Anathema," she raised the phial in salute, "and for myself, will I take what is owed in fullest measure."

Drinking the small measure of wine, she replaced the cap, and waited long minutes, expecting Trooh to have an immediate effect. Nothing. Nothing except for the beginnings of light-headedness, she thought was brought on by drinking wine so early in the morning on an empty stomach, and a warm fuzzy feeling at the ends of her fingers and toes. Disappointed, she turned the casket the right way up, and put the empty phial inside. From the web-silk shawl, she had unceremoniously bundled it in so long ago, Clara unwrapped the quiver. Too large to sit upon her hips, she slung it over one shoulder, and under the other.

"Clump will have a fit when he sees it. Well, he must have his tantrum, and when it is done, learn to accept I wear the symbol, not of Atrament, but of Amthyst."

The casket picked up, she carried it from the room and left the speak-cube buzzing silence with its subtle whirr, while the warm, wholesome scent of blackberries rode upon the still air.

Chapter 66.

It is said, the Way came into being at my contrivance, thus was the name they gave me, given to it.
It is said, the Way owns a voice both silken and mesmerizing.
It is said, the Way whispers in seductive tones to would be walkers, enticing them to set a foot upon its broadness.
It is said, in return for treading its broad surface, the Way makes brave the weakest heart, enabling it to do all things the avaricious mind desires.
It is said, the Way is carpeted with many promises, and never does it renege on reward, but imbues a walker with the will to act.
It is said, if a walker steps up onto its broadness, doors they dare not open, the Way flings wide.
It is said, the Way shows opportunity may improperly be grasped, and dreams the Way makes reality, for the walker to take hold of and have.
It is said, the Way shows the walke, how to achieve a thing desired, by means foul and nefarious, and into the bargain, slays the hindering conscience.
These sayings are very great lies.
Here, do I set out the truth, so you may know its true source.
Ever, has the Way existed.
The Way cannot be seen, nor touched, yet it is ever there, waiting for walkers to tread its broadness.
Take heed, all you, who would walk upon the Way. Treacherous and capricious it is, and very dangerous to put one single toe of a foot upon it.
If the Way should disappear behind the walker, there can be no going back, for the walker must forever travel upon it.
If the Way crumbles beneath the walker's feet, the Way has abandoned the walker, who in thinking to retrace the steps of an iniquitous journey, is cast from it to meet their doom.
If the Way stretches ever onward, and the walker joyfully treads its broadness to the end, that walker is most truly lost.
Know the Way for all it truly is.
The Way is free will.
The Way is self-delusion.
The Way is greedy want that cares not how it fosters wealth, or status, or all those things frail beings struggle to gather to their bosom, to the detriment of others.
Lend not my name to the Way, nor call me enticing seducer.
Call me not Anathema. That title, I never earned.
When the Way whispers, sweet and low...know the truth, it is your own desire that speaks.

When the Way speaks in velvet tones…it is your own base self that whispers.

A slight click resounded through the empty room. The speak-cube, ceasing its whirred buzz, Atrament spoke no more.

Atrament Speaks
The first book of the trilogy - Noor.

Glosssary.

Locations:

Lessadgh: An alternative Earth.
Noor, the place of perfect light: – a world full of garish colour constructed by the Disobedient Ones, and wrapped around Lessadgh, denying that place much light.

Humans of Lessadgh:

Clara Maddingley: Owner of a smallholding. Later High Lord of Almandine.
Thomas Makepeace: The eventual steward of her land.

Inhabitants of Nooor:
The Disobedient Ones: Beings with supernatural power, who broke a cardinal rule and earned themselves that name.
Faienya: The gigantic offspring of the Disobedient Ones, and their descendants.
Atrament: The sole survivor of firstborn children of the union between the Disobedient Ones and the women of Lessadgh.
Persimmony Clump: A Faienya, but one of the despised Stunted Ones, whose height and looks resemble Lessadgh's humans.
William: Clara Maddingley's adopted son.
Lingaradgh: Believed to have died, and once Ruler of Almandine.
Apatia: Lingaradgh's daughter.
Sinhaladgh: Apatia's High Chancellor.
Slubeadgh: Con-joined at the stomach with his mal-formed twin, whom he carries in a sling, giving the appearance of a paunch. The bonded servant of Apatia.
Galateo: Slubeadgh's brother.
Semyon: Apatia's lover and Commander of her Guards.
Ratanakiri: Mistress of Apatia's paint-box.
Reboia: One of Semyon's guards.
Cullinan: Doge of the Order of the Guardians – rulers in all but name of Noor.
Caryadgh: A novice of the Guardians.
Bezel: A would be Mendicant.
Mendicants: Vagabonds, the lowest rank of the Order of the Guardians, who wander throughout the Kingdom States.
Soude: A leader of a group of Mendicants.

Terminology used in Noor:

Third Trichotomy: The year is divided into three seasons, the third being last.
Urilatum: The only precious metal in Noor, it has a copper-silver gleam.
Life force: Blood.
Faded: Dead.
Making: The performance of seemingly miraculous deeds using talent and words. A making's potency is most effective, when the old language is used.
Trooh: Gold reduced to its basic constituents, through a process of smelting, and then used as an aid to enhance talent's performance.
Darkling: Night.
Brightling: Day.
Sparn: One year.
Starn: One month
Scarn: One week.
Span: One day.
Segment: One hour.
Sen: One minute.
Sistens: Musical instruments used by the Mendicants.

Animals of Noor:

Gostle: Resembling Caribou, smallest of the four-legged creatures in Noor.
Haran: Horse-like in form, hairless with scaled skin. The head, triangular with long ears spreading out from the top of the skull, which look like horns, and sharp quills run along an arching neck. Three-toes on each foot, with a talon at the end of each toe, their tails are whip-like.
Smu hundghs: Voiceless dogs, used for hunting.
Coobir: Red-feathered bird, similar to a dove.